# GOLF'S *Best*
## SHORT STORIES

# GOLF'S *Best*
## SHORT STORIES

Edited by Paul D. Staudohar

Souvenir Press

First published in the USA by
Chicago Review Press, Incorporated, Chicago

British edition first published 2000 by
Souvenir Press Ltd,
43 Great Russell Street, London WC1B 3PD

Reprinted 2001, 2002



ISBN 0 285 63576 X

Printed in Great Britain by
Creative Print and Design Group (Wales), Ebbw Vale

# CONTENTS

# ACKNOWLEDGMENTS

It is nice to be able to thank those who so generously made this collection of stories possible. A computer search was done by Roger Siebert, and interlibrary loan assistance was provided by Toni Holloway and Lynne LaFleur, from California State University, Hayward. Florence Bongard from Cal State was secretary for the project. Particularly helpful in getting me started on the research was Michael Salmon, librarian at the Amateur Athletic Foundation of Los Angeles. Thanks also to Saundra Sheffer, librarian at the Ralph W. Miller Golf Library in the City of Industry, California. The Miller library is a treasure trove of information on golf, both fiction and nonfiction. Three people who went the extra mile in locating resources were Paulina Bax, intern at *Harper's,* Erika Mansourian, fiction editor at *Esquire,* and Alice K. Turner, senior editor at *Playboy*. On several occasions my colleague Professor Richard Zock provided valuable assistance. E. D. Conklin, Mary Hill, Bob George, Nick McIntosh, and golf pro Tim Sullivan were wise counselors. Kudos to Treva Miles for a great job of typing the manuscript. Most of all, credit goes to Cynthia Sherry, senior editor at Chicago Review Press, who directed all facets of the project so capably. While Cynthia was away tending to her firstborn, daughter Sophia, her place was ably filled by associate publisher Linda Matthews.

Paul D. Staudohar

# INTRODUCTION

Golf is a great game because it takes one out in the open air, provides unsurpassed views of natural beauty, and promotes physical fitness. It also builds lasting friendships and encourages worthwhile business contacts. On the other hand, the game exasperates, perplexes, angers, embarrasses, and distresses its participants. It's a waste of time, a bad habit, a silly diversion, and a serious vice. Is there any game that is loved and hated so much at the same time?

The twenty-four stories in this book seek to capture the essence of the game, its pleasures as well as its frustrations. They reach beyond golf to reveal the nature of people who play the game and the experiences they take from it. In the stories the reader will meet duffers, pros, hustlers, finaglers, plodders, and an assortment of other characters. There are love stories, spoofs, dramas, fantasies, mysteries, and more. The authors of the stories, among the best at their craft, treat us to poignant glimpses of life, which are made more entertaining by linkage with the fascinating game of golf. Let's tee off!

Paul D. Staudohar

*This is the first of three stories in the book by Sir Pelham Grenville "Plummie" Wodehouse (1881–1975). Wodehouse, who held dual citizenship in Britain and America, is one of the most artful and humorous writers of all time. Critic Hilaire Belloc called him "the greatest writer working in English," and writer Evelyn Waugh always referred to him as "the Master." Wodehouse loved golf and was a fairly competent duffer. "The Clicking of Cuthbert" was one of his first golf stories. Many were to follow and are collected in* The Golf Omnibus *(1973). Wodehouse was a golf traditionalist who lamented that some of the old names for clubs were no longer in use. In his and other early golf stories we find reference to clubs like the mashie (a middle iron) and niblick (a wedge). Other club names that have faded into history are the baffy, brassie, cleek, and spoon.*

*P. G. Wodehouse*

# THE CLICKING OF CUTHBERT (1910)

THE YOUNG MAN CAME into the smoking-room of the club-house, and flung his bag with a clatter on the floor. He sank moodily into an arm-chair and pressed the bell.

"Waiter!"

"Sir?"

The young man pointed at the bag with every evidence of distaste.

"You may have these clubs," he said. "Take them away. If you don't want them yourself, give them to one of the caddies."

Across the room the Oldest Member gazed at him with a grave sadness through the smoke of his pipe. His eye was deep and dreamy–the eye of a man who, as the poet says, has seen Golf steadily and seen it whole.

"You are giving up golf?" he said.

He was not altogether unprepared for such an attitude on the young man's part: for from his eyrie on the terrace above the ninth green he had observed him start out on the afternoon's round and had seen him lose a couple of balls in the lake at the second hole after taking seven strokes at the first.

"Yes!" cried the young man fiercely. "For ever, dammit! Footling game! Blanked infernal fat-headed silly ass of a game! Nothing but a waste of time."

The Sage winced.

"Don't say that, my boy."

"But I do say it. What earthly good is golf? Life is stern and life is earnest. We live in a practical age. All round us we see foreign competition making itself unpleasant. And we spend our time playing golf! What do we get out of it? Is golf any *use*? That's what I'm asking you. Can you name me a single case where devotion to this pestilential pastime has done a man any practical good?"

The Sage smiled gently.

"I could name a thousand."

"One will do."

"I will select," said the Sage, "from the innumerable memories that rush to my mind, the story of Cuthbert Banks."

"Never heard of him."

"Be of good cheer," said the Oldest Member. "You are going to hear of him now."

It was in the picturesque little settlement of Wood Hills (said the Oldest Member) that the incidents occurred which I am about to relate. Even if you have never been in Wood Hills, that suburban paradise is probably familiar to you by name. Situated at a convenient distance from the city, it combines in a notable manner the advantages of town life with the pleasant surrounding and healthful air of the country. Its inhabitants live in commodious houses, standing in their own grounds, and enjoy so many luxuries–such as gravel soil, main drainage, electric light, telephone, baths (h. and c.), and company's own water, that you might be pardoned for imagining life to be so ideal for them that no possible improvement could be added to their lot. Mrs. Willoughby Smethurst was under no such delusion. What Wood Hills needed to make it perfect, she realized, was Culture. Material comforts are all very well, but, if the *summum bonum* is to be achieved, the Soul also demands a look in, and it was Mrs. Smethurst's unfaltering resolve that never while she had her strength should the Soul be handed the loser's end. It was her intention to make Wood Hills a centre of all that was most cultivated and refined, and golly! how she had succeeded. Under her presidency the Wood Hills Literary and Debating Society had tripled its membership.

But there is always a fly in the ointment, a caterpillar in the salad. The local golf club, an institution to which Mrs. Smethurst strongly objected, had also tripled its membership; and the division of the community into two rival camps, the Golfers and the Cultured, had become more marked than ever. This division, always acute, had attained now to the dimensions of a Schism. The rival sects treated one another with a cold hostility.

Unfortunate episodes came to widen the breach. Mrs. Smethurst's house adjoined the links, standing to the right of the fourth tee: and as the Literary Society was in the habit of entertaining visiting lecturers, many a golfer had foozled his drive owing to sudden loud outbursts of applause coinciding with his down-swing. And not long before this story opens a sliced ball, whizzing in at the open window, had come within an ace of incapacitating Raymond Parsloe Devine, the rising young novelist (who rose at the moment a clear foot and a half) from any further exercise of his art. Two inches, indeed, to the right and Raymond must inevitably have handed in his dinner-pail.

To make matters worse, a ring at the front-door bell followed almost immediately, and the maid ushered in a young man of pleasing appearance in a sweater and baggy knickerbockers who apologetically but firmly insisted on playing his ball where it lay, and, what with the shock of the lecturer's narrow escape and the spectacle of the intruder standing on the table and working away with a niblick, the afternoon's session had to be classed as a complete frost. Mr. Devine's determination, from which no argument could swerve him, to deliver the rest of his lecture in the coal-cellar gave the meeting a jolt from which it never recovered.

I have dwelt upon this incident, because it was the means of introducing Cuthbert Banks to Mrs. Smethurst's niece, Adeline. As Cuthbert, for it was he who had so nearly reduced the muster-roll of rising novelists by one, hopped down from the table after his stroke, he was suddenly aware that a beautiful girl was looking at him intently. As a matter of fact, everyone in the room was looking at him intently, none more so than Raymond Parsloe Devine, but none of the others were beautiful girls. Long as the members of Wood Hills Literary Society were on brain, they were short on looks, and, to Cuthbert's excited eye, Adeline Smethurst stood out like a jewel in a pile of coke.

He had never seen her before, for she had only arrived at her aunt's house on the previous day, but he was perfectly certain that life, even when lived in the midst of gravel soil, main drainage, and company's own water, was going to be a pretty poor affair if he did not see her again. Yes, Cuthbert was in love: and it is interesting to record, as showing the effect of the tender emotion on a man's game that twenty minutes after he had met Adeline he did the short eleventh in one, and as near as a toucher got a three on the four-hundred-yard twelfth.

I will skip lightly over the intermediate stages of Cuthbert's courtship and come to the moment when–at the annual ball in aid of the local Cottage Hospital, the only occasion during the year on which the lion, so to speak, lay down with lamb, and the Golfers and the Cultured met on terms of easy comradeship, their differences temporarily laid aside–he proposed to Adeline and was badly stymied.

That fair, soulful girl could not see him with a spy-glass.

"Mr. Banks," she said, "I will speak frankly."

"Charge right ahead," assented Cuthbert.

"Deeply sensible as I am of–"

"I know. Of the honour and the compliment and all that. But, passing lightly over all that guff, what seems to be the trouble? I love you to distraction–"

"Love is not everything."

"You're wrong," said Cuthbert earnestly. "You're right off it. Love–" And he was about to dilate on the theme when she interrupted him.

"I am a girl of ambition."

"And very nice, too," said Cuthbert.

"I am a girl of ambition," repeated Adeline, "and I realize that the fulfillment of my ambitions must come through my husband. I am very ordinary myself–"

"What!" cried Cuthbert. "You ordinary? Why, you are a pearl among women, the queen of your sex. You can't have been looking in a glass lately. You stand alone. Simply alone. You make the rest look like battered repaints."

"Well," said Adeline, softening a trifle, "I believe I am fairly good-looking–"

"Anybody who was content to call you fairly good-looking would describe the Taj Mahal as a pretty nifty tomb."

"But that is not the point. What I mean is, if I marry a nonentity I shall be a nonentity myself for ever. And I would sooner die than be a nonentity."

"And, if I follow your reasoning, you think that that lets *me* out?"

"Well, really, Mr. Banks, *have* you done anything, or are you likely ever to do anything worth while?"

Cuthbert hesitated.

"It's true," he said, "I didn't finish in the first ten in the Open, and I was knocked out in the semi-final of the Amateur, but I won the French Open last year."

"The–what?"

"The French Open Championship. Golf, you know."

"Golf! You waste all your time playing golf. I admire a man who is more spiritual, more intellectual."

A pang of jealousy rent Cuthbert's bosom.

"Like What's-his-name Devine?" he said, sullenly.

"Mr. Devine," replied Adeline, blushing faintly, "is going to be a great man. Already he has achieved much. The critics say that he is more Russian than any other young English writer."

"And is that good?"

"Of course it's good."

"I should have thought the wheeze would be to be more English than any other young English writer."

"Nonsense! Who wants an English writer to be English? You've got to be Russian or Spanish or something to be a real success. The mantle of the great Russians has descended on Mr. Devine."

"From what I've heard of Russians, I should hate to have that happen to *me*."

"There is no danger of that," said Adeline scornfully.

"Oh! Well, let me tell you that there is a lot more in me than you think."

"That might easily be so."

"You think I'm not spiritual and intellectual," said Cuthbert, deeply moved. "Very well. Tomorrow I join the Literary Society."

Even as he spoke the words his leg was itching to kick himself for being such a chump, but the sudden expression of pleasure on Adeline's face soothed him; and he went home that night with the feeling that he had taken on something rather attractive. It was only in the cold grey light of the morning that he realized what he had let himself in for.

I do not know if you have had any experience of suburban literary societies, but the one that flourished under the eye of Mrs. Willoughby Smethurst at Wood Hills was rather more so than the average. With my feeble powers of narrative, I cannot hope to make clear to you all that Cuthbert Banks endured in the next few weeks. And, even if I could, I doubt if I should do so. It is all very well to excite pity and terror, as Aristotle recommends, but there are limits. In the ancient Greek tragedies it was an ironclad rule that all the real rough stuff should take place off-stage, and I shall follow this admirable principle. It will suffice if I say merely that J. Cuthbert Banks had a thin time. After attending eleven debates and fourteen lectures on *vers libre* Poetry, the Seventeenth-Century Essayists, the

Neo-Scandinavian Movement in Portuguese Literature, and other subjects of a similar nature, he grew so enfeebled that, on the rare occasions when he had time for a visit to the links, he had to take a full iron for his mashie shots.

It was not simply the oppressive nature of the debates and lectures that sapped his vitality. What really got right in amongst him was the torture of seeing Adeline's adoration of Raymond Parsloe Devine. The man seemed to have made the deepest possible impression upon her plastic emotions. When he spoke, she leaned forward with parted lips and looked at him. When he was not speaking–which was seldom–she leaned back and looked at him. And when he happened to take the next seat to her, she leaned sideways and looked at him. One glance at Mr. Devine would have been more than enough for Cuthbert; but Adeline found him a spectacle that never palled. She could not have gazed at him with a more rapturous intensity than if she had been a small child and he a saucer of ice-cream. All this Cuthbert had to witness while still endeavouring to retain the possession of his faculties sufficiently to enable him to duck and back away if somebody suddenly asked him what he thought of the somber realism of Vladimir Brusiloff. It is little wonder that he tossed in bed, picking at the coverlet, through sleepless nights, and had to have all his waistcoats taken in three inches to keep them from sagging.

This Vladimir Brusiloff to whom I have referred was the famous Russian novelist, and, owing to the fact of his being in the country on a lecturing tour at the moment, there had been something of a boom in his works. The Wood Hills Literary Society had been studying them for weeks, and never since his first entrance into intellectual circles had Cuthbert Banks come nearer to throwing in the towel. Vladimir specialized in grey studies of hopeless misery, where nothing happened till page three hundred and eighty, when the moujik decided to commit suicide. It was tough going for a man whose deepest reading hitherto had been Vardon on the Push-Shot, and there can be no greater proof of the magic of love than the fact that Cuthbert stuck it without a cry. But the strain was terrible and I am inclined to think that he must have cracked, had it not been for the daily reports in the papers of the internecine strife which was proceeding so briskly in Russia. Cuthbert was an optimist at heart, and it seemed to him that, at the rate at which the inhabitants of that interesting country were murdering one another, the supply of Russian novelists must eventually give out.

One morning, as he tottered down the road for the short walk which was now almost the only exercise to which he was equal, Cuthbert met Adeline. A spasm of anguish flitted through all his nerve-centres as he saw that she was accompanied by Raymond Parsloe Devine.

"Good morning, Mr. Banks," said Adeline.

"Good morning," said Cuthbert hollowly.

"Such good news about Vladimir Brusiloff."

"Dead?" said Cuthbert, with a touch of hope.

"Dead? Of course not. Why should he be? No, Aunt Emily met his manager after his lecture at Queen's Hall yesterday, and he has promised that Mr. Brusiloff shall come to her next Wednesday reception."

"Oh, ah!" said Cuthbert, dully.

"I don't know how she managed it. I think she must have told him that Mr. Devine would be there to meet him."

"But you said he was coming," argued Cuthbert.

"I shall be very glad," said Raymond Devine, "of the opportunity of meeting Brusiloff."

"I'm sure," said Adeline, "he will be very glad of the opportunity of meeting you."

"Possibly," said Mr. Devine. "Possibly. Competent critics have said that my work closely resembles that of the great Russian Masters."

"Your psychology is so deep."

"Yes, yes."

"And your atmosphere."

"Quite."

Cuthbert in a perfect agony of spirit prepared to withdraw from this love-feast. The sun was shining brightly, but the world was black to him. Birds sang in the tree-tops, but he did not hear them. He might have been a moujik for all the pleasure he found in life.

"You will be there, Mr. Banks?" said Adeline, as he turned away.

"Oh, all right," said Cuthbert.

When Cuthbert had entered the drawing-room on the following Wednesday and had taken his usual place in a distant corner where, while able to feast his gaze on Adeline, he had a sporting chance of being overlooked or mistaken for a piece of furniture, he perceived the great Russian thinker seated in the midst of a circle of admiring females. Raymond Parsloe Devine had not yet arrived.

His first glance at the novelist surprised Cuthbert. Doubtless with the best motives, Vladimir Brusiloff had permitted his face to become almost entirely concealed behind a dense zareba of hair, but his eyes were visible through the undergrowth, and it seemed to Cuthbert that there was an expression in them not unlike that of a cat in a strange backyard surrounded by small boys. The man looked forlorn and hopeless, and Cuthbert wondered whether he had had bad news from home.

This was not the case. The latest news which Vladimir Brusiloff had had from Russia had been particularly cheering. Three of his principal creditors had perished in the last massacre of the *bourgeoisie,* and a man whom he owed for five years for a samovar and a pair of overshoes had fled the country, and had not been heard of since. It was not bad news from home that was depressing Vladimir. What was wrong with him was the fact that this was the eighty-second suburban literary reception he had been compelled to attend since he had landed in the country on his lecturing tour, and he was sick to death of it. When his agent had first suggested the trip, he had signed on the dotted line without an instant's hesitation. Worked out in roubles, the fees offered had seemed just about right. But now, as he peered through the brushwood at the faces round him, and realized that eight out of ten of those present had manuscripts of some sort concealed on their persons, and were only waiting for an opportunity to whip them out and start reading, he wished that he had stayed at his quiet home in Nijni-Novgorod, where the worst thing that could happen to a fellow was a brace of bombs coming in through the window and mixing themselves up with his breakfast egg.

At this point in his meditations he was aware that his hostess was looming up before him with a pale young man in horn-rimmed spectacles at her side. There was in Mrs. Smethurst's demeanour something of the unction of the master-of-ceremonies at the big fight who introduces the earnest gentleman who wishes to challenge the winner.

"Oh, Mr. Brusiloff," said Mrs. Smethurst, "I do so want you to meet Mr. Raymond Parsloe Devine, whose work I expect you know. He is one of our younger novelists."

The distinguished visitor peered in a wary and defensive manner through the shrubbery, but did not speak. Inwardly he was thinking how exactly like Mr. Devine was to the eighty-one other younger novelists to whom he had been introduced at various hamlets throughout the country. Raymond Parsloe Devine bowed courteously, while Cuthbert, wedged into his corner, glowered at him.

"The critics," said Mr. Devine, "have been kind enough to say that my poor efforts contain a good deal of the Russian spirit. I owe much to the great Russians. I have been greatly influenced by Sovietski."

Down in the forest something stirred. It was Vladimir Brusiloff's mouth opening, as he prepared to speak. He was not a man who prattled readily, especially in a foreign tongue. He gave the impression that each word was excavated from his interior by some up-to-date process of mining. He glared bleakly at Mr. Devine, and allowed three words to drop out of him.

"Sovietski no good!"

He paused for a moment, set the machinery working again, and delivered five more at the pithead.

"I spit me of Sovietski!"

There was a painful sensation. The lot of a popular idol is in many ways an enviable one, but it has the drawback of uncertainty. Here today and gone tomorrow. Until this moment Raymond Parsloe Devine's stock had stood at something considerably over par in Wood Hills intellectual circles, but now there was a rapid slump. Hitherto he had been greatly admired for being influenced by Sovietski, but it appeared now that this was not a good thing to be. It was evidently a rotten thing to be. The law could not touch you for being influenced by Sovietski, but there is an ethical as well as a legal code, and this it was obvious that Raymond Parsloe Devine had transgressed. Women drew away from him slightly, holding their skirts. Men looked at him censoriously. Adeline

Smethurst started violently, and dropped a tea-cup. And Cuthbert Banks, doing his popular imitation of a sardine in his corner, felt for the first time that life held something of sunshine.

Raymond Parsloe Devine was plainly shaken, but he made an adroit attempt to recover his lost prestige.

"When I say I have been influenced by Sovietski, I mean, of course, that I was once under his spell. A young writer commits many follies. I have long since passed through that phase. The false glamour of Sovietski has ceased to dazzle me. I now belong whole-heartedly to the school of Nastikoff."

There was a reaction. People nodded at one another sympathetically. After all, we cannot expect old heads on young shoulders, and a lapse at the outset of one's career should not be held against one who has eventually seen the light.

"Nastikoff no good," said Vladimir Brusiloff, coldly. He paused, listening to the machinery.

"Nastikoff worse than Sovietski."

He paused again.

"I spit me of Nastikoff!" he said.

This time there was no doubt about it. The bottom had dropped out of the market, and Raymond Parsloe Devine Preferred were down in the cellar with no takers. It was clear to the entire assembled company that they had been all wrong about Raymond Parsloe Devine. They had allowed him to play on their innocence and sell them a pup. They had taken him at his own valuation, and had been cheated into admiring him as a man who amounted to something, and all the while he had belonged to the school of Nastikoff. You never can tell. Mrs. Smethurst's guests were well-bred, and there was consequently no violent demonstration, but you could see by their faces what they felt. Those nearest Raymond Parsloe jostled to get further away. Mrs. Smethurst eyed him stonily through a raised lorgnette. One or two low hisses were heard, and over at the other end of the room somebody opened the window in a marked manner.

Raymond Parsloe Devine hesitated for a moment, then, realizing his situation, turned and slunk to the door. There was an audible sigh of relief as it closed behind him.

Vladimir Brusiloff proceeded to sum up.

"No novelists any good except me. Sovietski–yah! Nastikoff–bah! I spit me of zem all. No novelists anywhere any good except me. P. G. Wodehouse and Tolstoi not bad. Not good, but not bad. No novelists any good except me."

And, having uttered this dictum, he removed a slab of cake from a near-by plate, steered it through the jungle, and began to champ.

It is too much to say that there was a dead silence. There could never be that in any room in which Vladimir Brusiloff was eating cake. But certainly what you might call the general chit-chat was pretty well down and out. Nobody liked to be the first to speak. The members of the Wood Hills Literary Society looked at one another timidly. Cuthbert, for his part, gazed at Adeline; and Adeline gazed into space. It was plain that the girl was deeply stirred. Her eyes were opened wide, a faint flush crimsoned her cheeks, and her breath was coming quickly.

Adeline's mind was in a whirl. She felt as if she had been walking gaily along a pleasant path and had stopped suddenly on the very brink of a precipice. It would be idle to deny that Raymond Parsloe Devine had attracted her extraordinarily. She had taken him at his own valuation as an extremely hot potato, and her hero-worship had gradually been turning into love. And now her hero had been shown to have feet of clay. It was hard, I consider, on Raymond Parsloe Devine, but that is how it goes in this world. You get a following as a celebrity, and then you run up against another bigger celebrity and your admirers desert you. One could moralize on this at considerable length, but better not, perhaps. Enough to say that the glamour of Raymond Devine ceased abruptly in that moment for Adeline, and her most coherent thought at this juncture was the resolve, as soon as she got up to her room, to burn the three signed photographs he had sent her and to give the autographed presentation set of his books to the grocer's boy.

Mrs. Smethurst, meanwhile, having rallied somewhat, was endeavouring to set the feast of reason and flow of soul going again.

"And how do you like England, Mr. Brusiloff?" she asked.

The celebrity paused in the act of lowering another segment of cake.

"Dam good," he replied, cordially.

"I suppose you have traveled all over the country by this time?"

"You said," agreed the Thinker.

"Have you met many of our great public men?"

"Yais–Yais–Quite a few of the nibs–Lloyid Gorge, I meet him. But–" Beneath the matting a discontented expression came into his face, and his voice took on a peevish note. "But I not meet your *real* great men–your Arbmishel, your Arreevadon–I not meet them. That's what gives me the pipovitch. Have *you* ever met Arbmishel and Arreevadon?"

A strained, anguished look came into Mrs. Smethurst's face and was reflected in the faces of the other members of the circle. The eminent Russian had sprung two entirely new ones on them, and they felt that their ignorance was about to be exposed. What would Vladimir Brusiloff think of the Wood Hills Literary Society? The reputation of the Wood Hills Literary Society was at stake, trembling in the balance, and coming up for the third time. In dumb agony Mrs. Smethurst rolled her eyes about the room searching for someone capable of coming to the rescue. She drew blank.

And then, from a distant corner, there sounded a deprecating cough, and those nearest Cuthbert Banks saw that he had stopped twisting his right foot round his left ankle and his left foot round his right ankle and was sitting up with a light of almost human intelligence in his eyes.

"Er–" said Cuthbert, blushing as every eye in the room seemed to fix itself on him, "I think he means Abe Mitchell and Harry Vardon."

"Abe Mitchell and Harry Vardon?" repeated Mrs. Smethurst, blankly. "I never heard of–"

"Yais! Yais! Most! Very!" shouted Vladimir Brusiloff, enthusiastically. "Arbmishel and Arreevadon. You know them, yes, what, no, perhaps?"

"I've played with Abe Mitchell often, and I was partnered with Harry Vardon in last year's Open."

The great Russian uttered a cry that shook the chandelier.

"You play in ze Open? Why," he demanded reproachfully of Mrs. Smethurst, "was I not been introducted to this young man who play in opens?"

"Well, really," faltered Mrs. Smethurst. "Well, the fact is, Mr. Brusiloff–"

She broke off. She was unequal to the task of explaining, without hurting anyone's feelings, that she had always regarded Cuthbert as a piece of cheese and a blot on the landscape.

"Introduct me!" thundered the Celebrity.

"Why, certainly, certainly, of course. This is Mr. –." She looked appealingly at Cuthbert.

"Banks," prompted Cuthbert.

"Banks!" cried Vladimir Brusiloff. "Not Cootaboot Banks?"

"*Is* your name Cootaboot?" asked Mrs. Smethurst, faintly.

"Well, it's Cuthbert."

"Yais! Yais! Cootaboot!" There was a rush and swirl, as the effervescent Muscovite burst his way through the throng and rushed to where Cuthbert sat. He stood for a moment eyeing him excitedly, then, stooping swiftly, kissed him on both cheeks before Cuthbert could get his guard up. "My dear young man, I saw you win ze French Open. Great! Great! Grand! Superb! Hot stuff, and you can say I said so! Will you permit one who is but eighteen at Nijni-Novgorod to salute you once more?"

And he kissed Cuthbert again. Then, brushing aside one or two intellectuals who were in the way, he dragged up a chair and sat down.

"You are a great man!" he said.

"Oh, no," said Cuthbert modestly.

"Yais! Great. Most! Very! The way you lay your approach-putts dead from anywhere!"

"Oh, I don't know."

Mr. Brusiloff drew his chair closer.

"Let me tell you one vairy funny story about putting. It was one day I play at Nijni-Novgorod with the pro against Lenin and Trotsky, and Trotsky had a two-inch putt for the hole. But, just as he addresses the ball, someone in the crowd he tries to assassinate Lenin with a rewolwer–you know that is our great national sport, trying to assassinate Lenin with rewolwers–and the bang puts Trotsky off his stroke and he goes five yards past the hole, and then Lenin, who is rather shaken, you understand, he misses again himself, and we win the hole and match and I clean up three hundred and ninety-six thousand roubles, or fifteen shillings in your money. Some gameovitch! And now let me tell you one other vairy funny story–"

Desultory conversation had begun in murmurs over the rest of the room, as the Wood Hills intellectuals politely endeavoured to conceal the fact that they realized that they were about as much out of it at this re-union of twin souls as cats at a dogshow. From time to time they started as Vladimir Brusiloff's laugh boomed out. Perhaps it was a consolation to them to know that he was enjoying himself.

As for Adeline, how shall I describe her emotions? She was stunned. Before her very eyes the stone which the builders had rejected had become the main thing, the hundred-to-one shot had walked away with the race. A rush of tender admiration for Cuthbert Banks flooded her heart. She saw that she had been all wrong. Cuthbert, whom she had always treated with a patronizing superiority, was really a man to be looked up to and worshipped. A deep, dreamy sigh shook Adeline's fragile form.

Half an hour later Vladimir and Cuthbert Banks rose.

"Goot-a-bye, Mrs. Smet-thirst," said the Celebrity. "Zank you for a most charming visit. My friend Cootaboot and me we go now to shoot a few holes. You will lend me clobs, friend Cootaboot?"

"Any you want."

"The niblicksky is what I use most. Goot-a-bye, Mrs. Smet-thirst."

They were moving to the door, when Cuthbert felt a light touch on his arm. Adeline was looking up at him tenderly.

"May I come, too, and walk round with you?"

Cuthbert's bosom heaved.

"Oh," he said, with a tremor in his voice, "that you would walk round with me for life!"

Her eyes met his.

"Perhaps," she whispered, softly, "it could be arranged."

"And so" (concluded the Oldest Member), "you see that golf can be of the greatest practical assistance to a man in Life's struggle. Raymond

Parsloe Devine, who was no player, had to move out of the neighbourhood immediately, and is now, I believe, writing scenarios out in California for the Flicker Film Company. Adeline is married to Cuthbert, and it was only his earnest pleading which prevented her from having their eldest son christened Abe Mitchell Ribbed-Faced Mashie Banks, for she is now as keen a devotee of the great game as her husband. Those who know them say that theirs is a union so devoted, so–"

The Sage broke off abruptly, for the young man had rushed to the door and out into the passage. Through the open door he could hear him crying passionately to the waiter to bring back his clubs.

*This story, originally published in* Harper's, *is a fine example of how early golf literature can be surprisingly modern. Personal integrity is an intriguing aspect of golf and makes a good theme for a story. Golfers who play alone or whose shots are unwitnessed by playing partners may be tempted to take a "mulligan" (an uncounted shot) or to tee up in the rough. Golfers have also been known to have memory lapses. As Will Rogers said, "Only income tax has made more liars out of American people than golf." But there is also a diamond-hard integrity among many golfers about following the rules, in the spirit of true sportsmanship. In "The Phantom Card," a golfer is tormented by his guilty conscience when he wins a tournament by lying on his scorecard. Can there be absolution for such a sin?*

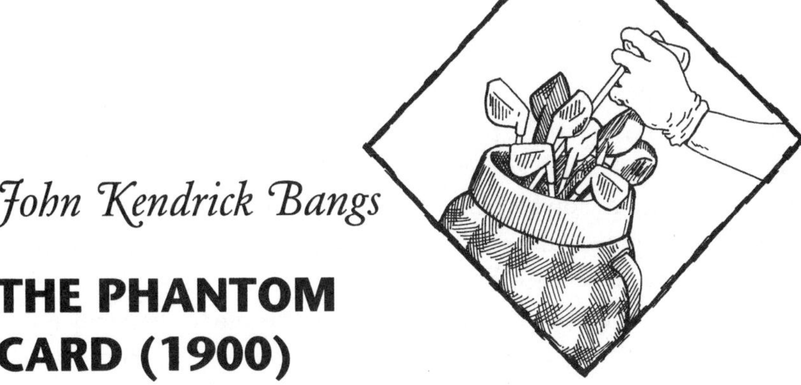

*John Kendrick Bangs*

# THE PHANTOM CARD (1900)

(*A Letter from Wilkinson Peabody, Esq., of New York, to Willie McGuffin, Greens-keeper at St. Willieboy's.*)

It is said, my dear McGuffin, that confession is good for the soul, and that in some cases it is the first step towards absolution. I am in urgent need of forgiveness for a sin for which I have suffered punishment a hundredfold in the past five years–nay, a thousandfold, for day and night, sleeping and waking, have I been haunted by a miserable golf-card that would not down, and has so preyed upon my nervous system that I am fast becoming the merest shadow of my former self. Time and again have I resolved to expose my crime to the world, and so rid my conscience of its withering secret. As many times have I foozled my approach to its beginning; but now I am resolved to lay bare my soul to you, and abide by whatever result may come from my act. It may be that I shall derive no benefit from my act of confession, but I shall not be deterred by that possibility, for I can no longer suffer in silence. Therefore, my dear McGuffin, I send you this awful tale of duplicity and woe. Just as the priest is confessor of an errant soul in his parish, so are you, as greens-keeper of the St. Willieboy's Links, the father confessor of the sinning golfer, and I approach you humbly, in a meekness of spirit which comports not well with my scarlet coat and green plaid stockings, but is none the less the sincere emotion of a contrite heart. Do with my confession as you will. Lock it up in your breast and let my secret die with you, or publish it broadcast to the world. I leave my fate wholly in your hands; but, as you love the game, O McGuffin, give me advice–advice which shall relieve my tortured heart of its load of iniquity and apprehension.

My story, to come to the point at once, is one of crime, and of a crime than which there is none greater in the list of golfing wrongdoing. Even a failure to replace the divots pales into insignificance beside it, for it is the crime of putting in a false card. McGuffin–a card that lied, and won by the lie! Do you remember the first time you and I met, McGuffin? Five years ago, on a beautiful June afternoon, you came into the lounging-room of the St. Willieboy's Club house, at Dunwoodie-on-the-Hudson, and congratulated me upon my winning of the Class B cup in the June handicap. Do you remember how I rose as you spoke, grew red of face, and stammered out my thanks, and how you slapped me on the back, and told me not to be rattled by a first victory? How you said every good golfer had to have his first victory before he could hope to win his second? How you added that if I kept on as I had begun, the winning of cups would soon be an every-day affair with me; and, furthermore, how my agitation increased instead of decreasing as you went on? Ah, McGuffin, you little knew how unworthy I was of all the kind and encouraging things you said to me, or how every allusion you made to my "victory" wrung my very soul!

You did not know then, as I did, McGuffin, that my card was a lie, a living lie, a bad lie–a lie which must be wiped from the face of earth before I could look myself in the eye again and call myself an honest man.

Every one noticed–they must have–and some spoke of, my modest bearing in the hour of triumph. I did not swell around and brag about it. I did not cable my wife in Europe that I had won the trophy. I did not send marked copies of the papers announcing my victory to my eldest son, as another man would have done–but there was a reason, McGuffin, a potent reason. I did not do these things *because my card was a lie;* and I felt myself not a champion at that time, but a liar–an unmitigated liar.

I did not even take the trophy home with me that night: you remember it, don't you McGuffin–the silver-backed hair-brush with the dragon's head etched upon it? Why? Again because my card was a lie, and every time I looked at it the dragon's mouth seemed to open and shout the words "Liar! Cheat! Scoundrel!" in my face; and once, upon my soul, McGuffin, as I tentatively ventured to touch it, the etched jaws of that dreadful beast opened sharply, and snapped at me with such violence that I fell back in dismay.

I went home that night and argued the situation over with myself. There were plenty of pros in favor of my keeping quiet and taking the honors, but for every one was the same insistent con: "Your card was a lie. You didn't make the round in ninety-two; you made it in ninety-four; and you won by the lie, for the second man was ninety-three."

Among the pros was the hard luck of it all, as you will yourself realize as you read on. I was away ahead of any one else up to the seventh hole, where I made my wizard drive–a full 230 yards, McGuffin–and found my ball trapped in the marsh. To be penalized for that was surely not right, and to lift and tee up back of the marsh for a loss of two was a terrible sacrifice. There should have been a rule to meet the case, or rather an exception–indeed, there is now such an exception. But there wasn't then, and I confess it, McGuffin, I made one for my own use and advantage. I took the ball back, teed it up without penalty, brasseyed to the green in two, and holed out in two more, making four for the hole.

My opponent took my word for it, and my caddie, who was looking for apples, or butterflies, or whatever it is that caddies always are looking for while a tournament is in progress, had not observed my act, and what was under the rules a six hole was put down at four, beating Bogey himself by a stroke.

"Rattling good work," said my opponent. "But you deserved it on that drive."

I made no reply, but my face burned with the hot flush that suffused my cheeks. Several times, as we played on, I was about to confess the truth, but I argued my conscience down at the moment. I had really taken only four strokes, and I didn't expect to win, so I let it go, and played on. "What is the use, now the thing is done?" I asked myself. "It won't hurt anybody but myself." But when I came in and found myself a winner by a stroke—ah, McGuffin, McGuffin, I wanted to drop in my tracks, to smash my club upon some convenient rock, to take every ball in my locker and pummel it into a shapeless mass of gutta-percha. And the cheers of the fellows when the announcement was made! They are ringing in my ears yet. It seemed as if Patton, in proposing them, had cried, "Three sneers for Wilkinson!" and the hurrahs were like so many "Yahs" and hoots; and instead of rising and receiving them joyously, I bent my head down over my folded arms upon the table to conceal the blush of shame that surged up into my cheeks. And everybody said I was rattled with joy! Joy! Think of it, McGuffin! A self-convicted liar being rattled with joy!

"Confess at once or be forever branded," said conscience, and I sprang up to obey, but the words died in my throat, and the resolution faded in my breast as I looked upon the expectant faces of my friends. Instead of acknowledging then and there my sin, I thanked them for their cheers, and told the steward to take their orders, which he did, and they all drank to my continued success. My Scotch and soda burned my throat, my cigar grew rank to my taste, and as I passed by the caddie-house, on my way out, it seemed as if every one of those grinning little ball-losing imps was pointing the finger of scorn at me.

"It's too late to confess now," I moaned to myself when I went to bed that night, heartsick and weary. "But I shall not be a thief even if I am a liar. That hair-brush will stay there until the silver crumbles into dust and the bristles fade before I will take it."

But, alas! it was not to be so. Circumstances over which I had no control forced me to be a thief as well, for a week later the accursed thing was sent to me by express, and with it came a letter from Catherington, our honorable secretary, telling me not to be so high-toned and sneer at the prizes the club put up; it was the honor of the victory, not the intrinsic worth of the prize, that counted; and I ought to be ashamed of myself to let the brush remain "knocking about the club-house as if it wasn't worth using on a bald head," like my own.

"Honor! Victory!" This to a man whose card was a lie!

I passed over the insulting allusion to my bald head, feeling myself unworthy to resent any disparaging references to my personal shortcomings.

I took the brush, paid the expressage on it, and pounded it with my brassey, stamped upon it with my hobnailed shoes, and lofted it over into the river with my jigger, a shapeless mass of silver, wood, and bristles; and at every crack with the brassey the infernal dragon's head on the back blared out: "Liar! Thief! Scoundrel!"

That night I tossed about, a prey to dreadful dreams. What if some one had seen and should tell? What if my caddie had observed my act, and should blackmail me? Think of that, McGuffin! Think of the terror of it all! Think of how the newspapers would gloat over the revelation, and what a startling headline "BLACKMAILED BY HIS CADDIE" would make for the New York *Whirald!* The idea was maddening, but I at last fell asleep, and I dreamed awful dreams. I dreamed that I was at the opera listening to *Siegfried.* Everyone I knew, whose good-will I wished, whose esteem I treasured, was present, and when the fire-breathing "Fafner" came out he was no longer "Fafner," but that other more terrible dragon from the back of the hair-brush, and instead of "Fafner's" barytone oozings of Wagner's measures, he bellowed forth to the audience: "There he is! Look at him! Wilkinson Peabody! The liar, thief, and scoundrel whose golf-card was a lie!" And the audience, with a mad cry of "Fore!" shrank away from me as from a leper. Can you imagine it, McGuffin?

But this was not all.

From that day to this, wherever I have gone, that card has followed me. If I have looked into my wife's eyes, it has been there, with the figure four constantly changing back and forth into a six. If I have gazed into my boy's face, the card has risen there, blurring his features. The very number was a mockery to me, and once at Newport, when a player behind me yelled "Fore!" I turned madly, and cried back at him, "Yes, hang you, four!" For six months afterward I did not play the game, but in the autumn I ventured back to St. Willieboy's and tried a single round. Every drive I made, every approach, every putt, that infernal card danced to and fro before my eye and took it off the ball. At the fourth hole, to my vision the disk bore the number six; at the sixth, the disk was numbered four. I was worn to a skeleton, and the doctors sent me South. At Aiken I played in the tournament, and for seventeen holes the phantom card left my vision and my mind, and I thought the hour of my release had come.

"Playing a stunning game," said Patlow, who was my opponent. "Quite up to your old form. I think you'll win again to-day."

But it was a vain thought, for with Patlow's remark up rose the spectral card once more, all the figures on it grinning derisively at me, and turning, it disclosed written upon its back in wriggling letters: "Win? Again? What have you ever won before?" The result was a foozle of my drive, a clean miss for my second, nine through the green, and eight putts, making seventeen for the hole; and the match was lost. I fled to St. Augustine, thence to Palm Beach–all through the South, seeking relief, but the card would not down.

Last spring I tried to make amends, and when in the May handicap at St. Willieboy's I came in a winner, I altered my card to show me a loser, although Whitman, who played with me, insisted that I had made a mistake in my count. I stuck to it, however, and a mug I had really won went to another man. But the phantom card would not be appeased. "Two lies don't make a truth," it cried out to me that night, and I groaned in despair. And so it has gone with me ever since. I cannot seem to rid myself of its awful presence.

That is the story, McGuffin. Under overwhelming temptation, and with no thought of profit, I put in a false card and won the trophy; but have I not suffered enough? Is there no reparation one can make? I appeal to you as a sort of high-priest of golfers for absolution, or for some hint as to how I may obtain it. For five years my wrong-doing has been ever with me. I have sought relief in every quarter, but have found none.

I implore you to relieve me, for if you cannot, I fear for the future. My very reason is tottering on its throne.

Yours humbly and imploringly,
WILKINSON PEABODY.

*(Note from Willie McGuffin to Wilkinson Peabody, Esq.)*
ST. WILLIEBOY'S LINKS, NEW YORK.
*OCTOBER 5, 1899.*

Dear Mr. Peabody,–Do you remember the exact date of the tournament to which you refer in your favor of yesterday? Was it June 10, 1894?

Yours respectfully,
W. MCGUFFIN.

*(Note from Wilkinson Peabody, Esq., to Willie McGuffin.)*
*NEW YORK, OCTOBER 7, 1899.*

My Dear McGuffin,–It was June 10, 1894. The date is burned indelibly upon my memory. I wish it were not. What has the date got to do with it?

Yours faithfully,
WILKINSON PEABODY.

*(Note from Willie McGuffin to Wilkinson Peabody, Esq.)*

Dear Mr. Peabody,–Four was right. The Greens Committee, according to the records which I have, at their meeting held June 2, 1894, unanimously passed a local rule that a ball driven from the seventh tee into the swamp, distance 223 yards, might be lifted and teed anywhere two club-lengths back of the swamp, without penalty. I should have posted it, but neglected to do so. Your dragon was a liar himself; and I never knew a dragon who wasn't.

Yours respectfully,
WILLIE MCGUFFIN.

* * *

The above is a copy of a correspondence found by me among the papers of the late Willie McGuffin, of St. Willieboy's Links, who recently departed from our club owing some $3000 for moneys collected but not accounted for. The names of the principals are, of course, changed. The correspondence seemed to me to be of sufficient interest to publish, not only from a psychological point of view, and as pointing a very important moral as to the integrity of a golf-card, but because it has brought up before my mind a very grave question:

Was Mr. Peabody really absolved by the prior action of the Greens Committee, of which he was unconscious? Or should he still consider himself unworthy to associate with true golfers?

I incline myself to the latter belief.

*John Updike is one of America's greatest living writers. He is the author of the celebrated* Rabbit *series, winning a Pulitzer Prize for* Rabbit Is Rich *(1981). Other prominent books from his pen are* The Centaurs *(1963),* Bech is Back *(1982),* The Witches of Eastwick *(1984), and* Rabbit At Rest *(1990). Altogether, he has written forty books. Updike is also a prolific writer of short stories. He is a regular contributor to* The New Yorker *and has written for* Harper's, Esquire, *and* Playboy. *Updike's "The Pro," originally published in* The New Yorker, *is the first of two stories in this book. In the story a duffer takes a golf lesson from the local pro and the reader gets to eavesdrop on the dialogue.*

*John Updike*

# THE PRO (1966)

I AM ON MY FOUR-HUNDRED-AND-TWELFTH GOLF LESSON, and my drives still have that pushed little tail, and my irons still take the divot on the wrong side of the ball. My pro is a big gloomy sun-browned man–age about thirty-eight, weight around 195. When he holds a club in his gloved hand and swishes it nervously (the nervousness comes over him after the first twenty minutes of our lesson), he makes it look light as a feather, a straw, a baton. Once I sneaked his 3-wood from his bag, and the head weighed more than a cannonball. "Easy does it, Mr. Wallace," he says to me. My name is not Wallace, but he smooths his clients toward one generic, acceptable name. I call him Dave.

"Easy does it, Mr. Wallace," he says. "That ball is not going anywhere by itself, so what's your hurry?"

"I want to clobber the bastard," I say. It took me two hundred lessons to attain this pitch of frankness.

"You dipped again," he tells me, without passion. "That right shoulder of yours dipped, and your knees locked, you were so anxious. Ride those knees, Mr. Wallace."

"I can't. I keep thinking about my wrists. I'm afraid I won't pronate them."

This is meant to be a joke, but he doesn't smile. "Ride those knees, Mr. Wallace. Forget your wrists. Look." He takes my 5-iron into his hands, a sight so thrilling it knocks the breath out of me. It is like, in the movies we all saw as children (oh, blessed childhood!), the instant when King Kong, or the gigantic Cyclops, lifts the beautiful blonde, who has blessedly fainted, over his head, and she becomes utterly weightless, a thing of sheer air and vision and pathos. I love it, I feel half sick with pleasure, when he lifts my club, and want to tell him so, but I can't. After four hundred and eleven lessons, I still repress.

"The hands can't *help* but be right," he says, "if the *knees* are right." He twitches the club, so casually I think he is brushing a bee from the ball's surface. There is an innocent click; the ball whizzes into the air and rises along a line as straight as the edge of a steel ruler, hangs at its remote apogee for a moment of meditation, and settles like a snowflake twenty yards beyond the shagging caddie.

"Gorgeous, Dave," I say, with an affectation of camaraderie, though my stomach is a sour churning of adoration and dread.

He says, "A little fat, but that's the idea. Did you see me grunt and strain?"

"No, Dave." This is our litany.

"Did you see me jerk my head, or freeze at the top of the backswing, or rock forward on my toes?"

"No, Dave, no."

"Well then, what's the problem? Step up and show me how."

I assume my stance, and take back the club, low, slowly; at the top, my eyes fog over, and my joints dip and swirl like barn swallows. I swing. There is a fruitless commotion of dust and rubber at my feet. "Smothered it," I say promptly. After enough lessons, the terminology becomes second nature. The whole process, as I understand it, is essentially one of self-analysis. The pro is merely a catalyst, a random sample, I have read somewhere, from the grab bag of humanity.

He insists on wearing a droll porkpie hat from which his heavy brown figure somehow downflows; his sloping shoulders, his hanging arms, his faintly pendulous belly, and his bent knees all tend toward his shoes, which are ideally natty–solid as bricks, black and white, with baroque stitching, frilled kilties, and spikes as neat as alligator teeth. He looks at me almost with interest. His grass-green irises are tiny, whittled by years of concentrating on the ball. "Loosen up," he tells me. I love it, I clench with gratitude, when he deigns to be directive. "Take a few practice swings, Mr. Wallace. You looked like a rusty mechanical man on that one. Listen. Golf is an effortless game."

"Maybe I have no aptitude," I say, giggling, blushing, hoping to deflect him with the humility bit.

He is not deflected. Stolidly he says, "Your swing is sweet. When it's there." Thus he uplifts me and crushes me from phrase to phrase. "You're blocking yourself out," he goes on. "You're not open to your own potential. You're not, as we say, *free*."

"I know, I know. That's why I'm taking all these expensive lessons."

"Swing, Mr. Wallace. Show me your swing."

I swing, and feel the impurities like bubbles and warps in glass: hurried backswing, too much right hand at impact, failure to finish high.

The pro strips off his glove. "Come over to the eighteenth green." I think we are going to practice chipping (a restricted but relaxed pendulum motion) for the fiftieth time, but he says, "Lie down."

The green is firm yet springy. The grounds crew has done a fine job watering this summer, through that long dry spell. Not since childhood have I lain this way, on sweet flat grass, looking up into a tree, branch above branch, each leaf distinct in its generic shape, as when, in elementary school, we used to press them between wax paper. The tree is a sugar maple. For all the times I have tried to hit around it, I never noticed its species before. In the fall, its dried-up leaves have to be brushed from the line of every putt. This spring, when the branches were tracery dusted with a golden budding, I punched a 9-iron right through the crown and salvaged a double bogey.

Behind and above me, the pro's voice is mellower than I remember it, with a lulling grittiness, like undissolved sugar in tea. He says, "Mr. Wallace, tell me what you're thinking about when you freeze at the top of your backswing."

"I'm thinking about my shot. I see it sailing dead on the pin, hitting six feet short, taking a bite with lots of backspin, and dribbling into the cup. The crowd goes *ooh* and cheers."

"Who's in the crowd? Anybody you know personally?"

"No. . . wait. There is somebody. My mother. She has one of those cardboard periscope things and shouts out, 'Gorgeous, Billy!'"

"She calls you Billy."

"That's my name, Dave. William, Willy, Billy, Bill. Let's cut out this Mr. Wallace routine. You call me Bill, I'll call you Dave." He is much easier to talk to, the pro, without the sight of his powerful passionless gloom, his hands (one bare, one gloved) making a mockery of the club's weight.

"Anybody else you know? Wife? Kids?"

"No, my wife's had to take the babysitter home. Most of the kids are at camp."

"What else do you see up there at the top of the backswing?"

"I see myself quitting lessons." It was out, *whiz,* before I had time to censor. Silence reigns in the leafy dome above me. A sparrow is hopping from branch to branch, like a pencil point going from number to number in those children's puzzles we all used to do.

At last the pro grunts, which, as we said, he never does.

"The last time you were out, Mr. Wallace, what did you shoot?"

"You mean the last time I kept count?"

"Mm."

"A hundred eight. But that was with some lucky putts."

"Mm. Better stand up. Any prolonged pressure, the green may get a fungus. This bent grass is hell to maintain." When I stand, he studies me, chuckles, and says to an invisible attendant, "A hundred eight, with a hot putter yet, and he wants to quit lessons."

I beg, "Not quit forever–just for a vacation. Let me play a few different courses. You know, get out into the world. Maybe even try a public course. Hell, or go to a driving range and whack out a bucket of balls. You know, learn to live with the game I've got. Enjoy life."

His noble impassivity is invested with a shimmering, twinkling humorousness; his leathery face softens toward a smile, and the trace of a dimple is discovered in his cheek. "Golf is life," he says softly, and his green eyes expand, "and life is lessons," and the humps of his brown muscles merge with the hillocks and swales of the course, whose red flags prick the farthest horizon, and whose dimmest sand traps are indistinguishable from galaxies. I see that he is right, as always, absolutely; there is no life, no world, beyond the golf course–just an infinite and terrible falling-off. "If I don't give *you* lessons," he is going on, "how will I pay for *my* lessons?"

"*You* take lessons?"

"Sure. I hook under pressure. Like Palmer. I'm too strong. Any rough on the left, there I am. You don't have that problem, with your nice pushy slice."

"You mean there's a sense," I ask, scarcely daring , "in which *you* need *me*?"

He puts his hand on my shoulder, the hand pale from wearing the glove, and I become a feather at the touch, all air and ease. "Mr. Wallace," he says, "I've learned a lot from your sweet swing. I hate it when, like now, the half hour's up."

"Next Tuesday, eleven-thirty?"

Solemnly my pro nods. "We'll smooth out your chipping. Here in the shade."

*Ring Lardner (1885–1933) is famous for his short stories about early twentieth-century America. While working as a sportswriter at the* Chicago Tribune, *he discovered that his real forte was writing fiction. Lardner's stories about baseball include such gems as "Alibi Ike" and "Horseshoes." He is also celebrated for his golf stories, and "Mr. Frisbie" is the best of these. Lardner was a gifted satirist and humorist, and this story provides a fine example of his talents. Typically, it is written in the colloquial jargon and fractured diction of the ill-educated but discerning observer, in this case a caddy. Some of the best of Lardner's other stories are in his book* Round-Up *(1929) and the* Collected Stories of Ring Lardner *(1941). "Mr. Frisbie" was first published in* Cosmopolitan.

*Ring Lardner*

# MR. FRISBIE (1928)

I AM MR. ALLEN FRISBIE'S CHAUFFEUR. Allen Frisbie is a name I made up because they tell me that if I used the real name of the man I am employed by that he might take offense and start trouble though I am sure he will never see what I am writing as he does not read anything except *The American Golfer*, but of course some of his friends might call his attention to it. If you knew who the real name of the man is, it would make more interesting reading as he is one of the 10 most wealthiest men in the United States and a man who everybody is interested in because he is so famous and the newspapers are always writing articles about him and sending high salary reporters to interview him but he is a very hard man to reproach or get an interview with and when they do he never tells them anything.

That is how I come to be writing this article because about two weeks ago a Mr. Kirk had an appointment to interview Mr. Frisbie for one of the newspapers and I drove him to the station after the interview was over and he said to me your boss is certainly a tough egg to interview and getting a word out of him is like pulling turnips.

"The public do not know anything about the man," said Mr. Kirk. "They know he is very rich and has got a wife and a son and a daughter and what their names are but as to his private life and his likes and dislikes he might just as well be a monk in a convent."

"The public knows he likes golf," I said.

"They do not know what kind of a game he plays."

"He plays pretty good," I said.

"How good?" said Mr. Kirk.

"About 88 or 90," I said.

"So is your grandmother," said Mr. Kirk.

He only meant the remark as a comparison but had either of my grandmothers lived they would both have been over 90. Mr. Kirk did not believe I was telling the truth about Mr. Frisbie's game and he was right though was I using real names I would not admit it as Mr. Frisbie is very sensitive in regards to his golf.

Mr. Kirk kept pumping at me but I am used to being pumped at and Mr. Kirk finally gave up pumping at me as he found me as closed mouth as Mr. Frisbie himself but he made the remark that he wished he was in my place for a few days and as close to the old man as I am and he would then be able to write the first real article which had ever been written about the old man. He called Mr. Frisbie the old man.

He said it was too bad I am not a writer so I could write up a few instance about Mr. Frisbie from the human side on account of being his caddy at golf and some paper or magazine would pay me big. He said if you would tell me a few instance I would write them up and split with you but I said no I could not think of anything which would make an article but after Mr. Kirk had gone I got to thinking it over and thought to myself maybe I could be a writer if I tried and at least there is no harm in trying so for the week after Mr. Kirk's visit I spent all my spare time writing down about Mr. Frisbie only at first I used his real name but when I showed the article they said for me not to use real names but the public would guess who it was anyway and that was just as good as using real names.

So I have gone over the writing again and changed the name to Allen Frisbie and other changes and here is the article using Allen Frisbie.

When I say I am Mr. Frisbie's chauffeur I mean I am his personal chauffeur. There are two other chauffeurs who drive for the rest of the family and run errands. Had I nothing else to do only drive I might well be turned a man of leisure as Mr. Frisbie seldom never goes in to the city more than twice a week and even less oftener than that does he pay social visits.

His golf links is right on the place an easy walk from the house to the first tee and here is where he spends a good part of each and every day playing alone with myself in the roll of caddy. So one would not be far from amiss to refer to me as Mr. Frisbie's caddy rather than his chauffeur but it was as a chauffeur that I was engaged and can flatter myself that there are very few men of my calling who would not gladly exchange their salary and position for mine.

Mr. Frisbie is a man just this side of sixty years of age. Almost ten years ago he retired from active business with money enough to put him in a class with the richest men in the United States and since then his investments have increased their value to such an extent so that now he is in a class with the richest men in the United States.

It was soon after his retirement that he bought the Peter Vischer estate near Westbury, Long Island. On this estate there was a 9 hole golf course in good condition and considered one of the best private 9 hole golf courses in the United States but Mr. Frisbie would have had it plowed up and the land used for some other usage only for a stroke of chance which was when Mrs. Frisbie's brother came over from England for a visit.

It was during while this brother-in-law was visiting Mr. Frisbie that I entered the last named employee and was an onlooker when Mr. Frisbie's brother-in-law persuaded his brother-in-law to try the game of golf.

As luck would have it Mr. Frisbie's first drive was so good that his brother-in-law would not believe he was a beginner till he had seen Mr. Frisbie shoot again but that first perfect drive made Mr. Frisbie a slave of the game and without which there would be no such instance as I am about to relate.

I would better explain at this junction that I am not a golfer but I have learned quite a lot of knowledge about the game by cadding for Mr. Frisbie and also once or twice in company with my employer have picked up some knowledge of the game by witnessing players like Bobby Jones and Hagen and Sarazen and Smith in some of their matches. I have only tried it myself on a very few occasions when I was sure Mr. Frisbie could not observe me and will confide that in my own mind I am convinced that with a little practise that I would have little trouble defeating Mr. Frisbie but will never seek to prove same for reasons which I will leave it to the reader to guess the reasons.

One day shortly after Mr. Frisbie's brother-in-law had ended his visit I was cadding for Mr. Frisbie and as had become my custom keeping the score for him when a question arose as to whether he had taken 7 or 8 strokes on the last hole. A 7 would have given him a total of 63 for the 9 holes while a 8 would have made it 64. Mr. Frisbie tried to recall the different strokes but was not certain and asked me to help him.

As I remember it he had sliced his 4th. wooden shot in to a trap but had recovered well and got on to the green and then had taken 3 putts which would make him a 8 but by some slip of the tongue when I started to say 8 I said 7 and before I could correct myself Mr. Frisbie said yes you are right it was a 7.

"That is even 7s," said Mr. Frisbie.

"Yes," I said.

On the way back to the house he asked me what was my salary which I told him and he said well I think you are worth more than that and from now on you will get $25.00 more per week.

On another occasion when 9 more holes had been added to the course and Mr. Frisbie was playing the 18 holes regular every day he came to the last hole needing a 5 to break 112 which was his best score.

The 18th. hole is only 120 yards with a big green but a brook in front and traps in back of it. Mr. Frisbie got across the brook with his second but the ball went over in to the trap and it looked like bad business because Mr. Frisbie is even worse with a niblick than almost any other club except maybe the No. 3 and 4 irons and the wood.

Well I happened to get to the ball ahead of him and it laid there burred in the deep sand about a foot from a straight up and down bank 8 foot high where it would have been impossible for any man alive to oust it in one stroke but as luck would have it I stumbled and gave the ball a little kick and by chance it struck the side of the bank and stuck in the grass and Mr. Frisbie got it up on the green in one stroke and was down in 2 putts for his 5.

"Well that is my record 111 or 3 over 6s," he said.

Now my brother had a couple of tickets for the polo at Meadowbrook the next afternoon and I am a great lover of horses flesh so I said to Mr. Frisbie can I go to the polo tomorrow afternoon and he said certainly any time you want a afternoon off do not hesitate to ask me but a little while later there was a friend of mine going to get married at Atlantic City and Mr. Frisbie had just shot a 128 and broke his spoon besides and when I mentioned about going to Atlantic City for my friend's wedding he snapped at me like a wolf and said what did I think it was the Xmas holidays.

Personally I am a man of simple tastes and few wants and it is very seldom when I am not satisfied to take my life and work as they come and not seek fear or favor but of course there are times in every man's life when they desire something a little out of the ordinary in the way of a little vacation or perhaps a financial accommodation of some kind and in such cases I have found Mr. Frisbie a king amongst men provide it one uses discretion in choosing the moment of their reproach but a variable tyrant if one uses bad judgment in choosing the moment of their reproach.

You can count on him granting any reasonable request just after he has made a good score or even a good shot where as a person seeking a favor when he is off his game might just as well ask President Coolidge to do the split.

I wish to state that having learned my lesson along these lines I did not use my knowledge to benefit myself alone but have on the other hand utilized same mostly to the advantage of others especially the members of Mr. Frisbie's own family. Mr. Frisbie's wife and son and daughter all realized early in my employment that I could handle Mr. Frisbie better than anyone else and without me ever exactly divulging the secret of my methods they just naturally began to take it for granted that I could succeed with him where they failed and it became their habit when they sought something from their respective spouse and father to summons me as their adviser and advocate.

As an example of the above I will first sight an example in connection with Mrs. Frisbie. This occurred many years ago and was the instance which convinced her beyond all doubt that I was a expert on the subject of managing her husband.

Mrs. Frisbie is a great lover of music but unable to perform on any instrument herself. It was her hope that one of the children would be a pianiste and a great deal of money was spent on piano lessons for both Robert the son and Florence the daughter but all in vain as neither of the two showed any talent and their teachers one after another gave them up in despair.

Mrs. Frisbie at last became desirous of purchasing a player piano and of course would consider none but the best but when she broached the subject to Mr. Frisbie he turned a deaf ear as he said pianos were made to be played by hand and people who could not learn same did not deserve music in the home.

I do not know how often Mr. and Mrs. Frisbie disgust the matter pro and con.

Personally they disgust it in my presence any number of times and finally being a great admirer of music myself and seeing no reason why a man of Mr. Frisbie's great wealth should deny his wife a harmless pleasure such as a player piano I suggested to the madam that possibly if she would leave matters to me the entire proposition might be put over. I can no more than fail I told her and I do not think I will fail so she instructed me to go ahead as I could not do worse than fail which she had already done herself.

I will relate the success of my plan as briefly as possible. Between the house and the golf course there was a summer house in which Mrs. Frisbie sat reading while Mr. Frisbie played golf. In this summer house she could sit so as not to be visible from the golf course. She was to sit there till she heard me whistle the strains of "Over There" where at she was to appear on the scene like she had come direct from the house and the fruits of our scheme would then be known.

For two days Mrs. Frisbie had to console herself with her book as Mr. Frisbie's golf was terrible and there was no moment when I felt like it would not be courting disaster to summons her on the scene but during the 3rd. afternoon his game suddenly improved and he had shot the 1st. 9 holes in 53 and started out on the 10th. with a pretty drive when I realized the time had come.

Mrs. Frisbie appeared promptly in answer to my whistling and walked rapidly up to Mr. Frisbie like she had hurried from the house and said there is a man at the house from that player piano company and he says he will take $50.00 off the price if I order today and please let me order one as I want one so much.

"Why certainly dear go ahead and get it dear," said Mr. Frisbie and that is the way Mrs. Frisbie got her way in regards to a player piano. Had I not whistled when I did but waited a little longer it would have spelt ruination to our schemes as Mr. Frisbie took a 12 on the 11th. hole and would have bashed his wife over the head with a No. 1 iron had she even asked him for a toy drum.

I have been of assistance to young Mr. Robert Frisbie the son with reference to several items of which I will only take time to touch on one item with reference to Mr. Robert wanting to drive a car. Before Mr. Robert was 16 years of age he was always after Mr. Frisbie to allow him to drive one of the cars and Mr. Frisbie always said him nay on the grounds that it is against the law for a person under 16 years of age to drive a car.

When Mr. Robert reached the age of 16 years old however this excuse no longer held good and yet Mr. Frisbie continued to say Mr. Robert nay in regards to driving a car. There is plenty of chauffeurs at your beckon call said Mr. Frisbie to drive you where ever and when ever you wish to go but of course Mr. Robert like all youngsters wanted to drive himself and personally I could see no harm in it as I personally could not drive for him and the other 2 chauffeurs in Mr. Frisbie's employee at the time were just as lightly to wreck a car as Mr. Robert so I promised Mr. Robert that I would do my best towards helping him towards obtaining permission to drive one of the cars.

"Leave it to me" was my bequest to Mr. Robert and sure enough my little strategy turned the trick though Mr. Robert did not have the patience like his mother to wait in the summer house till a favorable moment arrived so it was necessary for me to carry through the entire proposition by myself.

The 16th hole on our course is perhaps the most difficult hole on our course at least it has always been a variable tartar for Mr. Frisbie.

It is about 350 yards long in length and it is what is called a blind hole as you can not see the green from the tee as you drive from the tee up over a hill with a direction flag as the only guide and down at the bottom of the hill there is a brook a little over 225 yards from the tee which is the same brook which you come to again on the last hole and in all the times Mr. Frisbie has played around the course he has seldom never made this 16th. hole in less than 7 strokes or more as his tee shot just barely skins the top of the hill giving him a down hill lie which upsets him so that he will miss the 2d. shot entirely or top it and go in to the brook.

Well I generally always stand up on top of the hill to watch where his tee shot goes and on the occasion referred to he got a pretty good tee shot which struck on top of the hill and rolled half way down and I hurried to the ball before he could see me and I picked it up and threw it across the brook and when he climbed to the top of the hill I pointed to where the ball laid the other side of the brook and shouted good shot Mr. Frisbie. He was overjoyed and beamed with joy and did not suspect anything out of the way though in reality he could not hit a ball more than 60 yards if it was teed on the summit of Pike's Peak.

Fate was on my side at this junction and Mr. Frisbie hit a perfect mashie shot on to the green and sunk his 2d. putt for the only 4 of his career on this hole. He was almost delirious with joy and you may be sure I took advantage of the situation and before we were fairly off the green I said to him Mr. Frisbie if you do not need me tomorrow morning do you not think it would be a good time for me to learn Mr. Robert to drive a car.

"Why certainly he is old enough now to drive a car and it is time he learned."

I now come to the main instance of my article which is in regards to Miss Florence Frisbie who is now Mrs. Henry Craig and of course Craig is not the real name but you will soon see that what I was able to do for her was no such child's play like gaining consent for Mr. Robert to run a automobile or Mrs. Frisbie to purchase a player piano but this was a matter of the up most importance and I am sure the reader will not consider me a vain bragger when I claim that I handled it with some skill.

Miss Florence is a very pretty and handsome girl who has always had a host of suitors who paid court to her on account of being pretty as much as her great wealth and I believe there has been times when no less than half a dozen or more young men were paying court to her at one time. Well about 2 years ago she lost her heart to young Henry Craig and at the same time Mr. Frisbie told her in no uncertain turns that she must throw young Craig over board and marry his own choice young Junior Holt or he would cut her off without a dime.

Holt and Craig are not the real names of the two young men referred to though I am using their real first names namely Junior and Henry. Young Holt is a son of Mr. Frisbie's former partner in business and a young man who does not drink or smoke and has got plenty of money in his own rights and a young man who any father would feel safe in trusting their daughter in the bands of matrimony. Young Craig at that time had no money and no position and his parents had both died leaving nothing but debts.

"Craig is just a tramp and will never amount to anything," said Mr. Frisbie. "I have had inquiries made and I understand he drinks when anyone will furnish him the drinks. He has never worked and never will. Junior Holt is a model young man from all accounts and comes of good stock and is the only young man I know whose conduct and habits are such that I would consider him fit to marry my daughter."

Miss Florence said that Craig was not a tramp and she loved him and would not marry anyone else and as for Holt he was terrible but even if he was not terrible she would never consider undergoing the bands of matrimony with a man named Junior.

"I will elope with Henry if you do not give in," she said.

Mr. Frisbie was not alarmed by this threat as Miss Florence has a little common sense and would not be lightly to elope with a young man who could hardly finance a honeymoon trip on the subway. But neither was she showing any signs of yielding in regards to his wishes in regards to young Holt and things began to take on the appearance of a dead lock between father and daughter with neither side showing signs of yielding.

Miss Florence grew pale and thin and spent most of her time in her room instead of seeking enjoyment amongst her friends as was her custom. As for Mr. Frisbie he was always a man of iron will and things began to take on the appearance of a dead lock with neither side showing any signs of yielding.

It was when it looked like Miss Florence was on the verge of a serious illness when Mrs. Frisbie came to me and said we all realize that you have more influence with Mr. Frisbie than anyone else and is there any way you can think of to get him to change his status toward Florence and these 2 young men because if something is not done right away I am afraid of what will happen. Miss Florence likes you and has a great deal of confidence in you said Mrs. Frisbie so will you see her and talk matters over with her and see if you can not think up some plan between you which will put a end to this situation before my poor little girl dies.

So I went to see Miss Florence in her bedroom and she was a sad sight with her eyes red from weeping and so pale and thin and yet her face lit up with a smile when I entered the room and she shook hands with me like I was a long lost friend.

"I asked my mother to send you," said Miss Florence. "This case looks hopeless but I know you are a great fixer as far as Father is concerned and you can fix it if anyone can. Now I have got a idea which I will tell you and if you like it it will be up to you to carry it out."

"What is your idea?"

"Well," said Miss Florence, "I think that if Mr. Craig the man I love could do Father a favor why Father would not be so set against him."

"What kind of a favor?"

"Well Mr. Craig plays a very good game of golf and he might give Father some pointers which would improve Father's game."

"Your father will not play golf with anyone and certainly not with a good player and besides that your father is not the kind of a man that wants anyone giving him pointers. Personally I would just as leaf go up and tickle him as tell him that his stance is wrong."

"Then I guess my idea is not so good."

"No," I said and then all of a sudden I had a idea of my own. "Listen Miss Florence does the other one play golf?"

"Who?"

"Young Junior Holt."

"Even better than Mr. Craig."

"Does your father know that?"

"Father does not know anything about him or he would not like him so well."

Well I said I have got a scheme which may work or may not work but no harm to try and the first thing to be done is for you to spruce up and pretend like you do not feel so unkindly towards young Holt after all. The next thing is to tell your father that Mr. Holt never played golf and never even saw it played but would like to watch your father play so he can get the hang of the game.

And then after that you must get Mr. Holt to ask your father to let him follow him around the course and very secretly you must tip Mr. Holt off that your father wants his advice. When ever your father does anything wrong Mr. Holt is to correct him. Tell him your father is crazy to improve his golf but is shy in regards to asking for help.

There is a lot of things that may happen to this scheme but if it should go through why I will guarantee that at least half your troubles will be over.

Well as I said there was a lot of things that might have happened to spoil my scheme but nothing did happen and the very next afternoon Mr. Frisbie confided in me that Miss Florence seemed to feel much better and seemed to have changed her mind in regards to Mr. Holt and also said that the last named had expressed a desire to follow Mr. Frisbie around the golf course and learn something about the game.

Mr. Holt was a kind of a fat pudgy young man with a kind of a sneering smile and the first minute I saw him I wished him the worst.

For a second before Mr. Frisbie started to play I was certain we were lost as Mr. Frisbie remarked where have you been keeping yourself Junior that you never watched golf before. But luckily young Holt took the remark as a joke and made no reply. Right afterwards the storm clouds began to gather in the sky. Mr. Frisbie sliced his tee shot.

"Mr. Frisbie," said young Holt, "there are several things the matter with you then but the main trouble was that you stood too close to the ball and cut across it with your club head and besides that you swang back faster than Alex Smith and you were off your balance and you gripped too hard and you jerked instead of hitting with a smooth follow through."

Well, Mr. Frisbie gave him a queer look and then made up his mind that Junior was trying to be humorous and he frowned at him so as he would not try it again but when we located the ball in the rough and Mr. Frisbie asked me for his spoon young Holt said Oh take your mashie Mr. Frisbie never use a wooden club in a place like that and Mr. Frisbie scowled and mumbled under his breath and missed the ball with his spoon and missed it again and then took a midiron and just dribbled it on to the fairway and finally got on the green in 7 and took 3 putts.

I suppose you might say that this was one of the quickest golf matches on record as it ended on the 2d. tee. Mr. Frisbie tried to drive and sliced again. Then young Holt took a ball from my pocket and a club from the bag and said here let me show you the swing and drove the ball 250 yards straight down the middle of the course.

I looked at Mr. Frisbie's face and it was puffed out and a kind of a purple black color. Then he burst and I will only repeat a few of the more friendlier of his remarks.

"Get to hell and gone of my place. Do not never darken my doors again. Just show up around here one more time and I will blow out what you have got instead of brains. You lied to my girl and you tried to make a fool out of me. Get out before I sick my dogs on you and tear you to pieces."

Junior most lightly wanted to offer some word of explanation or to demand one on his own account but saw at a glance how useless same would be. I heard later that he saw Miss Florence and that she just laughed at him.

"I made a mistake about Junior Holt," said Mr. Frisbie that evening. "He is no good and must never come to this house again."

"Oh father and just when I was beginning to like him," said Miss Florence.

Well like him or not like him she and the other young man Henry Craig were married soon afterwards which I suppose Mr. Frisbie permitted the bands in the hopes that same would rile Junior Holt.

Mr. Frisbie admitted he had made a mistake in regards to the last named but he certainly was not mistaken when he said that young Craig was a tramp and would never amount to anything.

Well I guess I have rambled on long enough about Mr. Frisbie.

*Golfers like to bet on the outcome of their matches, as to low scores, first on green, winning holes, and so forth. Makes the game more fun. There are also golf hustlers who try to set up lesser players so as to win sucker bets. The Ooley-cow in this story is a rich fellow from Iowa who retires to southern California, takes up golf, and gullibly falls prey to a couple of crafty hustlers. Author Charles E. Van Loan (1876–1919) was a prolific writer of sports fiction with over a dozen books to his credit, such as* The Big League *(1911),* Taking the Count *(1915), and* Score by Innings *(1919).*

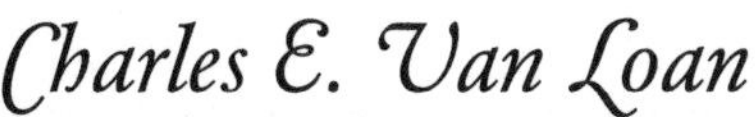


# THE OOLEY-COW (1918)

## I

AFTER THE EXPLOSION, and before Uncle Billy Poindexter and Old Man Sprott had been able to decide just what had hit them, Little Doc Ellis had the nerve to tell me that he had seen the fuse burning for months and months. Little Doc is my friend and I like him, but he resembles many other members of his profession in that he is usually wisest after the post mortem, when it is a wee bit late for the high contracting party.

And at all times Little Doc is full of vintage bromides and figures of speech.

"You have heard the old saw," said he. "A worm will turn if you keep picking on him, and so will a straight road if you ride it long enough. A camel is a wonderful burden bearer, but even a double-humped ship of the desert will sink on your hands if you pile the load on him a bale of hay at a time."

"A worm, a straight road, a camel and a sinking ship," said I. "Whither are we drifting?"

Little Doc did not pay any attention to me. It is a way he has.

"Think," said he, "how much longer a camel will stand up under punishment if he gets his load straw by straw, as it were. The Ooley-cow was a good thing, but Uncle Billy and Old Man Sprott did not use any judgment. They piled it on him too thick."

"Meaning," I asked, "to compare the Ooley-cow with a camel?"

"Merely a figure of speech," said Little Doc; "but yes, such was my intention."

"Well," said I, "your figures of speech need careful auditing. A camel can go eight days without a drink–"

Little Doc made impatient motions at me with both hands. He has no sense of humour, and his mind is a one-way track, totally devoid of spurs and derailing switches. Once started, he must go straight through to his destination.

"What I am trying to make plain to your limited mentality," said he, "is that Uncle Billy and Old Man Sprott needed a lesson in conservation, and they got it. The Ooley-cow was the easiest, softest picking that ever strayed from the home pasture. With care and decent treatment he would have lasted a long time and yielded an enormous quantity of nourishment, but Uncle Billy and Old Man Sprott were too greedy. They tried to corner the milk market, and now they will have to sign tags for their drinks and their golf balls the same as the rest of us. They have killed the goose that laid the golden eggs."

"A minute ago," said I, "the Ooley-cow was a camel. Now he is a goose–a dead goose, to be exact. Are you all done figuring with your speech?"

"Practically so, yes."

"Then," said I, "I will plaster up the cracks in your argument with the cement of information. I can use figures of speech myself. You are barking up the wrong tree. You are away off your base. It wasn't the loss of a few dollars that made Mr. Perkins run wild in our midst. It was the manner in which he lost them. Let us now dismiss the worm, the camel, the goose and all the rest of the menagerie, retaining only the Ooley-cow. What do you know about cows, if anything?"

"A little," answered my medical friend.

"A mighty little. You know that a cow has hoofs, horns and a tail. The same description would apply to many creatures, including Satan himself. Your knowledge of cows is largely academic. Now me, I was raised on a farm, and there were cows in my curriculum. I took a seven-year course in the gentle art of acquiring the lacteal fluid. Cow is my specialty, my long suit, my best hold. Believe it or not, when we christened old Perkins the Ooley-cow we builded better than we knew."

"I follow you at a great distance," said Little Doc. "Proceed with the rat killing. Why did we build better than we knew when we did not know anything?"

"Because," I explained, "Perkins not only looks like a cow and walks like a cow and plays golf like a cow, but he has the predominant characteristic of a cow. He has the one distinguishing trait which all country cows have in common. If you had studied that noble domestic animal as closely as I have, you would not need to be told what moved Mr. Perkins to strew the entire golf course with the mangled remains of the two old pirates before mentioned. Uncle Billy and Old Man Sprott were milking him, yes, and it is quite likely that the Ooley-cow knew that he was being milked, but that knowledge was not the prime cause of the late unpleasantness."

"I still follow you," said Little Doc plaintively, "but I am losing ground every minute."

"Listen carefully," said I. "Pin back your ears and give me your undivided attention. There are many ways of milking a cow without exciting the animal to violence. I speak now of the old-fashioned cow–the country cow–from Iowa, let us say."

"The Ooley-cow is from Iowa," murmured Little Doc.

"Exactly. A city cow may be milked by machinery, and in a dozen different ways, but the country cow does not know anything about new fangled methods. There is one thing–and one thing only–which will make the gentlest old mooley in Iowa kick over the bucket, upset the milker, jump a four-barred fence and join the wild bunch on the range. Do you know what that one thing is?"

"I haven't even a suspicion," confessed Little Doc.

Then I told him. I told him in words of one syllable, and after a time he was able to grasp the significance of my remarks. If I could make Little Doc see the point I can make you see it too. We go from here.

Wesley J. Perkins hailed form Dubuque, but he did not hail from there until he had gathered up all the loose change in Northeastern Iowa. When he arrived in sunny Southern California he was fifty-five years of age, and at least fifty of those years had been spent in putting aside something for a rainy day. Judging by the diameter of his bankroll, he must have feared the sort of a deluge which caused the early settlers to lay the ground plans for the Tower of Babel.

Now it seldom rains in Southern California–that is to say, it seldom rains hard enough to produce a flood–and as soon as Mr. Perkins became acquainted with climatic conditions he began to jettison his ark. He joined an exclusive downtown club, took up quarters there and spent his afternoons playing dominoes with some other members of the I've-got-mine Association. Aside from his habit of swelling up whenever he mentioned his home town, and insisting on referring to it as "the Heidelberg of America," there was nothing about Mr. Perkins to provoke comment, unfavourable or otherwise. He was just one more Iowan in a country where Iowans are no novelty.

In person he was the mildest-mannered man that ever foreclosed a short-term mortgage and put a family out in the street. His eyes were large and bovine, his mouth drooped perpetually and so did his jowls, and he moved with the slow, uncertain gait of a venerable milch cow. He had a habit of lowering his head and staring vacantly into space, and all these things earned for him the unhandsome nickname by which he is now known.

"But why the Ooley-cow?" some one asked one day. "It doesn't mean anything at all!"

"Well," was the reply, "neither does Perkins."

But this was an error, as we shall see later.

It was an increasing waistline that caused the Ooley-cow to look about him for some form of gentle exercise. His physician suggested golf, and that very week the board of directors of the Country Club was asked to consider his application for membership. There were no ringing cheers, but he passed the censors.

I will say for Perkins that when he decided to commit golf he went about it in a very thorough manner. He had himself surveyed for three knickerbocker suits, he laid in a stock of soft shirts, imported stockings and spiked shoes, and he gave our professional *carte blanche* in the matter of field equipment. It is not a safe thing to give a Scotchman permission to dip his hand in your change pocket, and MacPherson certainly availed himself of the opportunity to finger some of the Dubuque money. He took one look at the novice and unloaded on him something less than a hundredweight of dead stock. He also gave him a lesson or two, and sent him forth armed to the teeth with wood, iron and aluminum.

Almost immediately Perkins found himself in the hands of Poindexter and Sprott, two extremely hard-boiled old gentlemen who have never been known to take any interest in a financial proposition assaying less than seven per cent, and that fully guaranteed. Both are retired capitalists, but when they climbed out of the trenches and retreated into the realm of sport they took all their business instincts with them.

Uncle Billy can play to a twelve handicap when it suits him to do so, and his partner in crime is only a couple of strokes behind him; but they seldom uncover their true form, preferring to pose as doddering and infirm invalids, childish old men, who only think they can play the game of golf, easy marks for the rising generation. New members are their victims; beginners are just the same as manna from heaven to them. They instruct the novice humbly and apologetically, but always with a small side bet, and no matter how fast the novice improves he makes the astounding discovery that his two feeble old tutors are able to keep pace with him. Uncle Billy and Old Man Sprott are experts at nursing a betting proposition along, and they seldom win any sort of a match by a margin of more than two up and one to go. Taking into account the natural limitations of age they play golf very well, but they play a cinch even better–and harder. It is common scandal that Uncle Billy has not bought a golf ball in ten years. Old Man Sprott bought one in 1915, but it was under the mellowing influence of the third toddy and, therefore, should not count against him.

The Ooley-cow was a cinch. When he turned up, innocent and guileless and eager to learn the game, Uncle Billy and his running mate were quick to realise that Fate had sent them a downy bird for plucking, and in no time at all the air was full of feathers.

They played the Ooley-cow for golf balls, they played him for caddy hire, they played him for drinks and cigars, they played him for luncheons and they played him for a sucker–played him for everything, in fact, but the locker rent and the club dues. How they came to overlook these items is more than I know. The Ooley-cow would have stood for it; he stood for everything. He signed all the tags with a loose and vapid grin, and if he suffered from writer's cramp he never mentioned the fact. His monthly bill must have been a thing to shudder at, but possibly he regarded this extra outlay as part of his tuition.

Once in a while he was allowed to win, for Poindexter and Sprott followed the system practised by other confidence men; but they never forgot to take his winnings away from him the next day, charging him interest at the rate of fifty per cent for twenty-four hours. The Ooley-cow was so very easy that they took liberties with him, so good-natured about his losses that they presumed upon that good nature and ridiculed him openly; but the old saw sometimes loses a tooth, the worm turns, the straight road bends at last, so does the camel's back, and the prize cow kicks the milker into the middle of next week. And, as I remarked before, the cow usually has a reason.

## II

One morning I dropped into the downtown club which Perkins calls his home. I found him sitting in the reception room, juggling a newspaper and watching the door. He seemed somewhat disturbed.

"Good morning," said I.

"It is not a good morning," said he. "It's a bad morning. Look at this."

He handed me the paper, with his thumb at the head of the Lost-and-Found column, and I read as follows:

"LOST–A BLACK LEATHER WALLET, CONTAINING PRIVATE PAPERS AND A SUM OF MONEY. A SUITABLE REWARD WILL BE PAID FOR THE RETURN OF SAME, AND NO QUESTIONS ASKED. APPLY TO W. J. P., ARGONAUT CLUB, CITY."

"Tough luck," said I. "Did you lose much?"

"Quite a sum," replied the Ooley-cow. "Enough to make it an object. In large bills mostly."

"Too bad. The wallet had your cards in it?"

"And some papers of a private nature."

"Have you any idea where you might have dropped it? Or do you think it was stolen?"

"I don't know what to think. I had it last night at the Country Club just before I left. I know I had it then, because I took it out in the lounging room to pay a small bet to Mr. Poindexter–a matter of two dollars. Then I put the wallet back in my inside pocket and came straight here–alone in a closed car. I missed it just before going to bed. I telephoned to the Country Club. No sign of it there. I went to the garage myself. It was not in the car. Of course it may have been there earlier in the evening, but I think my driver is honest, and–"

At this point we were interrupted by a clean-cut looking youngster of perhaps seventeen years.

"Your initials are W. J. P., sir?" he asked politely.

"They are."

"This is your 'ad' in the paper?"

"It is."

The boy reached in his pocket and brought out a black leather wallet. "I have returned your property," said he, and waited while the Ooley-cow thumbed a roll of yellow-backed bills.

"All here," said Perkins with a sigh of relief. Then he looked up at the boy, and his large bovine eyes turned hard as moss agates. "Where did you get this?" he demanded abruptly. "How did you come by it?"

The boy smiled and shook his head, but his eyes never left Perkins' face. "No questions were to be asked, sir," said he.

"Right!" grunted the Ooley-cow. "Quite right. A bargain's a bargain. I–I beg your pardon, young man. . . . Still, I'd like to know. . . . Just curiosity, eh? . . .No? . . .Very well then. That being the case"–he stripped a fifty-dollar note from the roll and passed it over–"would you consider this a suitable reward?"

"Yes, sir, and thank you, sir."

"Good day," said Perkins, and put the wallet into his pocket. He stared at the boy until he disappeared through the street door.

"Something mighty queer about this," mused the Ooley-cow thoughtfully. "Mighty queer. That boy–he looked honest. He had good eyes and he wasn't afraid of me. I couldn't scare him worth a cent. Couldn't bluff him. . . .Yet if he found it somewhere, there wasn't any reason why he shouldn't have told me. He didn't steal it–I'll bet on that. Maybe he got it from some one who did. Oh, well, the main thing is that he brought it back. . . . Going out to the Country Club this afternoon?"

I said that I expected to play golf that day.

"Come out with me then," said the Ooley-cow. "Poindexter and Sprott will be there too. Yesterday afternoon I played Poindexter for the lunches to-day. Holed a long putt on the seventeenth green, and stuck him. Come along, and we'll make Poindexter give a party–for once."

"It can't be done," said I. "Uncle Billy doesn't give parties."

"We'll make him give one," chuckled the Ooley-cow. "We'll insist on it."

"Insist if you want to," said I, "but you'll never get away with it."

"Meet me here at noon," said the Ooley-cow. "If Poindexter doesn't give the party I will."

I wasn't exactly keen for the Ooley-cow's society, but I accepted his invitation to ride out to the club in his car. He regaled me with a dreary monologue, descriptive of the Heidelberg of America, and solemnly assured me that the pretty girls one sees in Chicago are all from Dubuque.

It was twelve-thirty when we arrived at the Country Club, and Uncle Billy and Old Man Sprott were there ahead of us.

"Poindexter," said Perkins, "you are giving a party to-day, and I have invited our friend here to join us."

Uncle Billy looked at Old Man Sprott, and both laughed uproariously. Right there was where I should have detected the unmistakable odour of a rodent. It was surprise number one.

"Dee-lighted!" cackled Uncle Billy. "Glad to have another guest, ain't we, Sprott?"

Sprott grinned and rubbed his hands. "You bet! Tell you what let's do, Billy. Let's invite everybody in the place–make it a regular party while you're at it!"

"Great idea!" exclaimed Uncle Billy. "The more the merrier!" This was surprise number two. The first man invited was Henry Bauer, who has known Uncle Billy for many years. He sat down quite overcome.

"You shouldn't do a thing like that, Billy," said he querulously. "I have a weak heart, and any sudden shock–"

"Nonsense! You'll join us?"

"Novelty always appealed to me," said Bauer. "I'm forever trying things that nobody has ever tried before. Yes, I'll break bread with you, but–why the celebration? What's it all about?"

That was what everybody wanted to know and what nobody found out, but the luncheon was a brilliant success in spite of the dazed and mystified condition of the guests, and the only limit was the limit of individual capacity. Eighteen of us sat down at the big round table, and sandwich-and-milk orders were sternly countermanded by Uncle Billy, who proved an amazing host, recommending this and that and actually ordering Rhine-wine cup for all hands. I could not have been more surprised if the bronze statue in the corner of the grill had hopped down from its pedestal to fill our glasses. Uncle Billy collected a great pile of tags beside his plate, but the presence of so much bad news waiting at his elbow did not seem to affect his appetite in the least. When the party was over he called the head waiter. "Mark these tags paid," said Uncle Billy, capping the collection with a yellow-backed bill, "and hand the change to Mr. Perkins."

"Yes sir," said the head waiter, and disappeared.

I looked at the Ooley-cow, and was just in time to see the light of intelligence dawn in his big soft eyes. He was staring at Uncle Billy, and his lower lip was flopping convulsively. Everybody began asking questions at once.

"One moment, gentlemen," mooed the Ooley-cow, pounding on the table. "One moment!"

"Now don't get excited, Perkins," said Old Man Sprott. "You got your wallet back, didn't you? Cost you fifty, but you got it back. Next time you won't be so careless."

"Yes," chimed in Uncle Billy, "you oughtn't to go dropping your money round loose that way. It'll teach you a lesson."

"It will indeed." The Ooley-cow lowered his head and glared first at one old pirate and then at the other. His soft eyes hardened and the moss-agate look came into them. He seemed about to bellow, paw up the dirt and charge.

"The laugh is on you," cackled Poindexter, "and I'll leave it to the boys here. Last night our genial host dropped his wallet on the floor out in the lounging room. I kicked it across under the table to Sprott and Sprott put his foot on it. We intended to give it back to him to-day, but this morning there was an 'ad' in the paper–reward and no questions asked–so we sent a nice bright boy over to the Argonaut Club with the wallet. Perkins gave the boy a fifty-dollar note–very liberal, I call it–and the boy gave it to me. Perfectly legitimate transaction. Our friend here has had a lesson, we've had a delightful luncheon party, and the joke is on him."

"And a pretty good joke, too!" laughed Old Man Sprott.

"Yes," said the Ooley-cow at last, "a pretty good joke. Ha, ha! A mighty good joke." And place it to his credit that he managed a very fair imitation of a fat man laughing, even to the shaking of the stomach and the wrinkles round the eyes. He looked down at the tray in front of him and fingered the few bills and some loose silver.

"A mighty good joke," he repeated thoughtfully, "but what I can't understand is this–why didn't you two jokers keep the change? It would have been just that much funnier."

## III

The Ooley-cow's party was generally discussed during the next ten days, the consensus of club opinion being that some one ought to teach Poindexter and Sprott the difference between humour and petty larceny. Most of the playing members were disgusted with the two old skinflints, and one effect of this sentiment manifested itself in the number of invitations that Perkins received to play golf with real people. He declined them all, much to our surprise, and continued to wallop his way round the course with Uncle Billy and Old Man Sprott, apparently on as cordial terms as ever.

"What are you going to do with such a besotted old fool as that?" asked Henry Bauer. "Here I've invited him into three foursomes this week–all good men, too–and he's turned me down cold. It's not that we want to play with him, for as a golfer he's a terrible thing. It's not that we're crazy about him personally, for socially he's my notion of zero minus; but he took his stinging like a dead-game sport and he's entitled to better treatment than he's getting. But if he hasn't any better sense than to pass his plate for more, what are you going to do about it?"

"'Ephraim is joined to idols,'" quoted Little Doc Ellis. "'Let him alone.'"

"No, it's the other way round," argued Bauer. "His idols are joined to him–fastened on like leeches. The question naturally arises, how did such a man ever accumulate a fortune? Who forced it on him, and when, and where, and why?"

That very afternoon the Ooley-cow turned up with his guest, a large, loud person, also from the Heidelberg of America, who addressed Perkins as "Wesley," and lost no time in informing us that Southern California would have starved to death but for Iowa capital. His name was

Cottle–Calvin D. Cottle–and he gave each one of us his card as he was introduced. There was no need. Nobody could have forgotten him. Some people make an impression at first sight–Calvin D. Cottle made a deep dent. His age was perhaps forty-five, but he spoke as one crowned with Methuselah's years and Solomon's wisdom, and after each windy statement he turned to the Ooley-cow for confirmation.

"Ain't that so, Wesley? Old Wes knows, you bet your life! He's from my home town!"

It was as good as a circus to watch Uncle Billy and Old Man Sprott sizing up this fresh victim. It reminded me of two wary old dogs circling for position, maneuvering for a safe hold. They wanted to know something about his golf game–what was his handicap, for instance?

"Handicap?" repeated Cottle. "Is that a California idea? Something new, ain't it?"

Uncle Billy explained the handicapping theory.

"Oh!" said Cottle. "You mean what do I go round in–how many strokes. Well, sometimes I cut under a hundred; sometimes I don't. It just depends. Some days I can hit 'em, some days I can't. That's all there is to it."

"My case exactly," purred Old Man Sprott. "Suppose we dispense with the handicap?"

"That's the stuff!" agreed Cottle heartily. "I don't want to have to give anybody anything; I don't want anybody to give me anything. I like an even fight, and what I say is, may the best man win! Am I right, gentlemen?"

"Absolutely!" chirped Uncle Billy. "May the best man win!"

"You bet I'm right!" boomed Cottle. "Ask old Wes here about me. Raised right in the same town with him, from a kid knee-high to a grasshopper! I never took any the best of it in my life, did I, Wes? No, you bet not! Remember that time I got skinned out of ten thousand bucks on the land deal? A lot of fellows would have squealed, wouldn't they? A lot of fellows would have hollered for the police; but I just laughed and gave 'em credit for being smarter than I was. I'm the same way in sport as I am in business. I believe in giving everybody credit. I win if I can, but if I can't–well, there's never any hard feelings. That's me all over. You may be able to *lick* me at this golf thing–likely you will; but you'll never *scare* me, that's a cinch. Probably you gentlemen play a better game than I do–been at it longer; but then I'm a lot younger than you are. Got more strength. Hit a longer ball when I do manage to land on one right. So it all evens up in the long run."

Mr. Cottle was still modestly cheering his many admirable qualities when the Perkins party went in to luncheon, and the only pause he made was on the first tee. With his usual caution Uncle Billy had arranged it so that Dubuque was opposed to Southern California, and he had also carefully neglected to name any sort of a bet until after he had seen the stranger drive.

Cottle teed his ball and stood over it, gripping his driver until his knuckles showed white under the tan. "Get ready to ride!" said he. "You're about to leave this place!"

The club head whistled through the air, and I can truthfully say that I never saw a man of his size swing any harder at a golf ball–or come nearer cutting one completely in two.

"Topped it, by gum!" ejaculated Mr. Cottle, watching the maimed ball until it disappeared in a bunker. "Topped it! Well, better luck next time! By the way, what are we playing for? Balls, or money, or what?"

"Whatever you like," said Uncle Billy promptly. "You name it."

"Good! That's the way I like to hear a man talk. Old Wes here is my partner, so I can't bet with him, but I'll have a side match with each of you gentlemen–say, ten great, big, smiling Iowa dollars. Always like to bet what I've got the most of. Satisfactory?"

Uncle Billy glanced at Old Man Sprott, and for an instant the old rascals hesitated. The situation was made to order for them, but they would have preferred a smaller wager to start with, being petty larcenists at heart.

"Better cut that down to five," said Perkins to Cottle in a low tone. "They play a strong game."

"Humph!" grunted his guest. "Did you ever know me to pike in my life? I ain't going to begin now. Ten dollars or nothing!"

"I've got you," said Old Man Sprott.

"This once," said Uncle Billy. "It's against my principles to play for money; but yes, this once."

And then those two old sharks insisted on a foursome bet as well.

"Ball, ball, ball," said the Ooley-cow briefly, and proceeded to follow his partner into the bunker. Poindexter and Sprott popped conservatively down the middle of the course and the battle was on.

Battle, did I say? It was a massacre of the innocents, a slaughter of babes and sucklings. Our foursome trailed along behind, and took note of Mr. Cottle, of Dubuque, in his fruitless efforts to tear the cover off the ball. He swung hard enough to knock down a lamp-post, but he seldom made proper connections, and when he did the ball landed so far off the course that it took him a dozen shots to get back again. He was hopelessly bad, so bad that there was no chance to make the side matches close ones. On the tenth tee Cottle demanded another bet–to give him a chance to get even, he said. Poindexter and Sprott each bet him another ten dollar note on the last nine, and this time Uncle Billy did not say anything about his principles.

After it was all over Cottle poured a few mint toddies into his system and floated an alibi to the surface.

"It was those confounded sand greens that did it," said he. "I'm used to grass, and I can't putt on anything else. Bet I could take you to Dubuque and flail the everlasting daylights out of you!"

"Shouldn't be surprised," said Uncle Billy. "You did a lot better on the last nine–sort of got into your stride. Any time you think you want revenge–"

"You can have it," finished Old Man Sprott, as he folded a crisp twenty-dollar note. "We believe in giving a man a chance–eh, Billy?"

"That's the spirit!" cried Cottle enthusiastically. "Give a man a chance; it's what I say and if he does anything, give him credit. You beat me to-day, but I never saw this course before. Tell you what we'll do: Let's make a day of it to-morrow. Morning and afternoon both. Satisfactory? Good! You've got forty dollars of my dough and I want it back. Nobody ever made me quit betting yet, if I figure to have a chance.

What's money? Shucks! My country is full of it! Now then, Wesley, if you'll come out on the practise green and give me some pointers on this sand thing, I'll be obliged to you. Ball won't run on sand like it will on grass–have to get used to it. Have to hit 'em a little harder. Soon as I get the hang of the thing we'll give these Native Sons a battle yet! Native Sons? Native Grandfathers! Come on!" Uncle Billy looked at Old Man Sprott and Old Man Sprott looked at Uncle Billy, but they did not begin to laugh until the Ooley-cow and his guest were out of earshot. Then they clucked and cackled and choked like a couple of hysterical old hens.

"His putting!" gurgled Uncle Billy. "Did he have a putt to win a hole all the way round?"

"Not unless he missed count of his shots. Say, Billy!"

"Well?"

"We made a mistake locating so far West. We should have stopped in Iowa. By now we'd have owned the entire state!"

## IV

I dropped Mr. Calvin D. Cottle entirely out of my thoughts; but when I entered the locker room shortly after noon the next day something reminded me of him. Possibly it was the sound of his voice.

"Boy! Can't we have 'nother toddy here? What's the matter with some service? How 'bout you, Wes? Oh, I forgot–you never take anything till after five o'clock. Think of all the fun you're missing. When I get to be an old fossil like you maybe I'll do the same. Good rule. . . . You gentlemen having anything? No? Kind of careful ain't you? Safety first, hey? . . . Just one toddy, boy, and if that mint ain't fresh, I'll. . . . Yep, you're cagey birds, you are, but I give you credit just the same. And some cash. Don't forget that. Rather have cash than credit any time, hey? I bet you would! But I don't mind a little thing like that. I'm a good sport. You ask Wes here if I ain't. If I ain't a good sport I ain't anything. . . . Still, I'll be darned if I see how you fellows do it! You're both old enough to have sons in the Soldiers' Home over yonder, but you take me out and lick me again–lick me and make me like it! A couple of dried-up mummies with one foot in the grave, and I'm right in the prime of life! Only a kid yet! It's humiliating, that's what it is, humiliating! Forty dollars apiece you're into me–and a flock of golf balls on the side! Boy! Where's that mint toddy? Let's have a little service here!"

I peeped through the door leading to the lounging room. The Dubuque-California foursome was grouped at a table in a corner. The Ooley-cow looked calm and placid as usual, but his guest was sweating profusely, and as he talked he mopped his brow with the sleeve of his shirt. Uncle Billy and Old Man Sprott were listening politely, but the speculative light in their eyes told me that they were wondering how far they dared go with this outlander from the Middle West.

"Why," boomed Cottle, "I can hit a ball twice as far as either one of you! 'Course I don't always know where it's going, but the main thing is I got the *strength*. I can throw a golf ball farther than you old fossils can hit one with a wooden club, yet you lick me easy as breaking sticks. Can't understand it at all. . . . Twice as strong as you are. . . . Why, say, I bet I can take one hand and outdrive you! *One hand*!"

"Easy, Calvin," said the Ooley-cow reprovingly. "Don't make wild statements."

"Well, I'll bet I can do it," repeated Cottle stubbornly. "If a man's willing to bet his money to back up a wild statement, that shows he's got the right kind of a heart anyway.

"I ought to be able to stick my left hand in my pocket and go out there and trim two men of your age. I ought to, and I'll be damned if I don't think I can!"

"Tut, tut!" warned the Ooley-cow. "That's foolishness."

"Think so?" Cottle dipped his hand into his pocket and brought out a thick roll of bills. "Well, this stuff here says I can do it–at least I can *try*–and I ain't afraid to back my judgment."

"Put your money away," said Perkins. "Don't be a fool!"

Cottle laughed uproariously and slapped the Ooley-cow on the back. "Good old Wes!" he cried. "Ain't changed a bit. Conservative! Always conservative! Got rich at it, but me I got rich taking chances. What's a little wad of bills to me, hey? Nothing but chicken-feed! I'll bet any part of this roll–I'll bet *all* of it–and I'll play these sun-dried old sports with one hand. Now's the time to show whether they've got any sporting blood or not. What do you say, gentlemen?"

Uncle Billy looked at the money and moistened his lips with the tip of his tongue.

"Couldn't think of it," he croaked at length.

"Pshaw!" sneered Cottle. "I showed you too much–I scared you!"

"He ain't scared," put in Old Man Sprott. "It would be too much like stealing it."

"I'm the one to worry about that," announced Cottle. "It's my money, ain't it? I made it, didn't I? And I can do what I damn please with it–spend it, bet it, burn it up, throw it away. When you've worried about everything else in the world it'll be time for you to begin worrying about young Mr. Cottle's money! This slim little roll–bah! Chickenfeed! Come get it if you want it!" He tossed the money on the table with a gesture which was an insult in itself. "There it is–cover it! Put up or shut up!"

"Oh, forget it!" said the Ooley-cow wearily. "Come in and have a bite to eat and forget it!"

"Don't want anything to eat!" was the stubborn response. "Seldom eat in the middle of the day. But I'll have 'nother mint toddy. . . . Wait a second, Wes. Don't be in such a rush. Lemme understand this thing. These–these gentlemen here, these two friends of yours, these dead-game old Native Sons have got eighty dollars of my money–not that it makes any difference to me, understand, but they've got it–eighty dollars that they won from me playing golf. Now I may have a drink or two in me and I may not, understand, but anyhow I know what I'm about. I make these –gentlemen a sporting proposition. I give 'em a chance to pick up a couple of hundred apiece, and they want to run out on me because it'll be like stealing it. What kind of a deal is that, hey? Is it sportsmanship? Is it what they call giving a man a chance? Is it–"

"But they know you wouldn't have a chance," interrupted the Ooley-cow soothingly. "They don't want a sure thing."

"They've had one so far, haven't they?" howled Cottle. "What are they scared of now? 'Fraid I'll squeal if I lose? Tell 'em about me, Wes.

Tell 'em I never squealed in my life! I win if I can, but if I can't–'s all right. No kick coming. There never was a piker in the Cottle family, was there, Wes? No, you bet not! We're sports, every one of us. Takes more than one slim little roll to send us up a tree! If there's anything that makes me sick, it's a cold-footed, penny-pinching, nickel-nursing, sure-thing player!"

"Your money does not frighten me," said Uncle Billy, who was slightly nettled by this time. "It is against my principles to play for a cash bet–"

"But you and your pussy-footed old side-partner got into me for eighty dollars just the same!" scoffed Cottle. "You and your principles be damned!"

Uncle Billy swallowed this without blinking, but he did not look at Cottle. He was looking at the roll of bills on the table.

"If you are really in earnest–" began Poindexter, and glanced at Old Man Sprott.

"Go ahead, Billy," croaked that aged reprobate. "Teach him a lesson. He needs it."

"Never mind the lesson," snapped Cottle. "I got out of school a long time ago. The bet is that I can leave my left arm in the clubhouse safe–stick it in my pocket–and trim you birds with one hand."

"We wouldn't insist on that," said Old Man Sprott. "Play with both hands if you want to."

"Think I'm a welsher?" demanded Cottle. "The original proposition goes. 'Course I wouldn't really cut the arm off and leave it in the safe, but what I mean is, if I use two arms in making a shot, right there is where I lose. Satisfactory?"

"Perkins," said Uncle Billy, solemnly wagging his head, "you are a witness that this thing has been forced on me. I have been bullied and browbeaten and insulted into making this bet–"

"And so have I," chimed in Old Man Sprott. "I'm almost ashamed–"

The Ooley-cow shrugged his shoulders.

"I am a witness," said he quietly. "Calvin, these gentlemen have stated the case correctly. You have forced them to accept your proposition–"

"And he can't blame anybody if he loses," finished Uncle Billy as he reached for the roll of bills.

"You bet!" ejaculated Old Man Sprott. "He was looking for trouble, and now he's found it. Count it, Billy, and we'll each take half."

"That goes, does it?" asked Cottle.

"Sir?" cried Uncle Billy.

"Oh, I just wanted to put you on record," said Cottle, with a grin. "Wesley, you're my witness too. I mislaid a five-hundred-dollar note the other day, and it may have got into my change pocket. Might as well see if a big bet will put these safety-first players off their game! Anyhow, I'm betting whatever's there. I ain't sure how much it is."

"I am," said Uncle Billy in a changed voice. He had come to the five-hundred-dollar bill, sandwiched in between two twenties. He looked at Old Man Sprott, and for the first time I saw doubt in his eyes.

"Oh, it's there, is it?" asked Cottle carelessly. "Well, let it all ride. I never backed up on a gambling proposition in my life–never pinched a bet after the ball started to roll. Shoot the entire works–'s all right with me!"

Uncle Billy and Old Man Sprott exchanged significant glances, but after a short argument and some more abuse from Cottle they toddled over to the desk and filled out two blank checks–for five hundred and eighty dollars apiece.

"Make 'em payable to cash," suggested Cottle. "You'll probably tear 'em up after the game. Now the next thing is a stakeholder–"

"Is that necessary?" asked Old Man Sprott.

"Sure!" said Cottle. "I might run out on you. Let's have everything according to Hoyle–stakeholder and all the other trimmings. Anybody'll be satisfactory to me; that young fellow getting an earful at the door; he'll do."

So I became the stakeholder–the custodian of eleven hundred and sixty dollars in coin and two checks representing a like amount. I thought I detected a slight nervousness in the signatures, and no wonder. It was the biggest bet those old petty larcenists had ever made in their lives. They went in to luncheon–at the invitation of the Ooley-cow, of course–but I noticed that they did not eat much. Cottle wandered out to the practise green, putter in hand, forgetting all about the mint toddy which, by the way, had never been ordered.

## V

"You drive first, sir," said Uncle Billy to Cottle, pursuing his usual system. "We'll follow you."

"Think you'll feel easier if I should hit one over into the eucalyptus trees yonder?" asked the man from Dubuque. "Little nervous, eh? Does a big bet scare you? I was counting on that. . . . Oh, very well, I'll take the honour."

"Just a second," said Old Man Sprott, who had been prowling about in the background and fidgeting with his driver. "Does the stakeholder understand the terms of the bet? Mr. Cottle is playing a match with each of us individually–"

"Separately and side by each," added Cottle.

"Using only one arm," said Old Man Sprott.

"If he uses both arms in making a shot," put in Uncle Billy, "he forfeits both matches. Is that correct, Mr. Cottle?"

"Correct as hell! Watch me closely, young man. I have no moustache to deceive you–nothing up my sleeve but my good right arm. Watch me closely!" He teed his ball, dropped his left arm at his side, grasped the driver firmly in his right hand and swung the club a couple of times in tentative fashion. The head of the driver described a perfect arc, barely grazing the top of the tee. His two-armed swing had been a thing of violence–a baseball wallop, constricted, bound up, without follow-through or timing, a combination of brute strength and awkwardness. Uncle Billy's chin sagged as he watched the easy, natural sweep of that wooden club–the wrist-snap applied at the proper time, and the long graceful follow-through which gives distance as well as direction. Old Man Sprott also seemed to be struggling with an entirely new and not altogether pleasant idea.

"Watch me closely, stakeholder," repeated Cottle, addressing the ball. "Nothing up my sleeve but my good right arm. Would you gentlemen like to have me roll up my sleeve before I start?"

"Drive!" grunted Uncle Billy.

"I'll do that little thing," said Cottle, and this time he put the power into the swing. The ball, caught squarely in the middle of the club-face, went whistling toward the distant green, a perfect screamer of a drive without a suspicion of hook or slice. It cleared the cross bunker by ten feet, carried at least a hundred and eighty yards before it touched grass, and then bounded ahead like a scared rabbit, coming to rest at least two hundred and twenty-five yards away. "You like that?" asked Cottle, moving off the tee. "I didn't step into it very hard or I might have had more distance. Satisfactory, stakeholder?" And he winked at me openly and deliberately.

"Wha–what sort of a game is this?" gulped Old Man Sprott, finding his voice with an effort.

"Why," said Cottle, smiling cheerfully, "I wouldn't like to say offhand and so early in the game, but you might call it golf. Yes, call it golf, and let it go at that."

At this point I wish to go on record as denying the rumour that our two old reprobates showed the white feather. That first tee shot, and the manner in which it was made, was enough to inform them that they were up against a sickening surprise party; but, though startled and shaken, they did not weaken. They pulled themselves together and drove the best they knew how, and I realised that for once I was to see their true golfing form uncovered.

Cottle tucked his wooden club under his arm and started down the course, and from that time on he had very little to say. Uncle Billy and Old Man Sprott followed him, their heads together at a confidential angle, and I brought up the rear with the Ooley-cow, who had elected himself a gallery of one.

The first hole is a long par four. Poindexter and Sprott usually make it in five, seldom getting home with their seconds unless they have a wind behind them. Both used brassies and both were short of the green. Then they watched Cottle as he went forward to his ball.

"That drive might have been a freak shot," quavered Uncle Billy.

"Lucky fluke, that's all," said Old Man Sprott, but I knew and they knew that they only hoped they were telling the truth.

Cottle paused over his ball for an instant, examined the lie and drew a wooden spoon from his bag. Then he set himself, and the next instant the ball was on its way, a long, high shot, dead on the pin.

"And maybe that was a fluke!" muttered the Ooley-cow under his breath. "Look! He's got the green with it!"

From the same distance I would have played a full mid-iron and trusted in Providence, but Cottle had used his wood, and I may say that never have I seen a ball better placed. It carried to the little rise of turf in front of the putting green, hopped once, and trickled onto the sand. I was not the only one who appreciated that spoon shot.

"Say," yapped Old Man Sprott, turning to Perkins, "what are we up against here? Miracles?"

"Yes, what have you framed up on us?" demanded Uncle Billy vindictively.

"Something easy, gentlemen," chuckled the Ooley-cow. "A soft thing from my home town. Probably he's only lucky."

The two members of the Sure-Thing Society went after their customary fives and got them but Cottle laid his approach putt stone dead at the cup and holed out in four. He missed a three by the matter of half an inch. I could stand the suspense no longer. I took Perkins aside while the contestants were walking to the second tee.

"You might tell a friend," I suggested. "In strict confidence, what are they up against?"

"Something easy," repeated the Ooley-cow, regarding me with his soft, innocent eyes. "They wanted it and now they've got it."

"But yesterday, when he played with both arms–" I began.

"That was yesterday," said Perkins. "You'll notice that they didn't have the decency to offer him a handicap, even when they felt morally certain that he had made a fool bet. Not that he would have accepted it–but they didn't offer it. They're wolves, clear to the bone, but once in a while a wolf bites off more than he can chew." And he walked away from me. Right there I began reconstructing my opinion of the Ooley-cow.

In my official capacity as stakeholder I saw every shot that was played that afternoon. I still preserve the original score card of that amazing round of golf. There are times when I think I will have it framed and present it to the club, with red-ink crosses against the thirteenth and fourteenth holes. I might even set a red-ink star against the difficult sixth hole, where Cottle sent another tremendous spoon shot down the wind, and took a four where most of our Class-A men are content with a five. I might make a notation against the tricky ninth, where he played a marvelous shot out of a sand trap to halve a hole which I would have given up as lost. I might make a footnote calling attention to his deadly work with his short irons. I say I think of all these things, but perhaps I shall never frame that card. The two men most interested will never forget the figures. It is enough to say that Old Man Sprott, playing such golf as I had never seen him play before, succumbed at the thirteenth hole, six down and five to go. Uncle Billy gave up the ghost on the fourteenth green, five and four, and I handed the money and the checks to Mr. Calvin D. Cottle, of Dubuque. He pocketed the loot with a grin.

"Shall we play the bye-holes for something?" he asked. "A drink–or a ball, maybe?" And then the storm broke. I do not pretend to quote the exact language of the losers. I merely state that I was surprised, yes, shocked at Uncle Billy Poindexter. I had no idea that a member of the Episcopal church–but let that pass. He was not himself. He was the biter bitten, the milker milked. It makes a difference. Old Man Sprott also erupted in an astounding manner. It was the Ooley-cow who took the centre of the stage.

"Just a minute, gentlemen," said he. "Do not say anything which you might afterward regret. Remember the stakeholder is still with us. My friend here is not, as you intimate, a crook. Neither is he a sure-thing player. We have some sure-thing players with us, but he is not one of them. He is merely the one-armed golf champion of Dubuque–and the Middle West."

Imagine an interlude here for fireworks, followed by pertinent questions.

"Yes, yes, I know," said Perkins soothingly. "He can't play a lick with two arms. He never could. Matter of fact, he never learned. He fell off a haystack in Iowa–how many years ago was it, Cal?"

"Twelve," said Mr. Cottle. "Twelve next July."

"And he broke his left arm rather badly," explained the Ooley-cow. "Didn't have use of it for–how many years, Cal?"

"Oh, about six, I should say."

"Six years. A determined man can accomplish much in that length of time. Cottle learned to play golf with his right arm–fairly well, as you must admit. Finally he got the left arm fixed up–they took a piece of bone out of his shin and grafted it in–newfangled idea. Decided there was no sense in spoiling a one-armed star to make a dub two-armed golfer. Country full of 'em already. That's the whole story. You picked him for an easy mark, a good thing. You thought he had a bad bet and you had a good one. Don't take the trouble to deny it. Gentlemen, allow me to present the champion one-armed golfer of Iowa and the Middle West!"

"Yes," said Cottle modestly, "when a man does anything, give him credit for it. Personally I'd rather have the cash!"

"How do you feel about it now?" asked the Ooley-cow.

Judging by their comments, they felt warm–very warm. Hot, in fact. The Ooley-cow made just one more statement, but to me that statement contained the gist of the whole matter.

"This," said he, "squares us on the wallet proposition. I didn't say anything about it at the time, but that struck me as a scaly trick. So I invited Cal to come out and pay me a visit. . . . Shall we go back to the clubhouse?"

I made Little Doc Ellis see the point; perhaps I can make you see it now.

Returning to the original simile, the Ooley-cow was willing to be milked for golf balls and luncheons and caddie hire. That was legitimate milking, and he did not resent it. He would have continued to give down in great abundance, but when they took fifty dollars from him, in the form of a bogus reward, he kicked over the bucket, injured the milkers and jumped the fence.

Why? I'm almost ashamed to tell you, but did you ever hear of a country cow–an Iowa cow–that would stand for being milked from the wrong side?

I think this will be all, except that I anticipate a hard winter for the golfing beginners at our club.

*This story was originally published in the* American Magazine *during the Great Depression. It's hard to imagine in these days of posh country clubs that many golfers in the past did not have access to such grand accommodations. This story is about two early golf course proprietors who compete with each other by trying to gussy up their facilities to attract customers. Their "can you top this?" maneuverings lead to a rollicking conclusion.*

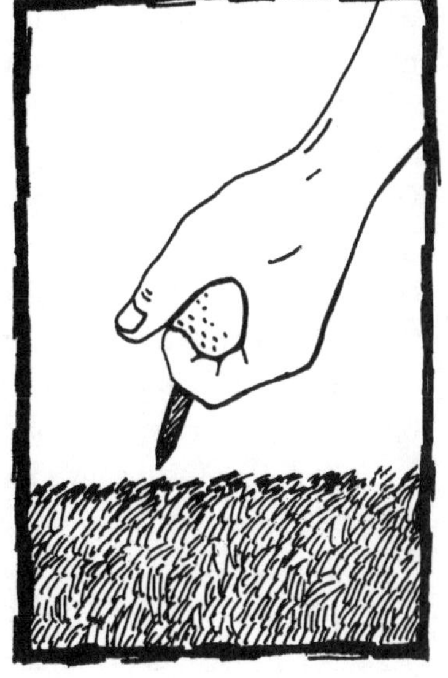

*Everett Rhodes Castle*

# PAY AS YOU PLAY (1932)

THE GENERAL IDEA IN PAY-AS-YOU PLAY circles seemed to be, at the time, that the deadly feud which sprang up overnight between the Sleepy Valley Country Club and the Carasota Hills Country Club began when "Pop" Pryker hired Miss Pansy Delancey as club professional, and that the events which followed were but natural consequences of this unconventional step in sales promotion. Pop was chairman of the House Committee, sole member of the Greens Committee, president and sole proprietor of Sleepy Valley.

As a matter of fact, the trouble between the two golf courses started several months prior to the appearance of Miss Delancey, when Pop Pryker gave a real Hollywood touch to his property by grouping a half-dozen fancy iron tables, surrounded by iron chairs in Chinese red and covered with fancy striped umbrellas, about the first tee.

Wiley Gibbs, whose property lay three miles farther down the road, considered the adornment an overt act. Not only was the Carasota Hills Country Club the oldest fee club in the district, but it was operated on the sound proposition that golf courses were designed for golf and not for the exercise of the social graces. The big red barn which, by the application of two coats of white paint and the introduction of a row of showers, had become the Carasota clubhouse was, in the opinion of Mr. Gibbs, an ample gesture toward *camaraderie.* It was twice as big and twice as white as Sleepy Valley's clubhouse, which was nothing more or less than a rejuvenated real estate office that had been left on the property by the original subdivision company.

At first, Mr. Gibbs inclined toward the position that if the old fool wanted to give away his shirt with every dollar he took in for eighteen holes of golf it was his own funeral. He told his young, curly-headed, and decidedly good-looking professional, Johnny Dexter, as much several times during the first week that the Hollywood ensemble was on view.

But young Mr. Dexter was not so sure. "These birds like that sort of stuff," he protested. "It makes the place look more like a real club."

"It don't turn a real estate shanty into a big clubhouse, though," retorted Mr. Gibbs.

"I hear Pop has already doubled his pop sales," murmured Johnny innocently. "Some of the players have their wives come out and meet them. I even heard he was thinking of serving meals."

Mr. Gibbs, who was short and fat, snorted contemptuously. "I don't believe it," he announced loudly. "Pryker always was a big talker."

"A few tables and umbrellas," began his professional, "would–"

"Cost money," his employer finished for him. Tartly. "I–I looked into that. You can't play golf with fancy tables, can you? I got a better course than he has, haven't I?" he demanded.

Johnny nodded diplomatically. "If we could get some turf on those big bare spots over on the third, seventh, and eighth holes," he went on cheerfully, "and got some sand into our traps, Sleepy Valley couldn't touch us. Even if we have a few rough spots on some of our greens–"

His employer stopped him with an upraised hand, brick-red from the sun.

"Listen, Johnny," he commanded, "the trouble with you is that all you think about is wearing yellow sweaters an' looking like Walter Hagen. If we have a few bare spots here and there and need a little sand it just makes the course that much more sportier, don't it?"

"But–"

"Besides," went on Mr. Gibbs coldly, "turf costs money. That's why I got you, who only three years ago was a caddy, instead of Johnny Farrell."

The erstwhile caddy winced. Then he shook his curly blond head proudly. "That may be so," he admitted, "but, just the same, some day I'm going to be a real professional and win the National Open. I had a seventy-three the other day with a four-putt green on Number Three–where the tile is sticking through. Really, I think, Mr. Gibbs, we should do something about that green. It–"

"We'll talk about that some other time," the head of Carasota put in hurriedly. "Just now we are talking about this fancy monkey business. I won't have anything to do with it. Not for a minute."

But three days later a truck bumped its way over the ruts leading into the Carasota Hills Country Club. Immediately Mr. Gibbs bounced out of his wicker rocker on the improvised veranda of the club, and, hurrying around to the half-shed, half-tent which served as the headquarters of his professional, grabbed that young man by the arm and led him out to the drive. Two men were unloading a large white sign from the truck.

"Look at that," Mr. Gibbs told him, his broad, red face wreathed in smiles, "and tell me if Pryker will sit up and take notice. Just compare that with your red chairs an' your green and yeller awnings."

Johnny Dexter read the large letters slowly:

THE CARASOTA HILLS COUNTRY CLUB
PAY AS YOU PLAY–
AND A BRAND-NEW BALL WITH EVERY TICKET
FREE! FREE! FREE!

"I guess that'll hold him," boasted Mr. Gibbs. "Teach him to get funny with me."

"Won't it cost a lot of money–I mean, in comparison with chairs–?"

Mr. Gibbs nodded, but a sly little twinkle in his brown eyes suggested an Ethiopian discount somewhere in the woodpile. "Sure," he confided, with a little snicker, "but not so much as it sounds. I only paid 'leven apiece for them. A company that was runnin' a lot of them miniature golf courses," he sniffed, "went broke, an' the receiver had a sale. They ain't the best ball in the world, but that makes the game all the sportier, don't it, Johnny?"

As an employee, young Johnny Dexter nodded in turn, but as a future Open Champion he could not repress a shudder. He was still shuddering, if anything more violently, an hour later, after driving a half-dozen of the new balls. The best distance he could get, even with the long downhill roll across the eighteenth fairway which he used for lessons, was one hundred and sixty yards! And yet, as he came around the corner of the clubhouse, there was the chubby figure of his employer standing before the big board, gloating. A dozen caddies formed an admiring background and furnished an attentive audience.

"You mark my words," his fat voice welled up in a final burst of triumph, "they won't have enough players down the road to wad a gun after this gets around. You boys are goin' to make a fortune. Red chairs! I'll show 'em."

For three mornings in succession this simple act of pity for smart-Aleck competition was repeated. The ritual was simple. Teetering happily backward and forward on his brown sneakers, his hands tucked into the bulging pockets of his white duck trousers, the president of Carasota Hills nodded happily. The news was getting around pay-as-you-play circles.

Then, on the fourth morning, the ritual ended abruptly with the first teeter of satisfaction. The happy smile of complacency became a spluttering, incoherent chant of hate. During the night somebody had inserted a large letter R in the first word of the third line. It sneered at the bare spots and the sandless traps. It flaunted the broken tile in Mr. Wiley Gibbs' scarlet face. The line now read:

PRAY AS YOU PLAY–

Personally, Mr. Gibbs had no doubt who the "somebody" was who had committed the outrage. He promptly climbed into his battered sedan and drove down the road toward the brown fairways of Sleepy Valley. Behind him, as soon as the dust of his going was laid, he left one grinning professional.

"I don't care who did it," that young man told his still younger assistant, who also dispensed the pop and candy bars, "but, whoever it was, he certainly put the truth into our advertising."

A matter of three miles away the battered sedan took the loose gravel drive leading up to Pop Pryker's golfing property on two wheels. It stopped with a scream of brakes beside the lanky figure of the proprietor himself, occupied for the moment in dusting off his China-red chairs. A red fist came through the window like a shot and menaced the long nose and the shaggy white eyebrows, arched like a rooster's tail, which were the principal physical characteristics of all mature male Prykers.

"I'll have the law on you!" The quivering scream of rage followed the fist with equal force. "Defacing property! Sneaking through the night like a common thief! I'll–I'll–"

"You better watch out, Wiley," his lanky rival advised him soothingly. "With that short neck o' yourn, anything might happen. What's bitin' you?"

The open window of the sedan framed a face which certainly intimated that something was amiss. The scarlet of it deepened to a rich chili sauce, as its owner noted the sly blandness in the gray eyes before him–a blandness all the more unbearable because of the mock solicitude in his competitor's tone.

"Don't you get funny with me, Pryker! You know mighty well what's wrong. Dirty competition! You pay me to have my sign fixed up or I'll have the law on you, like I said. Yes, an' damages, too!"

Pop Pryker mopped his forehead, covered with straggling gray hair, with his dust cloth.

"What sign?" he asked guilelessly.

Wiley Gibbs laughed loudly and bitterly. "What sign?" he repeated mockingly. "I'll tell you what sign! The sign that made your red chairs an' your fancy umbrellas look like two cents. The sign that increased my business twenty per cent in three days. That's the sign!"

Pop Pryker spat contemplatively. "I think I know what sign you mean now," he said finally. "You mean that sign about givin' away five-and-ten-cent-store golf balls?"

"They ain't!" In his rage Wiley Gibbs was almost at the point of throwing the price in his rival's teeth.

"Never mind about that," he glowered. "It's the rest of the sign I'm talking about. I suppose you don't know anything about what happened last night. Changin' my sign from 'Pay as You Play' to 'Pray as You Play.'"

"Sounds okay to me," murmured Mr. Pryker innocently. "I mean, with those traps an' everything."

"It won't sound okay to you when I get through with you," his competitor promised him grimly. "An' you got a lot of nerve to talk about my traps when you ain't got a fairway on your course that ain't as brown an' dried up as last year's hay."

Pop Pryker's gray eyes lost their blandness. The brownness of his fairways was a touchy point with him. The tails of his white eyebrows shot upward combatively.

"You get out of here, you crazy old coot!" he shouted suddenly. "Go an' have your fits in your own cow pasture an' don't come around to a first-class golf course and–"

"Golf course!" shrilled Mr. Gibbs. "You mean a broken-down real estate scheme, don't you?" He retreated prudently behind the wheel and raced his motor as Pop raised the dust cloth above his shaking head.

"Well, we'll see," he promised darkly, as the suddenly retreating wheels caught the gravel.

"You bet, we'll see," the president of the Sleepy Valley Country Club shouted into the dust. "An' listen, you–you potbellied little shrimp! You won't have to wait very long, either. Just drive by here again in a couple of days an' see what I do to that ten-cent-golf-ball offer of yours!"

But the news did not reach Mr. Gibbs visually. It was his young professional who carried the tidings to his employer that sex appeal had entered pay-as-you-play circles.

"Pryker has a new professional," he announced. "A–a girl named Miss Pansy Delancey!"

"A girl!" gasped Mr. Gibbs. "What kind of a girl?"

Young Johnny Dexter closed his eyes. He found a vivid, compelling image registered against the red-black darkness. A graceful, laughing image with big blue eyes, and a golden aura where most women only had yellow hair. A picture out of the magazines in her blue and white sports costume, with her bare brown arms and legs for delectable contrast. A dream of womanhood. A honey! Young Mr. Dexter sighed.

"She–she isn't half bad. Her father was old Archie Delancey that used to be the pro out at Hunting Valley. He died broke. The–the girl has been working in the sporting-goods department of some store."

Mr. Wiley Gibbs nodded. Then he smiled. "There ain't nothing to that," he decided. "Who ever heard of a woman golf professional? The old fool's crazy!"

"Crazy like a fox" was an expression which often popped into the mind of Johnny Dexter during the next few weeks. After the first week his employer dropped the little smile of pleased superiority which had been his chief facial adornment since the advent of the free ball. It appeared that the fools, especially the old fools, preferred dazzling teeth, big, baby-blue eyes, and a mop of yellow hair to free balls.

In desperation Mr. Gibbs bought a white linen coat for the pop boy and made him carry everything on a tray. But even this Simon-pure big-league touch failed to have any appreciable effect. With a sinking heart the little man heard that for the first time since 1929 it was necessary to arrange playing time ahead at Sleepy Valley for Saturday afternoons and Sundays.

"It's your department that's falling down on the job," he announced savagely, after the fourth week, to his young professional. "We got a real course an' a real clubhouse an' even a boy to serve refreshments. You got to do something about it."

"What can I do?" demanded Johnny indignantly. "I mean–That is–"

"How should I know what you should do?" snapped his superior heatedly. "I ain't no professional. If you spent a little time thinking instead of playing golf–"

"I'm not just playing golf. The Middle West Open begins in three weeks and I'm practicing. Maybe I'll win it, Mr. Gibbs."

The president of Carasota Hills stared coldly at the eager face of his professional. "Don't make me laugh," he commanded.

Johnny flushed. "I haven't been over seventy-three in a week," he protested. "Everybody has to start."

"People that prefer a pair of legs and some yellow hair to a couple of free golf balls wouldn't care if you shot a fifty every day of your life," retorted his chubby employer gloomily. "You get busy."

But it was the massive brain of Mr. Gibbs that solved the problem instead of his professional. For the first time in weeks his red cheeks were puffed out importantly. He almost danced into the little cubbyhole where Johnny was polishing his cherished irons.

"I got it!" he shouted. "I got it, Johnny! Pryker thought he could put it over Wiley Gibbs, did he? I'll show him!"

"What is it?"

Mr. Gibbs tiptoed cautiously to the doorway. No one was in sight. He returned, still stepping lightly. "You know that burlesque troupe that played in town last week?" he whispered hoarsely. "The Cherry Pickers? Well, they went broke Saturday night."

"Well?"

Mr. Wiley Gibbs leaned forward. "I've hired 'em!" he announced triumphantly. "Twenty-one of 'em. They'll all be out here tomorrow. Caddies! Think of it, Johnny. Will they make Pryker's one-horse female look like a last year's bird's nest? I'll say they will. Goin' to wear blue silk overalls that they wore in the show."

"You–you–"

His employer brought his fist down so heavily that the table danced. "If he wants sex appeal," he shouted, "I'll give it to him."

"Won't they cost a lot of money?"

Mr. Gibbs stared pityingly at his professional. "Tips," he explained finally. "Tips pay the difference. The girls only get what an ordinary boy would get."

"But what do they know about golf? Will they be able to find balls and carry big bags?"

"What does Pryker's woman know about golf ?" countered his boss. "Was she hired because she was a real golf professional? Ha, ha! I guess not!"

Young Mr. Dexter studied the shining face of a Number Two iron attentively. "P-Miss Delancey is a real golfer," he muttered finally. "She–"

"How do you know what kind of a golfer she is?" thundered his employer.

The color which mounted slowly to young Mr. Dexter's face stained the skin beneath the tan to rich mahogany.

"I–I only heard," he said finally.

Prosperity smiled upon the Carasota Hills Country Club in the weeks that followed. The story of the ripe pulchritude on view at Mr. Wiley Gibb's course made rapid headway. "The Battle of the Mashies" was written up with much gusto by an enterprising reporter for his afternoon paper, and several pictures appeared in the Sunday rotogravure sections of both the morning papers a week later. Mr. Wiley Gibbs bought a pair of white linen knickerbockers and a jade-green sweater with socks to match. The cash register played a symphony of prosperity unequaled in the district.

True, there were minor discords. A certain Miss Fifi Rooney, a large and handsome brunette, committed minor lacerations on the person of a thin golfer who insisted on reaching around Miss Rooney's person to get a desired club.

"She–she didn't know one club from another, so naturally I had to reach," wailed the assailed to Mr. Gibbs. "Then she pulled my necktie with one hand and hit me in the eye with the other."

"I'll say I hit the sap in the eye," agreed his fair caddy grimly. "An' I'll make the same play on any little two-by-four that thinks his little sticks are so important that he has to squeeze me to get one."

"I didn't try to squeeze you!"

Miss Rooney stared witheringly. First at the thin golfer, then at the teetering Mr. Gibbs.

"If you knew as much about golf as I know about that kind of palaver," she said, as she turned on her heel, "you could count all your strokes and still come in in par."

"See here, Miss–Miss–Whatever-your-name-is," said Mr. Gibbs after he had helped his suffering customer into his car, "we can't have you talking that way to the guests. It won't do. If it happens again I'll have to dismiss you."

At this Miss Rooney laughed shrilly.

"Says you?" she inquired impudently.

Somewhere in the rear a soprano laughed.

"You're fired!" shouted Mr. Gibbs.

"I quit," Miss Rooney corrected him calmly.

Then there was the episode of the minor embezzlements connected with the sale of pop. It developed after a searching probe by Mr. Gibbs that under the blandishments of soft eyes and smiling lips, ginger ale, lemonade, orange blush, root beer, and other thirst-quenching beverages were being dispensed without the formality of *quid pro quo.* In defense of his assistant, Johnny Dexter pointed out that the liquids in question were not being embezzled, as his superior insisted, but were sold on the deferred-payment plan, and he produced a large sheet of brown paper on which such debits were entered. Mr. Gibbs insisted, however, that the transactions were fraudulent in character, and proceeded, at the top of his voice, to read the riot act to the head-hanging culprit.

The reading was brought to an abrupt close by one of the debtors—a petite blonde with cold blue eyes and a large red mouth.

"Leave the kid alone," she broke in. "Who do you think you are anyway? Simon Legree?"

But Mr. Wiley Gibbs refused to be bearded aboard his own lugger.

"You're fired!" he bellowed. "You—"

"I quit." Like Miss Fifi Rooney's correction, this one was also accompanied by a loud, dramatic laugh.

Neither episode ended there. Several days later a seedy, sandy-haired man with a long, drooping underlip called at Carasota Hills to announce that he had been retained in the matter of the felonious assault committed on the person of his client by an employee of Mr. Gibbs'. He suggested a settlement on the basis of twenty-five hundred dollars, pointing out at the same time that the publicizing of the event would be very injurious to the prospective defendant.

Despite the fact that several foursomes were waiting to tee off not a dozen feet away, the proprietor of Carasota Hills almost laid himself open to a similar charge, with the seedy man as the victim. Dancing with rage, he did shake his tanned fist under Mr. Smiley's drooping underlip and call upon him to remove his person from the club grounds in two shakes of a lamb's tail or suffer the consequences.

"You—you can't scare me," asserted Mr. Smiley, retreating, however, from the threatened mayhem.

"You can't blackmail me!" thundered Mr. Gibbs. "I'll have you arrested for trespass! I'll—I'll—"

What might have happened had the little man known, as he knew two days later, that the seedy man was a brother-in-law of Pop Pryker's, will never be known. Because his professional was away, playing in the Middle Western Open, Mr. Gibbs could only obtain relief by discharging

Miss Cheri Montville, whom he caught shooting craps with the iceman. The fact that Miss Montville raised her plucked eyebrows and laughed merrily helped the situation not at all.

But the climax was reached three days later–the same day, incidentally, that the name of Johnny Dexter appeared among the leading fifteen professional golfers in the Middle Western Open–when Mr. Gibbs discovered that all three of his discharged caddies had been received with open arms at Sleepy Valley and that a vigorous campaign of propaganda was going forward to undermine the loyalty of the remaining Cherry Pickers.

The plot was discovered when a small boy, a former caddy, was caught in the act of loosing a box of rats in the caddy-house. Blood and bone could stand no more. Mr. Gibbs selected a broken driver as calmly and deliberately as D'Artagnan might have selected a doughty rapier, and swung himself into the battered sedan. His lips moved continuously, but no words came. He smashed beyond all further usefulness his favorite rocker, as he backed under the apple tree beside the clubhouse porch. His right fender clipped off the mail box, as he hurtled around the corner of the drive to the main road. Still moving his mouth soundlessly, he put his broad foot down to the floor and kept it there. Coughing and spitting, the sedan swayed up to thirty-five miles an hour and stayed there.

Staring grimly ahead, Mr. Gibbs picked up a small car coming rapidly toward him. The yellow of it was familiar. Several times during the past months he had occasion to compare the color of Pop Pryker's spirit to the color of his car. The yellow car drew closer, and all doubts were settled. With the scream of contracting brakes and a wrench of the wheel, Mr. Gibbs brought his car across the road–and waited.

"I was just going for you," he shouted, as the yellow car came to a halt.

The face framed in the yellow opening was no longer bland and smiling. Instead, there was a distinct menace in the convulsive workings of the rooster tails above the cold eyes.

"I was just coming for you–you cheap little snake in the grass."

Mr. Gibbs laughed bitterly. "Snake in the grass!" he sneered. "A fine lot of right you got to talk to me like that, Pryker. I suppose you didn't steal my caddies. I suppose you didn't give that Miller kid a dollar to bring that box of rats–"

Pop Pryker opened the yellow door.

"Sure, I hired the Miller kid," he conceded grimly. "I suppose you didn't send young Johnny Dexter up to try an' take Miss Delancey away from me."

Mr. Gibbs grasped his driver.

"You're a liar!"

"You're another. They've been meeting nearly every night up to the time Johnny went to play in that tournament."

"I don't believe it. Johnny is too loyal to go mixin' with a cheap little–"

Pop Pryker stepped out on the road. As he came toward the sedan, Mr. Gibbs brought the driver into view.

"You keep away," he warned, "or something'll happen."

"Something has happened. Where is my professional?"

"How should I know?"

"I suppose it's all news to you that she is at the Middle Western Open watchin' Johnny."

Though cold anger surged through his ample frame as he thought of the disloyalty of his trusted aide, Mr. Wiley Gibbs could not help but snicker at his rival's predicament.

"Serves you right," he announced unctuously, "for starting all this trouble. We were both making money until you had to come along with your fancy awnings an' your red chairs–"

"Who started to give away golf balls?"

"Yeah? Who hired a woman professional?"

"Who hired a lot of actress caddies?"

"Who put rats in my caddy-house?"

"Who stole my professional?"

"Who is going to have me sued?"

There were two stories as to how the fight started. Mr. Wiley Gibbs insisted that Pop Pryker reached through the window of his sedan and pulled his nose. Pop Pryker, on the other hand, claimed that, keeping well within the vantage of the sedan, Mr. Gibbs hit him over the head with a driver. The only concrete evidence brought before Justice-of-the-Peace Birdly was that of the state trooper who separated the combatants as they rolled along the concrete. He found that the Defendant Gibbs had a bloody nose and a badly ripped sweater, while the Defendant Pryker had a large lump on the side of his head and had lost the lower part of one trousers leg.

In the trial, two days later, the Law pointed out with the utmost severity the ridiculousness of the entire situation. As a friend of both men, Justice Birdly observed that there was no fool like an old fool.

"He started it, Asa," protested Mr. Gibbs, almost tearfully. "If he hadn't put out those red chairs an'–"

"Silence," thundered the court. "Your conduct has been a blot on the community. Chorus girls an' pieces in the papers."

"He hired those girls, first," Pop Pryker pointed out to the court. "I'm a business man. I don't –"

"Business men," chided the court over steel-rimmed glasses, "don't act like schoolboys. You fellows don't know the first thing about business. Did you both get along all right before this trouble started?"

"Those red chairs–"

"Silence," roared the court. "Did you? Did you both make money?"

The court accepted the nods of both defendants with a little nod of his own.

"Making any money now?"

"How can–?"

"Listen, Judge–"

"Silence! Are you?" Justice Asa Birdly was a man of few words. "Of course you're not. Now, here's my proposition. You two go into my private office. In ten minutes, if you can agree to settle this silly feud, let me know and I'll suspend the twenty dollars an' costs an' ten days in jail that I am now going to sentence you to."

It took the defendants only seven minutes to reach a decision. They emerged from the dusty little private office arm in arm.

"We've been a couple of old fools," Pop Pryker admitted on behalf of both, "but it's all over now. I'm going to fire my woman professional an' Wiley is going to fire them girls he's got up there."

"An' Johnny Dexter, too," announced Mr. Gibbs firmly. "When I think how that young whippersnapper went behind my back an' took up with that girl, I don't care if he is Middle Western Open Champion–"

Pop Pryker nodded firmly. "I'm goin' to send you a couple of them red chairs," he broke in, "an' one of the fancy umbrellas. You got your car here, Wiley?"

Mr. Gibbs lacked transportation. Mr. Pryker offered to run his old friend up to Carasota Hills. Justice Asa Birdly watched them leave the courtroom with a grin.

Pop Pryker, smoking a large cigar tendered by Mr. Gibbs, backed the yellow car out from the curb and started west.

"If you got a little time," he said, after the car was out of traffic, "I want to go out by Welland Road. That hundred an' fifty acres of Parsons' would make a swell golf course. Maybe some day we might go in together an' have a real golf course. I understand Parsons is willin' to put up the money if he was sure it would pay."

"Golf is always a good payer," his newly warmed friend suggested, "if you keep competition out–I–I mean cutthroat competition."

Pop Pryker nodded.

"Well, I guess we got that all fixed up."

Mr. Wiley Gibbs grinned. "The way I figger," he said finally, "with everything on a friendly basis we could raise the rates for eighteen holes to a dollar an' a quarter pretty soon."

Pop Pryker pulled valiantly upon his cigar.

"Sure, we could," he agreed smilingly. "Here's Parsons' property." Then, suddenly, "What's that big white sign say?"

Both men read it together–read it silently:

COMING!

BROOKHILL COUNTRY CLUB

Under the direction of Johnny Dexter–

MIDDLE WESTERN OPEN CHAMPION

–And Mrs. Dexter

PAY AS YOU PLAY!

*Kevin Cook is an Indiana-born freelance writer. He played golf for Butler University, once winning a closest-to-the-pin prize at an NCAA tourney. Unfortunately, he missed the putt. Cook has written for* GQ, Playboy, Sports Illustrated, Details, Vogue, *and the* Los Angeles Times Magazine. *He lives in California with his wife and young son, who is starting to swing like Ian Woosnam. Cook's story, "Lee and Me At the Open," originally appeared in* Playboy. *It's whimsical high-tech fantasy.*

*Kevin Cook*

# LEE AND ME AT THE OPEN (1982)

I GOT UP THAT MORNING feeling pretty good. Pretty loose, ready to go all the way around Pebble Beach one more time without losing my concentration. Sports are concentration as much as anything else. Any professional athlete will tell you that the competition is a lot more mental than physical when you get to a professional level. In my case, I guess you'd have to say it was almost all mental.

I think my varied background is what made my whole golf career possible. The acting came first, from high school right up through college.

Then I decided there was more security in software. By software, I don't mean Tupperware; I mean computer software–all the advanced new programs for the advanced new computers. I knew that was where the future was, and that was what finally made me the most loved and famous and awesome golfer of all time. And modest, too. I'm still modest, but now I've got real good reasons to be.

I was the most loved and famous and awesome for a while, anyway. For a while, they said Nicklaus was a decent club player compared with me. Jones was a high school hacker and everybody else, from Hogan to Watson, never should have left the Putt-Putt. It's damn sure nobody else ever shot 260 to win the Masters by 23 strokes. Dan Jenkins from *Sports Illustrated* was so star-struck, he used to knock over a Jack Daniel's bottle every time I came into the clubhouse. They were all like that.

Not anymore, damn 'em. Now they call my career "meteoric," with the emphasis on when I hit the ground.

Anyway, the guys at *Golf Magazine* called me up to see if I'd write a story on that last round at Pebble Beach. You'll notice they didn't ask for a *series* of stories, even though I was the biggest thing that ever happened to the game. Nowadays, most people want to forget about me. The blazer guys especially want to forget about me–Frank Hannigan and Beman and the rest of them. You'd think I was a baboon with the clap the way they stay away from me.

*Golf* didn't ask me to be on its advisory staff, either. Well, that's OK. I turned them down before, when I was hot. Who wants to sit around a table with Johnny Miller and Tom Weiskopf and three other guys who look just like Jerry McGee? *All* the young ones look like Jerry McGee. Must be their Amana hats.

No, *Golf* doesn't want me on its Jerry McGee staff now, but that's OK with me. I guess Weiskopf's off it now, anyway. I think he bogeyed his first article, withdrew and went home. Ha-ha. Little Tom Weiskopf joke there.

Used to be, magazines had to run after me just to get a quote to put in their book, and then they'd put my name on the cover, like I had a whole article inside or something. "ORVAL GREENE ON BUNKER PLAY," the cover would say, when all they had inside was something I said coming off the course, like, "I don't care if they fill up all the traps with Jell-O. I'm never in 'em."

So, looks like I've got this article to write. Might as well get on it–I need the money. Alimony. You probably remember Billie Lou. They had a whole issue of *People* about us when we got married under the press tent at the '82 Open. Maybe some of you guys remember her as the Playmate of the Year a few years ago. I think she's Warren Beatty's playmate now.

Like I said, I felt pretty loose that Sunday morning. Knew I could keep it going and make it look good. The program called for me to hit a tree on two and make a bogey, then get it back with a spectacular bird from the trap on three. It was a good program, and I was smiling and joking around with the writers while I knocked back a chicken-fried steak and three eggs for breakfast.

Then I went out to the putting green and dropped a few balls. I played Spalding Dots, even though Wilson made a ball called the Greene Champion, which was a solid piece of white stuff–kind of like a round tooth. I knew it was going to be a great day. I sniffed the sea breeze. I didn't know then that I was about to take seven on the Par Five of Life.

Let me tell you how I worked the whole thing out. A buddy of mine at Kansas Instruments helped me put together a microcomputer small enough to fit in a golf ball. We did it as a demonstration–to show the boss we could get a pretty sophisticated machine down to that size. It made for a great demonstration: "Look here, J.B., we've got a Titleist X-out here with all the knowledge of the Library of Congress inside."

It didn't go much further than that. There's not much call for smart golf balls in the Business Office of Tomorrow. The boss gave us a pat on the back and said maybe we could get the thing to make a hole in one every time, har-de-har.

Well, he was close.

If I had the layout of a golf course, I figured, I could lay out the yardage in two dimensions and feed the perfect placement of each shot into the memory of the little computer. Then it would just be a matter of setting all the perfect placements in order, so the ball would go into the fairway from the tee, then go to the next programmed spot, in the right sequence. It took about a month of tinkering before I had a ball that knew where to go for every shot in a whole round of golf.

The problem was that the ball didn't know how to get there. If you hit it from the tee with an inside-out swing, the baby would just hook right into the bushes, knowing all along that it ought to be in the middle of the fairway 290 yards out. The problem was propulsion. It took a while, but I solved it.

Now, they're not paying me near enough to get me to let the secret out, but I will tell you one thing. The reason I always used the Spalding Dot, when all the other pros played Pro-Staffs and Titleists and Tourneys, was the key. You know that little black spot on the Dot? Well, if you ever took a magnifying glass to my ball, you'd see it should really have been called a Spalding Exhaust Pipe. Clever, huh?

So, I had me a sophisticated little computer with an automatic-guidance system and propulsion from the oxygenation of the hydrogen fuel (which was in the liquid center). I was ready to take on the tour.

It worked pretty well, but some of the bugs weren't worked out right at the start. They gave me a few scares, like the time in the Byron Nelson when I hit a drive that went about 700 yards–"Hot damn! That wind in Texas shore do kick up, don't it?"–but I got them all straightened out and settled down to the business of becoming the most loved and awesome and all that stuff golfer.

You think it'd be really hard to get a computer in a golf ball? Then you just don't understand how advanced our technology is, pal. All I had to do was program the thing to go to its preordained spot every time it took a hard jolt. That way, it wouldn't take off like a rocket when I tried to putt. Since the sequence of 36-40 shots was all locked in the night before, when I sat down in the hotel with a layout of the course, nothing could go wrong.

I was on my own on the greens, of course, but then I hardly ever fixed it so I'd be more than ten feet away. If I three-putted, so what? I'd have five or six tap-in birdies a day, anyway, and I could always put in a few flag-biters the next day, if I missed too many.

The toughest thing was to make it *look* convincing. If you're going to beat Tom Watson by 15 strokes in the Crosby, you damn well better not look like Andy Williams when you swing or somebody's going to suspect something. I had played in college (number-two man at Kansas State in a down year), and I worked with video tapes of Sam Snead's swing for three months until our swings started to look quite a bit alike. So, then, all I had to do was look pretty reasonable out there and I could start practicing my wave to the crowd.

Guess you're probably ready to hear about that last day at Pebble Beach by now.

I was paired with Trevino and with Danny Sterling, the kid from Wake Forest who would wind up low amateur. They both put their tee shots on one right down the pipe, but nobody really cared, of course. I was the hot ticket, and the Greene Goblins were lined up ten deep in the gallery. I had a nine-stroke lead, and the program was for a straight, dead-solid-perfect drive off the first tee. It took off like an ICBM, about six feet off the ground the first 50 yards. Then it started to rise and didn't come down until the gasps did and I was a good 60 yards farther out than the other two guys.

I heard Ben Wright intone "Dear God . . ." into his ABC microphone and headed down the fairway the way you would if you'd just hit a 310-yard drive off the first tee on the last day of the Open.

Things went fine all day long. Made a couple of bogeys on eight and nine, just to keep the folks by their TVs, while Lee was starting to get real hot. I wasn't worried, though. Does General Motors worry if Schwinn sells a few extra bikes?

Lee and I were the only red numbers on the board as we came to the turn. I was 11 under and he was minus four. Crenshaw was even (Wright insisted he was "level"). Ben is the best damn second-and-third-place finisher in the majors the world will ever know.

The ball was working like a charm. I could have shot 63 on a good day, but the putts weren't falling. Maybe you remember that nobody ever called me a great putter, because I was actually just a club player out there with the guys on the tour. So I always missed my share of four-footers. Anyway, I still had four strokes on Lee, coming to 16. Everybody else was out of it by then. It was ticking me off a little that Lee was staying so close–I had at least ten strokes on the rest of the field. He kept cracking jokes and making birdies, but I knew my birdie-birdie-birdie finish was coming up, so the old Mex would need an eagle and two holes in one to catch me. I wasn't worried.

Sterling hit first, at 16. He'd just made birdie to bring him back to eight over for the day. The low ams usually don't shoot the lights out on the last day, playing late with their heroes, and I could tell the kid idolized the hell out of me. I hit next–a real thunderball, down the left side. We had to wait for Lee to finish telling a joke before he hit: "What's the difference between a nymphomaniac, a prostitute and a housewife? A nymphomaniac says, 'Is it over?' A prostitute says, 'It's over' and a housewife says, 'I think I'll paint the ceiling yellow.' "

Lee said his wife would get on him pretty good for that one, then he hit a high fade out into the middle and followed me into the fairway.

I waited for him to hit. He took a six iron and put it into the trap on the left. He looked over at me and smiled and said, "Well, *amigo,* unless you start taking sevens, this is about over, isn't it?"

Sterling hit a six about 40 yards over the green and nearly died of embarrassment.

I got to my ball and looked it over, took an eight and concentrated hard on making my swing look like Sam's. I knew that if I slipped and still hit the ball, or even if I forgot which way the green was and faced the tee and hit it that way, the ball would head straight for the heart of the green. It was important to keep up appearances.

Lee moseyed over and looked at my ball.

"How come you play a Dot?" he said.

"I like 'em."

"No click. Everybody else plays Pro-Staffs."

"Well, they tend to explode when I hit 'em." I thought I might as well lay it on thick.

He looked down at my ball. "Looks like that one already did."

"What?"

"The stuffings are coming out."

He was right. I tried to keep my eyes from bugging out of my head. I'd put a smile in the ball somewhere along the line.

"You got a jolly little golf ball," Lee said.

"Yeah. Must have skulled one somewhere."

"It's even got teeth."

"Huh?"

"The smile's even got teeth."

My little chips and microprocessors were trying to slip out though the smile.

"Well, I better hit it before it gets any worse."

I put a desperate Gerald Ford swing on it, and the ball acted like a missile with its guidance center falling out the bottom. It fluttered and pushed a little black smoke out of the exhaust pipe and hit about 60 feet past the pin. Still, the programming held true and the ball backed up 56 feet, until it was right next to the pin.

Lee looked a little suspicious by this time. "A lot of bite on that ball," he said.

I gave him a queasy grin. "Must have been the teeth, I guess." As I hustled up to the green, the crowd was giving me a standing ovation.

I was just reaching down to replace my ball with an intact backup ball when one of the blazer guys stopped me and asked to take a look. He was the tournament director.

He took it out of my hand and rubbed it on his blazer. Some of the chips were starting to fall out now. He squeezed and sparks popped out of the smile.

The tournament director looked at me and said, "I don't think this is a regulation ball."

I said, "*Damn* that Spalding company! I should have been playing ProStaffs all along, just like Lee said."

"We'll have to take them all and examine them. I'll have someone bring you a dozen new balls." He turned and got in his cart.

"Wait a minute!" I yelled. "You can't just take my balls!"

"What is this material on the inside of the ball?"

"How do I know? Maybe it's a bomb. Maybe somebody's trying to kill me."

As he zipped away through the gallery, he said, "We'll find out."

I stood there and watched the blazer chug away with my career in his pocket. A kid brought me a dozen regular Spalding Dots, helped me open a boat and take one out, then pushed me in the direction of the green. The crowd crunched in around me. My caddie handed me my putter and said, "Hey, you been cheatin', man?" All in all, it was a bad moment.

Lee came over and said he was sorry if he'd caused me any trouble. He mumbled something like, *"Muchachas siesta por favor, amigo, tostada burrito yoyo bolos,"* which he translated as, "You never stop trying as long as you've got the balls."

I was an 11 handicapper with good form and an ordinary golf ball. I had two holes to play and a four-stroke lead. My brains were trying to slide out through the smile in my face.

Just then, I realized I had found my way into every golfer's dream. There I was, standing over a putt for a five-stroke lead in the last round of the U. S. Open, looking across the green at Lee Trevino, who had just saved par to stay close. Millions of people were watching on TV.

I stood over the putt and looked at the hole, a long four feet away, and watched my hands shake. Then, over a monitor somewhere, I heard Jim McKay say, "And now Orval Greene, the Greene Machine, bids to close the door on Trevino and take his place in the lore of this great game . . ." and I knew I couldn't let down every duffer who ever dreamed this dream.

I glared at the hole, like Nicklaus, and gripped my putter and held on until it stopped shaking. I put it behind the ball and waited for minutes, and then I drew the blade back and brought it through.

I made it.

The crowd went nuts. Lee looked a little surprised, but he came over and patted me on the back. We went to 17, the par three. I had a five-stroke lead with two to play. I had the honor.

* * *

People have asked me ever since why I didn't just hang it up right then, knowing the blazers were going to find out about the ball and kick me out on my rear.

Did you ever think what you'd do if sometime you woke up and you were standing on the stage at the Met, with 200 people all dressed up behind you and a full house in front of you, and you were wearing a big helmet with horns? Well, you'd sing, wouldn't you?

I stood over the ball on the 17th tee and glared again, just like Nicklaus. I took a smooth practice swing and a deep breath, and then hit a worm burner off the tee. It bounced down over the ladies' tee and into the rough out in front of me and stopped a good 75 yards short of the green. The ball just sat there, dead, like a lump. It was a real ball, all right.

Sterling stuck a three about 12 feet from the flag, and then Lee threw in a two iron even closer.

I got to my ball and hit a wedge into the trap at the back left of the green. Didn't have to wait for anybody–I was still away. My caddie started running up toward the green, embarrassed to be connected with my last two shots.

My bunker shot just made it out onto the edge of the green. I was still away. I got the ball down in two, since my first putt rifled into the back of the hole and only went six inches by. Lee and the kid both made their birdie putts, and my lead on Lee was two strokes.

The 18th at Pebble Beach is that famous par five that winds its way around the Pacific. The Pacific is that famous ocean that drinks up balls that wind the wrong way on the 18th. The other two guys hit big drives down the left side, flirting with the water. My driver was shaking in my hand like an electric eel, but I held it down and popped one about 175 yards from the tee, out into the right rough. Then I rushed out and hacked at a three wood. That only went 100 yards.

I was still about 275 yards from the green. I could have taken a fairway wood and tried to get it close to the front, but I decided on a two iron. If Lee made par (and anybody who birdies the 18th at Pebble on the last day of the Open deserves to win and be made king besides), then a bogey would still win for me.

I turned to my caddie with my teeth clenched. "Gimme a two iron. I'm going to win this thing."

He said, "I can't understand you when you got your mouth closed."

"A two! I want a two!"

He handed it over, and I waggled a little. It was quiet everywhere in the world.

I backed away, waggled again. I saw Ben Hogan in my mind, and Palmer charging, and Player, and Miller on the last day at Oakmont, and Trevino at Merion and Nicklaus everywhere. I nailed that two, and it took off low and then rose and didn't come down again until it was just 20 yards short of the green.

The crowd went wild, and I grinned right in the face of Frank Hannigan and all the others blazers who wanted to do me in.

Well, you know how it all wound up. Lee made that beautiful eight-footer for his par, and I needed a downhill four-footer with a little left break on it for a one-stroke win.

It was just a little one, the kind you'd call a gimme if you were playing with your pals on Sunday morning. But they don't have gimmes in the Open.

I looked at it for a good five minutes, just standing there glaring at the black dot on the ball–that little black spot of paint with no exhaust pipe in it. I looked at it some more, and still the ball didn't move.

Lee said, "Winter's coming, *amigo.*"

Wright whispered, "And it appears that at last, the great man is going to strike his tiny spheroid, and will it find its way into that marvelous pit or will it stay, like a rebellious child, at the entrance and refuse to go in?"

My caddie whispered in my ear, "You better make it, honkie."

Like I said, it was downhill, so I just started it rolling.

It seemed to roll forever before it got in the neighborhood of the hole, picking up speed all the time.

It started its break late and just caught the right lip and spun all the way around, until it was on the right lip again and I was looking at that black dot on the ball as it hovered on the last blade of grass between it and the bottom of the cup.

You probably remember the whole scene. Lee and I both fainted dead away, and the kid Sterling fell to the green in imitation of us. We looked like the end of *Hamlet,* the three of us there flat on the green, our putters lying next to us like swords.

The ball wavered.

The blazers clustered around the back of the greens waving their arms like chickens. They were trying to decide which one of us should be revived first. They decided on Lee, since he had honors on the hole.

The TV guys were getting excited, shouting into their microphones, showing close-ups of us sprawled on the green, with insets of the ball, teetering.

Then the fans just lost control and broke through the ropes and came pouring out around us. And that, of course, jarred the ground, and the ball fell in.

When they put smelling salts under my nose and brought me around, they had my trophy and my permanent suspension waiting at a red-and-white-striped table in front of the clubhouse, and that was the end of my brilliant career.

So, it was fun while it lasted, even if they do treat me like a doggy scooper now.

I spend most of my time now watching video tapes of Garo Yepremian. You know, a football is a lot bigger than a golf ball, and I'm working on a real smart one.

I know no N.F.L. club is going to want to give me a tryout, but maybe I can force their hand.

Last week, I kicked a field goal at the Rams game. From section 24, row UU, seat 31.

*There were some great sports short stories written in the 1950s and this is one of them. Writers have had a special fascination with stories linking sports with romance. Because golf is an attractive game for women as well as men, it provides a natural setting for a romantic yarn. "Who Wants to Marry Money?" captures the reader's attention with plot and humor, is marvelously written, and has a nifty ending.*

# WHO WANTS TO MARRY MONEY? (1955)

IT WAS AROUND TEN O'CLOCK on a Friday morning and I was hurrying around the corner of the clubhouse, head down, when I ran square into Roger Bartholdy. I mumbled an apology and was about to go on when I realized who it was.

"Tallyho!" I said. "I didn't recognize you without your horse."

This was a logical observation. The sight of Roger Bartholdy patrolling the terrace of the Pinehurst Country Club in golfing clothes was worth at least a notice in the Pinehurst newspaper. After all, Roger was master of the Moore County hounds and went around with the horsy set. You could put it down as a fairly accurate rule of thumb that the fox-chasing mob regarded golf as a footling pursuit, followed by idlers with overlapping arteries and interlocking brain cells.

In fairness, you might also put down that the Pinehurst golf crowd regarded the county cavalry–if at all–as a gang of eccentric stable swipes who dressed up in pink coats two mornings a week to go chasing foxes before breakfast. In short, never were two worlds farther apart.

When I barged into him, Roger reared back, nostrils flaring and eyes rolling wildly. For a moment I thought he might drop the putter he was holding and start pawing the air with his forelegs. Skittish was the word.

"Whoa," I said softly. Roger began to quiet down and even managed a cold smile.

"Oh," he said. "It's you."

I backed off and studied his haberdashery. Roger Bartholdy was certainly dressed to the nines, whatever that means. He was wearing a fancy red cap, and his golf shoes were so new they creaked even when he was standing still.

"You're beautiful this morning," I said, nodding approval. "But I think we ought to remove the price tag from the putter."

Roger flushed and peeled off the marker and muttered something I didn't quite get. I thought I detected a general air of petulance and, as he glanced toward the door of the ladies locker, a faint suggestion of impatience.

"Well," I said, after a decent pause. I made a show of looking at my wrist watch. "I've got to get into town and back before our foursome tees off at noon, but I have time to listen to any kind of plausible explanation."

There's something about old Yale crewmen that annoys the hell out of me, and Roger Bartholdy was a real prototype. They have a generic tendency to be brusque and opinionated. That isn't just my own private observation; other Harvard men have remarked on it.

Roger was in one of his Napoleonic moods. He stared me up and down with a gaze that can only be described as steely. Then he pushed past me and strutted off. At the putting green he was joined by Mimi Elverson, and together they headed for the first tee.

I continued to watch, bemused by the scene, while Mimi teed off. As befits the perennial champion of the Pinehurst Women's Open, she whipped one well down the fairway. Then the master of the hounds, after nearly decapitating himself with his first effort, plopped one neatly onto the bowling green.

"View halloo!" I shouted and pointed to the bowling lawn. Mimi waved in reply, but Roger Bartholdy only glared and then trudged off behind his caddie. I noticed that the razor-sharp crease in his slacks was already losing its edge.

I sighed for Mimi. If Roger was going to trail the ball through bush and bracken without his horse, it would be a long afternoon for her. Just watching that kind of game can be pretty boring for a good golfer, and Mimi shot in the low eighties. There are those who argue that she ought to–she has nothing else to do since her father passed on and left her his millions.

As I turned back toward the clubhouse I saw Link Dreyer standing on the porch, watching Mimi and Bartholdy with a faint suggestion of a frown on his brow.

Dreyer was a big, easygoing guy who might have been a great golfer if his life hadn't been complicated by the fact that he had to earn a living. He might have been a good salesman too, if his craving for golf hadn't brought him in off the road like a homing pigeon every Thursday. As it was, he couldn't perfect his golf game; he had to waste too much time working. And he put in too many days playing golf to make any serious dent in the Carolina sales market.

Under the circumstances, of course, we all felt that the ends of justice and humanity would best be served if Mimi Elverson and Link Dreyer would quietly pair off and withdraw to some convenient rectory for the wedding. Then Link wouldn't have to waste Monday, Tuesday and Wednesday on the road. And Mimi could go about her golf with a high heart and a clear conscience, serene in the knowledge that she was serving society and not just reaping the fruits of compound-interest accounts.

Some astute observers of the social scene were inclined to believe that all this would one day come to pass. And certainly Link Dreyer was in there pitching to the pin; he was sensible enough to realize that he was missing a lot of fine golfing days. Mimi, on the other hand, was inclined to practice evasive tactics–but it was the consensus in the village that she just wanted to be chased a little bit. Women, I'm told, are like that.

Consequently, the sight of Link Dreyer watching his social security tack off down the fairway with Roger Bartholdy was most interesting. "It looks like somebody is playing your ball," I said gently.

Link turned to face me. A dark flush started up from his collar line. Perhaps that's why everyone was so genuinely fond of Link; he was such a total oaf; he even could blush.

"Isn't that Roger Bartholdy, the horse guy?" he said. Behind his horn-rimmed glasses, his eyes blinked in disbelief.

"Uh-huh."

Link turned this piece of intelligence over in his mind. "But he doesn't play golf," he said at length and rather suspiciously, as if testing the statement for a secret loophole.

I looked off down the fairway where Roger was emerging from the brush for the fourth time. "No," I said, "he sure doesn't."

Link frowned and pursed his lips. "Then," he went on stubbornly, "what's he doing out there with Mimi?"

"Well," I said airily, "he's not playing golf. We both agree on that point."

Link stared hard at me, and as he began to get the point his jaw dropped in astonishment. But I'll say this for Link Dreyer: Once he comes to grips with the subject he goes right to the mat. He looked quickly over his shoulder and then pulled me aside behind a pillar. "But Bartholdy's got lots of dough," he said hoarsely. Then, a bit anxiously, he added, "Hasn't he?"

I nodded. "They tell me his stable-boys make mops out of dirty old twenty-dollar bills and use 'em to clean the stalls," I said. "What's that got to do with it?"

"Well–" Link gestured weakly down the distant fairway.

I tapped him confidentially on the arm. "Don't let this get around town," I whispered, "but out there, in the world, people are still marrying for love."

Link stiffened and clenched his jaws. Poor guy. All his life he had either been in a bunker or under a shower when Dan Cupid posted the starting times. He recognized the word "romance" when he saw it, but he associated it vaguely with perfume advertisements.

"Love?" he said. And then he repeated it softly, over and over. I backed him to a wicker chair and gave a slight push. Then I shrugged and started off for town. Empires might totter and dynasties fall, but if I wasn't back by tee time, I'd have to spend the afternoon at gin rummy.

As luck would have it, whom do I meet on Broad Street but Victoria Nelson, the editor of the *Pinehurst Pilot.* After exploring the customary conversational gambits, I casually passed along the bulletin about Bartholdy and his new diversion. Victoria took it standing up.

"I'm not surprised," she said. "I heard he was selling his horses."

"How come?" I asked. "Did he bow a tendon or something?"

Victoria looked at me queerly. "He's broke," she said flatly. "And the government's put a plaster on his paint business up North until he kicks through with two years' back taxes."

I tipped my hat to her, accomplished my errand and hurried back out to the country club.

I found Link Dreyer there hovering weakly on the fringe of a gin game, still convalescing from the effects of the blockbuster. I dragged him out onto the porch and fed him the 11:00 A.M. newscast.

Righteous anger is beautiful to behold. Link gripped his hamlike hands into fists and the muscles of his forearms twitched convulsively. His normally cherubic face seemed to harden strangely. I was hoping that a small vein in his forehead would begin to throb, like it does in the movies, but nothing developed there except a few beads of perspiration. "Why, the lousy–" he began.

I cut him off. "Ah-ah," I chided him. "Temper never won the match. We've got to be cold and calculating, like Ben Hogan . . ."

Hogan's name worked magic. For a moment I thought the mention of Link's personal golfing deity would bring him to his knees. Instead he simply bowed his head momentarily. When he looked up again, the fury of the moment was gone. Gone, too, was the coiled-spring tenseness, though his eyes, behind the spectacles, were still glacier-cold.

He took my hand in a firm grip. "Thank you, Kelsey," he said humbly. "You're right. We must think." Then a look of panic came over his face. "But I'm not very good at that."

I poked his shoulder reassuringly. "Leave it to Kelsey," I said . . . .

Some people practice perfidy; others have conspiracy thrust upon them. I can't take full credit for what followed. The scheme was tossed into my lap, smoking hot, almost as soon as I got home: Jane, my wife, reported that her sister Margaret was en route for a visit.

Now, normally, a visit from Margaret fills me with the same sense of exhilaration as a ball out of bounds. Margaret is a schoolmarm of fairly formidable spirit who toils at her educational forge in distant Texas, hammering out sturdy little minds that someday will complete the winning of the West.

That is, if Margaret doesn't get impatient and decide to finish up the job herself.

"Margaret?" I said blankly. "What happened? Did she flunk out?"

My spouse seared me with a look. "It's spring vacation," she said. "She's flying here for the week."

She waited for me to return to the attack, but a nasty little idea was seeping into a dark corner of my brain. I carried it gingerly out to the porch, where I sat quietly with it through the full incubation period. Ten minutes later, the plot fully hatched and scratching, I went to the telephone.

With my helpmeet eavesdropping, I unfolded my scheme to Link Dreyer. When I hung up she was standing in the doorway, staring at me as if I were something that had just wriggled out of the kitchen faucet.

"You're insane," she announced without any preamble. "Do you think Margaret is going to stand for such nonsense? Imagine! Masquerading as the widow of a wealthy Texas oilman, looking for a place to settle in the Sandhills . . ."

She snorted. "And a horsewoman, at that," she went on. "Why, the idea! Margaret probably thinks a snaffle is the past tense of sniffle."

Under Jane's withering barrage my bold project began to look shabbier and shabbier. "You don't think she'd go along with the gag, huh?" I asked glumly.

To my surprise Jane began to laugh. "Go along with it?" she exclaimed. "If I know Margaret, she'll dress it up so even you won't recognize it!"

It just goes to show you about women. Like I say, they're balky as jennies ordinarily, but rig up a scheme to ease some poor goof into matrimony and no piece of knavery is too foul, no plot too diabolical.

And Margaret, sure enough, went along with the idea. She sniffed suspiciously at first, but with Jane and me both working at her, she began to thaw. Then a formidable glitter crept into her eye and she began to embroider on her role with growing enthusiasm.

"And you want me to lead the hounds off on another scent," she said finally. "Is that it?"

"Just the one hound–Roger Bartholdy," I explained. "A pretty mangy cur, if you ask me. But if you can get him baying after you, just for a few days, Link will move in and win the championship by default."

A strange little smile softened the strong line of Margaret's mouth. "Sounds like it might be fun," she said dreamily.

I'll say this for Margaret: she isn't bad looking. I came to the conclusion that it was just those steel-rimmed spectacles that gave her the appearance of a drill sergeant.

In fact, when she arrived at the Moultons' cocktail party the next evening, squired by Link Dreyer, I began to think I had misjudged her–either that, or else Texas does something for women.

Jane had done a good job of planting her propaganda stories. When Margaret entered the room the clatter of tongues stopped as if somebody had snapped of a switch. There's something about a million dollars when it walks into a room that seems to focus attention. Everyone at the party looked Margaret over as though she were a six-foot sidehill putt.

Me, I was watching Roger Bartholdy–who was there, of course, with Mimi Elverson. When Margaret came in, he lifted his head like a hound catching the scent of a fox. I noticed he lingered over their introduction–getting quite a brisk run out of it, as we say around the tackroom.

Bartholdy would like to have carried on the conversation the rest of the evening, but Link broke it up by dragging Margaret off just as Mimi, a trifle grim, reminded Bartholdy that her glass was empty again. I caught Link's eye in passing and winked. He grinned happily. . . .

Sure enough, on Sunday afternoon there was a telephone call for Margaret–from Bartholdy. But Margaret wasn't there to receive the call. She had driven up to Chapel Hill with Link Dreyer to see the state university and they didn't get home until rather late. In fact, Jane and I had gone to bed when Link's old sedan turned into the drive.

"Say," I said to Jane, "don't you think you'd better tell your sister to concentrate a little more on Roger Bartholdy?"

She muttered something I couldn't make out. "What?" I said.

Jane's voice was muffled and fuzzy when she spoke again, but I'm pretty sure I understood her clearly. "Don't forget," she said, "that the backswing is just as important as the follow-through."

I didn't see Link during the next three days. He was rocketing around the Carolinas, selling just enough kitchen crockery to pay for his weekend golf losses. But on Thursday, when he showed up at the country club, I was able to announce important advances all along the front.

"Bartholdy had Margaret up to look at his farm Monday," I told him.

Link tugged reflectively at his ear.

"And he took her to the hunt breakfast Tuesday," I added, a little disappointed by his lukewarm reaction.

Link took off his glasses, held them up to the light, and then began polishing the lenses thoughtfully.

"And they went up to his farm again yesterday," I said peevishly. The guy's total lack of response irked me. We were standing in front of the pro shop and I turned away and strode over to the putting green, where I dropped a couple of balls and began batting them furiously around and about.

I suppose that's why I didn't notice when Roger Bartholdy came up. The first inkling I got was when I heard Link's voice, choking with anger: "Bartholdy, I want to see you."

I looked up as Link charged past me and I turned my head in time to see Roger advancing with a dark gleam in his eyes.

It was a pretty pallid battle and both principals would have been thrown out of the ring at the Garden. I don't know who opened fire first. Link threw a right over Roger's head and then Roger retaliated with a right hook that missed by two feet. Link jabbed twice with his left and didn't connect, and Bartholdy uncorked a haymaker that tore a gaping hole in thin air. After that they grappled and began to roll around on the lawn.

By the time we bystanders had got the warriors separated, unhurt but breathing hard, the affair had attracted quite a gathering from the club and the pro shop. It was the first time anything of the sort had ever happened in the staid purlieus of the Pinehurst Country Club, and oldsters who interpreted all disputes in the light of the rules of golf were shaking their heads and clucking their dismay.

It was Link Dreyer who first recovered his breath. "That'll teach you," he gasped, "to play around with other men's women."

Bartholdy glared venomously at him, but before he could reply Mimi Elverson pushed her way through the spectators and stepped up beside him. She stared coldly at Link. "For your information, Mr. Dreyer," she said, "I don't appreciate being made the subject of a common street brawl."

Dreyer blinked and readjusted his spectacles.

"And for your further information," Mimi went on, turning to wipe a tiny smudge of dirt off Roger's cheek, "Mr. Bartholdy and I have reached an understanding. Your brutal attack has only confirmed my judgment." She leaned forward and planted a light kiss on Roger's cheek.

Link gaped at her, and then he glanced at Roger and back to Mimi again. "You mean"–he pointed from one to the other, his forefinger swinging like a metronome–"you and him? You mean, you and he are–"

Suddenly Link lunged toward them. Roger Bartholdy, in alarm, started to assume the appropriate Marquis of Queensberry defense, but Link merely seized his hand and shook it excitedly. Then, before Mimi could fend him off, he swept her up and kissed her loudly on the cheek.

"Congratulations," he cried. "Congratulations to both of you. I didn't realize. I thought–" he stopped and turned abruptly to me.

"Where's Margaret?" he said.

"Home, I suppose," I said, puzzled by his giddy behavior.

Without another word, Link darted through the ring of spectators and ran toward the parking area. In a few moments his old sedan careened down the driveway like a hot rod. I turned to Doc Kerrins.

"What do you make of it, Watson?" I asked.

Doc shrugged. "A clear case of a mixed foursome," he said as he drew me off toward the cardroom. "Anyone for gin rummy?"

It was a quiet wedding, Margaret's and Link's–nothing as elaborate as the one Mimi Elverson and Roger Bartholdy staged the following week. And Margaret made a handsome bride. She left her steel-rimmed spectacles at home.

She and Link are living now at the old Bartholdy place which they bought from Roger. Margaret has opened a private school. Of course, we don't see much of Link these days. He's just a Saturday-afternoon golfer and his iron shots lack that old crispness; but they say he's a crackajack salesman–he's even taken on a couple of new lines.

We miss Link in the regular foursome. But Roger Bartholdy plays with us quite a lot, and he's not too bad if you give him a couple of strokes a side. He can't putt, though. Personally, I think those bowlegs of his have something to do with it.

But he's turning out to be a pretty fair gin player–for a Yale man.

*There are several detective stories about sports, a few of which are about golf. England's doyenne of crime stories, Agatha Christie, wrote one of the best, called "The Sunningdale Mystery," featuring her likeable sleuths Tommy and Tuppence Beresford. Better still, though, is the story that follows, "The Sweet Shot." Here we meet the famous detective Philip Trent, as he shrewdly solves a cunning murder on the links. The author of the story, E. C. Bentley (1875–1956), is one of the great English mystery writers.*

*E. C. Bentley (1938)*

# THE SWEET SHOT

"NO, I HAPPENED TO BE abroad at the time," Philip Trent said. "I wasn't in the way of seeing the English papers, so until I came here this week I never heard anything about your mystery."

Captain Royden, a small, spare, brown-faced man, was engaged in the delicate and forbidden task of taking his automatic telephone instrument to pieces. He now suspended his labors and reached for the tobacco jar. The large window of his office in the Kempshill clubhouse looked down upon the eighteenth green of that delectable golf course, and his eye roved over the whin-clad slopes beyond as he called on his recollection.

"Well, if you call it a mystery," he said as he filled a pipe. "Some people do, because they like mysteries, I suppose. For instance, Colin Hunt, the man you're staying with, calls it that. Others won't have it, and say there was a perfectly natural explanation. I could tell you as much as anybody could about it, I dare say."

"As being secretary here, you mean?"

"Not only that. I was one of the two people who were in at the death, so to speak–or next door to it," Captain Royden said. He limped to the mantelshelf and took down a silver box embossed on the lid with the crest and mottoes of the Corps of Royal Engineers. "Try one of the cigarettes, Mr. Trent. If you'd like to hear the yarn, I'll give it you. You have heard something about Arthur Freer, I suppose?"

"Hardly anything," Trent said. "I just gathered that he wasn't a very popular character."

"No," Captain Royden said with reserve. "Did they tell you he was my brother-in-law? No? Well, now, it happened about four months ago, on a Monday–let me see–yes, the second Monday in May. Freer had a habit of playing nine holes before breakfast. Barring Sundays–he was strict about Sunday–he did it most days, even in the beastliest weather, going round all alone usually, carrying his own clubs, studying every shot as if his life depended on it. That helped to make him the very good player he was. His handicap here was two, and at Undershaw he used to be scratch, I believe.

"At a quarter to eight he'd be on the first tee, and by nine he'd be back at his house–it's only a few minutes from here. That Monday morning he started off as usual–"

"And at the usual time?"

"Just about. He had spent a few minutes in the clubhouse blowing up the steward about some trifle. And that was the last time he was seen alive by anybody–near enough to speak to, that is. No one else went off the first tee until a little after nine, when I started round with Browson–he's our local padre; I had been having breakfast with him at the vicarage. He's got a game leg, like me, so we often play together when he can fit it in.

"We had holed out on the first green, and were walking on to the next tee, when Browson said, 'Great Scott! Look there. Something's happened.' He pointed down the fairway of the second hole; and there we could see a man lying sprawled on the turf, face down and motionless. Now there is this point about the second hole–the first half of it is in a dip in the land, just deep enough to be out of sight from any other point on the course, unless you're standing right above it–you'll see when you go round yourself. Well, on the tee, you *are* right above it; and we saw this man lying there. We ran to the spot.

"It was Freer, as I had known it must be at that hour. He was dead, lying in a disjointed sort of way no live man could have lain in. His clothing was torn to ribbons, and it was singed too. So was his hair–he used to play bareheaded–and his face and hands. His bag of clubs was lying a few yards away, and the brassie, which he had just been using, was close by the body.

"There wasn't any wound showing, and I had seen far worse things often enough, but the padre was looking sickish, so I asked him to go back to the clubhouse and send for a doctor and the police while I mounted guard. They weren't long coming, and after they had done their job the body was taken away in an ambulance. Well, that's about all I can tell you at first hand, Mr. Trent. If you are staying with Hunt, you'll have heard about the inquest and all that, probably."

Trent shook his head. "No," he said. "Colin was just beginning to tell me, after breakfast this morning, about Freer having been killed on the course in some incomprehensible way, when a man came to see him about something. So, as I was going to apply for a fortnight's run of the course, I thought I would ask you about the affair."

"All right," Captain Royden said. "I can tell you about the inquest anyhow–had to be there to speak my own little piece, about finding the body. As for what had happened to Freer, the medical evidence was rather confusing. It was agreed that he had been killed by some tremendous shock, which had jolted his whole system to pieces and dislocated several joints, but had been not quite violent enough to cause any visible wound. Apart from that, there was a disagreement. Freer's own doctor, who saw the body first, declared he must have been struck by lightning. He said it was true there hadn't been a thunder storm, but that there had been thunder about all that week-end, and that sometimes lightning did act in that way. But the police surgeon, Collins, said there would be no such displacement of the organs from a lightning stroke, even if it did ever happen that way in our climate, which he doubted. And he said that if it had been lightning, it would have struck the steel-headed clubs; but the clubs lay there in their bag quite undamaged. Collins thought there must have been some kind of explosion, though he couldn't suggest what kind."

Trent shook his head. "I don't suppose that impressed the court," he said. "All the same, it may have been all the honest opinion he could give." He smoked in silence a few moments, while Captain Royden attended to the troubles of his telephone instrument with a camel-hair brush. "But surely," Trent said at length, "if there had been such an explosion somebody would have heard the sound of it."

"Lots of people would have heard it," Captain Royden answered. "But there you are, you see–nobody notices the sound of explosions just about here. There's the quarry on the other side of the road there, and any time after 7:00 A.M. there's liable to be a noise of blasting."

"A dull, sickening thud?"

"Jolly sickening," Captain Royden said, "for all of us living near by. And so that point wasn't raised. Well, Collins is a very sound man; but as you say, his evidence didn't really explain the thing, and the other fellow's did, whether it was right or wrong. Besides, the coroner and the jury had heard about a bolt from a clear sky, and the notion appealed to them. Anyhow, they brought it in death from misadventure."

"Which nobody could deny, as the song says," Trent remarked. "And was there no other evidence?"

"Yes; some. But Hunt can tell you about it as well as I can; he was there. I shall have to ask you to excuse me now," Captain Royden said. "I have an appointment in the town. The steward will sign you on for a fortnight, and probably get you a game too, if you want one today."

Colin Hunt and his wife, when Trent returned to their house for luncheon, were very willing to complete the tale. The verdict, they declared, was tripe. Dr. Collins knew his job, whereas Dr. Hoyle was an old footler, and Freer's death had never been reasonably explained.

As for the other evidence, it had, they agreed, been interesting, though it didn't help at all. Freer had been seen after he had played his tee-shot at the second hole, when he was walking down to the bottom of the dip towards the spot where he had met his death.

"But according to Royden," Trent said, "that was a place where he couldn't be seen, unless one was right above him."

"Well, this witness *was* right above him," Hunt rejoined. "Over one thousand feet above him, so he said. He was an R.A.F. man, piloting a bomber from Bexford Camp, not far from here. He was up doing some sort of exercise, and passed over the course just at that time. He didn't know Freer, but he spotted a man walking down from the second tee, because he was the only living soul visible on the course. Gossett, the other man in the plane, is a temporary member here, and he did know Freer quite well–or as well as anybody cared to know him–but he never saw him. However, the pilot was quite clear that he saw a man just at the time in question, and they took his evidence so as to prove that Freer was absolutely alone just before his death. The only other person who saw Freer was another man who knew him well; used to be a caddie here, and then got a job at the quarry. He was at work on the hillside, and he watched Freer play the first hole and go on to the second–nobody with him, of course."

"Well, that was pretty well established then," Trent remarked. "He was about as alone as he could be, it seems. Yet something happened somehow."

Mrs. Hunt sniffed skeptically, and lighted a cigarette. "Yes, it did," she said. "However, I didn't worry much about it, for one. Edith–Mrs. Freer, that is: Royden's sister–must have had a terrible life of it with a man like that. Not that she ever said anything–she wouldn't. She is not that sort."

"She is a jolly good sort, anyhow," Hunt declared.

"Yes, she is; too good for most men. I can tell you," Mrs. Hunt added for the benefit of Trent, "if Colin ever took to cursing me and knocking me about, my well-known loyalty wouldn't stand the strain for very long."

"That's why I don't do it. It's the fear of exposure that makes me the perfect husband, Phil. She would tie a can to me before I knew what was happening. As for Edith, it's true she never said anything, but the change in her since it happened tells the story well enough. Since she's been living with her brother she has been looking far better and happier than she ever succeeded in doing while Freer was alive."

"She won't be living with him for very long, I dare say," Mrs. Hunt intimated darkly.

"No. I'd marry her myself if I had the chance," Hunt agreed cordially.

"Pooh! You wouldn't be in the first six," his wife said. "It will be Rennie, or Gossett, or possibly Sandy Butler–you'll see. But perhaps you've had enough of the local tittle-tattle, Phil. Did you fix up a game for this afternoon?"

"Yes; with the Jarman Professor of Chemistry in the University of Cambridge," Trent said. "He looked at me as if he thought a bath of vitriol would do me good, but he agreed to play me."

"You've got a tough job," Hunt observed. "I believe he is almost as old as he looks, but he is a devil at the short game, and he knows the course blindfold, which you don't. And he isn't so cantankerous as he pretends to be. By the way, he was the man who saw the finish of the last shot Freer ever played–a sweet shot if ever there was one. Get him to tell you."

"I shall try to," Trent said. "The steward told me about that, and that was why I asked the professor for a game."

Colin Hunt's prediction was fulfilled that afternoon. Professor Hyde, receiving five strokes, was one up at the seventeenth, and at the last hole sent down a four-foot putt to win the match. As they left the green he remarked, as if in answer to something Trent had that moment said, "Yes; I can tell you a curious circumstance about Freer's death."

Trent's eye brightened; for the professor had not said a dozen words during their game, and Trent's tentative allusion to the subject after the second hole had been met merely by an intimidating grunt.

"I saw the finish of the last shot he played," the old gentleman went on, "without seeing the man himself at all. A lovely brassie it was, too–though lucky. Rolled to within two feet of the pin."

Trent considered. "I see," he said, "what you mean. You were near the second green, and the ball came over the ridge and ran down to the hole."

"Just so," Professor Hyde said. "That's how you play it–if you can. You might have done it yourself today, if your second shot had been thirty yards longer. I've never done it; but Freer often did. After a really good drive you play a long second, blind, over the ridge; and with a perfect shot, you may get the green. Well, my house is quite near that green. I was pottering about in the garden before breakfast, and just as I happened to be looking towards the green a ball came hopping down the slope and trickled right across to the hole. Of course, I knew whose it must be–Freer always came along about that time. If it had been anyone else, I'd have waited to see him get his three, and congratulate him. As it was, I went indoors, and didn't hear of his death until long afterwards."

"And you never saw him play the shot?" Trent said thoughtfully.

The professor turned a choleric blue eye on him. "How the deuce could I?" he said huffily. "I can't see through a mass of solid earth."

"I know, I know," Trent said. "I was only trying to follow your mental process. Without seeing him play the shot, you knew it was his second–you say he would have been putting for a three. And you said, too–didn't you–that it was a brassie shot."

"Simply because, my young friend"–the professor was severe–"I happened to know the man's game. I had played that nine holes with him before breakfast often, until one day he lost his temper more than usual, and made himself impossible. I knew he practically always carried the ridge with his second–I won't say he always got the green–and his brassie was the only club that would do it. It is conceivable, I admit," Professor Hyde added a little stiffly, "that some mishap took place and that shot in question was not actually Freer's second; but it did not occur to me to allow for that highly speculative contingency."

On the next day, after those playing a morning round were started on their perambulation, Trent indulged himself with an hour's practice, mainly on the unsurveyed stretch of the second hole. Afterwards he had a word with the caddie-master; then visited the professional's shop, and won the regard of that expert by furnishing himself with a new mid-iron. Soon he brought up the subject of the last shot played by Arthur Freer. A dozen times that morning, he said, he had tried, after a satisfying drive, to reach the green with his second; but in vain. Fergus MacAdam shook his head. Not many, he said, could strike the ball with yon force. He could get there himself, whiles, but never for certainty. Mr. Freer had the strength, and he kenned how to use it forbye.

What sort of clubs, Trent asked, had Freer preferred? "Lang and heavy, like himsel'. Noo ye mention it," MacAdam said, "I hae them here. They were brocht here after the ahccident." He reached up to the top of a rack. "Ay, here they are. They shouldna be, of course; but naebody came to claim them, and it juist slippit ma mind."

Trent, extracting the brassie, looked thoughtfully at the heavy head with the strip of hard white material inlaid in the face. "It's a powerful weapon, sure enough," he remarked.

"Ay, for a man that could control it," MacAdam said. "I dinna care for yon ivorine face mysel'. Some fowk think it gies mair reseelience, ye ken; but there's naething in it."

"He didn't get it from you, then," Trent suggested, still closely examining the head.

"Ay, but he did. I had a lot down from Nelsons while the fashion for them was on. Ye'll find my name," MacAdam added, "stampit on the wood in the usual place, if yer een are seein' right."

"Well, I don't–that's just it. The stamp is quite illegible."

"Tod! Let's see," the professional said, taking the club in hand. "Guid reason for its being illegible," he went on after a brief scrutiny. "It's been obleeterated–that's easy seen. Who ever saw sic a daft-like thing! The wood has juist been crushed some gait–in a vise, I wouldna wonder. Noo, why would onybody want to dae a thing like yon?"

"Unaccountable, isn't it?" Trent said. "Still, it doesn't matter, I suppose. And anyhow, we shall never know."

It was twelve days later that Trent, looking in at the open door of the secretary's office, saw Captain Royden happily engaged with the separated parts of some mechanism in which coils of wire appeared to be the leading motive.

"I see you're busy," Trent said.

"Come in! Come in!" Royden said heartily. "I can do this any time–another hour's work will finish it." He laid down a pair of sharp-nosed pliers. "The electricity people have just changed us over to A.C., and I've got to rewind the motor of our vacuum cleaner. Beastly nuisance," he added, looking down affectionately at the bewildering jumble of disarticulated apparatus on his table.

"You bear your sorrow like a man," Trent remarked; and Royden laughed as he wiped his hands on a towel.

"Yes," he said, "I do love tinkering about with mechanical jobs, and if I do say it myself, I'd rather do a thing like this with my own hands than risk having it faultily done by a careless workman. Too many of them about. Why, about a year ago the company sent a man here to fit a new main fuse box, and he made a short-circuit with his screwdriver that knocked him right across the kitchen and might very well have killed him." He reached down his cigarette box and offered it to Trent, who helped himself; then looked down thoughtfully at the device on the lid.

"Thanks very much. When I saw this box before, I put you down for an R.E. man. *Ubique,* and *Quo fas et gloria ducunt.* H'm! I wonder why Engineers were given that motto in particular."

"Lord knows," the captain said. "In my experience, Sappers don't exactly go where right and glory lead. The dirtiest of all the jobs and precious little of the glory–that's what they get."

"Still, they have the consolation," Trent pointed out, "of feeling that they are at home in a scientific age, and that all the rest of the Army are amateurs compared with them. That's what one of them once told me, anyhow. Well now, Captain, I have to be off this evening. I've looked in just to say how much I've enjoyed myself here."

"Very glad you did," Captain Royden said. "You'll come again, I hope, now you know that the golf here is not so bad."

"I like it immensely. Also the members. And the secretary." Trent paused to light his cigarette. "I found the mystery rather interesting, too."

Captain Royden's eyebrows lifted slightly. "You mean about Freer's death? So you made up your mind it *was* a mystery."

"Why, yes," Trent said. "Because I made up my mind he had been killed by somebody, and probably killed intentionally. Then, when I had looked into the thing a little, I washed out the 'probably.'"

Captain Royden took up a penknife from his desk and began mechanically to sharpen a pencil. "So you don't agree with the coroner's jury?"

"No: as the verdict seems to have been meant to rule out murder or any sort of human agency, I don't. The lightning idea, which apparently satisfied them, or some of them, was not a very bright one, I thought. I was told what Dr. Collins had said against it at the inquest; and it seemed to me he had disposed of it completely when he said that Freer's clubs, most of them steel ones, were quite undamaged. A man carrying his clubs puts them down, when he plays a shot, a few feet away at most; yet Freer was supposed to have been electrocuted without any notice having been taken of them, so to speak."

"H'm! No, it doesn't seem likely. I don't know that that quite decides the point, though," the captain said. "Lightning plays funny tricks, you know. I've seen a small tree struck when it was surrounded by trees twice the size. All the same, I quite agree there didn't seem to be any sense in the lightning notion. It was thundery weather, but there wasn't any storm that morning in this neighborhood."

"Just so. But when I considered what had been said about Freer's clubs, it suddenly occurred to me that nobody had said anything about *the* club, so far as my information about the inquest went. It seemed clear, from what you and the parson saw, that he had just played a shot with his brassie when he was struck down; it was lying near him, not in the bag. Besides, old Hyde actually saw the ball he had hit roll down the slope onto the green. Now, it's a good rule to study every little detail when you are on a problem of this kind. There weren't many left to study, of course, since the thing had happened four months before; but

I knew Freer's clubs must be somewhere, and I thought of one or two places where they were likely to have been taken, in the circumstances, so I tried them. First, I reconnoitred the caddie-master's shed, asking if I could leave my bag there for a day or two; but I was told that the regular place to leave them was the pro's shop. So I went and had a chat with MacAdam, and sure enough it soon came out that Freer's bag was still in his rack. I had a look at the clubs, too."

"And did you notice anything peculiar about them?" Captain Royden asked.

"Just one little thing. But it was enough to set me thinking, and next day I drove up to London, where I paid a visit to Nelsons, the sporting outfitters. You know the firm, of course."

Captain Royden, carefully fining down the point of his pencil, nodded. "Everybody knows Nelsons."

"Yes; and MacAdam, I knew, had an account there for his stocks. I wanted to look over some clubs of a particular make–a brassie, with a slip of ivorine let into the face, such as they had supplied to MacAdam. Freer had purchased one of them from him."

Again Royden nodded.

"I saw the man who shows clubs at Nelsons. We had a talk, and then–you know how little things come out in the course of conversation–"

"Especially," put in the captain with a cheerful grin, "when the conversation is being steered by an expert."

"You flatter me," Trent said. "Anyhow, it did transpire that a club of that particular make had been bought some months before by a customer whom the man was able to remember. Why he remembered him was because, in the first place, he insisted on a club of rather unusual length and weight–much too long and heavy for himself to use, as he was neither a tall man nor of powerful build. The salesman had suggested as much in a delicate way; but the customer said no, he knew exactly what suited him, and he bought the club and took it away with him."

"Rather an ass, I should say," Royden observed thoughtfully.

"I don't think he was an ass, really. He was capable of making a mistake, though, like the rest of us. There were some other things, by the way, that the salesman recalled about him. He had a slight limp, and he was, or had been, an Army officer. The salesman was an ex-Service man, and he couldn't be mistaken, he said, about that."

Captain Royden had drawn a sheet of paper towards him, and was slowly drawing little geometrical figures as he listened. "Go on, Mr. Trent," he said quietly.

"Well, to come back to the subject of Freer's death. I think he was killed by someone who knew Freer never played on Sunday, so that his clubs would be–or ought to be, shall we say?–in his locker all that day. All the following night, too, of course–in case the job took a long time. And I think this man was in a position to have access to the lockers in this clubhouse at any time he chose, and to possess a master key to those lockers. I think he was a skillful amateur craftsman. I think he had a good practical knowledge of high explosives. There is a branch of the Army"– Trent paused a moment and looked at the cigarette box on the table– "in which that sort of knowledge is specially necessary, I believe."

Hastily, as if just reminded of the duty of hospitality, Royden lifted the lid of the box and pushed it towards Trent. "Do have another," he urged.

Trent did so with thanks. "They have to have it in the Royal Engineers," he went on, "because–so I'm told–demolition work is an important part of their job."

"Quite right," Captain Royden observed, delicately shading one side of a cube.

"*Ubique*!" Trent mused, staring at the box-lid. "If you are 'everywhere,' I take it you can be in two places at the same time. You could kill a man in one place, and at the same time be having breakfast with a friend a mile away. Well, to return to our subject yet once more; you can see the kind of idea I was led to form about what happened to Freer. I believe that his brassie was taken from his locker on the Sunday before his death. I believe the ivorine face of it was taken off and a cavity hollowed out behind it; and in that cavity a charge of explosive was placed. Where it came from I don't know, for it isn't the sort of thing that is easy to come by, I imagine."

"Oh, there would be no difficulty about that," the captain remarked. "If this man you're speaking of knew all about H.E., as you say, he could have compounded the stuff himself from materials anybody can buy. For instance, he could easily make tetranitroaniline–that would be just the thing for him, I should say."

"I see. Then perhaps there would be a tiny detonator attached to the inner side of the ivorine face, so that a good smack with the brassie would set it off. Then the face would be fixed on again. It would be a delicate job, because the weight of the clubhead would have to be exactly right. The feel and balance of the club would have to be just the same as before the operation."

"A delicate job, yes," the captain agreed. "But not an impossible one. There would be rather more to it than you say, as a matter of fact; the face would have to be shaved down thin, for instance. Still, it could be done."

"Well, I imagine it done. Now, this man I have in mind knew there was no work for a brassie at the short first hole, and that the first time it would come out of the bag was at the second hole, down at the bottom of the dip, where no one could see what happened. What certainly did happen was that Freer played a sweet shot, slap on to the green. What else happened at the same moment we don't know for certain, but we can make a reasonable guess. And then, of course, there's the question what happened to the club–or what was left of it; the handle, say. But it isn't a difficult question, I think, if we remember how the body was found."

"How do you mean?" Royden asked.

"I mean, by whom it was found. One of the two players who found it was too much upset to notice very much. He hurried back to the clubhouse; and the other was left alone with the body for, as I estimate it, at least fifteen minutes. When the police came on the scene, they found lying near the body a perfectly good brassie, an unusually long and heavy club, exactly like Freer's brassie in every respect–except one. The name stamped on the wood of the clubhead had been obliterated by crushing. That name, I think, was not F. MacAdam but W. J. Nelson;

and the club had been taken out of a bag that was not Freer's–a bag which had the remains, if any, of Freer's brassie at the bottom of it. And I believe that's all." Trent got to his feet and stretched his arms. "You can see what I meant when I said I found the mystery interesting."

For some moments Captain Royden gazed thoughtfully out of the window; then he met Trent's inquiring eye. "If there was such a fellow as you imagine," he said coolly, "he seems to have been careful enough–lucky enough too, if you like–to leave nothing at all of what you could call proof against him. And probably he had personal and private reasons for what he did. Suppose that somebody whom he was much attached to was in the power of a foul-tempered, bullying brute; and suppose he found that the bullying had gone to the length of physical violence; and suppose that the situation was hell by day and by night to this man of yours; and suppose there was no way on earth of putting an end to it except the way he took. Yes, Mr. Trent; suppose all that!"

"I will–I do!" Trent said. "That man–if he exists at all–must have been driven pretty hard, and what he did is no business of mine anyway. And now–still in the conditional mood–suppose I take myself off."

*Stephen Leacock (1869–1944) was an economist and professor of political science at McGill University in Montreal. He is famous, however, for his literary work, as Canada's best-known writer of essays, novels, and biographies. Leacock's gifts as a short story writer and humorist are nicely demonstrated in "The Golfomaniac." The protagonist of the story—a delightfully-drawn character—has an unbounded enthusiasm for the game.*

*Stephen Leacock*

# THE GOLFOMANIAC (1943)

WE RIDE IN AND OUT pretty often together, he and I, on a suburban train.

That's how I came to talk to him. "Fine morning," I said as I sat down beside him yesterday and opened a newspaper.

"Great!" he answered, "the grass is drying out fast now and the greens will soon be all right to play."

"Yes," I said, "the sun is getting higher and the days are decidedly lengthening."

"For the matter of that," said my friend, "a man could begin to play at six in the morning easily. In fact, I've often wondered that there's so little golf played before breakfast. We happened to be talking about golf, a few of us last night–I don't know how it came up–and we were saying that it seems a pity that some of the best part of the day, say, from five o'clock to seven-thirty, is never used."

"That's true," I answered, and then, to shift the subject, I said, looking out of the window: "It's a pretty bit of country just here, isn't it?"

"It is," he replied, "but it seems a shame they make no use of it–just a few market gardens and things like that. Why, I noticed along here acres and acres of just glass–some kind of houses for plants or something–and whole fields full of lettuce and things like that. It's a pity they don't make something of it. I was remarking only the other day as I came along in the train with a friend of mine, that you could easily lay out an eighteen-hole course anywhere here."

"Could you?" I said.

"Oh, yes. This ground, you know, is an excellent light soil to shovel up into bunkers. You could drive some big ditches through it and make one or two deep holes–the kind they have on some of the French links. In fact, improve it to any extent."

I glanced at my morning paper. "I see," I said, "that it is again rumored that Lloyd George is at last definitely to retire."

"Funny thing about Lloyd George," answered my friend. "He never played, you know; most extraordinary thing–don't you think?–for a man in his position. Balfour, of course, was very different: I remember when I was over in Scotland last summer I had the honor of going around the course at Dumfries just after Lord Balfour. Pretty interesting experience, don't you think?"

"Were you over on business?" I asked.

"No, not exactly. I went to get a golf ball, a particular golf ball. Of course, I didn't go merely for that. I wanted to get a mashie as well. The only way, you know, to get just what you want is to go to Scotland for it."

"Did you see much of Scotland?"

"I saw it all. I was on the links at St. Andrews and I visited the Loch Lomond course and the course at Inverness. In fact, I saw everything."

"It's an interesting country, isn't it, historically?"

"It certainly is. Do you know they have played there for over five hundred years! Think of it! They showed me at Loch Lomond the place where they said Robert the Bruce played the Red Douglas (I think that was the other party–at any rate, Bruce was one of them), and I saw where Bonnie Prince Charlie disguised himself as a caddie when the Duke of Cumberland's soldiers were looking for him. Oh, it's a wonderful country historically."

After that I let a silence intervene so as to get a new start. Then I looked up again from my newspaper.

"Look at this," I said, pointing to a headline, *United States Navy Ordered Again to Nicaragua.* "Looks like more trouble, doesn't it?"

"Did you see in the paper a while back," said my companion, "that the United States Navy Department is now making golf compulsory at the training school at Annapolis? That's progressive, isn't it? I suppose it will have to mean shorter cruises at sea; in fact, probably lessen the use of the navy for sea purposes. But it will raise the standard."

"I suppose so," I answered. "Did you read about this extraordinary murder case on Long Island?"

"No," he said. "I never read murder cases. They don't interest me. In fact, I think this whole continent is getting over-preoccupied with them–"

"Yes, but this case had such odd features–"

"Oh, they all have," he replied, with an air of weariness. "Each one is just boomed by the papers to make a sensation–"

"I know, but in this case it seems that the man was killed with a blow from a golf club."

"What's that? Eh, what's that? Killed him with a blow from a golf club!!"

"Yes, some kind of club–"

"I wonder if it was an iron–let me see the paper–though, for the matter of that, I imagine that a blow with even a wooden driver, let alone one of the steel-handled drivers–where does it say it?–pshaw, it only just says 'a blow with golf club.' It's a pity the papers don't write these things up with more detail, isn't it? But perhaps it will be better in the afternoon paper. . . ."

"Have you played golf much?" I inquired. I saw it was no use to talk of anything else.

"No," answered my companion, "I am sorry to say I haven't. You see, I began late. I've only played twenty years, twenty-one if you count the year that's beginning in May. I don't know what I was doing. I wasted about half my life. In fact, it wasn't till I was well over thirty that I caught on to the game. I suppose a lot of us look back over our lives that way and realize what we have lost.

"And even as it is," he continued, "I don't get much chance to play. At the best I can only manage about four afternoons a week, though of course I get most of Saturday and all Sunday. I get my holiday in the summer, but it's only a month, and that's nothing. In the winter I manage to take a run South for a game once or twice and perhaps a little swack at it around Easter, but only a week at a time. I'm too busy–that's the plain truth of it." He sighed. "It's hard to leave the office before two," he said. "Something always turns up."

And after that he went on to tell me something of the technique of the game, illustrate it with a golf ball on the seat of the car, and the peculiar mental poise needed for driving, and the neat, quick action of the wrist (he showed me how it worked) that is needed to undercut a ball so that it flies straight up in the air. He explained to me how you can do practically anything with a golf ball, provided that you keep your mind absolutely poised and your eye in shape, and your body a trained machine. It appears that even Bobby Jones of Atlanta and people like that fall short very often from the high standard set up by my golfing friend in the suburban car.

So, later in the day, meeting some one in my club who was a person of authority on such things, I made inquiry about my friend. "I rode into town with Llewellyn Smith," I said. "I think he belongs to your golf club. He's a great player, isn't he?"

"A great player!" laughed the expert. "Llewellyn Smith? Why, he can hardly hit a ball! And anyway, he's only played about twenty years!"

*What follows is a wonderful story about a golfer who collects clubs once supposedly used by champion players. What happens when he plays with these clubs might be described as fantasy. Then again, it might be reality. Whatever it is, the story is lots of fun. Sir Bernard Darwin (1876–1961) was primarily a nonfiction writer, probably the best ever on golf. He was the grandson of the English evolutionist Charles Darwin. As a sportswriter covering the inaugural Walker Cup match between the United States and Great Britain, Darwin was pressed into service as a substitute for a member of the British team. He won his match. Among Darwin's most important books are a biography of the famous English novelist,* Dickens *(1933),* The Golf Courses of Great Britain *(1925),* The Game of Golf: Stroke Play *(1931), and* A History of Golf in Britain *(1952).*

*Bernard Darwin*

# THE WOODEN PUTTER (1924)

IT WAS NOT FOR WANT of clubs that Mr. Polwinkle's handicap obstinately refused to fall below sixteen. His rack full of them extended round three sides of the smoking room. In addition, there was an enormous box resembling a sarcophagus on the floor, and in one corner was a large loose heap of clubs. To get one out of the heap without sending the others crashing to the ground was as delicate and difficult as a game of spillikins, and the housemaid had bestowed on it many an early morning malediction.

The rack along one side of the wall was clearly of a peculiarly sacred character. The clips holding the clubs were of plush, and behind each clip there was pasted on the wall an inscription in Mr. Polwinkle's meticulously neat handwriting. There was a driver stated to have belonged to the great James Braid; a mashie of J. H. Taylor's; a spoon of Herd's.

Nor were illustrious amateurs unrepresented. Indeed, these were the greatest treasures in Mr. Polwinkle's collection, because they had been harder to come by. The midiron had quite a long pedigree, passing through a number of obscure and intermediate stages, and ending in a blaze of glory with the awful name of Mr. John Ball, who was alleged once to have played a shot with it at the request of an admirer. A putting cleek with a rather long, old-fashioned head and a battered grip bore the scrupulous inscription: ATTRIBUTED TO THE LATE MR. F. G. TAIT.

Mr. Polwinkle always sighed when he came to that cleek. Its authenticity was, he had to admit, doubtful. There were so many Freddie Tait putters. Half the clubhouses in England seemed to possess one; they could hardly all be genuine. His Hilton he no longer even pretended to believe in.

"I bought that," he would say, "when I was a very young collector, and I'm afraid I was imposed upon." But, at any rate, there was no doubt about his latest acquisition, before which he now paused lovingly. Here was the whole story, written down by a man, who knew another man, who knew the people with whom Mr. Wethered had been staying. Mr. Wethered had overslept himself, packed up his clubs in a hurry, and left his iron behind; so he had borrowed this one, and had graciously remarked that it was a very nice one.

It must not be supposed that Mr. Polwinkle was ever so daring as to play with these sacred clubs. He contented himself with gazing and, on rare occasions, with a reverent waggle.

Mr. Polwinkle, as I have said, was not a good player. He was aware of not playing consistently up to his sixteen handicap. If he did not always insist on his rights of giving two strokes to his friend Buffery, he might, he was conscious, have suffered the indignity of being beaten level by an eighteen handicap player; and with all this nonsense about scratch scores and a raising of the standard, he saw before him the horrid certainty of soon being eighteen himself.

This evening he was feeling particularly depressed. It had been a bad day. Buffery had won by five and four without using either of his strokes, and had hinted pretty strongly that he did not propose to accept them any more. Confound the tactless creature!

Mr. Polwinkle tried to soothe himself by looking at his treasures. Ah! If only he could just for one day be endued with the slash and power of those who had played with them. If only something of their virtue could have passed into their clubs, what a splendid heritage! Such a miracle might even be possible if he had but faith enough. Coué-suggestion–better and better and better–how wonderful it would be!

Suddenly he felt a glow of new hope and inspiration. Greatly daring, he took from the rack the driver WITH WHICH as the inscription lyrically proclaimed JAMES BRAID WON THE CHAMPIONSHIP AT PRESTWICK IN 1908, WITH THE UNEXAMPLED SCORE OF 291; EIGHT STROKES BETTER THAN THE SECOND SCORE, AND PLAYING SUCH GOLF AS HAD NEVER BEEN SEEN BEFORE ON THAT CLASSIC GOLF COURSE.

He took one glance to see that his feet were in the right place–long practice enabled him to judge to an inch of the position in which the furniture was safe–and then he swung.

Gracious goodness! What had happened? Back went the club, instinct with speed and power, and he felt a violent and unaccustomed wrenching round of his hips. Down it came more swiftly than ever, his knees seemed to crumple under him with the vehemence of the blow, and swish went the clubhead, right out and round in a glorious finish. A shower of glass fell all over him and he was left in darkness.

Never had he experienced anything before in the least like that tremendous sensation; the electric light had always been perfectly safe. With trembling fingers he struck a match and groped his way, crunching glass as he walked, to the two candles on the chimney piece. Once more he swung the club up; then paused at the top of the swing, as he had done so many hundreds of times before, and gazed at himself in the glass. Could it really be?

He rushed to the bookshelf, tore down *Advanced Golf,* turned to the appropriate page, and again allowed the club to swing and wrench him in its grip. There could be no doubt about it. Allowing for differences of form and feature he was Braid to the very life–the poise, the turn of the body, the very knuckles–all were the same.

The miracle had happened with one club. Would it happen with all? Out came the Taylor mashie from the rack. As he picked it up his head seemed to shake formidably, his wrists felt suddenly as if they were made of whipcord, his boots seemed to swell and clutch the ground; another second–crash!–down came the club and out came a divot of carpet, hurtling across the room, while Mr. Polwinkle's eyes were fixed in a burning and furious gaze on the gaping rent that was left.

Then it really was all right. If he could swing the club like the great masters, he could surely hit the ball like them, and the next time he played Buffery, by Jove, it would not be only two strokes he could give him.

He was in the middle of being Mr. Wethered when the door opened and Buffery walked in. Mr. Polwinkle had got his feet so wide apart in his admirable impersonation that he could not move; for a perceptible moment he could only straddle and stare.

"They told me you were in, old chap," began Buffery, "so I just walked in. What on earth are you at? I always said that light would get it in the neck some day!" Buffery's heartiness, though well meant, was sometimes hard to bear. "However," he went on, while Mr. Polwinkle was still speechless, "what I came about was this. You remember you said you'd come down to Sandwich with me some day. Well, I suddenly find I can get off for three days. Will you come?"

Mr. Polwinkle hesitated a moment. He did not feel very kindly disposed toward Buffery. He should like to practice his new styles a little before crushing him; but still, Sandwich! And he had never seen it.

"All right," he said; "I'll come!"

"Topping!" cried Buffery. "We'll have some great matches, and I'm going to beat you level–you see if I don't!"

Mr. Polwinkle gathered himself together for an effort.

"I will give you," he said slowly and distinctly, "a stroke a hole, and

I'll play you for"–and he hesitated on the brink of something still wilder–"five pounds!"

Buffery guffawed with laughter. He had never heard Mr. Polwinkle make so good a joke before.

The next evening saw them safely arrived and installed at the Bell.

The journey, though slow, had been for Mr. Polwinkle full of romance. When he changed at Minster he snuffed the air and thought that already he could smell the sea. His mind was a jumble of old championships and of the wondrous shots he was going to play on the morrow. At dinner he managed to make Buffery understand that he really did mean to give him a stroke a hole. And Buffery, when at last convinced that it was not a joke, merely observed that a fiver would be a pleasant little help toward his expenses.

After dinner he felt too restless and excited to sit still, and leaving Buffery to play bridge, wandered stealthily into the hall to see if his precious clubs were safe. He felt a momentary shiver of horror when he found someone examining his bag. Had news of the match been spread abroad? Was this a backer of Buffery's tampering with his clubs?

No; he appeared a harmless, friendly creature, and apologized very nicely. He was merely, he said, amusing himself by looking at the different sets of clubs.

"You've got some jolly good ones," he went on, making Mr. Polwinkle blush with pleasure. "And look here, your mashie and mine might be twins–they're as like as two peas!" And he produced his own from a neighboring bag. They certainly were exactly alike; both bore the signature of their great maker; in weight and balance they were identical.

"Taylor used to play with mine himself!" said Mr. Polwinkle in a voice of pride and awe. "And this is Herd's spoon, and here's a putter of–"

"I expect he'd have played just as well with mine," cut in the stranger–Jones was the unobtrusive name on his bag–with regrettable flippancy. "Anyhow, they're both good clubs. Wish I could play like Taylor with mine. Well, I'm going to turn in early–good night!"

Mr. Polwinkle, a little sad that Jones did not want to hear all about his collection, fastened up his bag, and thought he would go to bed, too. He lay awake for some time, for the cocks crow as persistently by night in the town of Sandwich as the larks sing by day upon the links; moreover, he was a little excited. Still, he slept at last, and dreamed of mashie shots with so much backspin on them that they pitched on Prince's and came back into the hole on St. George's.

"Well," said Buffery, as they stood next morning on the first tee at St. George's, "it's your honor–you're the giver of strokes," he added in a rather bitter tone.

Mr. Polwinkle took out the Braid driver with as nonchalant an air as he could muster. He could not help feeling horribly frightened, but no doubt the club would help him through. He gave one waggle with that menacing little shake of the club that Walton Heath knows so well, and then the ball sped away an incredible distance. It was far over the "kitchen," that grassy hollow that has caught and stopped so many hundreds of balls; but it had a decided hook on it, and ran on and on till it finished in the rough on the left.

One of the caddies gave a prolonged whistle of surprise and admiration. Who was this new, unknown, and infinitely mild-looking champion who made the club hum through the air like a hornet? Buffery, too, was palpably taken aback.

"I say, old chap," he remarked, "you seem to have been putting a lot on to your drive. Was that what you had up your sleeve?"

However, he managed to hit a very decent shot himself into the kitchen, and then, narrowly escaping that trappy little bunker on the right with his second, lay in a good strategic position in front of the big cross bunker.

Meanwhile, Mr. Polwinkle was following up his own vast tee shot in an agitated state of mind. Of course, he reflected, Braid *can* hook. It was, he had read, the one human weakness to which the great man was occasionally prone, but it seemed hard that this should be the occasion. The ball lay very heavy in the rough, and worse than all he had only his own niblick, with which he was singularly ineffective. He had once had the chance of acquiring a genuine Ray, but niblicks were clumsy, ugly things and did not interest him. Why had he been such a fool?

His first effort was a lamentable top, his second only just got the ball out of the rough, with a gaping wound in its vitals. Still, there was a hope if Herd's spoon would behave itself as it should, and he addressed himself to the shot with a desperate composure.

Heavens, what was the matter with him? Was he never going to hit the ball? He felt himself growing dizzy with all those waggles, a fierce little glance at the hole between each of them. There could be no possible doubt that this spoon was a genuine Herd. Just as he felt that he must scream if it went on much longer, up went the club, and away went the ball–the most divine spoon shot ever seen–cut up into the wind to perfection; the ball pitched over the bunker, gave a dying kick or two, and lay within a yard of the hole.

Even the ranks of Tuscany could scarce forbear to cheer. "Good shot!" growled Buffery grudgingly.

That was four–he would be down in five. The enemy with his stroke had three for the hole, but the big cross bunker yawned between him and the green. Drat the man, he had not topped it. He had pitched well over, and his approach putt lay so dead that Mr. Polwinkle, though in no generous mood, had to give it to him. One down.

At the second hole at Sandwich, as all the world knows, there is a long and joyous carry from the tee. A really fine shot will soar over the bunker and the hilltop beyond, and the ball will lie in a little green valley, to be pitched home on to the green; but the short driver must make a wide tack to the right and will have a more difficult second.

Buffery, inspired by his previous win, despite his opponent's mighty drive, decided to "go for it." And plump went his ball into the bunker.

The Braid driver was on its best behavior this time–a magnificent shot, straight as an arrow and far over the hill.

"H'm!" said Buffery, looking discontentedly at the face of his driver. "Is that any new patent kind of ball you are playing with?"

"No," returned Mr. Polwinkle frigidly. "You can weigh it after the round if you like." And they walked on in stony silence.

Buffery had to hack his ball out backward, and his third was away to the right of the green.

"Just a little flick with the mashie, sir," said Mr. Polwinkle's caddie, putting the club in his hand.

He took the mashie, but somehow he did not feel comfortable. He shifted and wriggled, and finally his eye was high in the heavens long before the ball was struck. When he looked down to earth again he found the ball had only moved about three yards forward–a total and ignominious fluff. He tried again; another fluff moved it forward but a few painful inches; again, and a third precisely similar shot deposited it in the bunker in front of his nose. Then he went berserk with his niblick, irretrievably ruined a second new ball, and gave up the hole.

"Let me look at the mashie!" he said to his caddie as he walked on toward the next tee. And, after microscopically examining its head, "I see what it is!" he exclaimed, in frantic accents. "It's that fellow–what's his damned name, who was looking at my clubs last night–he's mixed them up–he's got my mashie and I've got his! Do you know Mr. Jones by sight?" And he turned to his caddie.

"Yes, sir. I knows him. And that's a funny thing if you've got his mashie. I was just thinking to myself that them shots of yours was just like what he plays. 'Joneses,' his friends call them. He'll play like a blooming pro, for a bit, and then fluff two or three–"

"Where is he now? Is he in front of us?" Mr. Polwinkle interrupted. Yes, Jones had started some time ago.

"Then run as hard as you can and tell him I'm playing an important match and insist on having my mashie back. Quick now, run!"–as the caddie was going to say something. "I'll carry the clubs!" And the caddie disappeared reluctantly in the sandhills.

"Bad luck, old man!" said Buffery, his complacency restored by that wonderfully soothing medicine of two holes up. "But I'll tell you where to go. Now this is the Sahara. The hole's over there," pointing to the left, "but it's too long a carry for you and me–we must go round by the right."

"Which line would Braid take?" asked Mr. Polwinkle. "Straight at the flag, would he? Then I shall go straight for the flag!"

"Please yourself!" answered Buffery with a shrug, and played away to the right–a mild little shot and rather sliced, but still clear of the sand. Mr. Polwinkle followed with another superb tee shot. Far over all that tumultuous mass of rolling sandhills the ball flew, and was last seen swooping down on to the green. Buffery's second was weak and caught in the hollow; his third was half topped and ran well past; his fourth put him within a yard or so of the hole.

The best he could do would be a five, and all the while there stood Mr. Polwinkle, calm, silent, and majestic, six yards from the flag in one. He had only to get down in two putts to win the hole; but he had not yet had a putt, and which putter was he to use–the Tait or the Harry Vardon? He decided on the Tait. A moment later he wished he had not, for his putt was the feeblest imaginable, and the ball finished a good five feet short. Still he persevered, and again was pitifully short.

"By Jove, that's a let-off, old chap!" said the tactless one, and popped his own ball into the hole.

"I'll give you that one!" he added magnanimously, and picked up Mr. Polwinkle's ball, which was reposing some three inches from the hole.

"I was always afraid it was a forgery!" murmured Mr. Polwinkle, mechanically accepting the ball. "Freddie Tait was never short with his putts–the books all say that!"

Buffery looked at him wonderingly, opened his mouth as if to make some jocular comment, then thought better of it and led the way to the tee.

Much the same thing happened at the fourth. Two magnificent shots by Braid and Herd respectively, right up to the edge of the little plateau, where it stands defiantly with the black railings in the background; a series of four scrambles and scuffles by Buffery, which just escaped perdition. Two for the hole again, and this time the Vardon putter was tried. The first putt was beautiful. How sweetly and smoothly and with what a free wrist it was taken back! The ball, perfectly struck, seemed in, then it just slipped past and lay two feet away.

"Ah!" he said to himself with a long sigh of satisfaction, "at any rate this is genuine!"

Alas! It was but too true, for when it came to the short putt, Mr. Polwinkle's wrist seemed suddenly to become locked, there was a quick little jerk of the club and–yes, somehow or other the ball had missed the hole. Buffery was down in his two putts again, and it was another half, this time in five to six.

"I ought to have been all square by now if I could have putted as well as an old lady with a broomstick!" said poor Mr. Polwinkle.

"Well, I like that!" answered the other truculently. "I ought to have been four up if I could have played a decent second either time!" And this time there was a lasting silence.

Mr. Polwinkle felt depressed and miserable. Still his heart rose a little when he contemplated the bunker that had to be carried from the tee at the fifth, and beyond it the formidable Maiden with its black terraces. And, sure enough, Buffery got into the bunker in three–not into the black terraces, because, sad to say, men do not now play over the Maiden's crown, but only over the lower spurs–touching, as it were, but the skirts of her sandy garment. Still, he was in the bunker, and Mr. Polwinkle had only a pitch to reach the green. Here it was that he wanted a good caddie to put an iron in his hand–to put anything there but the mashie that had played him false. But Mr. Polwinkle was flustered.

"After all," he thought, "a mashie is a mashie, even if it is not a genuine Taylor, and if I keep my eye on the ball–"

Clean off the socket this time the ball flew away toward cover point, and buried itself in a clump of bents. Why did he not "deem it unplayable"? I do not know. But since Mr. Horace Hutchinson once ruined a medal round and probably lost the St. George's Vase at the Maiden by forgetting that he could tee and lose two, Mr. Polwinkle may be forgiven. When his ball ultimately emerged from the bents he had played five; they holed out in nine apiece, for Buffery had also had his adventures and the stroke settled in. Three down.

Worse was to come, for at the sixth Buffery had the impudence to get a three–a perfect tee shot and two putts; no one could give a stroke to that. At the seventh Mr. Polwinkle, club in hand, walked forward with elaborate care to survey the ground, walked backward, his eye still fixed on the green–and heeled his ball smartly backward like a rugby forward. For a moment he was bewildered. Then he looked at his club. His Wethered iron! Of course. It was the tragedy of the Open Championship at St. Andrews over again!

At Hades his Vardon putter again misbehaved at short range, and Mr. Polwinkle looked at it reproachfully.

"I always thought it belonged to a bad period!" he groaned, remembering some of those tragic years in which the greatest of all golfers could do everything but hole a yard putt. He would use the Vardon no more. But, then, what on earth was he to putt with? He tried the pseudo-Tait again at the ninth, and by dint of taking only three putts got a half; but still he was six down.

There was one ray of comfort. There was his caddie waiting for him, having no doubt run the villain Jones to earth, and under his arm protruded the handle of a club.

"Well," he shouted, "have you got it?"

"No, sir," the caddie answered–and embarrassment and amusement seemed to struggle together in his voice. "Mr. Jones says he's playing an important match, too, and as you didn't send back his mashie he's going on with yours. Said they were just the same, he did, and he wouldn't know any difference between yours and his own."

"Then what's that club you've got there?" demanded Mr. Polwinkle.

"The gentleman lent you this to make up, so he said," the caddie replied, producing a wooden putter. "I was particularly to tell you it belonged to someone who used it in a great match, and blessed if I haven't forgotten who it was."

Mr. Polwinkle took the putter in his hand and could not disguise from himself that it had no apparent merits of any description. The shaft was warped, not bent in an upward curve as a well-bred wooden putter should be, and decidedly springy; no name whatever was discernible on the head. Still, he badly need a putter, and if it had been used by an eminent hand–

"Think, man, think!" he exclaimed vehemently. "You must remember!" But the caddie racked his brain in vain. And then–

"Really," said Buffery, "we can't wait all day while your caddie tries to remember ancient history. This is the match we're thinking about, and I'm six up!" And he drove off–a bad hook into the thick and benty rough on the left.

And now, thank goodness, I have reached the end of Mr. Polwinkle's misfortunes. The tide is about to turn. At the second shot Mr. Wethered's iron, I regret to have to say, made another error. It just pulled the ball into that horrid trappy bunker that waits voraciously at the left-hand corner of the plateau green–and that after Buffery had played three and was not on the green.

Mr. Polwinkle's temper had been badly shaken once or twice, and now it gave out entirely.

"Give me any dashed club you like!" he snarled, seized the first that came handy, and plunged into the bunker.

"Good sort of club to get out of a bunker with!" he said to himself, finding that he had a midiron in his hand, and then–out came the ball, as if it was the easiest thing in the world, and sat down within four yards of the hole.

How had it happened? Why, it was Mr. Ball's iron–and did not the hero of Hoylake habitually pitch out of bunkers with a straight-faced iron? Of course he did–and played his ordinary pitches with it as well. What a thing it was to know history! Here at once was a magic niblick and a substitute for the mashie rolled into one. And just then his caddie smacked himself loudly and suddenly on the thigh.

"I've remembered it, sir. It was Tommy something–young Tommy, I think."

"Young Tommy Morris?" gasped Mr. Polwinkle breathlessly.

"Ah!" said caddie. "Morris–that was it!"

"Give me the wooden putter!" said Mr. Polwinkle–and the ball rattled against the back of the tin. That was a four against Buffery's six. Down to five with eight to play.

It is a well-known fact that when golf is faultless there is next to nothing to write about it. The golfing reporter may say that So-and-So pushed his drive and pulled his second; but the real fact is that the great So-and-So was on the course with his tee shot, on the green with his second, and down in two putts–and kept on doing it. That is all the reporter need have said but he says more because he has his living to earn. So have I; but, nevertheless, I shall not describe Mr. Polwinkle's home-coming at full length. More brilliantly faultless golf never was seen. Braid drove magnificently, Mr. Ball did all the pitching to perfection and even Mr. Wethered behaved impeccably. As for the wooden putter, most of the putts went in, and even those that did not gave Buffery a cold shiver down his spine. What could poor eighteen-handicap Buffery do against it? He must need wilt under such an onslaught. If he did a respectable five, Mr. Polwinkle did a "birdie" three. If he did a long hole in six, as he did at the Suez Canal, that wooden putter holed one for a four.

Here, for those who know the course, are the figures of Mr. Polwinkle's first eight holes coming home: four, three, three, four, four, four, two, four. That was enough. Buffery was a crushed man; hole after hole slipped away, and when he had reached the seventeenth green in eight, there was nothing for it but to give up the match. Six up at the turn and beaten by two and one!

As Mr. Polwinkle walked triumphantly into the clubhouse he met Jones, and almost fell on his neck.

"My dear fellow," he cried, "I can't thank you enough for that putter. I holed everything. Never saw anything like it! I suppose," he went on with a sudden desperate boldness, "there's no chance of your selling it me, is there?"

"Oh no, I won't sell it!" began Jones.

"I knew it was too much to ask!" said Mr. Polwinkle dejectedly.

"But I'll give it to you with pleasure!"

"Oh, but I couldn't let you do that! Give me it for nothing–a putter that belonged to young Tommy–the greatest putter that ever–"

"Well, you see," said Jones, "I only told the caddie to tell you that because I thought it might put you on your putting. And, by George, it seems to have done it, too. Wonderful what a little confidence will do. You're perfectly welcome to the putter–I bought it in a toy shop for eighteen pence!"

Mr. Polwinkle fell swooning to the floor.

*This story brings to mind the quotation from the sixth century B.C. Greek philosopher Heraclitus that "character is fate." Archibald is undoubtedly a fellow of excellent character, and his fate is determined in the story. It takes some finagling by a couple of wily conspirators to aid Archibald in his quest for glory. There is also a winsome young lady to give spice to the hunt. This is served up by the master comedian and storyteller P. G. Wodehouse, his second story in the collection. Wodehouse authored ninety-two books and many stories and plays in his illustrious career. Among his books are the acclaimed Jeeves series,* Ukridge *(1924), and* The Butler Did It *(1957). This story originally appeared in* Collier's.

*P. G. Wodehouse*

# ARCHIBALD'S BENEFIT (1910)

ARCHIBALD MEALING WAS ONE OF those golfers in whom desire outruns performance. Nobody could have been more willing than Archibald. He tried, and tried hard. Every morning before he took his bath he would stand in front of his mirror and practise swings. Every night before he went to bed he would read the golden words of some master on the subject of putting, driving, or approaching. Yet on the links most of his time was spent in retrieving lost balls or replacing America. Whether it was that Archibald pressed too much or pressed too little, whether it was that his club deviated from the dotted line which joined the two points A and B in the illustrated plate of the man making the brassy shot in the *Hints on Golf* book, or whether it was that he was pursued by some malignant fate, I do not know. Archibald rather favoured the last theory.

The important point is that, in his thirty-first year, after six seasons of untiring effort, Archibald went in for a championship, and won it.

Archibald, mark you, whose golf was a kind of blend of hockey, Swedish drill, and buck-and-wing dancing.

I know the ordeal I must face when I make such a statement. I see clearly before me the solid phalanx of men from Missouri, some urging me to tell it to the King of Denmark, others insisting that I produce my Eskimoes. Nevertheless, I do not shrink. I state once more that in his thirty-first year Archibald Mealing went in for a golf championship, and won it.

Archibald belonged to a select little golf club, the members of which lived and worked in New York, but played in Jersey. Men of substance, financially as well as physically, they had combined their superfluous cash and with it purchased a strip of land close to the sea. This land had been drained–to the huge discomfort of a colony of mosquitoes which had come to look on the place as their private property–and converted into links, which had become a sort of refuge for incompetent golfers. The members of the Cape Pleasant Club were easy-going refugees from other and more exacting clubs, men who pottered rather than raced round the links; men, in short, who had grown tired of having to stop their game and stand aside in order to allow perspiring experts to whiz past them. The Cape Pleasant golfers did not make themselves slaves to the game. Their language, when they foozled, was gently regretful rather than sulphurous. The moment in the day's play which they enjoyed most was when they were saying: "Well, here's luck!" in the club-house.

It will, therefore, be readily understood that Archibald's inability to do a hole in single figures did not handicap him at Cape Pleasant as it might have done at St. Andrews. His kindly clubmates took him to their bosoms to a man, and looked on him as a brother. Archibald's was one of those admirable natures which prompt their possessor frequently to remark: "These are on me!" and his fellow golfers were not slow to appreciate the fact. They all loved Archibald.

Archibald was on the floor of his bedroom one afternoon, picking up the fragments of his mirror–a friend had advised him to practise the Walter J. Travis lofting shot–when the telephone bell rang. He took up the receiver, and was hailed by the comfortable voice of McCay, the club secretary.

"Is that Mealing?" asked McCay. "Say, Archie, I'm putting your name down for our championship competition. That's right, isn't it?"

"Sure," said Archibald. "When does it start?"

"Next Saturday."

"That's me."

"Good for you. Oh, Archie."

"Hello?"

"A man I met to-day told me you were engaged. Is that a fact?"

"Sure," murmured Archibald, blushfully.

The wire hummed with McCay's congratulations.

"Thanks," said Archibald. "Thanks, old man. What? Oh, yes. Milsom's her name. By the way, her family have taken a cottage at Cape Pleasant for the summer. Some distance from the links. Yes, very convenient, isn't it? Good-bye."

He hung up the receiver and resumed his task of gathering up the fragments.

Now McCay happened to be of a romantic and sentimental nature. He was by profession a chartered accountant, and inclined to be stout; and all rather stout chartered accountants are sentimental. McCay was the sort of man who keeps old ball programmes and bundles of letters tied round with lilac ribbon. At country houses, where they lingered in the porch after dinner to watch the moonlight flooding the quiet garden, it was McCay and his colleague who lingered longest. McCay knew Ella Wheeler Wilcox by heart, and could take Browning without anaesthetics. It is not to be wondered at, therefore, that Archibald's remark about his fiancée coming to live at Cape Pleasant should give him food for thought. It appealed to him.

He reflected on it a good deal during the day, and, running across Sigsbee, a fellow Cape Pleasanter, after dinner that night at the Sybarites'

Club, he spoke of the matter to him. It so happened that both had dined excellently, and were looking on the world with a sort of cosy benevolence. They were in the mood when men pat small boys on the head and ask them if they mean to be President when they grow up.

"I called up Archie Mealing to-day," said McCay. "Did you know he was engaged?"

"I did hear something about it. Girl of the name of Wilson, or–"

"Milsom. She's going to spend the summer at Cape Pleasant, Archie tells me."

Then she'll have a chance of seeing him play in the championship competition."

McCay sucked his cigar in silence for a while, watching with dreamy eyes the blue smoke as it curled ceiling-ward. When he spoke his voice was singularly soft.

"Do you know, Sigsbee," he said, sipping his Maraschino with a gentle melancholy–"do you know, there is something wonderfully pathetic to me in this business. I see the whole thing so clearly. There was a kind of quiver in the poor old chap's voice when he said: 'She is coming to Cape Pleasant,' which told me more than any words could have done. It is a tragedy in its way, Sigsbee. We may smile at it, think it trivial; but it is none the less a tragedy. That warm-hearted, enthusiastic girl, all eagerness to see the man she loves do well–Archie, poor old Archie, all on fire to prove to her that her trust in him is not misplaced, and the end–Disillusionment–Disappointment–Unhappiness."

"He ought to keep his eye on the ball," said the more practical Sigsbee.

"Quite possibly," continued McCay, "he has told her that he will win the championship."

"If Archie's mutt enough to have told her that," said Sigsbee decidedly, "he deserves all he gets. Waiter, two Scotch highballs."

McCay was in no mood to subscribe to this stony-hearted view.

"I tell you," he said, "I'm *sorry* for Archie. I'm *sorry* for the poor old chap. And I'm more than sorry for the girl."

"Well, I don't see what we can do," said Sigsbee. "We can hardly be expected to foozle on purpose, just to let Archie show off before his girl."

McCay paused in the act of lighting his cigar, as one smitten with a great thought.

"Why not?" he said. "Why not, Sigsbee? Sigsbee, you've hit it!"

"Eh?"

"You have! I tell you, Sigsbee, you've solved the whole thing. Archie's such a bully good fellow, why not give him a benefit? Why not let him win this championship? You aren't going to tell me that you care whether you win a tin medal or not?"

Sigsbee's benevolence was expanding under the influence of the Scotch highball and his cigar. Little acts of kindness on Archie's part, here a cigar, there a lunch, at another time seats for the theatre, began to rise to the surface of his memory like rainbow-coloured bubbles. He wavered.

"Yes, but what about the rest of the men?" he said. "There will be a dozen or more in for the medal."

"We can square them," said McCay confidently. "We will broach the matter to them at a series of dinners at which we will be joint hosts. They are all sound men who will be charmed to do a little thing like this for a sport like Archie."

"How about Gossett?" asked Sigsbee.

McCay's face clouded. Gossett was an unpopular subject with members of the Cape Pleasant Golf Club. He was the serpent in their Eden. Nobody seemed quite to know how he had got in, but there, unfortunately, he was. Gossett had introduced into Cape Pleasant golf a cheerless atmosphere of the rigour of the game. It was to enable them to avoid just such golfers as Gossett that the Cape Pleasanters had founded their club. Genial courtesy rather than strict attention to the rules had been the leading characteristics of their play till his arrival. Up to that time it had been looked on as rather bad form to exact a penalty. A cheery give-and-take system had prevailed. Then Gossett had come, full of strange rules, and created about the same stir in the community which a hawk would create in a gathering of middle-aged doves.

"You can't square Gossett," said Sigsbee.

McCay looked unhappy.

"I forgot him," he said. "Of course, nothing will stop him trying to win. I wish we could think of something. I would almost as soon see him lose as Archie win. But, after all, he does have off days sometimes."

"You need to have a very off day to be as bad as Archie."

They sat and smoked in silence.

"I've got it," said Sigsbee suddenly. "Gossett is a fine golfer, but nervous. If we upset his nerves enough, he will go right off his stroke. Couldn't we think of some way?"

McCay reached out for his glass.

"Yours is a noble nature, Sigsbee," he said.

"Oh, no," said the paragon modestly. "Have another cigar?"

In order that the reader may get that mental half-Nelson on the plot of this narrative which is so essential if a short story is to charm, elevate, and instruct, it is necessary now, for the nonce (but only for the nonce), to inspect Archibald's past life.

Archibald, as he stated to McCay, was engaged to a Miss Milsom–Miss Margaret Milsom. How few men, dear reader, are engaged to girls with svelte figures, brown hair, and large blue eyes, now sparkling and vivacious, now dreamy and soulful, but always large and blue! How few, I say. You are, dear reader, and so am I, but who else? Archibald was one of the few who happened to be.

He was happy. It is true that Margaret's mother was not, as it were, wrapped up in him. She exhibited none of that effervescent joy at his appearance which we like to see in our mothers-in-law elect. On the contrary, she generally cried bitterly whenever she saw him, and at the end of ten minutes was apt to retire sobbing to her room, where she remained in a state of semi-coma till an advanced hour. She was by way of being a confirmed invalid, and something about Archibald seemed to get right in among her nerve centres, reducing them for the time being to a complicated hash. She did not like Archibald. She said she liked big, manly men. Behind his back she not infrequently referred to him as a "gaby"; sometimes even as that "guffin."

She did not do this to Margaret, for Margaret, besides being blue-eyed, was also a shade quick-tempered. Whenever she discussed Archibald, it was with her son Stuyvesant. Stuyvesant Milsom, who thought Archibald a bit of an ass, was always ready to sit and listen to his mother on the subject, it being, however, an understood thing that at the conclusion of the séance she yielded one or two saffron-coloured bills towards his racing debts. For Stuyvesant, having developed a habit of backing horses which either did not start at all or else sat down and thought in the middle of the race, could always do with ten dollars or so. His prices for these interviews worked out, as a rule, at about three cents a word.

In these circumstances it was perhaps natural that Archibald and Margaret should prefer to meet, when they did meet, at some other spot than the Milsom home. It suited them both better that they should arrange a secret tryst on these occasions. Archibald preferred it because being in the same room with Mrs. Milsom always made him feel like a murderer with particularly large feet; and Margaret preferred it because, as she told Archibald, these secret meetings lent a touch of poetry to what might otherwise have been a commonplace engagement.

Archibald thought this charming; but at the same time he could not conceal from himself the fact that Margaret's passion for the poetic cut, so to speak, both ways. He admired and loved the loftiness of her soul, but, on the other hand, it was a tough job having to live up to it. For Archibald was a very ordinary young man. They had tried to inoculate him with a love of poetry at school, but it had not taken. Until he was thirty he had been satisfied to class all poetry (except that of Mr. George Cohan) under the general heading of punk. Then he met Margaret, and the trouble began. On the day he first met her, at a picnic, she had looked so soulful, so aloof from this world, that he had felt instinctively that here was a girl who expected more from a man than a mere statement that the weather was great. It so chanced that he knew just one quotation from the classics, to wit, Tennyson's critique of the Island-Valley of Avilion.

He knew this because he had had the passage to write out one hundred and fifty times at school, on the occasion of his being caught smoking by one of the faculty who happened to be a passionate admirer of the "Idylls of the King."

A remark of Margaret's that it was a splendid day for a picnic and that the country looked nice gave him his opportunity.

"It reminds me," he said, "it reminds me strongly of the Island-Valley of Avilion, where falls not hail, or rain, or any snow, nor ever wind blows loudly; but it lies deep-meadow'd, happy, fair, with orchard lawns. . . ."

He broke off here to squash a hornet; but Margaret had heard enough.

"Are you fond of the poets, Mr. Mealing?" she said, with a far-off look.

"Me?" said Archibald fervently. "Me? Why, I eat 'em alive!"

And that was how all the trouble had started. It had meant unremitting toil for Archibald. He felt that he had set himself a standard from which he must not fall. He bought every new volume of poetry which was praised in the press, and learned the reviews by heart. Every evening he read painfully a portion of the classics. He plodded through the poetry sections of Bartlett's *Familiar Quotations.* Margaret's devotion to the various bards was so enthusiastic, and her reading so wide, that there were times when Archibald wondered if he could endure the strain. But he persevered heroically, and so far had not been found wanting. But the strain was fearful.

The early stages of the Cape Pleasant golf tournament need no detailed description. The rules of match play governed the contests, and Archibald disposed of his first three opponents before the twelfth hole. He had been diffident when he teed off with McCay in the first round, but, finding that he defeated the secretary with ease, he met one Butler in the second round with more confidence. Butler, too, he routed; with the result that, by the time he faced Sigsbee in round three, he was practically the conquering hero. Fortune seemed to be beaming upon him with almost insipid sweetness. When he was trapped in the bunker at the seventh hole, Sigsbee became trapped as well. When he sliced at the sixth tee,

Sigsbee pulled. And Archibald, striking a brilliant vein, did the next three holes in eleven, nine, and twelve; and, romping home, qualified for the final.

Gossett, that serpent, meanwhile, had beaten each of this three opponents without much difficulty.

The final was fixed for the following Thursday morning. Gossett, who was a broker, had made some frivolous objection about the difficulty of absenting himself from Wall Street, but had been overruled. When Sigsbee pointed out that he could easily defeat Archibald and get to the city by lunch-time if he wished, and that in any case his partner would be looking after things, he allowed himself to be persuaded, though reluctantly. It was a well-known fact that Gossett was in the midst of some rather sizeable deals at that time.

Thursday morning suited Archibald admirably. It had occurred to him that he could bring off a double event. Margaret had arrived at Cape Pleasant on the previous evening, and he had arranged by telephone to meet her at the end of the board-walk, which was about a mile from the links, at one o'clock, supply her with lunch, and spend the afternoon with her on the water. If he started his match with Gossett at eleven-thirty, he would have plenty of time to have his game and be at the end of the board-walk at the appointed hour. He had no delusions about the respective merits of Gossett and himself as golfers. He knew that Gossett would win the necessary ten holes off the reel. It was saddening, but it was a scientific fact. There was no avoiding it. One simply had to face it.

Having laid these plans, he caught his train on the Thursday morning with the consoling feeling that, however sadly the morning might begin, it was bound to end well.

The day was fine, the sun warm, but tempered with a light breeze. One or two of the club had come to watch the match, among them Sigsbee.

Sigsbee drew Gossett aside.

"You must let me caddie for you, old man," he said. "I know your temperament so exactly. I know how little it takes to put you off your stroke. In an ordinary game you might take one of these boys, I know, but on an important occasion like this you must not risk it. A grubby boy, probably with a squint, would almost certainly get on your nerves. He might even make comments on the game, or whistle. But I understand you. You must let me carry your clubs."

"It's very good of you," said Gossett.

"Not at all," said Sigsbee.

Archibald was now preparing to drive off from the first tee. He did this with great care. Everyone who has seen Archibald Mealing play golf knows that his teeing off is one of the most impressive sights ever witnessed on the links. He tilted his cap over his eyes, waggled his club a little, shifted his feet, waggled his club some more, gazed keenly towards the horizon for a moment, waggled his club again, and finally, with the air of a Strong Man lifting a bar of iron, raised it slowly above his head. Then, bringing it down with a sweep, he drove the ball with a lofty slice some fifty yards. It was rarely that he failed either to slice or pull his ball. His progress from hole to hole was generally a majestic zigzag.

Gossett's drive took him well on the way to the green. He holed out in five. Archibald, mournful but not surprised, made his way to the second tee.

The second hole was shorter. Gossett won it in three. The third he took in six, the fourth in four. Archibald began to feel that he might just as well not be there. He was practically a spectator.

At this point he reached in his pocket for his tobacco-pouch, to console himself with smoke. To his dismay he found that it was not there. He had had it in the train, but now it had vanished. This added to his gloom, for the pouch had been given to him by Margaret, and he had always thought it one more proof of the way her nature towered over the natures of the other girls that she had not woven a monogram on it in forget-me-nots. This record pouch was missing, and Archibald mourned for the loss.

His sorrows were not alleviated by the fact that Gossett won the fifth and sixth holes.

It was a quarter-past twelve, and Archibald reflected with moody satisfaction that the massacre must soon be over, and that he would be able to forget it in the society of Margaret.

As Gossett was about to drive off from the seventh tee, a telegraph boy approached the little group.

"Mr. Gossett," he said.

Gossett lowered his driver, and wheeled round, but Sigsbee had snatched the envelope from the boy's hand.

"It's all right, old man" he said. "Go right ahead. I'll keep it safe for you."

"Give it to me," said Gossett anxiously. "It may be from the office. Something may have happened to the market. I may be needed."

"No, no," said Sigsbee, soothingly. "Don't you worry about it. Better not open it. It might have something in it that would put you off your stroke. Wait till the end of the game."

"Give it to me. I want to see it."

Sigsbee was firm.

"No," he said, "I'm here to see you win this championship and I won't have you taking any risks. Besides, even if it was important, a few minutes won't make any difference."

"Well, at any rate, open it and read it."

"It is probably in cipher," said Sigsbee. "I wouldn't understand it. Play on, old man. You've only a few more holes to win."

Gossett turned and addressed his ball again. Then he swung. The club tipped the ball, and it rolled sluggishly for a couple of feet. Archibald approached the tee. Now there were moments when Archibald could drive quite decently. He always applied a considerable amount of muscular force to his efforts. It was in direction that, as a rule, he erred. On this occasion, whether inspired by his rival's failure or merely favoured by chance, he connected with his ball at precisely the right moment. It flew from the tee, straight, hard, and low, struck the ground near the green, bounded on and finally rocked to within a foot of the hole. No such long ball had been driven on the Cape Pleasant links since their foundation.

That it should have taken him three strokes to hole out from this promising position was unfortunate, but not fatal, for Gossett, who seemed suddenly to have fallen off his game, only reached the green in seven. A moment later a murmur of approval signified the fact that Archibald had won his first hole.

"Mr. Gossett," said a voice.

Those murmuring approval observed that the telegraph boy was once more in their midst. This time he bore two missives. Sigsbee dexterously impounded both.

"No," he said with decision, "I absolutely refuse to let you look at them till the game is over. I know your temperament."

Gossett gesticulated.

"But they must be important. They must come from my office. Where else would I get a stream of telegrams? Something has gone wrong. I am urgently needed."

Sigsbee nodded gravely.

"That is what I fear," he said. "That is why I cannot risk having you upset. Time enough, Gossett, for bad news after the game. Play on, man, and dismiss it from your mind. Besides, you couldn't get back to New York just yet, in any case. There are no trains. Dismiss the whole thing from your mind and just play your usual, and you're sure to win."

Archibald had driven off during this conversation, but without his previous success. This time he had pulled his ball into some long grass. Gossett's drive was, however, worse; and the subsequent movement of the pair to the hole resembled more than anything else the manoeuvres of two men rolling pea-nuts with toothpicks as the result of an election bet. Archibald finally took the hole in twelve after Gossett had played his fourteenth.

When Archibald won the next in eleven and the tenth in nine, hope began to flicker feebly in his bosom. But when he won two more holes, bringing the score to like-as-we-lie, it flamed up within him like a beacon.

The ordinary golfer, whose scores per hole seldom exceed those of Colonel Bogey, does not understand the whirl of mixed sensations which the really incompetent performer experiences on the rare occasions when he does strike a winning vein. As stroke follows stroke, and he continues to hold his opponent, a wild exhilaration surges through him, followed by a sort of awe, as if he was doing something wrong, even irreligious. Then all these yeasty emotions subside and are blended into one glorious sensation of grandeur and majesty, as of a giant among pigmies.

By the time that Archibald, putting with the care of one brushing flies off a sleeping Venus, had holed out and won the thirteenth, he was in the full grip of this feeling. And as he walked to the fifteenth tee, after winning the fourteenth, he felt that this was Life, that till now he had been a mere mollusc.

Just at that moment he happened to look at his watch, and the sight was like a douche of cold water. The hands stood at five minutes to one.

Let us pause and ponder on this point for a while. Let us not dismiss it as if it were some mere trivial, everyday difficulty. You, dear reader, play an accurate, scientific game and beat your opponent with ease every time you go to the links, and so do I; but Archibald was not like us. This was the first occasion on which he had ever felt that he was playing well enough to give him a chance of defeating a really good man. True, he had beaten McCay, Sigsbee and Butler in the earlier rounds; but they were ignoble rivals compared with Gossett. To defeat Gossett, however, meant the championship. On the other hand, he was passionately devoted to Margaret Milsom, whom he was due to meet at the end of the board-walk at one sharp. It was now five minutes to one, and the end of the board-walk still a mile away.

The mental struggle was brief but keen. A sharp pang, and his mind was made up. Cost what it might, he must stay on the links. If Margaret broke off the engagement–well, it might be that Time would heal the wound, and that after many years he would find some other girl for whom he might come to care in a wrecked, broken sort of way. But a chance like this could never come again. What is Love compared with holing out before your opponent?

The excitement now became so intense that a small boy, following with the crowd, swallowed his chewing-gum; for a slight improvement had become noticeable in Gossett's play, and a slight improvement in the play of almost anyone meant that it became vastly superior to Archibald's. At the next hole the improvement was not marked enough to have its full effect, and Archibald contrived to halve. This made him two up and three to play. What an average golfer would consider a commanding lead. But Archibald was no average golfer. A commanding lead for him would have been two up and one to play.

To give the public of his best, your golfer should have his mind cool and intent upon the game. Inasmuch as Gossett was worrying about the telegrams, while Archibald, strive as he might to dismiss it, was haunted by a vision of Margaret standing alone and deserted on the board-walk, play became, as it were, ragged. Fine putting enabled Gossett to do the sixteenth hole in twelve, and when, winning the seventeenth in nine, he brought his score level with Archibald's, the match seemed over. But just then–

"Mr. Gossett!" said a familiar voice.

Once more was the much-enduring telegraph boy among those present.

"T'ree dis time!" he observed.

Gossett sprang, but again the watchful Sigsbee was too swift.

"Be brave, Gossett–be brave," he said. "This is a crisis in the game. Keep your nerve. Play just as if nothing existed outside the links. To look at these telegrams now would be fatal."

Eye-witnesses of that great encounter will tell the story of the last hole to their dying day. It was one of those Titanic struggles which Time cannot efface from the memory. Archibald was fortunate in getting a good start. He only missed twice before he struck his ball on the tee. Gossett had four strokes ere he achieved the feat. Nor did Archibald's luck desert him in the journey to the green. He was out of the bunker in eleven. Gossett emerged only after sixteen. Finally, when Archibald's twenty-first stroke sent the ball trickling into the hole, Gossett had played his thirtieth.

The ball had hardly rested on the bottom of the hole before Gossett had begun to tear the telegrams from their envelopes. As he read, his eyes bulged in their sockets.

"Not bad news, I hope," said a sympathetic bystander.

Sigsbee took the sheaf of telegrams.

The first ran: "Good luck. Hope you win. McCay." The second also ran: "Good luck, Hope you win. McCay." So, singularly enough, did the third, fourth, fifth, sixth, and seventh.

"Great Scott!" said Sigsbee. "He seems to have been pretty anxious not to run any risk of missing you, Gossett."

As he spoke, Archibald, close behind him, was looking at his watch. The hands stood at a quarter to two.

Margaret and her mother were seated in the parlour when Archibald arrived. Mrs. Milsom, who had elicited the fact that Archibald had not kept his appointment, had been saying "I told you so" for some time, and this had not improved Margaret's temper. When, therefore, Archibald, damp and dishevelled, was shown in, the chill in the air nearly gave him frost-bite. Mrs. Milsom did her celebrated imitation of the Gorgon, while Margaret, lightly humming an air, picked up a weekly paper and became absorbed in it.

"Margaret, let me explain," panted Archibald. Mrs. Milsom was understood to remark that she dared say. Margaret's attention was riveted by a fashion plate.

"Driving in a taximeter to the ferry this morning," resumed Archibald, "I had an accident."

This was the net result of some rather feverish brainwork on the way from the links to the cottage.

The periodical flapped to the floor.

"Oh, Archie, are you hurt?"

"A few scratches, nothing more; but it made me miss my train."

"What train did you catch?" asked Mrs. Milsom sepulchrally.

"The one o'clock. I came straight on here from the station."

"Why," said Margaret, "Stuyvesant was coming home on the one o'clock train. Did you see him?"

Archibald's jaw dropped slightly.

"Er–no," he said.

"How curious," said Margaret.

"Very curious," said Archibald.

"Most curious," said Mrs. Milsom.

They were still reflecting on the singularity of this fact when the door opened, and the son of the house entered in person.

"Thought I should find you here, Mealing," he said. "They gave me this at the station to give to you; you dropped it this morning when you got out of the train."

He handed Archibald the missing pouch.

"Thanks," said the latter huskily. "When you say this morning, of course you mean this afternoon, but thanks all the same–thanks–thanks."

"No, Archibald Mealing, he does *not* mean this afternoon," said Mrs. Milsom. "Stuyvesant, speak! From what train did that guf–did Mr. Mealing alight when he dropped the tobacco-pouch?"

"The ten o'clock, the fellow told me. Said he would have given it back to him then only he sprinted off in the deuce of a hurry."

Six eyes focused themselves upon Archibald.

"Margaret," he said, "I will not try to deceive you–"

"You may try," observed Mrs. Milsom, "but you will not succeed."

"Well, Archibald?"

Archibald fingered his collar.

"There was no taximeter accident."

"Ah!" said Mrs. Milsom.

"The fact is, I have been playing in a golf tournament."

Margaret uttered an exclamation of surprise.

"Playing golf!"

Archibald bowed his head with manly resignation.

"Why didn't you tell me? Why didn't you arrange for us to meet on the links? I should have loved it."

Archibald was amazed.

"You take an interest in golf, Margaret? You! I thought you scorned it, considered it an unintellectual game. I thought you considered all games unintellectual."

"Why, I play golf myself. Not very well."

"Margaret! Why didn't you tell me?"

"I thought you might not like it. You were so spiritual, so poetic. I feared you would despise me."

Archibald took a step forward. His voice was tense and trembling.

"Margaret," he said, "this is no time for misunderstandings. We must be open with one another. Our happiness is at stake. Tell me honestly, *do* you like poetry really?"

Margaret hesitated, then answered bravely:

"No, Archibald," she said, "it is as you suspect. I am not worthy of you. I do *not* like poetry. Ah, you shudder! You turn away! Your face grows hard and scornful!"

"I don't!" yelled Archibald. "It doesn't! It doesn't do anything of the sort! You've made me another man!"

She stared, wild-eyed, astonished.

"What! Do you mean that you, too–"

"I should just say I do. I tell you I hate the beastly stuff. I only pretended to like it because I thought you did. The hours I've spent learning it up! I wonder I've not got brain fever."

"Archie! Used you to read it up, too? Oh, if I'd only known!"

"And you forgive me–this morning, I mean?"

"Of course. You couldn't leave a golf tournament. By the way, how did you get on?"

Archibald coughed.

"Rather well," he said modestly. "Pretty decently. In fact, not badly. As a matter of fact, I won the championship."

"The championship!" whispered Margaret. "Of America?"

"Well, not *absolutely* of America," said Archibald. "But all the same a championship."

"My hero."

"You won't be wanting me for a while, I guess?" said Stuyvesant nonchalantly. "Think I'll smoke a cigarette on the porch."

And sobs from the stairs told that Mrs. Milsom was already on her way to her room.

*This story initially appeared in* Esquire. *It's about a man who loses his job. With a family to support and a new baby coming, he is struggling to cope with life. Can golf provide any salvation? Author Charles Dickinson is an accomplished writer with four novels and a book of short stories to his credit. The latter is called* With or Without and Other Stories *(1987), and his most recent novel is* Rumor Has It *(1991).*

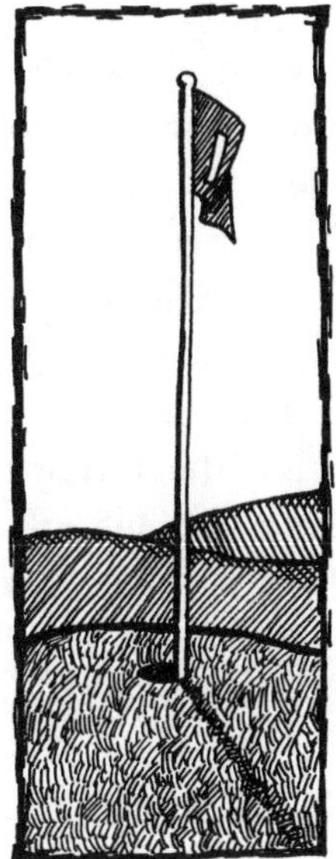

*Charles Dickinson*

# MY LIVELIHOOD (1982)

I LOST MY DAIRY JOB and was not troubled. One of my brothers-in-law said he could get me into the carpenters' union. He said he'd lend me the tools and instruct me in their use. I was tired of the dairy, all that whiteness every day, and the hairnets we had to wear. Hair in milk. Shows right up.

But I didn't want to be a carpenter, either. I wasn't looking for work. This bothered the hell out of my Stella, who was expecting our second child, hoping for a girl this time. She was six months' gone. Two-thirds there, her belly was nice and round. Her cheeks were fat. My Stel is tall and took it well. She is very close to being pretty. My son's name is Ray.

My Stella's father is a contractor of some renown. He told me I was lazy. Her brothers, seven carpenters, said the same thing. Ray even picked it up: Daddy's lazy. Stella's family makes me nervous. They are too hearty in their work, out all day driving nails. They have muscles and great tans. They told me I could be a carpenter too and called me lazy when I said no thanks. I was waiting, I told myself. I felt something happening.

I'm thirty-three years old. I've been out of work a number of times in my life. Never like this, though, Stel tells me. She's right. I must avoid panic. I mustn't get roped into the first thing that pays. That is the old me. I was raised to hate work but to do it. I always had to have a job. This time I'm going slow.

The dairy told me adios April fifteenth. My foreman called me into his office and said, "Kids ain't drinking the milk they used to." I didn't have the seniority to weather such a trend, but I liked the irony; Ray Boy drinks the stuff by the ton. Me and three other guys in hairnets went out the door. One guy started to cry and shake right there in the parking lot. A young guy, married but no kids, he went right to pieces before my eyes. I shook hands all around, told the crying guy to grab hold. I got in my car and went straight home. Me for a sandwich and beer.

Along the way home I saw ads for things I couldn't afford anymore. On my dairy pay I couldn't afford most things, but there was always the chance; now, no way. The world was hung with ads, I noticed. All those deluxes beyond my reach.

I got out of my whites at home and threw them down the laundry chute. This was a small favorite with me, the boy in me coming out. I held on to the clothes until I could get my head in the chute to watch them fall; they got smaller falling, they stayed in flight longer than I expected. It was a cheap special effect and reminded me of science fiction.

Ray came home a little later and screamed when he saw me. I was out of place lying on the couch in the middle of the afternoon with a beer on my stomach. I gave him a hug. He said my arms smelled like cheese.

"Where's Mom?" I asked. He didn't know. I took him out back and we threw the Frisbee until Stella came home.

She brought an armload of old clothes with her. More Goodwill crap.

Her face glowed with the pleasure of doing good for others. She dropped a black shoe when she came to the door to call Ray and saw me running after the flying saucer.

"Why are you home?" she asked.

"I lost my job."

My Stella wet her lips with her tongue. She carried the old clothes into the utility room and dropped them on the floor. I picked up the black shoe and followed her. She gave me a kiss. Wet salt taste. Her stomach bumping me. I felt a rising. When was the last time we'd done it in the afternoon? I was always working. Ray Boy. Something. See, I told myself, a positive thing already.

"It's not so bad," I told her. "Nothing to worry about."

I looked outside at Ray. He was talking to a kid on a bike and throwing the Frisbee up and catching it. I suggested to my Stella, "Let' go upstairs."

She stepped behind the pile of clothes. She wanted that crap between us, I guess. Her face had changed. I felt the moment getting away from me. My Stel wanted me to be afraid for our quality of life. She'd kissed me, sure, but she'd also bumped me with her hard belly. Number two, hello in there.

"Nothing to be worried about?" she said. She was tapping one of her feet, which are big.

"It'll be all right," I said.

She was not ready for this. My Stella is the baby of her family, though she is older than two of her brothers. Stella and her mother and her father and seven brothers. Her father paid for our house as a wedding present. Her brothers built it. I remember that as a hard time for me. Her brothers had something to do, they laughed at each other's jokes. I just sat on the lumber and watched. I fetched them beers to make myself useful.

Stella had been raised in a world that was a happy place. All lines were plumb, all nails were straight. Her grandfather was dead a year, flattened by a slipped ton of bricks, before Stel was told. She was not prepared for a husband out of work. I saw her start to cry. Her mother's tears. It was the lone soft spot in the men in Stella's family, and that spot was mush. Don't use it too often, I could hear Stella's mother coaching her, dry-eyed. Use it sparingly and it will hit home every time.

I took a step forward, kissed my wife, and smiled. I would not be bullied. If she kept it up, I'd go outside and play with Ray.

"Pretty soon . . . pretty soon," my Stella sobbed, bringing one of her big feet up through the pile of Goodwill crap, filling the air with it, "we'll be wearing this stuff ourselves."

I got into a poker game with some of the dairy guys, and though I won $122 I went home sad. All that dairy talk, it made me miss it. Tales of women on the routes. Stray things that dropped in the milk. A driver named Del was being sued for running over a champion Afghan. He laughed and said the dog looked like an old flame, and that was why he went after it, but still he was being sued. They let me play but I didn't belong. I imagined they were mad because I was ungrateful enough to win, too.

My Stella saw me sitting at home and decided I was sad and bored. She dragged me along on her Goodwill rounds. "It will do you good to get out of the house," she said. "It will lift your spirits until you find another job."

"My spirits aren't low."

"Yes, they are," she told me.

At every place we stopped she worked the fact of my unemployment into the conversation. I'd stand out by the car and she'd point at me, and I'd wave and smile. She might have asked for something in my size. She used me as an example of the type of person all those rags would help.

When I asked her not tell everybody I'd lost my job, she answered with words that even made a little sense. "These people are very successful, and you never know who might offer you a job."

We stopped at the Blatt house. Mrs. Blatt was going to donate an old set of golf clubs to Goodwill. I offered to buy them from her for ten dollars.

"You'll do no such thing," my Stella protested.

"Here." I folded the bill in Mrs. Blatt's hand. I saw it in her eyes: charity was fine, but profit was holy. "You can get rid of the clubs," I told her, "and make a little money."

I slung that bag of jangling sticks over my shoulder. "People who need Goodwill don't have time to play golf," I told Stella. "They're too busy looking for firewood."

I took my clubs to the public course the next day. The new ball I teed up reminded me guiltily of an egg that should have been on Ray Boy's plate, and that reminded me of my joblessness. But then I hit the ball and it swooped out of sight. The feeling was solid in my hands. A motion down the fairway caught my eye. My ball landing. It hit and rolled, it might have gone forever but the ground was damp. I set off after it. I played thirty-six holes that day.

I never was an athlete. My father owned a grocery and I went to work for him when I was seven years old, cheap help, a roof over my head, and a dollar allowance a week making me, in my father's words, "rich enough." I worked in that store for an hour before school, then after school until we closed at seven, and all day on the weekends. I was ringing sales on the cash register when I was nine years old and all the kids my age were outdoors hitting baseballs or shooting free throws. These kids came indoors in winter, red-faced, to buy gum or oatmeal cookies, skates hanging from their necks. Their taped sticks and black disks were exotic tools to me. I was a flop in gym. I once brained myself getting under a fly ball and probably survived only because we were playing softball.

One day, I was fifteen, I stopped to watch the golfers on my way to work. For more than two years they had been building the course and all that land hadn't meant much to me. I had seen the yellow graders and the scalloped dents filled with sand and the troops of Mexicans brought in to lay rolls of sod. It had meant nothing to me. I clerked in a grocery for my old man.

Then the golf course opened. I was passing by and saw a guy on the tee, and I watched him whip his club around and smack that ball a mile, though I couldn't see where it landed. The guy watched it and watched it, then he slid his club into a bag and covered it with a tasseled sock.

This was golf. It looked like something I might like. There were no moving balls to hit or control. I would not be required to be quick, or to do something instantly for the good of the team. But I didn't dare tell my father. I had a job; that was all I needed. Eighteen years would pass before I would tee it up.

I have two brothers, three sisters. I think that's part of why I fell in love with Stella; she understood the big-family life. All of us worked in the store. My mother, too. When my sister Diana got up the money and nerve to leave and was planning to move to Phoenix, my old man snuck into her room the night before she was to leave and cut up her bus ticket. Diana avenged this by upending every pyramid of cans in the store at the height of the Saturday rush. A terrific racket. We watched and cheered and refused to restack them. We never came closer to open revolt.

Why did we stay and work there so long? It was part of our training. All of us realize that now. My father hated that store. He told us so often how he hated it that we hated it, too. Now none of us can stand the things we do for a living. To the old man, work was a curse. Now it is to us, too. We may like the money or maybe the people on the job, or the end of the day, but none of us get anything from the actual work. It makes me angry. My father had no right. This is one reason I'm not looking right now.

Diana finally got to Phoenix and became a cocktail waitress and hooker. I've seen pictures of her taken there. She's a pretty girl, though I don't recognize her as my sister. She says she hates her jobs. Rachel is a nurse and hates it. She writes me long letters from Boston, filled with complaint. She hates the old man's ghost for what he gave her. That ghost has driven us all away. Me here, Rachel in Boston, Diana in Arizona, Tim in Paris, of all places, Rosie in Vancouver. Vic owns a bait and tackle shop in the Upper Peninsula of Michigan, on the shore of Lake Superior, and hires kids to run it for him. He told me they rob him blind, but he accepts this as the price he has to pay to be able to stay away from the place.

My father died when I was twenty-one. My mother sold the store and split the proceeds evenly among herself and her children. It made a nice lump, and it is this, to some extent, that feeds my family now. Vic bought the bait shop with his share. Rachel put hers into nursing-school tuition.

My mother took her share and moved to New Orleans. I visited her once and she made me cry, she was so content. She lived in a large apartment that had a thousand plants, French doors, and a thin strip of balcony you could stand on and smell the Gulf of Mexico. She cooked a ton of shrimp for us. She played Bingo every night. She sat in that smoky room and inhaled deeply. She was good. She claimed to have increased her inheritance by a fourth. I liked that she had her groceries delivered by lanky black boys eager for the good tip she was known for. She's still there.

So my father's death and the store's being sold was my first taste of being out of work. I stashed my inheritance and panicked. I took the first job I could find, going to work in a factory that made gizmos for detecting police radar. I sat on a high stool under perfect light doing the same four steps over and over again. It was boring work and I kind of liked it the first three hours. But the business was on the rise, and automation came along and did my job better. Last hired, I was first fired. That was only fair. A second time I was out of work.

I knocked around a few years. I worked odd jobs and tested my reactions to losing them. It was like giving myself increasing jolts of electricity to see how much I could stand. The longest I went without work, without looking for work, was three weeks. I started waking up depressed, bathed in sweat. I knew I had to find work right away. It was not lack of money that drove me, but something deeper. It was the values of my father, what he had nailed in me with all those hours in the store. Hating work was in my blood.

I'm a glib guy when I have to be. Getting a job has never been a problem. I come across as earnest, reliable, eager to do the job. I knew that once I started looking I'd find something right away. When I was twenty-five, I took a job working for the city at a recycling center, real moron's work that paid $7.70 an hour, a king's ransom. My job was to sort all the crap people brought in to have recycled, weigh the stuff, and throw it in the respective dumpsters to be hauled away. We took in only glass bottles, aluminum cans, and newspapers.

We paid twenty cents a pound for aluminum cans. A tall young lady with a kind of obsessed look on her face argued with me one day that our scales were off, that I was cheating her. I explained that the scales were accurate, that she'd have to trust me, but that if she wanted to complain, she could go up to the village hall and talk to them. She said she just might. I weighed her cans and wrote out her receipt. I watched her walk to her car, an emerald Lincoln Continental, and maneuver her body into it. She had large hips, breasts, and feet and was almost six feet tall. She didn't seem comfortable with all she had been given. It looked like too much for her to handle. I guessed she was twenty or twenty-one and would learn to be graceful later. Of course, this girl was my Stella.

She was back in a week with more cans, bags of them stuffed in the trunk and back seat of her Lincoln. I asked where she got them all.

"Along the highway," she said. "Everywhere you look. People can be such pigs."

I asked if that was how she paid for her car, smiling to let her know I was flirting.

"My daddy bought my car for me."

She kept returning with cans all that summer, and when I drove home I always was surprised to see any cans along the road, I was sure she had gotten them all. She had an anxious face. She was eager for something and late in July I began to have dreams that it was me. I asked her for a date the next time she was in. She agreed and volunteered to drive. We went miniature golfing and had a pizza on our first date. On other dates we necked in her wide back seat. She was clumsy with her size only until she got into my arms. Then her grace and invention were startling. She began driving me to and from work; on occasion, we scouted the highway together for cans, though I lacked her prospector's lust. The first time I took her clothes off I was amazed at all that was involved. My Stella, big, smooth-skinned riddle. We were married in a year. Ray Boy soon followed. I was making $10.11 an hour at the recycling center and hating it so much it had the feel of a career. Then about a year ago my Stella came home and told me her father knew someone at the dairy, that he could get me a job if I was interested.

I played 180 holes the first week of May. My Goodwill clubs were in sorry condition but I didn't mind. After I scraped the crud from their faces they worked fine. When I wasn't on the course, I was practicing in my yard with plastic golf balls.

The pro at the public course where I played told me my swing was "a natural" and that it could really be spruced up with a few lessons. I had no use for lessons. If I was taking a lesson, that would mean less time I'd be out on the course actually playing. I was afraid to take golf seriously. I was afraid I'd learn to hate the game.

The pro told me I was lazy. "You have to put some effort into it," he told me.

"Effort," I said, "implies resistance."

I hit the ball long and straight from the first. I didn't lust after scores like so many guys who were out to break a hundred, then ninety, then eighty. I was living on that fascination for the game planted eighteen years earlier when I'd seen that guy hitting his drive on my way to work. I was playing. It was a strange thing: work and play. Some days, if I was short or didn't feel like spending my money on a round, I worked it off in the pro shop washing balls, cleaning clubs, or filling driving-range buckets for Dave, who ran the place. When I did finally get out on the course, I wasn't ashamed of my clubs or my shoes (which I paid two dollars for at a garage sale; they fit perfectly but one was missing a heel cleat). I had a sport. And when my playing partners had to quit to go back to work, I could play all afternoon.

June came. The summer was dry and hot. I could feel the greens quickening by the moment. My Stella's face got fatter. I was in the front yard practicing my nine iron when one of my brothers-in-law appeared. This one was named Jack. He was about forty years old, with thick forearms, a tan, and a cigarillo in his mouth.

"How's she holding up?" he asked.

"Just fine."

"No leaks?"

"Stella?"

Jack broke off a laugh and walked up to the house he had helped build. He smacked the wall. "No, man! Our house. A damn fine job we did for you."

"The house is fine," I assured him. I had seven plastic balls lined up at my feet. One by one I would hit them down the yard. I looked forward to Jack leaving so I could get on with it.

"Stel tells us you're still out of work."

"Stel tells everybody that," I said. "I expect to see it on the news."

"Been a while, hasn't it?"

I swung smoothly through the first ball and it floated away with a faint *snick!* sound. I liked Jack best of that hopeless knot of carpenters I had married into. He was the oldest, and the only one to thank me for the beers I fetched while they built our house. Not much of a swap, I know, beers for a house, but I appreciate good manners wherever they occur.

"We'll be okay," I said. "Thanks for your concern."

"You got any prospects?"

"Prospects for a job? I haven't been looking too hard."

"You've got a pregnant wife in there, pal," Jack said.

"No. She's not home."

He grimaced. Me, the smart-ass. "What do you do with yourself all day?"

"I play a lot of golf. You play?"

"No. Look, how about being a carpenter? We can get you in the union."

"No, thanks."

"Dad said he can call in a few favors. It's good money. The work is seasonal, sure, but when you work, the money is damn good."

"I can't even hammer a nail, Jack." With the softest *tick!* I sent the next ball away down a sweet, high path.

Jack dismissed my ineptitude. "That can be taught. Any asshole can drive a nail. We'll lend you some tools until you can get your own. With a little pull from Dad we can even skip your apprenticeship. You'll start right off in the serious money."

"You've given us enough already," I told him. I settled myself over the next ball. Jack momentarily ceased to be. I hit it nicely. "This house," I said, "and I know your father gives Stella money. I can't take another job from you, too."

"Is that so terrible? Taking something from your family during hard times?"

"Yeah, Jack. It's gotten to that point."

"It's not easy getting into the union. The waiting list is a mile long."

"Let someone in who wants to be a carpenter."

"It's true, I guess, what Stel says."

"Probably," I agreed.

"She says you're lazy. She says you like being out of a job."

"My Stella speaks the truth."

My Stella gave us a daughter on a steamy August morning. Cecilia Joan was a big girl like her mother, coming in an ounce shy of ten pounds. I laid my hand on Stella's wet forehead and put my ear to her chest to listen to her heart. She had worked hard. The baby was red and creased. We took our mothers' first names, flipping a coin to determine the order.

The elevator dumped a load of carpenters. We heard them coming and Stella laughed. She rolled her tired eyes at me and hooked her lank hair behind her ears. She knew I'd be leaving soon.

Her father led them in. He carried a giant stuffed panda.

"So here's the numbnuts who's too good to be a carpenter," he said. "Too good to be helped out by his family that works up a sweat on the job."

"Daddy!" Stella protested.

They filled the room with the smell of pine. Shavings hung in their hair. Their pants were functionally adorned with loops and slots to hold the gizmos of their calling. They had brought fragile nightery and bluebird mobiles.

"Mr. Out-of-Work don't know what a sweet deal he blew," Stella's father pressed.

I kissed my pretty wife good-bye. Her forehead tasted of salt. Already her face looked not so fat.

"See you, boys," I said to the carpenters, and made my way through them to the door.

I met three strangers and we went out. I played my round to an eighty-nine. The others finished in the high nineties and low one hundreds. These men were quick to anger; they beat themselves. I counted a half dozen times when each of them could have made a run at me, but I knew they wouldn't. Over the summer I'd learned to read my opponents by the hunch of their shoulders or the smoke from their ears, and to know when another bad shot was about to emerge to compound their anguish. I waited for these moments and threw a bet their way just before they shot. They would straighten up, glare at me, and accept. They hated themselves for being less than perfect; now they had bet on it. A vein of cash ran from their brains to my wallet.

Toward the end of the day, I waited in the pro shop drinking lemonade.

"Didn't do much today," observed Dave.

"Too hot," I agreed.

"Too hot for anything."

"Hey, Dave! I'm a father!"

Dave smiled at me. "No shit?"

"Second time around," I said. "But undeniably no shit."

"That's great." He shook my hand. "You got any cigars?"

I patted my pockets: "Sorry."

"That's a screwy tradition anyhow," Dave said. "The father'll be paying out the nose all his life. He should be the one getting the see-gars."

"Amen," I said.

"So what can I give you, Dad?"

"New set of sticks."

"Be serious, Dad."

"A free round?"

"Play on, Dad."

I found a foursome. We moved over the course through a cooling dusk. Bugs swirled in the pro shop's lights. I was pushing up the fairway on my thirty-sixth hole of the day. I planned to shower, have a beer, then get Ray Boy and go visit his mother and sister. I felt pretty grand. I was on in three. Nobody could stop me from winning money on the round. And nobody said I couldn't win a little more.

My opponents had been at work and had come to catch the late-afternoon reduced fees. They played the front nine as though still in suits and ties. They bitched about their work between shots. They expected too much. Their anger increased and I skimmed it like cream.

On the eighteenth green I turned to one of them, a guy named Herb. He could not believe he trailed me by seven strokes. He was on in three, too.

"Ten to whoever gets down from here first?" I said.

"Yeah." He jumped at the chance.

I let him go first because I liked to savor any day's last putts. They always made me a little sad. What promise did I have I'd ever play again? Away from the game I was just another guy out of work.

Herb jerked his first putt eight feet past the cup. I easily rolled mine within a foot. I tapped in to get out of his way. No problem, he went wide. I swear his eyes were glowing.

They paid me my due in the twilight. Herb had to write me a check (he kept his checkbook in his bag, as though he suspected something about himself), and I accepted it gracefully. Another guy paid me in quarters.

All this money amazed me; my livelihood was seasonal, like carpentry.

A coin fell through my fingers while I was putting my earnings in my wallet. I left it there on the green for a fellow player to mark his ball.

*This is the oldest story in the book, and an endearing one it is. An earnest but hopelessly inept duffer acquires a magic golf ball. We have heard of juiced-up golf balls before in the story by Kevin Cook ("Lee and Me At the Open"). But the ball in "The Hong-Kong Medal" is devilishly inspired rather than a high-tech wonder. The ball is similarly agreeable, however: it goes where you want it to. Wouldn't it be nice to play just one round with such a ball? Author W. G. Van T. Sutphen (1861–1945) was a revered writer who turned out plays and novels as well as short stories. His popular science fiction book* The Doorsman *(1906) was reissued in 1975.*

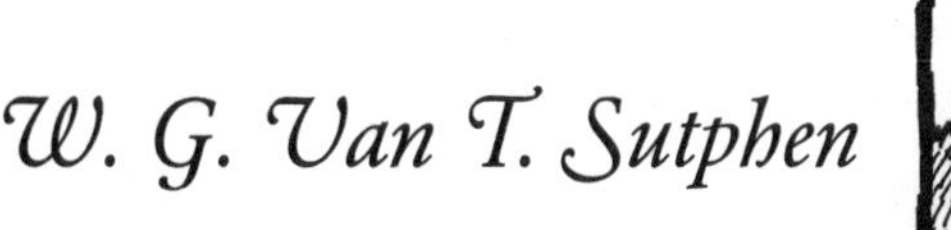


# THE HONG-KONG MEDAL (1898)

AT THE AGE OF THIRTY-FIVE but one illusion remained to Henry Alderson, rich, single, and a member in good and regular standing of the Marion County Golf Club. It is hardly necessary to add that it was only in his capacity as a golfer that he lived again in the rose-colored atmosphere of youth, for after the third decade there is no other possible form of self-deception. And it is equally superfluous to remark that he was a very poor golfer, for it is only the duffers at the royal and ancient game who have any leisure for the exercise of the imagination; the medal-winners are obliged to confine their attention to hitting the ball clean and to keeping their eye in for short putts. It was for Henry Alderson and his kind to keep trade brisk for the ball and club makers, and to win phenomenal matches against the redoubtable *Col. Bogey*–a game which may be magnificent, but which is certainly not golf. Still, the diversion was unquestionably a harmless one, and served to keep him in the open air and from an overclose application to business. Moreover, it was absolutely certain that the secret of success lay well within his grasp. A few more days of practice, the final acquisition of that peculiar turn of the wrist, and then!–Henry Alderson took a fresh grip on the familiar lofting-iron that had deceived him so often, and topped another ball along the turf. Of course the delusion was a hopeless one, but he was happy in its possession; and if we who look on have become wiser in our day and generation–why, so much the worse for us.

It was a bright autumn morning, and Henry Alderson stood at the tee looking at the little red flag that marked the location of the tenth hole, two hundred and thirty yards away. He had done fairly well on the outgoing course, but this hole had always been a stumbling-block to him, and that dreadful double hazard, a scant hundred yards down the course, looked particularly savage on this particular morning. On the left lurked an enormous sand-pit, which was popularly known as the "Devil"; and the "Deep Sea," in the shape of an ice pond, was only a few yards to the right. Straight between them lay the path to glory, but for a "slice" or a "foozle" there remained only destruction and double figures.

Henry Alderson shuddered as he looked, and incontinently forgot all about "slow back." Crack! and the "gutty" had disappeared beneath the treacherous waters of the "Deep Sea." With painful deliberation he teed another ball and mentally added two to his score. The club-head swung back, and for one fatal instant his eye wandered from the ball. Bang! and it had gone to the "Devil." Without a word Mr. Alderson took his expensive collection of seventeen clubs from the hands of his caddie and descended into the bunker to meet the Evil One.

It was just fifteen minutes after eleven when Henry Alderson entered upon his ghostly conflict with all the Powers of Darkness. At twenty minutes of twelve the caddie, tired of inaction, crept cautiously to the edge of the bunker and looked in. His master held in his hand a costly patented "driver" that was alleged to be unbreakable. Placing one foot upon the head of the club, he kicked judiciously but with determination at the precise place where the "scare" is whipped to the shaft, and then carefully added the fragments to the heap of broken putters, cleeks, and brasseys that lay before him. The boy, who was wise in his generation, waited for no more, but fled to the club-house.

Henry Alderson came up out of the bunker, took half a dozen new balls from the pocket of his red coat, and deliberately flung them into the "Deep Sea." He then tore his score-card into bits, divested himself of cap and shoes, laid his watch and purse where they would be readily observed, and walked with a firm step to the border of the pond.

Suddenly a quickly moving shadow projected itself over his shoulder, and a cheerful, albeit an unfamiliar, voice hailed him. He turned and saw a stranger standing close beside him. The new-comer was an odd-looking personage, dressed in a semi-clerical suit of rusty black, and carrying an old cotton umbrella and a well-stuffed carpet-bag. He had a keen-looking, smooth-shaven face, with piercing black eyes and an aggressive nose. His complexion was of a curious pallor, as though untouched by wind or sun, but there was nothing in his appearance to indicate either ill-health or decrepitude.

"Possibly a colporteur," thought Henry Alderson. "At any rate, he's no golfer."

"How are you making out?" inquired the stranger, in a tone of polite interest.

It was on the tip of Henry Alderson's tongue to answer, "Fifty-five for nine holes" (his actual score being sixty-three), but at this awful moment, when all the solid realities of life were crumbling away beneath his feet, the lie seemed so small, so pitiful, so mean, and he replied, "Came out in forty-two, but then I lost a shot through having my ball lifted by a dog."

The stranger did not seem to be visibly impressed. "Pooh!" he said, airily; "I should hardly call that golf."

"Perhaps you play yourself," returned Alderson, with what he considered to be a sarcastic inflection.

"Not as a general thing, though I do a round or so occasionally," said the dark gentleman, placidly. Then opening his carpet-bag and taking out a golfball, "It's a very pretty drive from where we stand. If you will allow me."

He teed the ball, and, with what seemed to be an almost contemptuous disregard of all rules for correct driving, swung against it the crook handle of his old cotton umbrella. Crack! and it went away like a rifle-bullet, close to the ground for one hundred and twenty yards, and then, towering upward in the manner of a rocketing pigeon, caught the full strength of the breeze for a hundred yards of further carry, and dropped dead on the putting-green. Henry Alderson gasped.

"Shall we walk on?" said the stranger.

It was a long putt onto the green, but the umbrella was again equal to the occasion. Henry Alderson's eyes sparkled. This was an umbrella worth having.

"It makes no difference what kind of a club you use," said the gentleman in black, apparently reading his thoughts. "But with this particular make of ball you can accomplish any shot at will, no matter how difficult."

"I'd like to try that kind of ball," said Alderson, eagerly. "Can you give me the maker's address?"

"If you will accept this one, it is entirely at your service."

Henry Alderson stretched out his hand, and then as quickly withdrew it. He remembered now that when the obliging stranger had opened his bag it had appeared to be filled with what looked like legal papers–contracts perhaps–and there was a dreadful significance in the fact that all the signatures were in red. Of course it might have been carmine ink, and probably was, but it looked suspicious.

"If it's a question of signing my name to anything," he faltered, "I don't think that I can accept. I've made it a rule–er–never to go upon anybody's paper. It's–er–business, you know."

The stranger smiled indulgently. "You are quite right. Nevertheless, you need have no scruples about accepting my gift, for there is no obligation of any kind involved in the transaction."

Henry Alderson trembled, and looked furtively at the dark gentleman's feet, which, as he now observed, were encased in a pair of arctic galoshes some four sizes too large. Clearly there was no definite information to be gained in that quarter; and as the field that they were in was used as pasture for cattle, the presence of hoof-marks could mean nothing either way. There was nothing to do but to chance it, and he was not long in making up his mind. He took the ball and stowed it away in his pocket.

The stranger nodded approvingly. "I think that I may congratulate you in advance upon your success in winning the club handicap this afternoon."

"But suppose that I lose the ball?" said Alderson, with a sudden accession of doubtfulness.

"Impossible. If your caddie has been negligent, you have only to whistle, and the ball will keep on answering 'Here' until you come up with it. And, moreover, it is indestructible."

"It makes no difference what club I use?"

"None whatever. If you care to, you can drive that ball two hundred yards with a feather bolster."

"I shall endeavor to do so," laughed Alderson. "You won't–er–come and have a bite of luncheon with me?"

"Not to-day," said the stranger, politely. "But we shall probably meet again. Good luck to you, and may your success end only with the winning of the Hong-Kong Medal."

The two men bowed, and the dark gentleman walked off. He went to the edge of the "Devil" sand-bunker, marched straight into it, and disappeared. Moved by a sudden impulse, Henry Alderson followed and looked in. There was nothing to be seen, but he thought that he could detect a slight trace of sulphur in the air. However, one may be easily deceived in such matters.

As Henry Alderson trudged back to the club-house it seemed as though the events of the last half-hour had been nothing more than the disordered fancies of a noon-day nightmare. But there was the ball in his hand, the tangible evidence of what had happened. And, after all, the bargain had been entirely in his favor. Whoever the dark gentleman may have been, and Henry Alderson shuddered as he reflected upon one unholy possibility, he was certainly no business man. The wonderful ball was in his, Henry Alderson's, possession, and his chances of eternal salvation were as good as ever.

"Somebody has been stupid," chuckled Mr. Alderson to himself as he entered the grill-room of the club and took up the luncheon card.

The handicap match had been put down for three o'clock. It was a monthly affair, and the winner had the proud distinction of wearing a silver cross for the following period of thirty days. It was a coveted honor, but of course not to be compared with the Hong-Kong Medal, which was always played for at the end of the golfing year. No one knew why it was called the Hong-Kong Medal, and it was certain that its donor had never in his life been out of the Middle States. But the appellation seemed to chime in with the somewhat fanciful phraseology that prevails in all things pertaining to golf, and it possessed a sonorous clang tint that was suggestive of tomtoms and barbaric victories.

It is needless to say that Henry Alderson invariably entered all the club competitions, and as invariably came out at the bottom of the list. And yet no one had worked harder to insure success. He was absolutely saturated with the theory and literature of golf, and could rattle off the roster of open and amateur champions with the fluency of a prize Sunday-school scholar reciting the names of the kings of Judah and Israel. He neglected nothing in the way of precept or practice, and when the club champion got married he had even thought of following his example for its possible effect upon his game. But when he ventured to propose the expedient to Miss Kitty Crake he met with a decided rebuff.

"I shall never," said Miss Crake, "marry a man who is not on the scratch list. When you have won the Hong-Kong Medal, why then we shall see."

Of course, such an answer could be nothing less than the most absolute of refusals. Even in his wildest dreams he had never hoped to come in better than fourth in the monthly handicaps, and that too with an allowance of thirty-six strokes. It is true that there were other young ladies who might have accepted a less heroic standard of excellence than the winning of the Hong-Kong, but Henry Alderson felt that the matrimonial experiment was not worth trying unless Kitty Crake could be induced to take part in it. And so there the matter rested.

When Mr. Alderson stepped to the teeing-ground that afternoon for his first drive he felt unaccountably cool and collected, in spite of the fact that Miss Crake stood in the very forefront of the "gallery." It was one hundred and seventy-seven yards to the first hole, and he usually "hooked" his ball into the "Punch-bowl" hollow at the left, or else feebly topped it along the ground in the one consuming desire to get away from the spectators. But to-day there should be another tale to tell. For an instant he thought of directing the magic ball to land upon the putting-green dead at the hole, but he reflected that such a phenomenal stroke would undoubtedly be put down as a fluke. It was the part of wisdom to go quietly, and so he picked out a spot some twenty yards short of the green but in good line, and affording a generous "lie."

As he lifted his club and swung through he was uncomfortably conscious of having transgressed at least eighteen out of the twenty-three cardinal precepts for correct driving, but already the ball was on its way, and, amidst a hearty burst of applause, led, as he could see, by Kitty Crake, it fell precisely as he had determined. A skilful approach laid him dead, and the hole was his in three. A subdued buzz ran around the circle of the "gallery," and everybody bent forward to watch his second drive across the "Punch-bowl." Straight over the yawning hollow flew the ball, and the crowd clapped again; but the play was now too far away to watch, and there were others ready to drive off. Henry Alderson disappeared in the direction of the "meadow" hole, and Miss Crake went to the club-house piazza to make tea. "Poor fellow," she thought, "his foozling will be all the worse when it does come."

It was a very successful tournament, and Henry Alderson won it by a credible score of eighty net. He blushed as the President handed him the silver cross, but the spectators clapped vigorously; for he had always been a good fellow, albeit a bad golfer, and his victory was a popular one.

"Splendid!" said Miss Kitty Crake, and Henry Alderson ascended forthwith into the seventh heaven.

During the month that followed there were some tremendous surprises in store for the record-holders. Three days after the handicap Alderson did the course in eighty-two, thereby breaking the amateur record, and that same afternoon he tied the best professional score. The Green Committee promptly reduced him to the scratch list, and there was some informal talk of sending him to represent the club at the National Amateur meeting. Montague, the holder of the Hong-Kong Medal for two years running, was visibly uneasy. He began to spend more time on the links, and held surreptitious conversations with Alderson's favorite caddie.

But there was a friend as well as an enemy to keep close watch upon Henry Alderson. There was a change in him that only Kitty Crake noticed at first–a change that both annoyed and alarmed her. The becoming modesty with which he had achieved his first successes had entirely disappeared. Almost imperceptibly he had grown self-sufficient and opinionated, and his attitude towards his fellow-players was at times little short of offensive. He seemed to take an insolent delight in openly flouting the hoary traditions of the game, and in giving the lie direct to each and every venerable truism incrusted in golfing lore. He invariably used a wrong grip; he played with a full swing for all distances, including the shortest of putts, and he never under any circumstances condescended to keep his eyes upon the ball. It was maddening to his fellow-golfers, but his scores were a sufficient answer to all remonstrances. Indeed, it may be said that his steadily decreasing averages were beginning to cause the Green Committee considerable uneasiness. For a player to return cards of sixty-four and then fifty-six and then forty-nine seemed to argue unfavorably for the sporting character of the links. Such kind of play was plainly injuring the reputation of the club, and at least the Honorary Secretary was emboldened to hint as much. The very next day Henry Alderson returned a total of eighteen for the full round of holes and handed it with a mocking smile to the Honorary Secretary himself. This was too much, and Henry Alderson was promptly summoned to appear before the outraged majesty of the Green Committee. But it all ended in smoke. No one could deny that extraordinary scores of a hole in one stroke had been made on several occasions, and in this case it was simply an established phenomenon multiplied by itself eighteen times. "And, gentlemen," concluded Henry Alderson," I did it all with a wooden putter."

The Green Committee had nothing more to say, but they were plainly dissatisfied, and at once set about putting in some new hazards.

And yet–will it be believed?–Henry Alderson was not a happy man. Egotistical and arrogant as he had become, he yet could not fail to perceive that he had lost immensely in the esteem of his clubmates. Nobody cared to play a match with him; and although at first he had put it down to jealousy, he was gradually forced to admit to himself that the reason lay deeper. Worst of all, Kitty Crake was decidedly cool in her manner towards him. He could not understand it, for his golf was certainly above reproach, and he knew that nothing now could prevent him from winning the Hong-Kong Medal. Once it was pinned upon his breast he would be in a position to demand an explanation and the fulfillment of her promise. But there was still another reason for his wishing that the match was over. Strange as it may appear, the very name of golf had become an abhorrence to him. And yet it was not so strange, after all, when one stops to consider. There is nothing so tiresome as perfection, and this especially applies to golf, as possessing an essentially feminine nature. It is the capriciousness, the inconstancy, of golf that makes it a folly so adorable, and Henry Alderson's game had arrived at a pitch of intolerable perfection. He had long ago discovered that the ball would not be a party to a poor shot. Goaded into fury by the monotonous consistency of his play, he had tried the experiment of ordering the ball into a bunker, or at least a bad lie. But the soulless piece of gutta-percha would have none of his foozling. It simply would not be denied, and after a few trials Henry Alderson resigned himself to his fate, comforting himself with the reflection that, having won the medal (and Kitty Crake), he would give up golf forever.

The day of the contest for the Hong-Kong Medal had come at last, and all golfdom had assembled to see the battle. A round-robin protesting against the admission of Henry Alderson as a competitor had been presented to the Green Committee, but that autocratic body had decided to ignore the protest. "It will be better," said a wise man, "to let him win rather than to give him a handle for a grievance. Let him take the medal, and then we can settle upon some pretext to expel him from the club. Montague has had detectives on the case, and thinks he can prove that Alderson has been playing tennis within the last two months. That will be sufficient in the eyes of all true golfers."

As it happened, Alderson and Montague were paired for the great event, and, of course, they had the gallery with them. Just before they started Alderson mustered up his courage and walked over to where Kitty Crake was standing. She did not raise her eyes as he approached, and he was obliged to speak twice before he could gain her attention.

"I trust that I am to have the benefit of your good wishes," he said, meaningly.

She looked at him in frosty surprise.

"I don't think that they will help you much." And then, with cutting deliberation, "I devoutly wish that the Hong-Kong Medal had never existed."

"Mr. Montague and Mr. Alderson," called out the referee. The two contestants came forward, and Kitty Crake ostentatiously turned her back as the play began.

In all the annals of the Marion County Golf Club a closer and more exciting match had never been played. Montague was certainly putting up the game of his life; and Alderson, while not showing any phenomenal work, was nevertheless returning a faultless score. Not a mistake had been made on either side, and at the end of the seventeenth hole honors were exactly even. But Montague was visibly breaking under the strain.

When Montague stepped forward to drive for the home hole it was plain that he was very nervous. Twice he tried to tee his ball, but his trembling fingers refused their office, and he was obliged to call upon a caddie for assistance. As he came up for the "address" he was deathly pale, and little beads of sweat were standing upon his forehead. The club swung back, and then descended upon the ball, but with a feeble, crooked blow that "sliced" it hopelessly into the bushes. A groan went up. Montague had "cracked," and the match was lost.

Up to this point Henry Alderson had played as though in a dream. At last he understood–those cold, stinging words of Kitty Crake could have but one meaning. *She did not wish him to win!* It was only too plain that she had never loved him, and that she regretted her idle words about the winning of the medal and the promise that they implied. What was he to do?

One thing was certain: he had no chance, in any event, with Kitty Crake. Of course he might go on and win the medal, and then humiliate her by contemptuously refusing to press his claim; but the revenge was an unmanly one, and he could not bring himself to adopt it. Again, he might withdraw, and so give the prize to Montague. He knew that the latter was desperately anxious to retain possession of the trophy. It was the pride, the joy, the treasure, of his otherwise empty life. The Montague infants had all cut their teeth upon the medal's firm and glittering edge. It was the family fetich; the one thing that distinguished them from the common herd of their neighbors, who lived in precisely the same pattern of suburban villa, but whose interest in life never rose above the discussion of village improvements or the election of a vestryman. Henry Alderson hesitated; his heart grew soft within him. And yet to give it up after it had cost him so much!

"Oh yes, a fair enough player, but a trifle short in his driving."

It was Montague who spoke, and Henry Alderson felt instinctively that the remark referred to him. His cheeks burned as he heard the half-veiled insult that only a golfer can understand in its full significance, and he incontinently forgot all about his generous resolution to withdraw. He stepped up to the tee.

"I dare say I can reach the green in two," he said, carelessly.

The hole was some four hundred yards away, and Montague smiled sarcastically. His enemy was about to be delivered into his hands.

"I've done two hundred and forty yards of straight carry," continued Alderson.

"Hym!" coughed Montague.

"And I'd back myself to make it three hundred."

"Why not four?" said Montague.

"Six hundred, if you say so," returned Alderson, hotly.

"Or perhaps out of sight," sneered Montague.

"Off the earth," retorted Alderson.

Montague made no reply, but turned away to hide his satisfaction. Alderson was deliberately going to "press," and every student of the art of golf knows what that implies. But there is nothing more uncertain than a certainty–in golf.

Henry Alderson swung down upon the ball. Shades of St. Rule! but was there ever such a mighty drive? Three hundred yards away, and it was still rising into the blue ether. Another instant and it had passed entirely out of sight, lost in infinite space. The spectators gasped, and Montague turned livid. But stop a bit. Where *was* the ball? The referee looked puzzled, and the caddies stared open-mouthed into the sky. And then in a flash it dawned upon Henry Alderson that his boast had been literally made good. *He had driven his ball off the earth.*

For a moment his heart stood still. With the ball was gone his golfing reputation, and gone forever. Was there anything else for him in life? The answer came in another flash of inspiration. Yes; he was a free man; now he could play golf again–his *own* game. Forgotten was the Hong-Kong Medal; forgotten for the nonce was Kitty Crake herself. The fit was upon him–the berserker rage of the true duffer. He turned to the referee.

"I acknowledge," he said, "the penalty for lost ball, and play a new one."

He teed a ball, an ordinary gutta-percha, and, swinging down upon it, made the most bungling of "tops." A roar of laughter went up, and Henry Alderson joined in it, the heartiest of all. He caught Kitty Crake's eye, and she was smiling too. Taking a brassey, he advanced for his second shot, and "missed the globe" twice running. But what a delightful sensation it was!–this was something like golf.

Finally, he succeeded in playing inside of Montague, who followed with a splendidly played iron shot out of the bushes. Alderson drove into a bunker, and noted, with an exquisite thrill of pleasure, that his ball had buried itself completely in the sand. It took him three to get out, and the crowd applauded. He "foozled" a shot into a clump of evergreens, and Kitty Crake clapped her hands. Montague made a phenomenal approach, and landed his ball dead at the hole. Alderson "hooked" one ball, "sliced" another, and banged a third into the flag, securing a lucky "rub." He missed two short putts, and then managed to hit Montague's ball, holing it, and leaving his own outside. The laughter of the "gallery" gods cleft the skies, and the referee stepped forward.

"Mr. Montague eighty strokes, Mr. Alderson ninety-six. Mr. Montague wins the tournament, and retains possession of the Hong-Kong Medal."

Curiously enough, it seemed as though the applause that followed the announcement was intended for Alderson rather than the for the victor. Men with whom he had not been on speaking terms for months crowded around him to shake his hand. From being the most unpopular man in the club he had suddenly become a hero. It was incomprehensible. Last of all came up Kitty Crake. The crowd had drifted away, and they were alone. Her eyes were wet and shining, and she held out her hand. He took it, trembling inwardly.

"Well," said she at length, "the match is over: have you nothing to say to me!"

"But–but I lost it," faltered Henry Alderson.

"Exactly; and in so doing you just managed to save yourself. You have evidently no idea how simply intolerable a champion at golf may be."

"Oh, Kitty–" he began; but they were already at the club-house.

After they were married he told her the whole story.

"But there is one thing I never understood," he concluded, thoughtfully. "If it really were the enemy of mankind, he certainly acted very stupidly in not getting my signature in the good old orthodox way. What had he to show for his side of the bargain?"

"Oh, that is plain enough," answered Mrs. Alderson. "So long as pride continues to be one of the seven deadly sins–"

"Well?"

"Why, the devil is quite justified in feeling cocksure of a medal-winner at golf. Poor Mr. Montague!"

*Ethan Canin is as distinguished as any young writer in America. He was just twenty-seven when he published his first collection of short stories,* Emperor of the Air *(1988), which the* London Sunday Times *called "the work of a phenomenally skilled writer." Perhaps more remarkable: at the time, Canin was in his last year at Harvard Medical School. Since then he has written a novel,* Blue River *(1991), and another book of short stories called* The Palace Thief *(1994), while completing his medical residency in California. "The Year of Getting to Know Us," first published in the* Atlantic Monthly, *is a poignant drama of a dying father and a son who recalls their family life, including the significance of golf in bringing them together.*

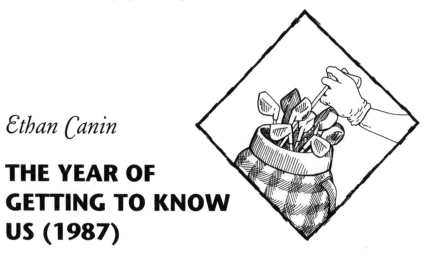

*Ethan Canin*

# THE YEAR OF GETTING TO KNOW US (1987)

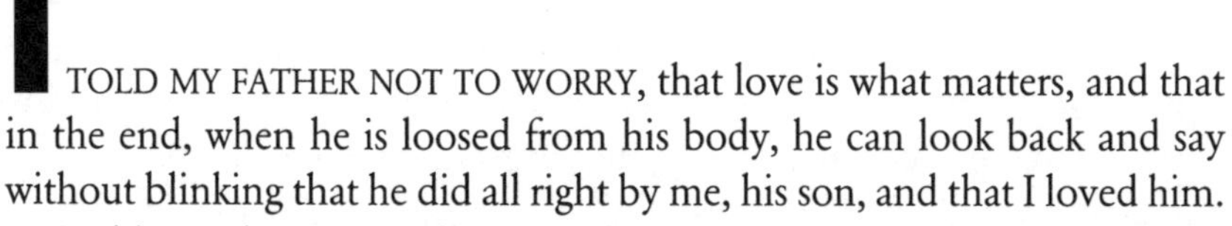

I TOLD MY FATHER NOT TO WORRY, that love is what matters, and that in the end, when he is loosed from his body, he can look back and say without blinking that he did all right by me, his son, and that I loved him.

And he said, "Don't talk about things you know nothing about."

We were in San Francisco, in a hospital room. IV tubes were plugged into my father's arms; little round Band-Aids were on his chest. Next to his bed was a table with a vase of yellow roses and a card that my wife, Anne, had brought him. On the front of the card was a photograph of a golf green. On the wall above my father's head an electric monitor traced his heartbeat. He was watching the news on a TV that stood in the corner next to his girlfriend, Lorraine. Lorraine was reading a magazine.

I was watching his heartbeat. It seemed all right to me: the blips made steady peaks and drops, moved across the screen, went out at one end and then came back at the other. It seemed that this was all a heart could do. I'm an English teacher, though, and I don't know much about it.

"It looks strong," I'd said to my mother that afternoon over the phone. She was in Pasadena. "It's going right across, pretty steady. Big bumps. Solid."

"Is he eating all right?"

"I think so."

"Is *she* there?"

"Is Lorraine here, you mean?"

She paused. "Yes, Lorraine."

"No," I said. "She's not."

"Your poor father," she whispered.

I'm an only child, and I grew up in a big wood-frame house on Huron Avenue in Pasadena, California. The house had three empty bedrooms and in the backyard a section of grass that had been stripped and leveled, and then seeded and mowed like a putting green. Twice a week a Mexican gardener came to trim it wearing special moccasins my father had bought him. They had soft hide soles that left no imprints.

My father was in love with golf. He played seven times every week and talked about the game as if it were a science that he was about to figure out. "Cut through the outer rim for a high iron," he used to say at dinner, looking out the window into the yard while my mother passed him the carved-wood salad bowl. Or "In hot weather hit a high-compression ball." When conversations paused, he made little putting motions with his hands. He was a top amateur and in another situation might have been a pro. When I was sixteen, the year I was arrested, he let me caddie for the first time. Before that all I knew about golf was his clubs–the Spalding made-to-measure woods and irons, Dynamiter sand wedge, St. Andrew's putter –which he kept in an Abercrombie & Fitch bag in the trunk of his Lincoln, and the white leather shoes with long tongues and screw-in spikes, which he stored upside down in the hall closet. When he wasn't playing, he covered the club heads with socks that had little yellow dingo balls on the ends.

He never taught me to play. I was a decent athlete–could run, catch, throw a perfect spiral–but he never took me to the golf course. In the summer he played every day. Sometimes my mother asked if he would take me along with him. "Why should I?" he answered. "Neither of us would like it."

Every afternoon after work he played nine holes; he played eighteen on Saturday, and nine again on Sunday morning. On Sunday afternoon, at four o'clock, he went for a drive by himself in his white Lincoln Continental. Nobody was allowed to come with him on the drives. He was usually gone for a couple of hours. "Today I drove in the country," he would say at dinner as he put out his cigarette. Or "This afternoon I looked at the ocean," and we were to take from this that he had driven north on the coastal highway. He almost never said more, and across our blue and white tablecloth, when I looked at him, my silent father, I imagined in his eyes a pure gaze with which he read the waves and currents of the sea. He had made a fortune in business and owed it to being able to see the truth in any situation. For this reason, he said, he liked to drive with all the windows down. When he returned from his trips his face was red from the wind and his thinning hair lay fitfully on his head. My mother baked on Sunday afternoons while he was gone, walnut pies or macaroons that she prepared on the kitchen counter, which looked out over his putting green.

I teach English in a high school now, and my wife, Anne, is a journalist. I've played golf a half dozen times in ten years and don't like it any more than most beginners, though the two or three times I've hit a drive that sails, that takes flight with its own power, I've felt something that I think must be unique to the game. These were the drives my father used to hit. Explosions off the tee, bird flights. But golf isn't my game, and it never has been, and I wouldn't think about it at all if not for my father.

Anne and I were visiting in California, first my mother, in Los Angeles, and then my father and Lorraine, north in Sausalito, and Anne suggested that I ask him to play nine holes one morning. She'd been wanting me to talk to him. It's part of the project we've started, part of her theory of what's wrong–although I don't think that much is. She had told me that twenty-five years changes things, and, since we had the time, why not go out to California.

She said, "It's not too late to talk to him."

My best friend in high school was named Nickie Apple. Nickie had a thick chest and a voice that had been damaged somehow, made a little hoarse, and sometimes people thought he was twenty years old. He lived in a four-story house that had a separate floor for the kids. It was the top story, and his father, who was divorced and a lawyer, had agreed never to come up there. That was where we sat around after school. Because of the agreement, no parents were there, only kids. Nine or ten of us, usually. Some of them had slept the night on the big pillows that were scattered against the walls: friends of his older brothers', in Stetson hats and flannel shirts; girls I had never seen before.

Nickie and I went to Shrier Academy, where all the students carried around blue-and-gray notebooks embossed with the school's heraldic seal. "*Sumus Primi,*" the seal said. Our gray wool sweaters said it; our green exam books said it; the rear-window decal my mother brought home said it. My father wouldn't put the sticker on the Lincoln, so she pressed it onto the window above her kitchen sink instead. "*Sumus Primi,*" I read whenever I washed my hands. At Shrier we learned Latin in the eighth grade and art history in the ninth, and in the tenth I started getting into some trouble. Little things: cigarettes, graffiti. Mr. Goldman, the student counselor, called my mother in for a premonition visit. "I have a premonition about Leonard," he told her in the counseling office one afternoon in the warm October when I was sixteen. The office was full of plants and had five floor-to-ceiling windows that let in sun like a greenhouse. They looked over grassy, bushless knolls. "I just have a feeling about him."

That October he started talking to me about it. He called me in and asked me why I was friends with Nickie Apple, a boy going nowhere. I was looking out the big windows, opening and closing my fists beneath the desk top. He said, "Lenny, you're a bright kid–what are you trying to tell us?" And I said, "Nothing, I'm not trying to tell you anything."

Then we started stealing, Nickie and I. He did it first, and took things I didn't expect: steaks, expensive cuts that we cooked on a grill by the window in the top story of his house; garden machinery; luggage. We didn't sell it and we didn't use it, but every afternoon we went someplace new. In November he distracted a store clerk and I took a necklace that we thought was diamonds. In December we went for a ride in someone else's car, and over Christmas vacation, when only gardeners were on the school grounds, we threw ten rocks, one by one, as if we'd paid for them at a carnival stand, through the five windows in Mr. Goldman's office.

"You look like a train station," I said to my father as he lay in the hospital bed. "All those lines coming and going everywhere."

He looked at me. I put some things down, tried to make a little bustle. I could see Anne standing in the hall just beyond the door.

"Are you comfortable, Dad?"

"What do you mean 'comfortable'? My heart's full of holes, leaking all over the place. Am I comfortable? No. I'm dying."

"You're not dying," I said, and I sat down next to him. "You'll be swinging the five iron in two weeks."

I touched one of the tubes in his arm. Where it entered the vein, the needle disappeared under a piece of tape. I hated the sight of this. I moved the bedsheets a little bit, tucked them in. Anne had wanted me to be alone with him. She was in the hall, waiting to head off Lorraine.

"What's the matter with her?" he asked, pointing at Anne.

"She thought we might want to talk."

"What's so urgent?"

Anne and I had discussed it the night before. "Tell him what you feel," she said. "Tell him you love him." We were eating dinner in a fish restaurant. "Or if you don't love him, tell him you don't."

"Look, Pop," I said now.

"What?"

I was forty-two years old. We were in a hospital and he had tubes in his arms. All kinds of everything: needles, air, tape. I said it again.

"Look, Pop."

Anne and I have seen a counselor, who told me that I had to learn to accept kindness from people. He saw Anne and me together, then Anne alone, then me. Children's toys were scattered on the floor of his office. "You sound as if you don't want to let people near you," he said. "Right?"

"I'm a reasonably happy man," I answered.

I hadn't wanted to see the counselor. Anne and I have been married seven years, and sometimes I think the history of marriage can be written like this: People Want Too Much. Anne and I have suffered no plague; we sleep late two mornings a week; we laugh at most of the same things; we have a decent house in a suburb of Boston, where, after the commuter traffic has eased, a quiet descends and the world is at peace. She writes for a newspaper, and I teach the children of lawyers and insurance men. At times I'm alone, and need to be alone; at times she does too. But I can always count on a moment, sometimes once in a day, sometimes more, when I see her patting down the sheets on the bed, or watering the front-window violets, and I am struck by the good fortune of my life.

Still, Anne says I don't feel things.

It comes up at dinner, outside in the yard, in airports as we wait for planes. You don't let yourself feel, she tells me; and I tell her that I think it's a crazy thing, all this talk about feeling. What do the African Bushmen say? They say, Will we eat tomorrow? Will there be rain?

When I was sixteen, sitting in the backseat of a squad car, the policeman stopped in front of our house on Huron Avenue, turned around against the headrest, and asked me if I was sure this was where I lived.

"Yes, sir," I said.

He spoke through a metal grate. "Your daddy owns this house?"

"Yes, sir."

"But for some reason you don't like windows."

He got out and opened my door, and we walked up the porch steps. The swirling lights on the squad car were making crazy patterns in the French panes of the living room bays. He knocked. "What's your daddy do?"

I heard lights snapping on, my mother moving through the house. "He's in business," I said. "But he won't be home now." The policeman wrote something on his notepad. I saw my mother's eye through the glass in the door, and then the locks were being unlatched, one by one, from the top.

When Anne and I came to California to visit, we stayed at my mother's for three days. On her refrigerator door was a calendar with men's names marked on it–dinner dates, theater –and I knew this was done for our benefit. My mother has been alone for fifteen years. She's still thin, and her eyes still water, and I noticed that books were lying open all through the house. Thick paperbacks–*Dr. Zhivago, The Thorn Birds*–in the bathroom and the studio and the bedroom. We never mentioned my father, but at the end of our stay, when we had packed the car for our drive north along the coast, after she'd hugged us both and we'd backed out of the driveway, she came down off the lawn into the street, her arms crossed over her chest, leaned into the window, and said, "You might say hello to your father for me."

We made the drive north on Highway 1. We passed mission towns, fields of butter lettuce, long stretches of pumpkin farms south of San Francisco. It was the first time we were going to see my father with Lorraine. She was a hairdresser. He'd met her a few years after coming north, and one of the first things they'd done together was take a trip around the world. We got postcards from the Nile delta and Bangkok. When I was young, my father had never taken us out of California.

His house in Sausalito was on a cliff above a finger of San Francisco Bay. A new Lincoln stood in the carport. In his bedroom was a teak-framed king-size waterbed, and on the walls were bits of African artwork–opium pipes, metal figurines. Lorraine looked the same age as Anne. One wall of the living room was glass, and after the first night's dinner, while we sat on the leather sofa watching tankers and yachts move under the Golden Gate Bridge, my father put down his Scotch and water, touched his jaw, and said, "Lenny, call Dr. Farmer."

It was his second one. The first had been two years earlier, on the golf course in Monterey, where he'd had to kneel, then sit, then lie down on the fairway.

At dinner the night after I was arrested, my mother introduced her idea. "We're going to try something," she said. She had brought out a chicken casserole, and it was steaming in front of her. "That's what we're going to do. Max, are you listening? This next year, starting tonight, is going to be the year of getting to know us better." She stopped speaking and dished my father some chicken.

"What do you mean?" I asked.

"I mean it will be to a small extent a theme year. Nothing that's going to change every day of our lives, but in this next year I thought we'd all make an attempt to get to know each other better. Especially you, Leonard. Dad and I are going to make a better effort to know you."

"I'm not sure what you mean," my father said.

"All kinds of things, Max. We'll go to movies together, and Lenny can throw a party here at the house. And I personally would like to take a trip, all of us together, to the American Southwest."

"Sounds all right to me," I said.

"And Max," she said, "you can take Lenny with you to play golf. For example." She looked at my father.

"Neither of us would like it," he said.

"Lenny never sees you."

I looked out the window. The trees were turning, dropping their leaves onto the putting green. I didn't care what he said, one way or the other. My mother spooned a chicken thigh onto my plate and covered it with sauce. "All right," he said. "He can caddie."

"And as preparation for our trip," my mother said, "can you take him on your Sunday rides?"

My father took off his glasses. "The Southwest," he said, wiping the lenses with a napkin, "is exactly like any other part of the country."

Anne had an affair once with a man she met on an assignment. He was young, much younger than either of us–in his late twenties, I would say from the one time I saw him. I saw them because one day on the road home I passed Anne's car in the lot of a Denny's restaurant. I parked around the block and went in to surprise her. I took a table at the back, but from my seat in the corner I didn't realize for several minutes that the youngish-looking woman leaning forward and whispering to the man with a beard was my wife.

I didn't get up and pull the man out with me into the parking lot, or even join them at the table, as I have since thought might have been a good idea. Instead I sat and watched them. I could see that under the table they were holding hands. His back was to me, and I noticed that it was broad, as mine is not. I remember thinking that she probably liked this broadness. Other than that, though, I didn't feel very much. I ordered another cup of coffee just to hear myself talk, but my voice wasn't quavering or fearful. When the waitress left, I took out a napkin and wrote on it, "You are a forty-two-year-old man with no children and your wife is having an affair." Then I put some money on the table and left the restaurant.

"I think we should see somebody," Anne said to me a few weeks later. It was a Sunday morning, and we were eating breakfast on the porch.

"About what?" I asked.

On a Sunday afternoon when I was sixteen I went out to the garage with a plan my mother had given me. That morning my father had washed the Lincoln. He had detergent-scrubbed the finish and then sun-dried it on Huron Avenue, so that in the workshop light of the garage its highlights shone. The windshield molding, the grille, the chrome side markers, had been cloth-dried to erase water spots. The keys hung from their magnetic sling near the door to the kitchen. I took them out and opened the trunk. Then I hung them up again and sat on the rear quarter panel to consider what to do. It was almost four o'clock. The trunk of my father's car was large enough for a half dozen suitcases and had been upholstered in a gray medium-pile carpet that was cut to hug the wheel wells and the spare-tire berth. In one corner, fastened down by straps, was his toolbox, and along the back lay the golf bag. In the shadows the yellow dingos of the club socks looked like baby chicks. He was going to come out in a few minutes. I reached in, took off four of the club socks, and made a pillow for my head. Then I stepped into the trunk. The shocks bounced once and stopped. I lay down with my head propped on the quarter panel and my feet resting in the taillight berth, and then I reached up, slammed down the trunk, and was in the dark.

This didn't frighten me. When I was very young, I liked to sleep with the shades drawn and the door closed, so that no light entered my room. I used to hold my hand in front of my eyes and see if I could imagine its presence. It was too dark to see anything. I was blind then, lying in my bed, listening for every sound. I used to move my hand back and forth, close to my eyes, until I had the sensation that it was there but had in some way been amputated. I had heard of soldiers who had lost limbs but still felt them attached. Now I held my open hand before my eyes. It was dense black inside the trunk, colorless, without light.

When my father started the car, all the sounds were huge, magnified as if they were inside my own skull. The metal scratched, creaked, slammed when he got in; the bolt of the starter shook all the way through to the trunk; the idle rose and leveled; then the gears changed and the car lurched. I heard the garage door glide up. Then it curled into its housing, bumped once, began descending again. The seams of the trunk lid lightened in the sun. We were in the street now, heading downhill. I lay back and felt the road, listened to the gravel pocking in the wheel wells.

I followed our route in my mind. Left off Huron onto Telscher, where the car bottomed in the rain gulley as we turned, then up the hill to Santa Ana. As we waited for the light, the idle made its change, shifting down, so that below my head I heard the individual piston blasts in the exhaust pipe. Left on Santa Ana, counting the flat stretches where I felt my father tap the brakes, numbering the intersections as we headed west toward the ocean. I heard cars pull up next to us, accelerate, slow down, make turns. The blinkers echoed inside the quarter panels. I pulled off more club socks and enlarged my pillow. We slowed down, stopped, and then we accelerated, the soft piston explosions becoming a hiss as we turned onto the Pasadena freeway.

"Dad's rides," my mother had said to me the night before, as I lay in bed, "would be a good way for him to get to know you." It was the first week of the year of getting to know us better. She was sitting at my desk.

"But he won't let me go," I said.

"You're right." She moved some things around on a shelf. The room wasn't quite dark, and I could see the outline of her white blouse. "I talked to Mr. Goldman," she said.

"Mr. Goldman doesn't know me."

"He says you're angry." My mother stood up, and I watched her white blouse move to the window. She pulled back the shade until a triangle of light from the streetlamp fell on my sheets. "Are you angry?"

"I don't know," I said. "I don't think so."

"I don't think so either." She replaced the shade, came over and kissed me on the forehead, and then went out into the hall. In the dark I looked for my hand.

A few minutes later the door opened again. She put her head in. "If he won't let you come," she said, "sneak along."

On the freeway the thermal seams whizzed and popped in my ears. The ride had smoothed out now, as the shocks settled into the high speed, hardly dipping on curves, muffling everything as if we were under water. As far as I could tell, we were still driving west, toward the ocean. I sat halfway up and rested my back against the golf bag. I could see shapes now inside the trunk. When we slowed down and the blinker went on, I attempted bearings, but the sun was the same in all directions and the trunk lid was without shadow. We braked hard. I felt the car leave the freeway. We made turns. We went straight. Then more turns, and as we slowed down and I was stretching out, uncurling my body along the diagonal, we made a sharp right onto gravel and pulled over and stopped.

My father opened the door. The car dipped and rocked, shuddered. The engine clicked. Then the passenger door opened. I waited.

If I heard her voice today, twenty-six years later, I would recognize it.

"Angel," she said.

I heard the weight of their bodies sliding across the back seat, first hers, then his. They weren't three feet away. I curled up, crouched into the low space between the golf bag and the back of the passenger compartment. There were two firm points in the cushion where it was displaced. As I lay there, I went over the voice again in my head: it was nobody I knew. I heard a laugh from her, and then something low from him. I felt the shift of the trunk's false rear, and then, as I lay behind them, I heard the contact: the crinkle of clothing, arms wrapping, and the half-delicate, muscular sounds. It was like hearing a television in the next room. His voice once more, and then the rising of their breath, slow; a minute of this, maybe another; then shifting again, the friction of cloth on the leather seat and the car's soft rocking. "Dad," I whispered. Then rocking again; my father's sudden panting, harder and harder, his half words. The car shook violently. "Dad," I whispered. I shouted, "Dad!"

The door opened.

His steps kicked up gravel. I heard jingling metal, the sound of the key in the trunk lock. He was standing over me in an explosion of light.

He said, "Put back the club socks."

I did and got out of the car to stand next to him. He rubbed his hands down the front of his shirt.

"What the hell," he said.

"I was in the trunk."

"I know," he said. "What the goddamn."

The year I graduated from college, I found a job teaching junior high school in Boston. The school was a cement building with small windows well up from the street, and dark classrooms in which I spent a lot of time maintaining discipline. In the middle of an afternoon that first winter a boy knocked on my door to tell me I had a phone call. I knew who it was going to be.

"Dad's gone," my mother said.

He'd taken his things in the Lincoln, she told me, and driven away that morning before dawn. On the kitchen table he'd left a note and some cash. "A lot of cash," my mother added, lowering her voice. "Twenty thousand dollars."

I imagined the sheaf of bills on our breakfast table, held down by the ceramic butter dish, the bank notes ruffling in the breeze from the louvered windows that opened onto his green. In the note he said he had gone north and would call her when he'd settled. It was December. I told my mother that I would visit in a week, when school was out for Christmas. I told her to go to her sister's and stay there, and then I said that I was working and had to get back to my class. She didn't say anything on the other end of the line, and in the silence I imagined my father crisscrossing the state of California, driving north, stopping in Palm Springs and Carmel, the Lincoln riding low with the weight.

"Leonard," my mother said, "did you know anything like this was happening?"

During the spring of the year of getting to know us better I caddied for him a few times. On Saturdays he played early in the morning, when the course was mostly empty and the grass was still wet from the night. I learned to fetch the higher irons as the sun rose over the back nine and the ball, on drying ground, rolled farther. He hit skybound approach shots with backspin, chips that bit into the green and stopped. He played in a foursome with three other men, and in the locker room, as they changed their shoes, they told jokes and poked one another in the belly. The lockers were shiny green metal, the floor clean white tiles that clicked under the shoe spikes. Beneath the mirrors were jars of combs in green disinfectant. When I combed my hair with them it stayed in place and smelled like limes.

We were on the course at dawn. At the first fairway the other men dug in their spikes, shifted their weight from leg to leg, and dummy-swung at an empty tee while my father lit a cigarette and looked out over the hole. "The big gun," he said to me, or, if it was a par three, "the lady." He stepped on his cigarette. I wiped the head with the club sock before I handed it to him. When he took the club, he felt its balance point, rested it on one finger, and then, in slow motion, he gripped the shaft.

Left hand first, then right, the fingers wrapping pinkie to index. Then he leaned down over the ball. On a perfect drive the tee flew straight up in the air and landed in front of his feet.

Over the weekend his heart lost its rhythm for a few seconds. It happened Saturday night when Anne and I were at the house in Sausalito and we didn't hear about it until Sunday. "Ventricular fibrillation," the intern said. "Circus movements." The condition was always a danger after a heart attack. He had been given a shock and his heartbeat had returned to normal.

"But I'll be honest with you," the intern said. We were in the hall. He looked down, touched his stethoscope. "It isn't a good sign."

The heart gets bigger as it dies, he told me. Soon it spreads across the X ray. He brought me with him to a room and showed me strips of paper with the electric tracings: certain formations. The muscle was dying in patches, he said. He said things might get better, they might not.

My mother called that afternoon. "Should I come up?"

"He was a bastard to you," I said.

When Lorraine and Anne were eating dinner, I found the intern again. "I want to know," I said. "Tell me the truth." The intern was tall and thin, sick-looking himself. So were the other doctors I had seen around the place. Everything in that hospital was pale–the walls, the coats, the skin.

He said, "What truth?"

I told him that I'd been reading about heart disease. I'd read about EKGs, knew about the medicines–lidocaine, propranolol. I knew that the lungs filled up with water, that heart failure was death by drowning. I said, "The truth about my father."

The afternoon I had hidden in the trunk, we came home while my mother was cooking dinner. I walked up the path from the garage behind my father, watching the pearls of sweat on his neck. He was whistling a tune. At the door he kissed my mother's cheek. He touched the small of her back. She was cooking vegetables, and the steam had fogged up the kitchen windows and dampened her hair. My father sat down in the chair by the window and opened the newspaper. I thought of the way the trunk rear had shifted when he and the woman had moved into the back of the Lincoln. My mother was smiling.

"Well?" she said.

"What's for dinner?" I asked.

"Well?" she said again.

"It's chicken," I said. "Isn't it?"

"Max, aren't you going to tell me if anything unusual happened today?"

My father didn't look up from the newspaper. "Did anything unusual happen today?" he said. He turned the page, folded it back smartly. "Why don't you ask Lenny?"

She smiled at me.

"I surprised him," I said. Then I turned and looked out the window.

"I have something to tell you," Anne said to me one Sunday morning in the fifth year of our marriage. We were lying in bed. I knew what was coming.

"I already know," I said.

"What do you already know?"

"I know about your lover."

She didn't say anything.

"It's all right," I said.

It was winter. The sky was gray, and although the sun had risen only a few hours earlier, it seemed like late afternoon. I waited for Anne to say something more. We were silent for several minutes. Then she said, "I wanted to hurt you." She got out of bed and began straightening out the bureau. She pulled my sweaters from the drawer and refolded them. She returned all our shoes to the closet. Then she came back to the bed, sat down, and began to cry. Her back was toward me. It shook with her gasps, and I put my hand out and touched her. "It's all right," I said.

"We only saw each other a few times," she answered. "I'd take it back if I could. I'd make it never happen."

"I know you would."

"For some reason I thought I couldn't really hurt you."

She had stopped crying. I looked out the window at the tree branches hung low with snow. It didn't seem I had to say anything.

"I don't know why I thought I couldn't hurt you," she said. "Of course I can hurt you."

"I forgive you."

Her back was still toward me. Outside, a few snowflakes drifted up in the air.

"You shouldn't forgive me."

"Why not?"

"Or not so fast, at least. You should hate me."

"I don't hate you," I said. "It's something you did. It's like running over an animal. It's passed."

The night he died, Anne stayed awake with me in bed. "Tell me about him," she said.

"What about?"

"Stories. Tell me what it was like growing up, things you did together."

"We didn't do that much," I said. "I caddied for him. He taught me things about golf."

That night I never went to sleep. Lorraine was at a friend's apartment and we were alone in my father's empty house, but we pulled out the sheets anyway, and the two wool blankets, and we lay on the fold-out sofa in the den. I told stories about my father until I couldn't think of any more, and then I talked about my mother until Anne fell asleep.

In the middle of the night I got up and went into the living room. Through the glass I could see lights across the water, the bridges, Belvedere and San Francisco, ships. It was clear outside, and when I walked out to the cement carport the sky was lit with stars. The breeze moved inside my nightclothes. Next to the garage the Lincoln stood half lit in the porch floodlight. I opened the door and got in. The seats were red leather and smelled of limes and cigarettes. I rolled down the window and took the key from the glove compartment. I thought of writing a note for Anne, but didn't. Instead I coasted down the driveway in neutral and didn't close the door or turn on the lights until the bottom of the hill, or start the engine until I had swung around the corner, so that the house was out of sight and the brine smell of the marina was coming through the open windows of the car. The pistons were almost silent.

I felt urgent, though I had no route in mind. I ran one stop sign, then one red light, and when I reached the ramp onto Highway 101, I squeezed the accelerator and felt the surge of the fuel-injected, computer-sparked V-8. The dash lights glowed. I drove south and crossed over the Golden Gate Bridge at seventy miles an hour, its suspension cables swaying in the wind and the span rocking slowly, ocean to bay. The lanes were narrow. Reflectors zinged when the wheels strayed. If Anne woke, she might come out to the living room and then check for me outside. A light rain began to fall. Drops wet my knees, splattered my cheek. I kept the window open and turned on the radio; the car filled up with wind and music. Brass sounds. Trumpets. Sounds that filled my heart.

The Lincoln drove like a dream. South of San Francisco the road opened up, and in the gulley of a shallow hill I took it up over a hundred. The arrow nosed rightward in the dash. Shapes flattened out. "Dad," I said. The wind sounds changed pitch. I said, "The year of getting to know us." Signposts and power poles were flying by. Only a few cars were on the road, and most moved over before I arrived. In the mirror I could see the faces as I passed. I went through San Mateo, Pacifica, Redwood City, until, underneath a concrete overpass, the radio began pulling in static and I realized that I might die at this speed. I slowed down. At seventy drizzle wandered in the windows again. At fifty-five the scenery stopped moving. In Menlo Park I got off the freeway.

It was dark still, and off the interstate I found myself on a road without streetlights. It entered the center of town and then left again, curving up into shallow hills. The houses were large on either side. They were spaced far apart, three and four stories tall, with white shutters or ornament work that shone in the perimeter of the Lincoln's headlamps. The yards were large, dotted with eucalyptus and laurel. Here and there a light was on. Sometimes I saw faces: someone on an upstairs balcony; a man inside the breakfast room, awake at this hour, peering through the glass to see what car could be passing. I drove slowly, and when I came to a high school with its low buildings and long athletic field I pulled over and stopped.

The drizzle had become mist. I left the headlights on and got out and stood on the grass. I thought, "This is the night your father has passed." I looked up at the lightening sky. I said it, "This is the night your father has passed," but I didn't feel what I thought I would. Just the wind on my throat, the chill of the morning. A pickup drove by and flashed its lights at me on the lawn. Then I went to the trunk of the Lincoln, because this was what my father would have done, and I got out the golf bag. It was heavier than I remembered, and the leather was stiff in the cool air. On the damp sod I set up: dimpled white ball, yellow tee. My father would have swung, would have hit drives the length of the football field, high irons that disappeared into the gray sky, but as I stood there I didn't even take the clubs out of the bag. Instead I imagined his stance. I pictured the even weight, the deliberate grip, and after I had stood there for a few moments, I picked up the ball and tee, replaced them in the bag, and drove home to my wife.

The year I was sixteen we never made it to the American Southwest. My mother bought maps anyway, and planned our trip, talking to me about it at night in the dark, taking us in her mind across the Colorado River at the California border, where the water was opal green, into Arizona and along the stretch of desert highway to New Mexico. There, she said, the canyons were a mile deep. The road was lined with sagebrush and a type of cactus, jumping cholla, that launched its spines. Above the desert, where a man could die of dehydration in an afternoon and a morning, the peaks of the Rocky Mountains turned blue with sun and ice.

We didn't ever go. Every weekend my father played golf, and at last, in August, my parents agreed to a compromise. One Sunday morning, before I started the eleventh grade, we drove north in the Lincoln to a state park along the ocean. Above the shore the cliffs were planted with ice plant to resist erosion. Pelicans soared in the thermal currents. My mother had made chicken sandwiches, which we ate on the beach, and after lunch, while I looked at the crabs and swaying fronds in the tide pools, my parents walked to the base of the cliffs. I watched their progress on the shallow dunes. Once when I looked, my father was holding her in his arms and they were kissing.

She bent backward in his hands. I looked into the tide pool where, on the surface, the blue sky, the clouds, the reddish cliffs, were shining. Below them rock crabs scurried between submerged stones. The afternoon my father found me in the trunk, he introduced me to the woman in the backseat. Her name was Christine. She smelled of perfume. The gravel drive where we had parked was behind a warehouse, and after we shook hands through the open window of the car, she got out and went inside. It was low and long, and the metal door slammed behind her. On the drive home, wind blowing all around us in the car, my father and I didn't say much. I watched his hands on the steering wheel. They were big and red-knuckled, the hands of a butcher or a carpenter, and I tried to imagine them on the bend of Christine's back.

Later that afternoon on the beach, while my mother walked along the shore, my father and I climbed a steep trail up the cliffs. From above, where we stood in the carpet of ice plant, we could see the hue of the Pacific change to a more translucent blue–the drop-off and the outline of the shoal where the breakers rose. I tried to see what my father was seeing as he gazed out over the water. He picked up a rock and tossed it over the cliff. "You know," he said without looking at me, "you could be all right on the course." We approached the edge of the palisade, where the ice plant thinned into eroded cuts of sand. "Listen," he said. "We're here on this trip so we can get to know each other a little bit." A hundred yards below us waves broke on the rocks. He lowered his voice. "But I'm not sure about that. Anyway, you don't *have* to get to know me. You know why?"

"Why?" I asked.

"You don't have to get to know me," he said, "because one day you're going to grow up and then you're going to *be* me." He looked at me and then out over the water. "So what I'm going to do is teach you how to hit." He picked up a long stick and put it in my hand. Then he showed me the backswing. "You've got to know one thing to drive a golf ball," he told me, "and that's that the club is part of you." He stood behind me and showed me how to keep the left arm still. "The club is your hand," he said. "It's your bone. It's your whole arm and your skeleton and your heart." Below us on the beach I could see my mother walking the waterline. We took cut after cut, and he taught me to visualize the impact, to sense it. He told me to whittle down the point of energy so that the ball would fly. When I swung he held my head in position. "Don't just watch," he said. *"See."* I looked. The ice plant was watery looking and fat, and at the edge of my vision I could see the tips of my father's shoes. I was sixteen years old and waiting for the next thing he would tell me.

*John Updike can really turn a phrase, referring to a golfer in this story as "another warty pickle blanching in the brine of time." Farrell's caddy, Sandy, is a canny fellow who gives unexpectedly sage advice on a bewildering variety of topics. Updike's extraordinary talents have won, in addition to the Pulitzer Prize, the National Book Award, the American Book Award, and the Howells Medal. The latter award, from the American Academy of Arts and Letters, is for the most distinguished work of American fiction in the past five years. Updike won this medal for* Rabbit At Rest (1990). *"Farrell's Caddie" was originally published in the* New Yorker.

*John Updike*

# FARRELL'S CADDIE (1991)

WHEN FARRELL SIGNED UP, WITH seven other aging members of his local Long Island club, for a week of golf at the Royal Caledonian Links in Scotland, he didn't foresee the relationship with the caddies. Hunched little men in billed tweed caps and rubberized rain suits, they huddled in the misty gloom as the morning foursomes got organized, and reclustered after lunch, muttering as unintelligibly as sparrows, for the day's second eighteen.

Farrell would never have walked thirty-six holes a day in America, but here in Scotland golf was not an accessory to life, drawing upon one's marginal energy, it *was* life, played out of the center of one's being. At first, stepping forth on legs, one of which had been broken in a college football game forty years before, and which damp weather or a night of twisted sleep still provoked to a reminiscent twinge, he missed the silky glide and swerve of the accustomed electric cart, its magic-carpet suspension above the whispering fairway; he missed the rattle of spare balls in the retaining shelf, and the round plastic holes to hold drinks, alcoholic or carbonated, and the friendly presence on the seat beside him of another gray-haired sportsman, another warty pickle blanching in the brine of time, exuding forbearance and the expectation of forbearance, and resigned, like Farrell, to a golfing mediocrity that would poke its way down the sloping dogleg of decrepitude to the level green of death.

Here, however, on the heather-rimmed fairways, cut as close as putting surfaces back home, yet with no trace of mower tracks, and cheerfully marred by the scratchings and burrows of the nocturnal rabbits that lived and bred beneath the impenetrably thorny, waist-high gorse, energy came up through the turf, as if Farrell's cleats were making contact with primal spirits beneath the soil, and he felt he could walk forever. The rolling treeless terrain, the proximity of the wind-whipped sea, the rain that came and went with the suddenness of thought–they composed the ancient matrix of the game, and the darkly muttering caddies were also part of this matrix.

That first morning in the drizzly shuffle around the golf bags, his bag was hoisted up by a hunched shadow who, as they walked together in pursuit of Farrell's first drive (good contact, but pulled to the left, toward some shaggy mounds), muttered half to himself, with those hiccups or glottal stops the Scots accent inserts, "Sandy's wha' they call me."

Farrell hesitated, then confessed, "Gus." His given name, Augustus, had always embarrassed him, but its shortened version seemed a little short on dignity, and at the office, as he had ascended in rank, his colleagues had settled on his initials, "A.J."

"Ye want now tae geh oover th' second boosh fra' th' laift," Sandy said, handing Farrell a 7-iron. The green was out of sight behind the shaggy mounds, which were covered with a long tan grass that whitened in waves as gusts beat in from the sea.

"What's the distance?" Farrell was accustomed to yardage markers–yellow stakes, or sprinkler heads.

The caddie looked reflectively at a sand bunker not far off, and then at the winking red signal light on the train tracks beyond, and finally at a large bird, a gull or a crow, winging against the wind beneath the low, tattered, blue-black clouds. "Ah hunnert thirty-eight tae th' edge o' th' green, near a hunnert fifty tae th' pin, where they ha' 't."

"I can't hit a 7-iron a hundred fifty. I can't hit it even one forty, against the wind."

Yet the caddie's fist, in a fingerless wool glove, did not withdraw the offered club. "Seven's what ye need."

As Farrell bent his face to the ball, the wet wind cut across his eyes and made him cry. His tears turned one ball into two; he supposed the brighter one was real. He concentrated on taking the clubhead away slowly and low to the turf, initiating his downswing with a twitch of the left hip, and suppressing his tendency to dip the right shoulder. The shot seemed sweet, soaring with a gentle draw precisely over the second bush. He looked toward the caddie, expecting congratulations or at least some small sign of shared pleasure. But the man, whose creased face was weathered the strangely even brown of a white actor playing Othello, followed the flight of the ball as he had that of the crow, reflectively. "Yer right hand's a wee bit tae into 't," he observed, and the ball, they saw as they climbed to the green, was indeed pulled to the left, into a deep pot bunker. Furthermore, it was fifteen yards short. The caddie had underclubbed him, but showed no sign of remorse as he handed Farrell the sand wedge. In Sandy's dyed-looking face, pallid gray eyes showed like touches of morning light; it shocked Farrell to suspect that the other man, weathered though he was, and bent beneath the weight of a perpetual golf bag, was younger than himself–a prematurely wizened Pict, a concentrate of Farrell's diluted, Yankeefied Celtic blood.

The side of the bunker toward the hole was as tall as Farrell and sheer, built up of bricks of sod in a way he had never seen before, not even at Shinnecock Hills. Rattled, irritated at having been unrepentantly underclubbed, Farrell swung five times into the damp, brown sand, darker and denser than any sand on Long Island; each time, the ball thudded short of the trap's lip and dribbled back at his feet. " 'it at it well beheend," the caddie advised, "and dinna stop th' cloob." Farrell's sixth swing brought the ball bobbling up onto the green, within six feet of the hole.

His fellow-Americans lavished ironical praise on the tardily excellent shot but the caddie, with the same deadpan solemnity with which Farrell had repeatedly struck the ball, handed him putter. "Ae ball tae th' laift," he advised, and Farrell was so interested in this quaint concept–the ball as a unit of measure–that his putt stopped short. "Ye forgot tae 'it it, Goos," Sandy told him.

Farrell tersely nodded. The caddie made him feel obliged to keep up a show of golfing virtues. Asked for his score, he said loudly, in a stagey voice, "That was a honest ten."

"We'll call it a six," said the player keeping score, in the forgiving, corrupting American way.

As the round progressed, through a rapid alternation of brisk showers and silvery sunshine, with rainbows springing up around them and tiny white daisies gleaming underfoot, Farrell and his caddie began to grow into one another, as a foot in damp weather grows into a shoe. Sandy consistently handed Farrell one club too short to make the green, but Farrell came to accept the failure as his own; his caddie was handing the club to the stronger golfer latent in Farrell, and it was Farrell's job to let this superior performer out, to release him from his stiff, soft, more than middle-aged body. On the twelfth hole, called "Dunrobin"–a seemingly endless par 5 with a broad stretch of fairway, bleak and vaguely restless like the surface of the moon, receding over a distant edge marked by two small pot bunkers, with a pale-green arm of gorse extending from the rabbit-undermined thickets on the left–his drive clicked. Something about the ghostly emptiness of this terrain, the featurelessness of it, had removed Farrell's physical inhibitions; he felt the steel shaft of the driver bend in a subtle curve at his back, and a corresponding springiness awaken in his knees, and he knew, as his weight elastically moved from the right foot to the left, that he would bring the clubface squarely into the ball, and indeed did, so that the ball–the last of his new Titleists, the others having already been swallowed by gorse and heather and cliffside scree—was melting deep into the drizzle straight ahead almost before he looked up, his head held sideways, as if pillowed on his right ear, just like the pros on television. He cocked an eye at Sandy. "O.K.?" asked Farrell, mock-modest but also genuinely fearful of some hazard, some trick of the layout, that he had missed taking into account.

"Gowf shot, sir," the caddie said, and his face, as if touched by a magic wand, crumpled into a smile full of crooked gray teeth, his constantly re-lit cigarette adhering to one corner. Small matter that Farrell, striving for a repetition of his elastic sensations, topped the following 3-wood, hit a 5-iron fat and short, and skulled his wedge shot clear across the elevated green. He had for a second awakened the golf giant sleeping among his muscles, and imagined himself cutting a more significant figure in the other man's not quite colorless, not quite indifferent eyes.

Dinner, for this week of foreign excursion, was a repeating male event, involving the same eight Long Island males, their hair growing curly and their faces ruddy away from the arid Manhattan canyons and air-conditioned offices where they had accumulated their small fortunes. They discussed their caddies as men, extremely unbuttoned, might discuss their mistresses. What does a caddie want? "Come on, Freddie, 'it it fer once!" the very distinguished banker Frederic M. Panoply boasted that his had cried out to him as, on the third day of displaying his cautious, successful, down-the-middle game, he painstakingly addressed his ball.

Another man's caddie, when asked what he thought of Mrs. Thatcher, had responded with a twinkle, "She'd be a good 'ump."

Farrell, prim and reserved by nature, though not devoid of passion, had relatively little to offer concerning Sandy. He worried that the man's incessant smoking would kill him. He wondered if the tips he gave him were too far below what a Japanese golfer would have bestowed. He feared that Sandy was becoming tired of him. As the week went by, their relationship had become more intuitive. "A 6 iron?" Farrell would now say, and without a word would be handed the club. Once he had dared declined an offered 6, asked for the 5, and sailed his unusually well-struck shot into the sedge beyond the green. On the greens, where he at first had been bothered by the caddie's explicit directives, so that he forgot to stroke the ball firmly, Farrell had come to depend upon Sandy's advice, and would expertly cock his ear close to the caddie's mouth, and try to envision the curve of the ball into the center of the hole from "an inch an' a fhingernail tae th' laift." He began to sink putts. He began to get pars, as the whitecaps flashed on one side of the links and on the other the wine-red electric commuter trains swiftly glided up to Glasgow and back. This was happiness, bracketed between sea and rail, and freedom, of a wild and windy sort. On the morning of his last day, having sliced his first drive into the edge of the rough, between a thistle and what appeared to be a child's weathered tombstone, Farrell bent his ear close to the caddie's mouth for advice, and heard, "Ye'd be better leavin' 'er."

"Beg pardon?" Farrell said, as he had all week, when the glottal, hiccuping accent had become opaque. Today the acoustics were especially bad; a near-gale off the sea made his rain pants rattle like machine guns and deformed his eyeballs with air pressure as he tried to squint down. When he could stop seeing double, his lie looked fair–semi-embedded. The name on the tombstone was worn away. Perhaps it was merely an ancient railroad right-of-way marker.

"Yer missus," Sandy clarified, passing over the 8-iron. "Ere it's tae late, mon. She was never yer type. Tae proper."

"Shouldn't this be a wedge?" Farrell asked uncertainly.

"Nay, it's sittin' up guid enough," the caddie said, pressing his foot into the heather behind the ball so it rose up like ooze out of mud. "Ye kin reach with th' 8," he said. "Go fer yer par, mon. Yer fauts er a' in yer mind; ye tend t' play a hair defainsive."

Farrell would have dismissed his previous remarks, as a verbal mirage amid the clicks and skips of windblown Scots, had they not seemed so uncannily true. "Too proper" was exactly what his college friends had said of Sylvia, but he had imagined that her physical beauty had been the significant thing, and her propriety a pose she would outgrow, whereas thirty-five married years had revealed the propriety as enduring and the beauty as transient. As to leaving her, this thought would never have entered his head until recently; the mergers-and-acquisitions branch had recently taken on a certain Irma Finegold, who had heavy-lidded eyes, full lips painted vermilion, and a curious presumptuous way of teasing Farrell in the eddies of chitchat before and after conferences, or in the elevator up to the boardroom. She had been recently divorced, and when she talked to Farrell she manipulated her lower lip with a pencil eraser and shimmied her shoulders beneath their pads. On nights when the office worked late—he liked occasionally to demonstrate that, well-along though he was, he could still pull an all-nighter with the young bucks—there had been between him and Irma shared Chinese meals in greasy takeout cartons, and a joint limo home in the dawn light, through the twinned arches and aspiring tracery of the Brooklyn Bridge. On one undreamed-of occasion, there had been an invitation, which he did not refuse, to delay his return to Long Island with an interlude at her apartment in Park Slope. Though no young buck, he had not done badly, it seemed to him, even factoring in the flattery quotient from a subordinate.

The 8-iron pinched the ball clean, and the Atlantic gale brought the soaring shot left-to-right toward the pin. "Laift edge, but dinna gi' th' hole away," Sandy advised of the putt, and Farrell sank it, for the first birdie of his week of golf.

Now, suddenly, out of the silvery torn sky, sleet and sunshine poured simultaneously, and as the two men walked at the same tilt to the next tee, Sandy's voice came out of the wind, "An' steer clear o' th' MiniCorp deal. They've laiveraged th' company tae daith."

Farrell studied Sandy's face. Rain and sleet bounced off the brown skin as if from a waxy preservative coating. Metallic gleams showed as the man studied, through narrowed eyelids, the watery horizon. Farrell pretended he hadn't heard. On the tee he was handed a 3-wood, with the advice, "Ye want tae stay short o' th' wee burn. Th' wind's come around beheend, bringin' th' sun with it."

As the round wore on , the sun did struggle through, and a thick rainbow planted itself over the profile of the drab town beyond the tracks, with its black steeples and distillery chimneys. By the afternoon's eighteen, there was actually blue sky, and the pockets of lengthening shadow showed the old course to be everywhere curvacious, crest and swale, like the body of a woman. Forty feet off the green on the fourteenth ("Whinny Brae"), Farrell docilely accepted the caddie's offer of a putter, and rolled it up and over the close-mown irregularities within a gimme of the hole. His old self would have skulled or fluffed a chip. "Great advice," he said, and in his flush of triumph challenged the caddie: "But Irma *loves* the MiniCorp deal."

"Aye, 't keeps th' twa o' ye taegither. She's fairful ye'll wander off, i' th' halls o' corporate power."

"But what does she see in me?"

"Lookin' fer a father, th' case may be. Thet first husband o' hers was meikle immature, an' also far from yer own income bracket."

Farrell felt his heart sink at the deflating shrewdness of the analysis. His mind elsewhere, absented by bittersweet sorrow, he hit one pure shot after another. Looking to the caddie for praise, however, he met the same impassive, dour, young-old visage, opaque beneath the billed tweed cap. Tomorrow, he would be caddying for someone else, and Farrell would be belted into a business-class seat within a 747. On the home stretch of holes–one after the other strung out beside the railroad right-of-way, as the Victorian brick clubhouse, with its turrets and neo-Gothic windows, enlarged in size–Farrell begged for the last scraps of advice. "The 5-wood, or the 3-iron? The 3 keeps it down out of the wind, but I feel more confident with the wood, the way you've got me swinging."

"Th' 5'll be ower an' gone; ye're a' poomped up. Take th' 4-iron. Smooth it on, laddie. Aim fer th' little broch."

"Broch?"

"Wee stone fortress, frae th' days we had our own braw king." He added, "An' ye might be thinkin' aboot takin' early retirement. Th' severance deals won't be so sweet aye, with th' coomin' resaission. Ye kin free yerself up, an' take on some consults, fer th' spare change."

"Just what I was thinking, if Irma's a will-o'-the-wisp."

"Will-o'-the-wisp, do ye say? Ye're a speedy lairner, Goos."

Farrell felt flattered and wind-scoured, here in this surging universe of green and gray. "You really think so, Sandy?"

"I *ken* sae. Aye, ye kin tell a' aboot a mon, frae th' way he gowfs."

*The cast of characters in this story includes King John of England, who signed the Magna Carta in 1215, and a Saxon chap named Robin Hood, who hailed from Sherwood Forest. The reader may remember the archery contest between Mr. Hood and his rival, Hubert the Norman. Hollywood has taken a turn or two on this incident. What we have here is a change of venue to golf, and a similarly bizarre result. Author Stephen Leacock demonstrates his international reputation for caricature in this playful tale of yore. Apart from P. G. Wodehouse, no one has produced more high-quality golf humor than Leacock.*

*Stephen Leacock*

# A MEDIAEVAL HOLE IN ONE (1929)

THE MIDDLE AGES, FROM WHAT we know about them, were days of pretty tall deeds and pretty tall talk. In the Middle Ages if a man accomplished a feat of arms, or a feat of dexterity, or a feat of anything, he didn't let it get spoiled for want of telling. In witness of which take the marvellous accounts of archery, swordsmanship, strength, skill, and magic which fill the pages of mediaeval romance from the Chanson de Roland to Walter Scott.

And there is no doubt that the "tall talk" of the Middle Ages was greatly helped along by the prevailing habit of tall drinking. They drank in those days not by the glass but by the barrel. They knew nothing of "flasks" or "cups" or "glasses," or such small degenerate measures as those of their descendants. When they wanted a real drink they knocked in the head of a "cask" or "tun" and gathered round it and drank it to the bottom of the barrel.

Even for a modest individual drink they needed a "flagon"–and a "flagon" in the Middle Ages was of the same size as one of our garden watering pots. A man who had inside him a couple of flagons of old "Malmsey" or old "Gascony," had a power of talk and energy in him no longer known among us. When it is added that old "Malmsey" only cost ten pennies for a full imperial gallon–six of our quarts–one can see that even the dark age had its bright spots and that history was not so dry as it is called.

As a result, not only were the deeds and feats of arms of the Middle Ages bigger than ours, but even the narration of them had more size. And the spectators and witnesses, having sopped up on their own account a few "hogsheads" of "mead" or sack, could see more, far more, than our poor dried-out audiences. In witness of which take any account of any tournament, bear fight, bullfight, archery match or rat hunt anywhere from 1000 to 1500 a.d.

For all of which deeds and performances, the running accompaniment of knocking in hogsheads and draining flagons kept the whole event in character.

No king in the Middle Ages ever appeared at a public tournament or joust without ordering the ends of half a dozen casks of sack to be knocked in. No royal christening was ever held without "tuns" of ale being distributed or "broached" for the populace, and "pipes" of wine being pumped into the nobility. At all big celebrations there were huge bonfires. Oxen were roasted whole. Any good man would get away with fifteen pounds of roast meat, six gallons of ale and a flagon of brandy, and go roaring home with an atmosphere round him like the mist round a brewery.

Those were great days. We cannot compete with them.

But in just one point the superiority is ours. The mediaeval people didn't have our opportunities. Their archery and their tournaments were poor stuff beside our games of to-day. Just think what would have happened if they had had such a thing as golf in the Middle Ages! Imagine the way in which, with their flagons of sack and their hogsheads of Malmsey right on the ground, they could have carried out a golf match. Imagine what they could have done in the narration of it afterwards! Conceive what could have been made of a mediaeval Hole in One. Our poor unimaginative truth-telling generation can form but little idea as to how they would have dealt with it.

What follows below represents an account of a Hole in One, as achieved in the year 1215 A.D. and related after the style of mediaeval romance. It is based on the account of the famous tournament and meeting at Ashby de la Zouche (which is in England) during the reign of King John. On that famous occasion, as Walter Scott related in his *Ivanhoe,* there was an archery match between Hubert the Norman, the protégé of King John, and the Mysterious Bowman, Locksley, otherwise Robin Hood the Saxon Outlaw. In this contest Hubert "sped his arrow" (that's the mediaeval name for what he did) with such consummate skill that it pierced the very centre of the bull's-eye, three hundred yards away. But Locksley had a still more consummate touch. He sped his shaft with such unerring dexterity that the point of it struck fair in the notch of Hubert's arrow, still sticking in the bull's-eye, and split it into two exactly even halves! After which even the stingy King John had to treat the crowd, a whole meadowful, to about two firkins each.

Imagine what would happen if people who could write that kind of thing and people who could believe it had had a chance at a golf story.

Come! Let us turn Hubert and Locksley into their twentieth-century form and make the contest a Hole-in-One-Shot! Thus–

All was now prepared. The vast concourse of spectators, both Norman and Saxon, crowded the vacant spaces of the course, and even invaded the fairways from which the heralds and poursuivants sought in vain to dislodge them. The humbler churls, or jarls, clustered in the branches of the trees.

At intervals along the course great "butts" or "tuns," by which we mean "vats," had been placed, from which not only the yeomanry but even the commonry were permitted that day to drink at the King's expense.

King John was seated on a dais beside the sand-box of Tee No. 1, at the edge of which the pious Archbishop Stephen Langton knelt in prayer for the success of the Norman Hubert. Around and about the tee, on tiers of rudely contrived benches, the Knights of the Household in full (autumn) armour were mingled with the resplendent Ladies of the Court.

"Sirrah!" said the King, turning sternly to Hubert, "dost think thou canst outswat this Saxon fellow?"

"My grandsire," said Hubert, "played in the Hastings handicap, and it shall go hard with me an I fall short of his score."

The King scowled but said nothing.

"What is bogey?" whispered Roger Bigod, Earl of Bygod, to Sir John Montfaucon de la Tour, who stood beside him near the tee.

"Three, so it thinks me," answered Sir John.

"And gives either of the contestants as it were a bisque or holeth he in one stroke the fewer?"

"Nay," said Montfaucon, "they play as man to man, or as who should say at scratch."

At this moment the loud sound of a tucket armoured by the winding of a hobo from the second tee announced that the lists were clear.

"Let the course be measured!" commanded the Chief Marshal.

On this Sir Roger Mauleverer of the Tower and Sir Eustace, the Left-handed, Constable of the Constable, attended by six poursuivants carrying a line of silken yarn, measured the distance.

"How stands it?" asked the King.

"Four hundred ells, six firkins, and a demilitre," answered the Marshal.

At the mention of this distance–which corresponds in our modern English to more than four hundred yards–an intense hush fell upon the attendant crowd. That a mere ball no larger than a pheasant's egg could be driven over this tremendous distance by a mere blow from a mere wand of hickory, daunted the mere imagination.

The King, who well knew that the approaching contest was in reality one between Norman and Saxon and might carry with it the loss of his English crown, could ill conceal the fears that racked his evil conscience. In vain his cupbearer fetched him goblet after goblet of Gascony. Even the generous wine failed to enliven the mind or to dissipate the fears of the doomed monarch. A great silence had fallen upon the assembled knights and ladies, broken only by the murmured prayers of the saintly archbishop kneeling beside the sand-box. Even the stout hearts of such men as Sir Roger Bigod de Bygod and Sir Walter de la Tenspot almost ceased to beat.

"Have done with this delay," exclaimed the King. "Let the men begin."

Hubert the Norman stepped first onto the tee. His lithe frame, knit to a nicety, with every bone and joint working to its full efficiency, was encased in a jerkin of Andalusian wool, over a haut-de-chausse, or plus eight, of quilted worsted. He carried in his right hand a small white ball, while in his left he bore a shaft or club of hickory, the handle bound with cordovan leather and the end, or tip, or as the Normans called it the *bout,* fashioned in a heavy knot flattened on one side to a hexagonal diagonal.

The manner of the Norman Hubert was grave, but his firm movements and his steady eye showed no trace of apprehension as he adjusted the ball upon a small heap of sand upon the forward, or front, part of the tee.

"Canst do it?" queried the agonizing King, his hands writhing nervously on the handle of his sceptre.

"My grandsire . . ." began Hubert.

"You said that before," cried John. "Shoot!"

Hubert bowed and paused a moment to drink a flagon of Amsterdam gin handed to him by the King's bouteillier or bottle-washer. Then, standing poised on the balls of his feet at a distance of two Norman demis (twenty-six and a half English inches) from the ball, he waved his club in the air as if testing its weight, while his keen eye measured the velocity of the wind.

Then, as the crowd waited in breathless silence, Hubert suddenly swung the hickory to his full reach behind his shoulder and brought it down in a magnificent sweep, striking the ball with its full impact.

There was a loud resilient "click," distinctly heard by the spectators at the second tee, while a great shout arose from all the Normans as the ball rose in the air describing a magnificent parabola in its flight.

"A Hubert! A Hubert!" they shouted. "*Par le Sang de Dieu,*" exclaimed Sir Roger Bigod de Bygod, "some stroke!"

Meantime the ball, glistening in the sunshine and seeming to gather force in its flight, swept above the fairway and passed high in the air over the ground posts that marked the hundred, the two hundred, and the three hundred ells, still rushing to its goal.

"By the body of St. Augustine!" cried the pious Guillaume de la Hootch, "'twill reach the green itself!"

"It has!" shouted Sir Roger Bigod. "Look! Look! They are seizing and lifting the flag! 'Tis on! 'Tis in! By the shirt of St. Ambrose, the ball is in the can!"

And as Sir Roger spoke a great shout went up from all the crowd, echoed even by the Saxon churls who lined the branches of the trees. "A Hole in One! A Hole in One!" cried the multitude, while an immediate rush was made to the barrels or vats of mead which lined the course, into which the exultant populace precipitated themselves head first.

For such readers as do not understand the old Norman game of Goffe, or Gouffe–sometimes also called Guff–it is proper to explain that in the centre of each *parterre* or *terrace,* sometimes called a *Green* or *Pelouse*–it was customary to set a sunken receptacle or can, of the kind used by the Normans to can tomatoes, into which the ball must ultimately be driven. The virtue of Hubert's stroke was that he had driven the ball into the can (a feat for which many Normans required eight, ten, or even twenty strokes) in one single blow, an achievement called in old Norman a "Hole in One."

And now the voice of the Chief Herald could be heard calling through hautboy or megaphone:

"Hole No. 1; stroke No. 1. Hubert of Normandy scores Hole in One. Player in hand, J. Locksley, of Huntingdon, England. Clear the fairway for shot No. 2."

All eyes now turned to where the splendid figure of the mysterious Locksley, the Unknown Golfer or Gopher, ascended the first tee. It was known to all that this was in reality none other, or little other, than the

Saxon outlaw Robin Hood, who was whispered to be the Earl of Huntingdon and half whispered to be, by his descent from his own grandmother, the Saxon claimant to the throne.

"How now, Locksley!" sneered the triumphant John as the Saxon appeared beside him, "canst beat that?"

Every gaze rested upon Locksley as he stood leaning upon his hickory club. His mysterious appearance at Ashby de la Zouche and the whispers as to his identity lent to him a romantic, and almost fearsome interest, while his magnificent person marked him as the beau ideal of the Saxon Golfer still seen at times even in the mimic contests of to-day.

His powerful form could have touched the balance at two hundred and eighty-five pounds avoirdupois. The massive shoulders would have seemed out of proportion but for the ample sweep of the girth or waistline and the splendid breadth of the netherward or rearward hind-quarters.

He was clad, like Hubert, in woollen jerkin and plus eights, and he bore on his feet the terrific spiked sandals of the Saxon, capable of inflicting a mortal blow.

Locksley placed his ball, and then, grasping in his iron grip the leather-bound club-headed hickory hexagonal, he looked about him with complete sang-froid and even something of amusement.

The King's boozelier, or booze-hound, now approached Locksley and, after the courtesy of the age, offered him a horn, or "jolt" of gin. The Saxon put it aside and to the astonishment of the crowd called only for water, contenting himself with a single bucketful.

"Drink'st not?" said the scowling King.

"Not in hours of busyness," said Locklsey firmly.

"And canst thou outdo Hubert's shot?" sneered John.

"I know not," said Locksley carelessly; "Hubert's shot was not half bad, but I'll see if I can touch up his ball for him in the tomato can."

"Have done with boasting!" cried the King. "Tell the archbishop to count three, and then let the fellow shoot. If he fail, my lord Montfaucon and you, Roger Bigod of Bygod, see that he does not leave the tee alive."

The archbishop raised his saintly face towards the skies and began to count.

"Unum!" he said, using the neuter gender of the numeral adjective in accordance with the increasing deterioration of the Latin language which had already gone far in the year 1215 A.D.

"Duo," said the archbishop, and then in a breathless hush, as the word "tres" quivered on the lips of the ecclesiastic, Locksley's club cleft the air in a single flash of glittering sunlight and descended upon the ball with such force that the sound of the concussion echoed back from the woods beyond the farthest green.

In a moment the glittering trajectory of the missile could be followed high in its flight and then the curve of its rushing descent towards the green. For a moment the silence was so intense that even the faint rustling of the grass was audible to the ear, then the crashing concussion of the driven ball against the inner tin of the tomato can showed that Locksley also had achieved a Hole in One! But the gasp or gulp of astonishment had hardly passed when the crowd became aware that Locksley's skilled marksmanship had far surpassed the mere feat of a Hole in One accomplished by his opponent. His ball, driven with a power and accuracy that might well-nigh seem incredible, had struck against Hubert's ball inside the can at exactly the angle necessary to drive it out with great force and start it back in flight towards the first tee.

To the amazement of all beholders, Hubert's ball, easily distinguishable by two little dots on its lower face, was seen rushing in rapid flight to retrace its course above the fairway. So true was its path that it landed back precisely on the tee from which Hubert had shot it and came to rest on the little pile of sand on which the Norman gopher had originally placed it.

"By God!" shouted Bigod of Bygod, as Locksley picked up the ball and handed it with a bow to King John.

A wild shout that rose alike from the Saxon Thanes, the Danes, and even the Normans, rent the air, while even the ladies of the court, carried away in a burst of chivalrous admiration, tore off their silken baldrics and threw them at the feet of the victor.

Nobles and commons alike, Norman and Saxon together seized axe or bill and began beating in the heads of the casks in their eagerness to drink the health of the victor.

"A Locksley! A Locksley!" cried the multitude. For the moment the King paused. His ear caught in the roaring plaudits of the crowd the first note of that mighty unison of Saxon and Norman voices which was destined to cast him from his power.

He knew that any attempt against the life or person of the Saxon chieftain was without avail.

He turned to the venerable archbishop, who was prostrate beside the tee, eating sand.

"Fetch me the Magna Carta," he said, "and I'll sign it."

*This witty story was originally published in the* Saturday Evening Post. *It's a period piece from the World-War-II era. William Fowler is a sales-promotion manager for a golf equipment company whose job is threatened by a shortage of rubber for making golf balls. The owner of the company cooks up a golf match between himself and the owner of a rival company, with each tycoon teaming up with one of the golf professionals on his payroll. It's a high-stakes match for the rubber allotment, and Fowler is trying to figure out how to get his company to win. Author Paul Gallico (1897–1976) was a rococo and flamboyant sportswriter for the* New York Daily News. *Like Ring Lardner, he soon became famous for his writing on subjects beyond sports. Among Gallico's twenty-seven books are* Farewell to Sport *(1937),* The Snow Goose *(1941),* Lou Gehrig, Pride of the Yankees *(1942), and* The Poseidon Adventure *(1969).*

*Paul Gallico*

# GOLF IS A NICE FRIENDLY GAME (1942)

WHEN THE BUZZER ON MY desk snarled three times, meaning that old A. R. was yearning to bend my ear, I paused just long enough to bid a fond farewell to the rest of the staff before stepping in onto the carpet to get the can tied to me. Your Uncle William was a sure thing to get fired.

Of what use was a sales-promotion manager to a golf-equipment company when pretty soon there wasn't going to be anything to sell?

Sooner or later, of course, Uncle Sam was going to hand me one of those nice new Garands that can hole out at a thousand yards, but while I was waiting for my number to come up it was nice to go on eating.

True, I'd read in the papers where the Priorities Board had released a small quantity of second-grade rubber to be rationed to the four leading makers of golf balls, in the interest of morale. But when a golf ball gets that rare, you don't need a top promotion guy to figure out ways to get rid of them. Well, what was going to happen to me was no worse than what had happened to a lot of others.

Oh yeah?

You could have knocked me over with a score card when I walked into A. R.'s office. Instead of being parked behind his desk scowling at reports, he was swinging a mashie in the middle of the floor.

"Ha! Harrrrmph!" he barked, missing the chandelier by an inch. "Come in, Fowler. Don't stand there gawking."

I flattened up against the wall. So the Old Man had finally fallen for the game. Every time I came in to see him I had to listen to his beef about what a bunch of no-good loafers our pros were and why couldn't they win every tournament since that was what they were paid for? Maybe he'd be a little easier to handle now. Which gives you an idea of William Fowler's skullwork.

"I–I didn't know you had taken up golf, A. R."

"Ha! Ahm'mm'm. Lot of things you don't know, Fowler. Started four months ago. Doctor's orders. Not getting enough exercise. Simple game. Mastered it at once. Sit down, sit down, Fowler. Want to talk to you."

I figured: "Here it comes, and there I go." But it was just as easy to take it sitting down as standing up. I wouldn't have so far to fall.

A. R. sat down too. He was a little bit of a guy, no bigger than a pepper-box, but twice as sharp. He had Antarctic eyes and a mouth like the edge of a number-three iron.

"Joined the Skipping Brook Country Club, Fowler. Learned golf. Ridiculously easy game. Confirmed a suspicion I have entertained for many years. Those professionals on our payroll. Bunch of good-for-nothing, lazy loafers. Absolutely no excuse for them to lose. Look at me. Play only Saturdays and Sundays. Completely familiar with the rudimentary science of the game. No doubt if I were to devote my entire time to it as they do, I would become perfect. Lot of fakers and idlers, those professionals. Lame excuses about nerves and strain. Outrageous!"

Well now, I don't go much for that hero stuff about golfers, but I've got a pretty fair idea what some of the lads go through trying to knock off a big championship, or just win eating money for that matter, and I couldn't let him get by with that, so I started to say: "Aw, now A. R.–"

"Hmmffff! Never mind, Fowler. We'll discuss that some other time. You know Fairfield Greenly, president of Fairgreen Company?"

"Sure."

"Humph! Exactly! Pompous ass. Always bragging and blowing. Sickening. Play with him on Sundays. Member at Skipping Brook. Doesn't know first rudiments of the game. Just lucky. Had to take him down a peg, eh, Fowler, my boy?"

Beware of the boss when he calls you "my boy." I ventured: "Did you beat him, sir?"

"Eh? Haaarm'fff! Well, not exactly. That is to say, on skill and knowledge, of course, but he's damnably lucky. Crows afterwards. Had to fix his kite once and for all. Challenged him, Fowler, that's what I did. That's where you come in."

I thought: "Oh-oh! Careful, Fowler." Out loud I said: "Me, sir?"

"Precisely. You know all those indolent, incompetent pros I have been supporting. Want you to pick the best of a bad lot and have him at Skipping Brook next Sunday morning. Relying upon your choice."

"I don't exactly get the picture, A. R."

"Haaarumph! Well, perhaps we *were* all imbibing a bit. Customary at the end of a game. Wasn't enough I paid Greenly his money. Had to listen to his blowing. Fairgreen clubs! Fairgreen professionals! Got sick of it. Challenged him. Myself and best Mallow professional against Greenly and a Fairgreen pro. Scotchman's fourball."

"You mean a Scotch foursome, sir?"

"Eh? That's what I said. Strict rules. Eighteen holes. Play our own equipment. Made a wager on it. That will fix him. Now you get me a man who can win."

Did I breathe a sigh of relief. Here I was expecting to be fired, and all it was about was a grudge match between a couple of old coots. They'd probably agreed on a five-dollar Nassau, which wasn't going to hurt anybody. Still, just for the record I asked: "How much is the bet, A. R.?"

I should have known something was coming, because he didn't answer right away, but fiddled with stuff on his desk, hemming and hawing and getting red.

"Hraaagh! Oh yes, the wager. Well now, Fowler, it was necessary to put him in his place. We–ah–hroomp–agreed that the stakes should be our share of the–ah–rubber allotment we are getting from the–"

"The *what?*"

"Now, now, Fowler! Don't shout. I can hear you. It was Greenly's idea. Naturally, I couldn't let him bluff–"

"But great Jehosaphat, A. R.! If we lose we might as well go out of business. We won't be able to make a golf ball. . . ."

A. R. gave me that ice-box stare. "Exactly, Fowler. You know the professionals. It's up to you to see that we don't lose, or else–"

He didn't have to finish that "or else." That was a dilleroo, wasn't it? We had a lot of ace pros on our payroll, but Fairgreen was a sure thing to play Angus MacDonough, their open champion. And what did I know about A. R.'s game, or Greenly's either, for that matter?

I said: "Gee, A. R., this is a pretty important match. What kind of a score do you shoot? Maybe we'd better play around together some day this week so that I could study your–"

"Eh? What for, Fowler? Wholly unnecessary. It isn't the figures that count. Told you there's nothing about the game I don't understand."

I had to use bait. "It's just plain strategy, A. R. For instance, if you're a long hitter I'd naturally assign you a pro with the best approaching shots–" I had the decency to blush. "Ah–someone who will back up your game."

He swallowed it. "Well, if you put it that way, Fowler. Wouldn't want a man who would hold me down. Supposing you come up to Skipping Brook next Wednesday morning. Might be able to give you a few pointers. That's all."

But when I got to the door he called me back. "Ah, Fowler! Just one moment. Do you know of a golf professional by the name of Lane, Jimmy Lane?"

"Jimmy Lane? Sure, A. R. He's a kid we signed up last year. Hasn't had a chance to do much yet, but he sure raised hell around Texas, where he comes from. Lot of the boys think he'll grab the Open in a couple of years. We were lucky to–"

Now what had I done? A. R. was looking as black as a tar pit. That blade mouth of his was set like a trap.

"On my payroll, eh? Well then, you just tell him to stay away from my niece Eleanor, do you hear? I'm responsible for her and I don't intend having her take up with a lazy, good-for-nothing golf loafer. Tell him if I catch him hanging around her again, he's fired. Hmurrrrf!"

Did I tell you that your Uncle William is the guy everything happens to? Or do I have to?

Believe me, by the time I hit the third tee with A. R. out at Skipping Brook in Westchester the following Wednesday, I had forgotten about Jimmy Lane and Mallow's niece and everything else. I had troubles of my own.

I won't try to describe A. R.'s game to you beyond saying that the way he played golf it would have taken him three years of solid practice to work up to the point where he could be called a duffer.

Brethren, now that it can be told, it was to weep. He sliced, he jabbed, he jumped, he hacked, he sclaffed, he shanked, he dribbled, he dug, he gouged, he shimmied, he whiffied, he pressed and depressed, he jounced and jiggled, he swayed and swiveled, he bent at the knees, and likewise at the instep, the thighs, and the fourth vertebra; he closed his eyes, he looked up, he slashed, swooped, leaped, lurched, ducked, bobbed, heaved, and wrenched.

But that wasn't even the worst. He was convinced he knew all about the game and never stopped saying so. That bevel-edged mouth of his didn't quit working from tee to green, between alibiing his shots, giving me instruction, blasting the pros who made such a fuss over a simple game, and jawing the caddies.

As near as I can remember without stenographic notes, a sample hole went something like this:

"Hoop! Know what I did then? Didn't keep my elbow out. Ugh! Dratted car going along the road disturbed me. Wagh! Caddie, you rattled those clubs. Do it again and back you go to the clubhouse. Fowler, you're getting too much shoulder into your swing. Here, watch me! Oops! Had it right, but the club slipped that time. Come on, Fowler, hurry up and hit it. Don't keep me waiting. There. See how that one went? It's because I don't break my wrists. Own discovery. Those crazy pros tell you to break your wrists. Lot of fakers. Bah! There was a lump of dirt back of the ball. That's why I didn't hit it right. Fowler, you're standing wrong. Wunh! Had something in my eye that time. Couldn't see the ball. . . ."

But you get the idea. Bob Jones, the year he made the grand slam, couldn't have beaten a couple of three-year-old kids, teamed with a guy like that. And your Uncle William was supposed to dig up a Mallow pro who would bring home the rubber.

As we plowed up the fourth fairway, we could see across to number nine, where it looked like one of those war photos in the picture magazines when a land mine goes up. Chunks of the scenery were leaping into the air. A. R. grunted and said: "There you are. That's Greenly. Look at him. Man like that ought to stay off a golf course."

When some of the dust of battle settled, I could see there was a man involved in the scene, a long, thin, dried-up guy with a fine Badminton swing. It was a minor comfort to ascertain that Mr. Greenly was the second worst golfer in the world. And not even that comfort lasted. I hadn't seen anything yet.

I won't insult your intelligence by asking you to guess who walked out of the bushes back of the sixth tee, using a club for a walking-stick, his patent-leather hair looking like one of those "Try Slicko" ads, his lemon-meringue puss parted in the middle to show four fangs. It was the smile that curdles, and its owner was the one guy in the world that I can do without in large quantities–J. Sears Hammett of the Fairgreen Company.

And did he move in!

"How d'e do, Mr. Mallow? Enjoying a little healthful exercise again, I see. Making some fine shots too. Watched you coming up the fifth. . . ." He twitched that flea-bite mustache of his and gave that half strangle, half sneeze he used in place of a laugh: "HA-aaaargh! Must say the company you're in won't help your game much. Ah there, Fowler."

"Oh, yeah?" I said. "Oh, yeah?"

Yes sir, a regular Fred Allen for repartee, that's your Uncle William. I'm the guy who comes up with the right crack about three hours later.

"Hah!" said A. R. "You've noticed those shots, eh, Hammett? New discovery of mine. Don't keep your eye on the ball. Keep it on the line of flight. See where it's going that way. Damned pros don't know anything at all."

"You're absolutely right, Mr. Mallow," said J. Sears Hammett, doing a double smirk. "Those pros will put you off your game. You do it your own way."

It wasn't even any use trying to tip A. R. off to what Hammett was trying to put over on him. It was obvious that they had become palsy-walsy. J. Sears kept buttering A. R., supporting him in his revolting theories about the game and egging him on to try new stances, grips, and swings. The old fool just lapped it all up.

Then the louse did just the thing I was afraid of. He said: "You see that Fowler assigns you a good man to play against Angus MacDonough, the Open Champion, Mr. Mallow. He's got some awful lemons on his list. Ah-ah, Fowler, too much left hand on that shot. Just as Mr. Mallow told you. That's why you knocked it out of bounds."

I said: "Oh, is that so?" That was a killer, wasn't it?

Coming up to the sixteenth, Mallow went into a deep bunker alongside the green and started excavating. He had taken eight socks at it and even his alibis were growing weaker when Hammett said: "Here, Mr. Mallow, try this one," and handed down the club he had been using for a walking-stick. A. R. took one gorblimey swipe and out popped the ball and dropped onto the carpet.

"Hah! Knew there was something the matter with my niblick all the time. Thanks, young man." He started to hand the club back when Hammett gave a magnanimous wave of his hand:

"Oh, that's all right, Mr. Mallow. Just stick it in your bag and keep it. I could see from here that club you were using wasn't properly balanced for you."

Walking up the home hole, A. R. said to me: "Fine chap, that Hammett, Fowler. Knows his stuff. Alert. Keen. Suggest you try to emulate him a little more. . . ."

I didn't even bat an eye at that one. I had other worries. You didn't forget about that rubber, did you? Whom was I going to assign to A. R. to play against Greenly and Angus MacDonough?

Well, whom? You know the list of A. R. Mallow professionals as well as I. Freddy McRae, our best shot-maker? Ever see him in a tournament? Hair-trigger nerves. If somebody sneezes in the gallery he starts to shake. A. R. would drive him stark, raving mad in two minutes.

Elmer Brown and Jed Scraggins were two even-tempered guys, but they were both in Florida. I didn't dare give him Archie Crobb, who was playing for us now. Archie is a poisonous, dried-up misanthropic old Scotchman who believes that dubs and duffers shouldn't be allowed to desecrate golf courses. He once threw a niblick at a kid in the gallery who was jiggling a balloon. I know, I know–Whitey Brompton. But what you don't know is that Whitey had had some kind of run-in with A. R. and hated his shadow. Pete Clary? No good. Great iron player–nasty, sarcastic tongue. One crack out of A. R., and Pete would tear him to pieces. And I couldn't use Reggie Ring because Angus MacDonough had the Indian sign on him.

What I needed was a guy with Craig Wood's tee shots, the short game of Paul Runyon, and the disposition of a saint. There wasn't any such animal. Classmates, I was low, walking back to the clubhouse from the eighteenth green. The match was in the bag for Fairgreen, and so was William Fowler, Esq., and the firm unless we could figure some way to make golf balls out of chewing gum.

I was so low I didn't even care when A. R. and Hammett, their arms about each other's shoulders, went into the grill room for a drink and didn't ask me to come along. I needed solitude. I went into the locker room and ordered a double whisky cocktail which consists of two parts whisky to three parts of whisky; add a jigger of whisky, shake well with a dash of whisky, pour in a glass with a little whisky, and drink while holding on to something firm.

After the third, when I discovered I had left my change of clothes in the car, I figured maybe the air would do me some good, so I went to get the bag myself instead of sending the Senegambian.

It was surprising how much one car looked like another at that point, so the only thing to do was try them all. I was just about to crawl into the back of the fifth when I heard a voice that was familiar on account of the Texas in it, saying:

"Gee, Eleanor, I jes' cain't help telling you. I'll bust ef I don't. I–I jes' love you, that's all."

"Oh-oh, Fowler!" I said to myself. "Blow!"

But you know how it is. I just couldn't resist taking a gander. Yop! You guessed it. It was the crusher too. I told you I'd forgotten about A. R. warning me about Jimmy Lane, our kid pro, and his niece Eleanor. When I have trouble it comes likes asparagus, in bunches.

They were in the front seat, and when I peeked again she was in his arms, and for keeps too. Friends, it was Capital El-Oh-Vee-Eee, except that your old pardner William wasn't exactly in the mood. She was pretty too, a soft little brunette with doe eyes. I couldn't see the mouth because it was occupied. Now, why couldn't I have found out that A. R. had a looker like that in the family?

Then, all of a sudden, they were apart and the girl had begun to cry. Well, you wouldn't expect me to check out at that point, would you? That's like tearing up the magazine with the last installment in it. I heard her say:

"Oh, Jim, I'm so miserable. I don't know what to do about Uncle Argyle. He can make everything so unpleasant. Oh, Jim–Jim. . . ."

Yeah, and a nice little package I had wrapped up for Jim too. The old heave-o. But he was still blissfully unaware of that. He just looked at her and said:

"Honey, I'll jes' make that man like me. I'll make him. There's nothing I won't do for you, darling. I'll try anything to win him over, El. I know I cain do it. Why, I'd plumb go through hell for you, honey."

She said: "Oh, Jim, I know you will," and got back into his arms again, at which point little Willie snuck away from there.

I could hardly wait to get back to that locker room. I wanted to be somewhere alone where I could hug myself. I've told you about me, haven't I? I don't get ideas often, but when I do, it's frightening.

That kid was so eager to go plumb through hell for his girl that I was going to fix it for him. I was just going to let him play eighteen holes of Scotch foursome with Argyle Rutherford Mallow, Inc.

Simple, wasn't it? In that frame of mind there was nothing he wouldn't take from A. R. for the sake of the girl. And by the time I got through steaming him up he might even bring home the latex for her too.

I had another shot of formula in the locker room before going into the grill. You see, I still had to sell it to A. R.

Whew! X marks the spot where he hit the ceiling when I told him I had picked Jimmy Lane to play with him. Even Hammett was scared and helped pour a couple of drinks into him while I talked fast.

I told him that McRae had broken his ankle in a blackout, that Brompton was in jail and Reggie Ring was at the bedside of his ailing grandmother. I gave him fast alibis for Pete and Archie and all the rest and then got down to business.

"Look, A. R.," I said, "I know all about what you said with regard to Jim in the office that day, but this is a time to put personal prejudices aside for the good of the Mallow team. He's young, but he's a fine golfer and, above all, he'll take advice and instruction. He's not like those old mossback know-it-alls. You'll be able to teach that kid. . . ."

I could see that part of it appealed to A. R., but he wasn't sold by a long shot. When what do you think happened? You could have knocked me flat with a whisk-broom. Hammett suddenly turned those Tomcod eyes of his on A. R., and said:

"Ah hem! I think perhaps Fowler has something there, Mr. Mallow, if I may say so. Lane is a comer. Best natural swing in years. Wish we had him signed up. Couldn't make a better choice myself."

Of course I got Hammett's angle. Jim was still a year or so away from top tournament golf and figured to be a soft touch for an old hand like Angus MacDonough. But wouldn't you think A. R. would have more sense?

Well, the dew was still on his beautiful friendship with J. Sears Hammett. He was probably figuring to give him my job. He turned to me and said:

"Young man, I have a great deal of faith in Mr. Hammett's judgment. Wish I could say the same for you. In this instance I shall take his advice. You may tell Lane to be here at two o'clock on Sunday afternoon. Hrrmph!"

Anyway, I was in. Uhuh. Right up to my ears.

You've played a Scotch foursome, haven't you? Two men on a side and you play alternate strokes. It's a variation of golf invented to try men's souls, with a perfect record of having busted up more deep and lasting friendships than women. When your partner fluffs the ball into a trap or hooks it into a brier patch and leaves *you* to play it out, you find your love and respect for him cooling rapidly.

Well, there we were, the six of us, on the first tee Sunday afternoon, Hammett all tricked out in white flannels and Angus looking like one of those red-faced Scotchmen they use on whisky ads. Fairfield Greenly was a long, jittery gent with a sour face. When he stood next to A. R. they looked like Mutt and Jeff. Jim Lane was a nice-looking kid with a bony nose and plenty of chin. He had do-or-die written all over his face. I had the shakes. That was our party.

I suppose it was purely by accident that Eleanor Mallow, dressed up in one of those fluffy, pink angora things, wandered over from the practice tee just as we were about to start.

A. R. didn't even speak to Jim on the tee, but just stood there giving him sour looks, with one eye on Eleanor to see that she didn't get too close to him. We won the toss and Jim knelt down to tee up his ball when A. R. barked:

"What do you think you're doing, young man? I'm driving first."

Jim gave him a nice smile. "Sure, Mr. Mallow. I just thought–"

"Hrooomph! I'll do the thinking. Stand back out of my way, now. You, Fowler, stop moving your feet. Everybody quiet, now."

He took a swing like a man with a wasp under his shirt and his pants on fire trying to impale a butterfly on the end of a scythe. The ball flew up into the air and settled in some rose bushes in front of the clubhouse on the right.

"Gaaaa! I hit it perfectly. You put me off, Lane, you and your butting in to drive. I ought to get another one." He turned to Hammett for confirmation, but Sears happened to be looking out the window.

"I'm terribly sorry, sir," Jim began, "I didn't mean–"

"Go on, you old bluffer," Greenly rasped pleasantly. "Get off the tee. You know the rules."

It was going to be a lovely match. And listen. If you don't think Eleanor's black eyes weren't shooting sparks–I'm telling you.

After Angus poled a honey right down the middle, I went over with Jim to inspect the extent of the disaster. It was a nasty lie. The kid laid hold of a number-three iron and whaled. He took out about eighteen dollars' worth of yellow-flowering *Rosa lutea,* but it was a magnificent shot and the ball wound up in the middle of the fairway not more than thirty yards behind Angus's drive.

When we got to it, A. R. glared at it and then at Jim. "Why aren't we up to where they are?" he demanded. "What did you use there, an iron? You should have used a wooden club. Hereafter you consult me what club you're to use. Understand?"

Jim gave him a smile like an angel. "Why, yes, sir. Surely I'll be glad to take yore advice."

Greenly, nervously playing out of turn, twitched at the ball, topping it, but it scuttered along the ground to the edge of the green.

"Of all the luck!" snorted A. R. He had an easy approach, but he shanked the ball off to the right into some knee-high weeds. "Ugh! Ball was lying in a hole. Partner's fault. Couldn't get at it. All right, Lane. What are you staring at? Hit it up onto the green."

The kid did, too, a sweetheart of a niblick out that dropped the ball eight inches from the cup. Angus ran his chip up to within three feet, but Greenly blew the putt. A. R. sank the eight-incher and then looked around as though he had made a hole in one.

"Fine putt, Mr. Mallow," Jim applauded. "We halved them."

"Bah!" snarled A. R. "We could have won the hole if you had played it right. A half isn't good enough."

"I'll try to do better next time, sir." The boy was just like honey. And was William Fowler, Esq., tickled with this brainwork. Lane was right in there pitching for that girl. The only thing that worried me at the moment was how long Eleanor was going to be able to hold out. That girl had spirit, and she was plenty sore.

And she kept getting madder and madder as the match went on until I began to feel pretty rotten at having done that to her and young Jimmy. The farther we went, the worse A. R. got. He griped and squawked and bullied the kid, and when he wasn't picking on Lane personally, he was handing it out to pros in general. Lane just kept on taking it and coming back for more.

Love must be a wonderful thing, because that boy performed miracles. A. R. was making him play woods out of mid-fairway bunkers, misjudging distances to greens and forcing him to use pitch clubs on shots that called for long irons. Once he even made him change his swing. All Lane would do was smile and say:

"Guess you're right, Mr. Mallow. You sure know a lot about golf."

And then I noticed a funny thing when we turned the tenth. Eleanor was still hopping mad, but it wasn't at A. R. any more. It was at Jim. I caught her looking at him and saw her lip curl. After a while she dropped back and walked with Hammett. I thought maybe I'd better say something, so crossing the bridge over the brook at twelve, I stepped alongside and murmured—"That's a shame what Jimmy has to take from A. R., but he's doing a great job. . . ."

She gave me one of those smiles right down from Greenland and said: "If you are referring to Mr. Lane, Mr. Fowler, I haven't the slightest interest in what he is doing."

And four days ago she was in his arms, crying over him. *You* figure 'em out.

The match was a seesaw ding-donger. Luckily Greenly was nervous and almost as bad as Mallow. Angus was playing that smooth, perfect golf that made him Open Champion, and not saying much. Then we hit a bad streak and were three down at the twelfth. A. R. was fit to be tied. "What's the matter, Lane?" he bawled. "Haven't you any guts? That's why you professionals blow up. Yellow!"

I didn't dare look at Eleanor. And for once Jimmy lost his sweet smile and didn't say anything. Luckily, Angus ran into a streak of bad putting and our side picked up three holes in a row before Angus changed their ball and apparently got his touch back.

We went one down on fifteen. I thought we were going to blow another on sixteen when Jimmy hit into a bunker because A. R. made him use an eight iron on a shot that called for a number five. My heart was rattling against my teeth when Mallow went down into the pit. But I have to hand it to A. R. He made the only good stroke of his whole round, and how we needed it there! He swung. The ball sailed out and dropped a foot from the can, for Jim to tap in for the half.

Even old Angus said: "Weel played, sor. A bonnie hit," while Jim beamed: "Splendid, sir. Wonderful shot."

A. R. just glared at the kid and said: "Somebody's got to know how to play this game. I don't need you to tell me when I make a good shot."

But I felt pretty sick when we came to the eighteenth, because we were still one down. We had to win the hole to keep the match alive. A half would mean we were licked. Old Greenly was getting more and more nervous, but I couldn't count on that. Even Eleanor came up close with Hammett to see what would happen.

I would rather not go into details about that eighteenth, but when the smoke cleared away, Fairgreen's ball lay on the green, four inches from the cup in six, for a sure seven. We were on the green too, in five, but about nine feet from the hole. Lane had played the greatest shot I ever saw, with the ball an inch under water at the edge of the pond where Mallow had dumped it.

And it was Mallow's and Greenly's turn to putt.

A. R. marched right up to the ball and began to sight it. I had to give him credit. I didn't know he had that much nerve. Then I heard an unpleasant rasping noise which I identified as the voice of J. Hammett Sears.

"You've got to sink this one, Mallow, old boy!"

A. R. looked up, frowning. "Eh?" he said. "What for? We're five to your six."

J. Sears parted that lemon he uses for a face. "If you miss it, all you can get is a half. We're one up now and that means we win. That's what for."

A. R. turned as white as his collar. "Wha-what? What do you mean?"

Greenly gave a snort like a horse. "It means, you old buzzard, that you've run out of holes. And rubber too. Haw-haw-haw! This is the eighteenth. There aren't any more. If you sink it we play an extra hole. If you don't–" He made that pretty gesture of the finger across the throat.

A lot of the bounce had suddenly gone out of A. R. He stared at the ball, then at the hole and finally at Jim and me. "D-do I really have to s-sink it?" he quavered.

I said: "Guess you do, sir, but Hammett ought to have kept his big mouth shut."

Jim encouraged him. "There's nothing to it, sir. It's a straight putt. Just step right up and knock it into the bucket. The hole looks as big as a washtub."

"Hummmmrf," said A. R. But it wasn't the old Mallow snort any more. It was a plaintive moan that sounded like first cousin to a whine.

Did you ever see a man who is really frightened? Not pretty, is it? That putt meant bucks and more. It meant maybe we were going out of business. And as it finally dawned on him, Argyle Rutherford Mallow began to come apart at the seams.

As he studied the putt he began to shake so his teeth chattered. He turned from white to a beautiful pea-green color. I thought his eyes were going to pop right out of his head. His chest heaved up and down; his knees knocked together. He examined the ball, the grass, the hole, the putter; and the longer he took, the worse he got.

Greenly, Angus, and Hammett had big grins on their faces, but I noticed that Jim Lane wasn't smiling any more as he watched A. R. Instead he had a queer expression on his face, one I had never seen there before.

Days turned into weeks, and weeks into months, and still A. R. hadn't putted. He wiped his sweaty hands. He loosened his collar and walked around. He lit a cigarette, threw it away, and put the match in his mouth. He was quaking so he couldn't hold the putter on the ground.

Gee, nobody wanted to see Mallow and Company win more than I, but I could have cheered at that moment. The Old Man was learning something about golf when the chips are down.

I've talked to the boys. I knew just what he was going through. That hole looked as big as a pea, and a thousand miles away. The close-cropped green was a jungle and every irregularity in the ground was Mount Everest.

Sweat began to pour from his face. All he had to do was tap the ball in a straight line and it would roll into the hole. But what was the line? And how hard to tap it? And how to hit a smooth, even stroke when every nerve in his body was screaming? If he could have done something explosive at that point, like hit a drive, it might have been different. But what was called for was a little bit of a delicate movement. On the complete accuracy and control of that movement everything depended.

A quivering wreck, A. R. tried to line up the putt again. I felt like hollering: "So you want to know why pros blow up in a big-money tournament, do you?" I knew what he was thinking. As long as he hadn't putted, he still had a chance. But if he missed. . . . And he *had* to putt. He saw the ball short, over, past the cup on one side or the other, but never in. Why, oh why did everything–honor, money, victory, or defeat–have to hang on that one damnable movement that he couldn't bring himself to make?

All of a sudden, A. R. gave a horrible groan, closed his eyes, and putted.

Oh, it was a lulu! He took up a foot of turf and the ball moved exactly one inch. Then his legs gave way and he fell right down on his knees while Hammett and Angus MacDonough patted each other's backs and whooped. It was all over.

With a fine disregard for rules, Fairfield Greenly stepped up to tap his four-incher into the cup and addressed it carefully. Nobody stopped him.

*"Easy now, Mr. Greenly!"*

The rasping voice of J. Sears Hammett exploded on the quiet like a concealed four-inch rifle. Greenly jumped as though somebody had stabbed him in the rear and knocked the ball ten feet past the hole.

"Dod blast you for a triple-plated clown!" he roared at Hammett. "Look what you made me do!"

"Mfffff!" mumbled A. R., still on his knees. "You missed! We've got another chance. Come on, Jim. Putt it in. You can do it."

I couldn't figure out what was coming from Jim. He stood there for a moment looking down at A. R. with that queer expression on his face. The he said evenly:

"I cain, Mr. Mallow, but I ain't a-goin' to."

"What? What the devil do you mean?"

Jim turned and gazed at Eleanor for a moment in a sort of sad way and then said to A. R.: "Exactly what I said. I'm not a-goin' to hit thet putt for you. I'm goin back to the clubhouse and leave it lay. Yo're no golfer, no sportsman, no gentleman. Yo're just a disgrace to golf. You been pickin' on me and all the other boys who play the game for you. I'd have taken it if you'd showed the courage of a mouse when the blue chips was down. But you folded up just like an old woman. I don't care for you, or the doggone rubber, or the match, or the job either. An' that's that."

He turned to Eleanor, whose dark eyes were shining like headlamps out of her white face. "Honey, I'm sorry. Lawd knows I love yo' an' tried hard, but I got to go on livin' with myself and lookin' myself in the face. I wasn't made to be a doormat. I jes' had to tell him. I guess it's good-by."

She got to him before he had taken more than three steps. "Darling! Darling! Oh, you're wonderful! I was *so* afraid you *weren't* going to do that. I was simply furious with you for letting him walk all over you. Oh, I adore you now. . . ." Her arms were around his neck. His were pretty busy too.

But that ball of ours was still nine feet from the hole. And A. R. was still kneeling on the green looking like a man who has been hit by lightning.

"Jim darling," Eleanor said suddenly when they had got through making up, "you said everything you had to say. Won't you sink it now–for me?"

Lane walked over to Mallow. Gee, he could look tough. "Is there going to be any more trouble about Eleanor and me?"

The experience of the putt had taken all the fight out of A. R. He just moaned and shook his head.

"Are you ever a-goin' to say again that pros have no guts and are lazy, good-for-nothing–"

"N-no, no, my boy. I was wrong. Pay no attention. Wonderful set of fellows."

"O.K.!" Jim stepped up to the ball, gave it a careless once-over, and tapped it. Boy, I never heard a sweeter sound than it made clattering into the bottom of that can.

"Come on!" I whooped. "We'll get 'em at the next hole."

A. R. got up with a moan. His knees were still shaking. "Another hole. Don't know if I can make it. All unstrung. Terrible experience."

J. Sears Hammett stepped forward. His voice dropped oil and treacle. He said: "I think I can spare you that trouble, Mallow, old boy. I claim that match and the bet for Fairgreen."

"You *what*? What are you talking about?"

Hammett looked at A. R. coldly. "You know the terms of the bet. Play your own equipment. The fine shot you hit out of that bunker on sixteen was made with that Fairgreen Shoor-Out sand wedge I gave you last Wednesday. Here it is in your bag."

Smart old Fowler! Will I never learn that J. Sears Hammett always has an edge? I had forgotten all about the Fairgreen club that louse had planted on A. R. We were sunk!

Mallow turned on Hammett and shouted: "You are a villain, sir. I trusted you–" when Jim Lane cut him short.

"Skip it, A. R. And you too, Hammett. If you're going to stick that close to the terms of the bet we'll jes' cancel it out. Angus MacDonough there has been playing the A. R. Mallow Thunderbolt ball for the last six holes."

Did we make a dive for those golf balls! It was true. They were both Thunderbolts. A. R. looked at Jim Lane with a new respect in his eyes.

Now it was Greenly's turn to scream. "MacDonough! What the devil does this mean? I pay you to play with–"

Friends, there was mutiny in the air. Angus cut Greenly off with a cold stare. "It means, sor, that I canna play wi' you blosted ball. Thot domned diamond chip rottlin' aroond inside it makes me nairvous, and ye can take it or leave it. As for your bet–"

"Hah!" I yelled. "The bet!" They weren't going to keep William Fowler, Esq., out of the insurrection if it cost me my job. And all that squawking about sticking to the terms of the bet had popped off an idea in my skull.

"The bet! It's all over. The terms of the match were eighteen holes. Well, you've played eighteen and you're even. Nothing was said about extra holes. Outside of being the two lousiest golfers in the world, you're a couple of old foofs trying to cut each other's throats for a little bit of rubber at a time when we all ought to be pulling together and trying to help each other out. Go on, shake hands, you two, and let's get out of here."

The pair of them looked just like a couple of kids caught in the cookie jar. A. R. heaved a sigh of relief like the Overland Limited blowing off steam.

"Gad!" he said. "Damned relieved. Couldn't play another stroke."

"Whew!" grunted Greenly. "Neither could I." They shook.

"Fowler," said A. R., "proud of you. You're a genius. I'll buy a drink."

"You bet you will," I said.

It wasn't that I was still being fresh. It just made me so darned happy to see Jim and Eleanor, their arms around each other, disappearing past the corner of the clubhouse.

*This is the third story in the book by the bard of the links, P. G. Wodehouse. It contains ingredients often found in his stories: golf and love, plus narration by the "Oldest Member of the club." Wodehouse once jokingly wrote, "Love has a lot of press-agentry from the oldest times; but there are higher, nobler things than love. A woman is only a woman, but a hefty drive is a slosh." Wodehouse was mad about golf even though his handicap never fell below eighteen. This story originally appeared in* McClure's *magazine.*

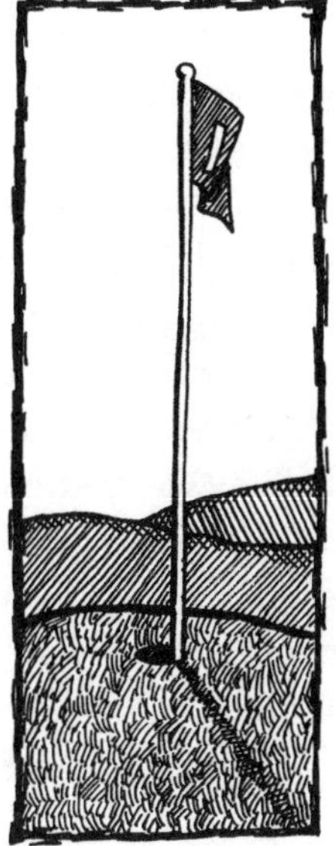

*P. G. Wodehouse*

# SUNDERED HEARTS (1920)

IN THE SMOKING-ROOM OF THE club-house a cheerful fire was burning, and the Oldest Member glanced from time to time out of the window into the gathering dusk. Snow was falling lightly on the links. From where he sat, the Oldest Member had a good view of the ninth green; and presently, out of the greyness of the December evening, there appeared over the brow of the hill a golf-ball. It trickled across the green and stopped within a yard of the hole. The Oldest Member nodded approvingly. A good approach-shot.

A young man in a tweed suit clambered on to the green, holed out with easy confidence, and, shouldering his bag, made his way to the club-house. A few moments later he entered the smoking-room, and uttered an exclamation of rapture at the sight of the fire.

"I'm frozen stiff!"

He rang for the waiter and ordered a hot drink. The Oldest Member gave a gracious assent to the suggestion that he should join him.

"I like playing in winter," said the young man. "You get the course to yourself, for the world is full of slackers who only turn out when the weather suits them. I cannot understand where they get the nerve to call themselves golfers."

"Not everyone is as keen as you are, my boy," said the Sage, dipping gratefully into his hot drink. "If they were, the world would be a better place, and we should hear less of all this modern unrest."

"I *am* pretty keen," admitted the young man.

"I have only encountered one man whom I could describe as keener. I allude to Mortimer Sturgis."

"The fellow who took up golf at thirty-eight and let the girl he was engaged to marry go off with someone else because he hadn't the time to combine golf with courtship? I remember. You were telling me about him the other day."

"There is a sequel to that story, if you would care to hear it," said the Oldest Member.

"You have the honour," said the young man. "Go ahead!"

Some people (began the Oldest Member) considered that Mortimer Sturgis was too wrapped up in golf, and blamed him for it. I could never see eye to eye with them. In the days of King Arthur nobody thought the worse of a young knight if he suspended all his social and business engagements in favour of a search for the Holy Grail. In the Middle Ages a man could devote his whole life to the Crusades, and the public fawned upon him. Why, then, blame the man of today for a zealous attention to the modern equivalent, the Quest of Scratch! Mortimer Sturgis never became a scratch player, but he did eventually get his handicap down to nine, and I honour him for it.

The story which I am about to tell begins in what might be called the middle period of Sturgis's career. He had reached the stage when his handicap was a wobbly twelve; and, as you are no doubt aware, it is then that a man really begins to golf in the true sense of the word. Mortimer's fondness for the game until then had been merely tepid compared with what it became now. He had played a little before, but now he really buckled to and got down to it. It was at this point, too, that he began once more to entertain thoughts of marriage. A profound statistician in this one department, he had discovered that practically all the finest exponents of the art are married men; and the thought that there might be something in the holy state which improved a man's game, and that he was missing a good thing, troubled him a great deal. Moreover, the paternal instinct had awakened in him. As he justly pointed out, whether marriage improved your game or not, it was to Old Tom Morris's marriage that the existence of young Tommy Morris, winner of the British Open Championship four times in succession, could be directly traced. In fact, at the age of forty-two, Mortimer Sturgis was in just the frame of mind to take some nice girl aside and ask her to become a step-mother to his eleven drivers, his baffy, his twenty-eight putters, and the rest of the ninety-four clubs which he had accumulated in the course of his golfing career. The sole stipulation, of course, which he made when dreaming his day-dreams, was that the future Mrs. Sturgis must be a golfer. I can still recall the horror in his face when one girl, admirable in other respects, said that she had never heard of Harry Vardon, and didn't he mean Dolly Vardon? She has since proved an excellent wife and mother, but Mortimer Sturgis never spoke to her again.

With the coming of January, it was Mortimer's practice to leave England and go to the South of France, where there was sunshine and crisp dry turf. He pursued his usual custom this year. With his suit-case and his ninety-four clubs he went off to Saint Brüle, staying as he always did at the Hôtel Superbe, where they knew him, and treated with an amiable tolerance his habit of practising chip-shots in his bedroom. On the first evening, after breaking a statuette of the Infant Samuel in Prayer, he dressed and went down to dinner. And the first thing he saw was Her.

Mortimer Sturgis, as you know, had been engaged before, but Betty

Weston had never inspired the tumultuous rush of emotion which the mere sight of this girl set loose in him. He told me later that just to watch her holing out her soup gave him a sort of feeling you get when your drive collides with a rock in the middle of a tangle of rough and kicks back into the middle of the fairway. If golf had come late in life to Mortimer Sturgis, love came later still, and just as the golf, attacking him in middle life, had been some golf, so was the love considerable love. Mortimer finished his dinner in a trance, which is the best way to do it at some hotels, and then scoured the place for someone who would introduce him. He found such a person eventually and the meeting took place.

She was a small and rather fragile-looking girl, with big blue eyes and a cloud of golden hair. She had a sweet expression, and her left wrist was in a sling. She looked up at Mortimer as if she had at last found something that amounted to something. I am inclined to think it was a case of love at first sight on both sides.

"Fine weather we're having," said Mortimer, who was a capital conversationalist.

"Yes," said the girl.

"I like fine weather."

"So do I."

"There's something about fine weather!"

"Yes,"

"It's–it's–well, fine weather's so much finer than weather that isn't fine," said Mortimer.

He looked at the girl a little anxiously, fearing he might be taking her out of her depth, but she seemed to have followed his train of thought perfectly.

"Yes, isn't it?" she said. "It's so–so fine."

"That's just what I meant," said Mortimer. "So fine. You've just hit it."

He was charmed. The combination of beauty with intelligence is so rare.

"I see you've hurt your wrist," he went on, pointing to the sling.

"Yes. I strained it a little playing in the championship."

"The championship?" Mortimer was interested. "It's awfully rude of me," he said, apologetically, "but I didn't catch your name just now."

"My name is Somerset."

Mortimer had been bending forward solicitously. He overbalanced and nearly fell off his chair. The shock had been stunning. Even before he had met and spoken to her, he had told himself that he loved this girl with the stored-up love of a lifetime. And she was Mary Somerset! The hotel lobby danced before Mortimer's eyes.

The name will, of course, be familiar to you. In the early rounds of the Ladies' Open Golf Championship of that year nobody had paid much attention to Mary Somerset. She had survived her first two matches, but her opponents had been nonentities like herself. And then, in the third round, she had met and defeated the champion. From that point on, her name was on everybody's lips. She became favourite. And she justified the public confidence by sailing into the final and winning easily. And here she was, talking to him like an ordinary person, and, if he could read the message in her eyes, not altogether indifferent to his charms, if you could call them that.

"Golly!" said Mortimer, awed.

Their friendship ripened rapidly, as friendships do in the South of France. In that favoured clime, you find the girl and Nature does the rest. On the second morning of their acquaintance Mortimer invited her to walk round the links with him and watch him play. He did it a little diffidently, for his golf was not of the calibre that would be likely to extort admiration from a champion. On the other hand, one should never let slip the opportunity of acquiring wrinkles on the game, and he thought that Miss Somerset, if she watched one or two of his shots, might tell him just what he ought to do. And sure enough, the opening arrived on the fourth hole, where Mortimer, after a drive which surprised even himself, found his ball in a nasty cuppy lie.

He turned to the girl.

"What ought I to do here?" he asked.

Miss Somerset looked at the ball. She seemed to be weighing the matter in her mind.

"Give it a good hard knock," she said.

Mortimer knew what she meant. She was advocating a full iron. The only trouble was that, when he tried anything more ambitious than a half-swing, except off the tee, he almost invariably topped. However, he could not fail this wonderful girl, so he swung well back and took a chance. His enterprise was rewarded. The ball flew out of the indentation in the turf as cleanly as though John Henry Taylor had been behind it, and rolled, looking neither to left nor to right, straight for the pin. A few moments later Mortimer Sturgis had holed out one under bogey, and it was only the fear that, having known him for so short a time, she might be startled and refuse him that kept him from proposing then and there. This exhibition of golfing generalship on her part had removed his last doubts. He knew that, if he lived for ever, there could be no other girl in the world for him. With her at his side, what might he not do? He might get his handicap down to six–to three–to scratch–to plus something! Good heavens, why, even the Amateur Championship was not outside the range of possibility. Mortimer Sturgis shook his putter solemnly in the air, and vowed a silent vow that he would win this pearl among women.

Now, when a man feels like that, it is impossible to restrain him long. For a week Mortimer Sturgis's soul sizzled within him: then he could contain himself no longer. One night, at one of the informal dances at the hotel, he drew the girl out on to the moonlit terrace.

"Miss Somerset–" he began, stuttering with emotion like an imperfectly corked bottle of ginger-beer. "Miss Somerset–may I call you Mary?"

The girl looked at him with eyes that shone softly in the dim light.

"Mary?" she repeated. "Why, of course, if you like–"

"If I like!" cried Mortimer. "Don't you know that it is my dearest wish? Don't you know that I would rather be permitted to call you Mary than do the first hole at Muirfield in two? Oh, Mary, how I have longed for this moment! I love you! I love you! Ever since I met you I have known that you were the one girl in this vast world whom I would die to win! Mary, will you be mine? Shall we go round together? Will you fix up a match with me on the links of life which shall end only when the Grim Reaper lays us both a stymie?"

She drooped towards him.

"Mortimer!" she murmured.

He held out his arms, then drew back. His face had grown suddenly tense, and there were lines of pain about his mouth.

"Wait!" he said, in a strained voice. "Mary, I love you dearly, and because I love you so dearly I cannot let you trust your sweet life to me blindly. I have a confession to make. I am not–I have not always been"–he paused–"a good man," he said, in a low voice.

She started indignantly.

"How can you say that? You are the best, the kindest, the bravest man I have ever met! Who but a good man would have risked his life to save me from drowning?"

"Drowning?" Mortimer's voice seemed perplexed. "You? What do you mean?"

"Have you forgotten the time when I fell in the sea last week, and you jumped in with all your clothes on–"

"Of course, yes," said Mortimer. "I remember now. It was the day I did the long seventh in five. I got off a good tee-shot straight down the fairway, took a baffy for my second, and–But that is not the point. It is sweet and generous of you to think so highly of what was the merest commonplace act of ordinary politeness, but I must repeat, that judged by the standards of your snowy purity, I am not a good man. I do not come to you clean and spotless as a young girl should expect her husband to come to her. Once, playing in a foursome, my ball fell in some long grass. Nobody was near me. We had no caddies, and the others were on the fairway. God knows–" His voice shook. "God knows I struggled against the temptation. But I fell. I kicked the ball on to a little bare mound, from which it was an easy task with a nice half-mashie to reach the green for a snappy seven. Mary, there have been times when, going round by myself, I have allowed myself ten-foot putts on three holes in succession, simply in order to be able to say I had done the course in under a hundred. Ah! You shrink from me! You are disgusted!"

"I'm not disgusted! And I don't shrink! I only shivered because it is rather cold."

"Then you can love me in spite of my past?"

"Mortimer!"

She fell into his arms.

"My dearest," he said presently, "what a happy life ours will be. That is, if you do not find that you have made a mistake."

"A mistake!" she cried, scornfully.

"Well, my handicap is twelve, you know, and not so darned twelve at that. There are days when I play my second from the fairway of the next hole but one, days when I couldn't putt into a coal-hole with 'Welcome!' written over it. And you are a Ladies' Open Champion. Still, if you think it's all right–. Oh, Mary, you little know how I have dreamed of some day marrying a really first-class golfer! Yes, that was my vision–of walking up the aisle with some sweet plus two girl on my arm. You shivered again. You are catching cold."

"It is a little cold," said the girl. She spoke in a small voice.

"Let me take you in, sweetheart," said Mortimer. "I'll just put you in a comfortable chair with a nice cup of coffee, and then I think I really must come out again and tramp about and think how perfectly splendid everything is."

They were married a few weeks later, very quietly, in the little village church of Saint Brüle. The secretary of the local golf-club acted as best man for Mortimer, and a girl from the hotel was the only bridesmaid. The whole business was rather a disappointment to Mortimer, who had planned out a somewhat florid ceremony at St. George's, Hanover Square, with the Vicar of Tooting (a scratch player excellent at short approach shots) officiating, and "The Voice That Breathed O'er St. Andrews" booming from the organ. He had even had the idea of copying the military wedding and escorting his bride out of the church under an arch of crossed cleeks. But she would have none of this pomp. She insisted on a quiet wedding, and for the honeymoon trip preferred a tour through Italy. Mortimer, who had wanted to go to Scotland to visit the birthplace of James Braid, yielded amiably, for he loved her dearly. But he did not think much of Italy. In Rome, the great monuments of the past left him cold. Of the Temples of Vespasian, all he thought was that it would be a devil of a place to be bunkered behind. The Colosseum aroused a faint spark of interest in him, as he speculated whether Abe Mitchell would use a full brassey to carry it. In Florence, the view over the Tuscan Hills from the Torre Rosa, Fiesole, over which his bride waxed enthusiastic, seemed to him merely a nasty bit of rough which would take a deal of getting out of.

And so, in the fullness of time, they came home to Mortimer's cosy little house adjoining the links.

Mortimer was so busy polishing his ninety-four clubs on the evening of their arrival that he failed to notice that his wife was preoccupied. A less busy man would have perceived at a glance that she was distinctly nervous. She started at sudden noises, and once, when he tried the newest of his mashie-niblicks and broke one of the drawing-room windows, she screamed sharply. In short her manner was strange, and, if Edgar Allan Poe had put her into "The Fall of the House of Usher," she would have fitted it like the paper on the wall. She had the air of one waiting tensely for the approach of some imminent doom. Mortimer, humming gaily to himself as he sand-papered the blade of his twenty-second putter, observed nothing of this. He was thinking of the morrow's play.

"Your wrist's quite well again now, darling, isn't it?" he said.

"Yes. Yes, quite well."

"Fine!" said Mortimer. "We'll breakfast early–say at half-past seven–and then we'll be able to get in a couple of rounds before lunch. A couple more in the afternoon will about see us through. One doesn't want to over-golf oneself the first day." He swung the putter joyfully. "How had we better play do you think? We might start with you giving me a half."

She did not speak. She was very pale. She clutched the arm of her chair tightly till the knuckles showed white under the skin.

To anybody but Mortimer her nervousness would have been even more obvious on the following morning, as they reached the first tee. Her eyes were dull and heavy, and she started when a grasshopper chirruped. But Mortimer was too occupied with thinking how jolly it was having the course to themselves to notice anything.

He scooped some sand out of the box, and took a ball out of her bag. His wedding present to her had been a brand-new golf-bag, six dozen balls, and a full set of the most expensive clubs, all born in Scotland.

"Do you like a high tee?" he asked.

"Oh, no," she replied, coming with a start out of her thoughts. "Doctors say it's indigestible."

Mortimer laughed merrily.

"Deuced good!" he chuckled. "Is that your own or did you read it in a comic paper? There you are!" He placed the ball on a little hill of sand, and got up. "Now let's see some of that championship form of yours!"

She burst into tears.

"My darling!"

Mortimer ran to her and put his arms round her. She tried weakly to push him away.

"My angel! What is it?"

She sobbed brokenly. Then, with an effort, she spoke.

"Mortimer, I have deceived you!"

"Deceived me?"

"I have never played golf in my life! I don't even know how to hold the caddie!"

Mortimer's heart stood still. This sounded like the gibberings of an unbalanced mind, and no man likes his wife to begin gibbering immediately after the honeymoon.

"My precious! You are not yourself!"

"I am! That's the whole trouble! I'm myself and not the girl you thought I was!"

Mortimer stared at her, puzzled. He was thinking that it was a little difficult and that, to work it out properly, he would need a pencil and a bit of paper.

"My name is not Mary!"

"But you said it was."

"I didn't. You asked if you could call me Mary, and I said you might, because I loved you too much to deny your smallest whim. I was going on to say that it wasn't my name, but you interrupted me."

"Not Mary!" The horrid truth was coming home to Mortimer. "You were not Mary Somerset?"

"Mary is my cousin. My name is Mabel."

"But you said you had sprained your wrist playing in the championship."

"So I had. The mallet slipped in my hand."

"The mallet!" Mortimer clutched at his forehead. "You didn't say 'the mallet'?"

"Yes, Mortimer! The mallet!"

A faint blush of shame mantled her cheek, and into her blue eyes there came a look of pain, but she faced him bravely.

"I am the Ladies' Open Croquet Champion!" she whispered.

Mortimer Sturgis cried aloud, a cry that was like the shriek of some wounded animal.

"Croquet!" He gulped, and stared at her with unseeing eyes. He was no prude, but he had those decent prejudices of which no self-respecting man can wholly rid himself, however broad-minded he may try to be. "Croquet!"

There was a long silence. The light breeze sang in the pines above them. The grasshoppers chirruped at their feet.

She began to speak again in a low, monotonous voice.

"I blame myself! I should have told you before, while there was yet time for you to withdraw. I should have confessed this to you that night on the terrace in the moonlight. But you swept me off my feet, and I was in your arms before I realized what you would think of me. It was only then that I understood what my supposed skill at golf meant to you, and then it was too late. I loved you too much to let you go! I could not bear the thought of you recoiling from me. Oh, I was mad–mad! I knew that I could not keep up the deception for ever, that you must find me out in time. But I had a wild hope that by then we should be so close to one another that you might find it in your heart to forgive. But I was wrong. I see it now. There are some things that no man can forgive. Some things," she repeated, dully, "which no man can forgive."

She turned away. Mortimer awoke from his trance.

"Stop!" he cried. "Don't go!"

"I must go."

"I want to talk this over."

She shook her head sadly and started to walk slowly across the sunlit grass. Mortimer watched her, his brain in a whirl of chaotic thoughts. She disappeared through the trees.

Mortimer sat down on the tee-box, and buried his face in his hands. For a time he could think of nothing but the cruel blow he had received. This was the end of those rainbow visions of himself and her going through life side by side, she lovingly criticizing his stance and his back-swing, he learning wisdom from her. A croquet-player! He was married to a woman who hit coloured balls through hoops. Mortimer Sturgis writhed in torment. A strong man's agony.

The mood passed. How long it had lasted, he did not know. But suddenly, as he sat there, he became once more aware of the glow of the sunshine and the singing of the birds. It was as if a shadow had lifted. Hope and optimism crept into his heart.

He loved her. He loved her still. She was part of him, and nothing that she could do had power to alter that. She had deceived him, yes. But why had she deceived him? Because she loved him so much that she could not bear to lose him. Dash it all, it was a bit of a compliment.

And, after all, poor girl, was it her fault? Was it not rather the fault of her upbringing? Probably she had been taught to play croquet when a mere child, hardly able to distinguish right from wrong. No steps had been taken to eradicate the virus from her system, and the thing had become chronic. Could she be blamed? Was she not more to be pitied than censured?

Mortimer rose to his feet, his heart swelling with generous forgiveness. The black horror had passed from him. The future seemed once more bright. It was not too late. She was still young, many years younger than he himself had been when he took up golf, and surely, if she put herself into the hands of a good specialist and practised every day, she might still hope to become a fair player. He reached the house and ran in, calling her name.

No answer came. He sped from room to room, but all were empty.

She had gone. The house was there. The furniture was there. The canary sang in its cage, the cook in the kitchen. The pictures still hung on the walls. But she had gone. Everything was at home except his wife.

Finally, propped up against the cup he had once won in a handicap competition, he saw a letter. With a sinking heart he tore open the envelope.

It was a pathetic, a tragic letter, the letter of a woman endeavouring to express all the anguish of a torn heart with one of those fountain-pens which suspend the flow of ink about twice in every three words. The gist of it was that she felt she had wronged him; that, though he might forgive, he could never forget; and that she was going away, away out into the world alone.

Mortimer sank into a chair, and stared blankly before him. She had scratched the match.

I am not a married man myself, so have had no experience of how it feels to have one's wife whiz off silently into the unknown; but I should imagine that it must be something like taking a full swing with a brassey and missing the ball. Something, I take it, of the same sense of mingled shock, chagrin, and the feeling that nobody loves one, which attacks a man in such circumstances, must come to the bereaved husband. And one can readily understand how terribly the incident must have shaken Mortimer Sturgis. I was away at the time, but I am told by those who saw him that his game went all to pieces.

He had never shown much indication of becoming anything in the nature of a first-class golfer, but he had managed to acquire one or two decent shots. His work with the light iron was not at all bad, and he was a fairly steady putter. But now, under the shadow of this tragedy, he dropped right back to the form of his earliest period. It was a pitiful sight to see this gaunt, haggard man with the look of dumb anguish behind his spectacles taking as many as three shots sometimes to get past the ladies' tee. His slice, of which he had almost cured himself, returned with such virulence that in the list of ordinary hazards he had now to include the tee-box. And, when he was not slicing, he was pulling. I have heard that he was known, when driving at the sixth, to get bunkered in his own caddie, who had taken up his position directly behind him. As for the deep sand-trap in front of the seventh green, he spent so much of his time in it that there was some informal talk among the members of the committee of charging him a small weekly rent.

A man of comfortable independent means, he lived during these days on next to nothing. Golf-balls cost him a certain amount, but the bulk of his income he spent in efforts to discover his wife's whereabouts. He advertised in all the papers. He employed private detectives. He even, much as it revolted his finer instincts, took to travelling about the country, watching croquet matches. But she was never among the players. I am not sure that he did not find a melancholy comfort in this, for it seemed to show that, whatever his wife might be and whatever she might be doing, she had not gone right under.

Summer passed. Autumn came and went. Winter arrived. The days grew bleak and chill, and an early fall of snow, heavier than had been known at that time of the year for a long while, put an end to golf. Mortimer spent his days indoors, staring gloomily through the window at the white mantle that covered the earth.

It was Christmas Eve.

The young man shifted uneasily on his seat. His face was long and sombre.

"All this is very depressing," he said.

"These soul tragedies," agreed the Oldest Member, "are never very cheery."

"Look here," said the young man, firmly, "tell me one thing frankly, as man to man. Did Mortimer find her dead in the snow, covered except for her face, on which still lingered that faint, sweet smile which he remembered so well? Because, if he did, I'm going home."

"No, no," protested the Oldest Member. "Nothing of that kind."

"You're sure? You aren't going to spring it on me suddenly?"

"No, no!"

The young man breathed a relieved sigh.

"It was your saying that about the white mantle covering the earth that made me suspicious."

The Sage resumed.

It was Christmas Eve. All day the snow had been falling, and now it lay thick and deep over the countryside. Mortimer Sturgis, his frugal dinner concluded–what with losing his wife and not being able to get any golf, he had little appetite these days–was sitting in his drawing-room, moodily polishing the blade of his jigger. Soon wearying of this once congenial task, he laid down the club and went to the front door to see if there was any chance of a thaw. But no. It was freezing. The snow, as he tested it with his shoe, crackled crisply. The sky above was black and full of cold stars. It seemed to Mortimer that the sooner he packed up and went to the South of France, the better. He was just about to close the door, when suddenly he thought he heard his own name called.

"Mortimer!"

Had he been mistaken? The voice had sounded faint and far away.

"Mortimer!"

He thrilled from head to foot. This time there could be no mistake. It was the voice he knew so well, his wife's voice, and it had come from somewhere down near the garden-gate. It is difficult to judge distance where sounds are concerned, but Mortimer estimated that the voice had spoken about a short mashie-niblick and an easy putt from where he stood.

The next moment he was racing down the snow-covered path. And then his heart stood still. What was that dark something on the ground just inside the gate? He leaped towards it. He passed his hands over it. It was a human body. Quivering, he struck a match. It went out. He struck another. That went out, too. He struck a third, and it burnt with a steady flame; and, stooping, he saw that it was his wife who lay there, cold and stiff. Her eyes were closed, and on her face still lingered that faint, sweet smile which he remembered so well.

The young man rose with a set face. He reached for his golf-bag.

"I call that a dirty trick," he said, "after you promised–" The Sage waved him back to his seat.

"Have no fear! She had only fainted."

"You said she was cold."

"Wouldn't you be cold if you were lying in the snow?"

"And stiff."

"Mrs. Sturgis was stiff because the train-service was bad, it being the holiday-season, and she had had to walk all the way from the junction, a distance of eight miles. Sit down and allow me to proceed."

Tenderly, reverently, Mortimer Sturgis picked her up and began to bear her into the house. Half-way there, his foot slipped on a piece of ice and he fell heavily, barking his shin and shooting his lovely burden out on to the snow.

The fall brought her to. She opened her eyes.

"Mortimer, darling!" she said.

Mortimer had just been going to say something else, but he checked himself.

"Are you alive?" he asked.

"Yes," she replied.

"Thank God!" said Mortimer, scooping some of the snow out of the back of his collar.

Together they went into the house, and into the drawing-room. Wife gazed at husband, husband at wife. There was a silence.

"Rotten weather!" said Mortimer.

"Yes, isn't it!"

The spell was broken. They fell into each other's arms. And presently they were sitting side by side on the sofa, holding hands, just as if that awful parting had been but a dream.

It was Mortimer who made the first reference to it.

"I say, you know," he said, "you oughtn't to have nipped away like that!"

"I thought you hated me!"

"Hated *you*! I love you better than life itself! I would sooner have smashed my pet driver than have had you leave me!"

She thrilled at the words.

"Darling!"

Mortimer fondled her hand.

"I was just coming back to tell you that I loved you still. I was going to suggest that you took lessons from some good professional. And I found you gone!"

"I wasn't worthy of you, Mortimer!"

"My angel!" He pressed his lips to her hair, and spoke solemnly. "All this has taught me a lesson, dearest. I knew all along, and I know it more than ever now, that it is you–you that I want. Just you! I don't care if you don't play golf. I don't care–" He hesitated, then went on manfully. "I don't care even if you play croquet, so long as you are with me!"

For a moment her face showed rapture that made it almost angelic. She uttered a low moan of ecstasy. She kissed him. Then she rose.

"Mortimer, look!"

"What at?

"Me. Just look!"

The jigger which he had been polishing lay on a chair close by. She took it up. From the bowl of golf-balls on the mantelpiece she selected a brand new one. She placed it on the carpet. She addressed it. Then, with a merry cry of "Fore!" she drove it hard and straight through the glass of the china-cupboard.

"Good God!" cried Mortimer, astounded. It had been a bird of a shot.

She turned to him, her whole face alight with that beautiful smile.

"When I left you, Mortie," she said, "I had but one aim in life, somehow to make myself worthy of you. I saw your advertisements in the papers, and I longed to answer them, but I was not ready. All this long, weary while I have been in the village of Auchtermuchtie, in Scotland, studying under Tamms McMickle."

"Not the Tamms McMickle who finished fourth in the Open Championship of 1911, and had the best ball in the foursome in 1912 with Jock McHaggis, Andy McHeather, and Sandy McHoots!"

"Yes, Mortimer, the very same. Oh, it was difficult at first. I missed my mallet, and longed to steady the ball with my foot and use the toe of the club. Wherever there was a direction post I aimed at it automatically. But I conquered my weakness. I practised steadily. And now Mr. McMickle says my handicap would be a good twenty-four on any links." She smiled apologetically. "Of course, that doesn't sound much to you! You were a twelve when I left you, and now I suppose you are down to eight or something."

Mortimer shook his head.

"Alas, no!" he replied, gravely. "My game went right off for some reason or other, and I'm twenty-four, too."

"For some reason or other!" She uttered a cry. "Oh, I know what the reason was! How can I ever forgive myself! I have ruined your game!"

The brightness came back to Mortimer's eyes. He embraced her fondly.

"Do not reproach yourself, dearest," he murmured. "It is the best thing that could have happened. From now on, we start level, two hearts that beat as one, two drivers that drive as one. I could not wish it otherwise. By George! It's just like that thing of Tennyson's."

He recited the lines softly:

*My bride,*
*My wife, my life. Oh, we will walk the links*
*Yoked in all exercise of noble end,*
*And so thro' those dark bunkers off the course*
*That no man knows. Indeed, I love thee: come,*
*Yield thyself up: our handicaps are one;*
*Accomplish thou my manhood and thyself;*
*Lay thy sweet hands in mine and trust to me.*

She laid her hands in his.

"And now, Mortie, darling," she said, "I want to tell you all about how I did the long twelfth at Auchtermuchtie in one under bogey."

*While this is the newest story in the book, it is one of the oldest in terms of setting. It features one of the greatest of all detectives, the magnificent Sherlock Holmes. Along with his boon companion Watson, Holmes travels to the ancient links at St. Andrews to solve a mystery. Whodunit? And why? It's a story that Holmes' creator, Arthur Conan Doyle, would have been proud of. Author Merrell Noden has been writing since 1986 for* Sports Illustrated, *where this story first appeared. He's a 15 handicap golfer who has played at St. Andrews and other famous Scottish courses. Noden lives with his wife and young daughter in New York City.*

*Merrell Noden*

# THE ADVENTURE OF THE TREACHEROUS TRAPS (1995)

"OF ALL THE FRIVOLOUS ACTIVITIES we supposedly higher apes have devised in the name of entertainment, surely there is none as silly as golf," declared my friend Sherlock Holmes one day. "Why a man who is free to do so many things would choose to spend the better part of a day striking and then hunting down a small ball is a mystery beyond even my powers to solve."

Although Holmes had never made a secret of his disdain for athletic competition, which he deemed a pointless expenditure of energy, the bitterness of his outburst took me by surprise. We were in our Baker Street chambers, I with a book, while he lay motionless on the divan in a posture of utter lassitude. It was the summer of 1895, and we had just completed one of the busiest periods in Holmes's great career. In the past few months he had brought to a halt the curious harassment of Miss Violet Smith, the "solitary cyclist" of Charlington, and had traveled to the Continent at the request of Leo XII to investigate the mysterious death of Cardinal Tosca. Soon, Holmes would put his considerable talent for disguise to good use in solving the case of Black Peter. I knew from experience that gloomy depressions often followed periods of intense excitement, so I did not despair.

"I see you have been reading the *Times*' preview of the upcoming Open championship," I remarked as casually as possible.

"Bravo, Watson!" said Holmes, leaping to his feet. "You know my methods well. You've noted a fact–that I've offered my opinion of golf, which is rather low. You've combined it with another fact, namely that I retrieved the paper from our doorstep not an hour ago. And from the two you have drawn a quite reasonable inference, albeit a rudimentary one. I have been reading the *Times'* piece on the Open. It. . . ."

But before he could finish, a knock came at the door. Poking her head around the corner, Mrs. Hudson said, "There's a gentleman to see you, sir. Says it's most urgent."

It must indeed have been urgent, for no sooner had she spoken this word than a young gentleman stepped into the room. From his demeanor, it was impossible not to receive the impression that he was being eaten alive by his own nerves. He was a good four inches under six feet, I would judge, with sandy-brown hair and a stocky build. He wore a neatly trimmed mustache and a tweed suit, and he seemed utterly incapable of standing still.

"I'm terribly sorry to intrude," said our visitor, his eyes darting from one of us to the other. "But I must speak to Mr. Sherlock Holmes."

"I am Sherlock Holmes. Please sit down," said my friend, gesturing to a chair while he studied our visitor keenly. "How are things at Westward Ho!? I trust you've worked the kinks out of your sand game?"

I thought our poor visitor would collapse. "This is astonishing," he said, recovering himself. "My accent, I suppose, identifies me as Devonian. But how can you possibly know that I am a golfer and have been working these past few weeks at the Westward Ho! club on improving my sand game?"

Holmes smiled. "Westward Ho! is the only real course in the west country. I took an educated guess. And as to the sand, when you sat down a few grains of sand fell from your trouser cuffs." Holmes stooped to examine the floor. "Here they are on the rug. I am the author of a small monograph on the 17 distinct types of sand found from Land's End to John o' Groat's. This sand is of the fine variety quarried in Cornwall and used predominantly in golf-course bunkers in that area. You are either an extraordinarily bad golfer, or an extremely diligent one who has spent the morning standing ankle deep in the stuff, practicing."

"Truly, Mr. Holmes, your reputation scarcely does you justice," said our visitor. "It is true: The bunker shot, which used to be the one constant in my game, has deserted me. I hit 100 balls at the club this morning and then raced to catch my train. I've just arrived on the 10:08 from Barnstaple, and I mean to leave London today for Edinburgh and thence for St. Andrews, where I am to play in the Open. I am the defender, having won the title last summer at Sandwich."

"My congratulations," Holmes said to Taylor. "But I'm sure it is not for the purpose of advertising your prowess as a golfer that you've come to consult me."

"To tell the truth, Mr. Holmes, I do not know whether the matter that brings me to you is worthy of your attention. I don't know whether it's a mystery–or just a silly prank. My name is John Henry Taylor, though in the golf world I am known as just J. H. I am 24 years old and, as you have already divined, I am from Devon. I was born in Northam, a tiny village on the north coast. My father was a laborer, a proud man who worked himself to death while I was still a boy.

"Though he left me little in the way of material gifts, he was more than generous in providing me with a large dose of ambition. Not far from my home was Westward Ho!, the cliffside premises of the Royal North Devon Golf Club. I learned from a friend that the club was always on the lookout for trustworthy lads to caddie for the members on weekends. I applied and was accepted.

"One of my regulars–at least when he was down from Oxford–was Horace Hutchinson, the amateur champion. Mr. Horace was a kind man. He would always allow me to borrow a club or two while he ate lunch or had a drink with his mates. We caddies regularly conducted our own fierce little tournaments behind the caddie hut, and before long I was the most proficient player among the caddies.

"Yet for some reason–perhaps because I had my poor father's example always before me–I could not bring myself to think of golf as work. So in those first few years of my professional life, I sampled other kinds of employment. I was a gardener's boy for three years, then a mason's laborer, carrying bricks and mortar up ladders for 15 shillings a week. I tried repeatedly to enlist in the army, but was rejected for poor eyesight and flat feet. I was turned down by the navy, as well, and was too short for the police. Finally all these rejections and false starts pointed me to one inescapable conclusion: Golf was the life I was meant for. There was no fighting it.

"With my own reservations at last quelled, I returned to the game with a new fervor. By the time the first working man's club in England was founded at Northam in North Devon seven years ago, I was playing off scratch and had the great honor of beating Mr. Horace 3 and 2. I began to travel to matches at clubs in Somerset, Cornwall and Hampshire and, what's more, to win them.

"Two years ago, when the Open was held at Prestwick, I began the tournament by playing as well as I ever had. I was out in 35, and not only was my 75 the first-round leader, it was a course record and gave me a three-stroke advantage. I think the excitement of my success must have played on my mind, for I shot 89 for the afternoon round and was never again in contention.

"Last year, however, at Sandwich, I led from the first day and won the Challenge Cup, becoming the first English professional to do so."

"Yes," said Holmes. "By coincidence, before you came, I was reading of the ceremony in which the cup is passed from the outgoing champion to his successor."

A terrible groan came from Mr. Taylor. "You anticipate the very reason for my visit, Mr. Holmes," he said, hanging his head. "I no longer have the trophy."

"You've lost it?" asked Holmes, leaning forward in excitement.

"No–at least I don't think so."

"Come, man. Don't be so cryptic."

"These past 12 months, I have kept it in the trophy case at Westward Ho! Last night I took it from its case and carried it home to pack it for the trip to Scotland. I left my living room for no more than a minute, and when I came back downstairs, the cup, which I'd left on my own mantel, was gone. The front door was ajar, so I suppose the thief entered and left by that means."

"Who knew of your plans to take the cup home?"

"Only a few of my closest friends at the club, but I cannot seriously suspect any of them. It's my great misfortune that the Open is being contested this year at St. Andrews. As you know, if I lose, I must present the cup to my successor. The ceremony is to be held at perhaps the most famous spot in all of golf, the 18th green at St. Andrews. If I don't have the cup," Mr. Taylor said, closing his eyes and taking a deep breath, "it will be a terrible blow, not just to my honor but to the honor of English golf."

"There's not much we can do at this moment, I'm afraid," said Holmes. "It seems any number of people could have entered your house and taken it."

"Please, Mr. Holmes, if you won't help me. . . ."

"Calm yourself, I only meant that there was nothing we can do here in London. If I'm not mistaken, there's a two o'clock express to Edinburgh. If we hurry to the station now, we may just be able to catch it."

Mr. Taylor proved to be an entertaining traveling companion. He may not have had a formal education, but his father would have been proud of the way he'd compensated. He was, it turned out, one of the game's great innovators, his many contributions including an overlapping manner of gripping the club, the expanded use of a club he called the "mashie" and a style of foul-weather play he referred to as "flat-footed golf," which I understood to mean spreading his feet wider and striking the ball with a short, compact swing.

It was evening when we changed trains in Edinburgh and from there crossed the rolling hills of Fife. As we approached our destination, Mr. Taylor's spirits rose higher and higher, and he seemed briefly to cast off his worry. "It is the great ambition of my life, Mr. Holmes, to bring golf to ordinary working people who at the moment have nowhere to play." He chuckled upon seeing the look of deep skepticism that crossed Holmes's face. "Ah, it's a great game, Mr. Holmes! I grant it might seem a bit daft to a cerebral chap like yourself, but once the fever has invaded your blood, it is hard to root out."

"Yes," said Holmes dryly, "I have little doubt that the Thane of Fife's wife–had she the misfortune of living in these golf-besotted times–would have been a golf widow."

At Leuchars Junctions we transferred to the local carriage that would take us the remaining few miles to St. Andrews. The first part of this stretch was through woodland. Then we rounded a bend, and directly before us was one of the most glorious sights in all the world. To our left was the dark expanse of linksland, which the late-afternoon sun had turned the dark brown of old oil paintings, and beyond it the still darker line I knew to be St. Andrews Bay. We could make out, here and there, the brighter yellow blotches of what the Scots call whins, but the scene was for the most part utterly lacking the bright greens of English courses. In the years since, I have seen many courses, but none possessed the stark beauty of St. Andrews.

Mr. Taylor had a room reserved at the Grand Hotel, an imposing red sandstone block standing right on the edge of the 18th green, and we learned, upon enquiring, that one suite remained. Exhausted by our hasty journey, I bid my companions good night and went up to bed. I must have begun dreaming the instant that my head touched the pillow because I fancied I heard, growing out of the rhythmic surge of the sea, the mournful drone of bagpipes.

I was awakened the next morning by the sun shining brightly in my window. Checking the adjoining room, I was surprised to find that Holmes had left. After a delicious breakfast of eggs and Scottish salmon, I had just wandered out the hotel's front door when Holmes came striding around the corner of the clubhouse, his face burnished red from the wind.

"Watson, you slugabed, I peeked in on you when I awoke, and I am pleased to say that you looked positively cherubic. I have been exploring the links. Truly, there is nothing as invigorating as a morning walk along the sea."

"You really should have waked me, Holmes," I said. But our conversation went no further for at that moment Mr. Taylor burst through the hotel door and rushed up to us. "I found this slipped in under my door," he said, handing Holmes a scrap of paper on which two lines were written:

*Burning to play?*
*Tom has the time.*

"What can it mean, Mr. Holmes?" asked Taylor, his voice tight with anxiety.

"It means our adversary is a playful soul," said Holmes slowly. "Is there anyone in the field named Tom?"

"Not that I'm aware of," said Taylor, "though until recently you'd have found two Toms in the field at every Open, and both very likely near the front. Between them, Old Tom Morris and his son, Young Tom, won eight of the first dozen Opens. Young Tom died a mysterious death on Christmas Day in 1875, and all agree the cause was a broken heart. The 18th hole, which you see before you, is now called Tom Morris, in honor of Old Tom."

"Do all the holes have names?" Holmes inquired of Taylor.

"Yes, the 1st is called Burn because of the stream that cuts in front of the green."

"That's it!" Holmes exclaimed. "Burn-ing to play. Tom has the time. If there's a further clue, we'll find it in the vicinity of these two holes."

He turned slowly, surveying the grand hotels and humble shops that stretched up the 18th fairway. When he had turned almost all the way around, his gaze fell upon the solid stone box of the clubhouse, and there it stopped. A satisfied smile crossed his face.

Holmes was staring at the clock on the southwest corner of the Royal & Ancient's clubhouse. Seeing nothing out of place or amiss with the clock itself, the three of us rushed inside and up to the corner room on whose outside wall the clock was fixed. There, pinned to the wall, was a note written in an elegant, spidery hand. It read:

*Well done, Mr. Holmes, you've*
*interpreted my first clue. Then again,*
*it was not that difficult, was it?*
*We'll call it even up. For now.*

"We can do nothing now but await our adversary's next clue," said Holmes. "Mr. Taylor, I suggest you make whatever preparations are necessary for your round today. Just in case our friend tries anything, Watson and I will follow you as inconspicuously as possible."

I had never attended a golf tournament so the entire day was a revelation to me. The Scottish weather, so renowned for its capriciousness, was sunny and calm. Unfortunately, Mr. Taylor was not. He started well, scoring 4s on each of the first two holes, but on the 3rd, which was called Cartgate Out, the strain of the past 24 hours began to take its toll. His first shot was a corker. The ball streaked down the middle of the fairway and aided in part by the wind and in part by its own perverse spin, turned abruptly right and headed straight for a knot of spectators clustered beside a clump of whins. Mr. Taylor stood as if paralyzed. My own voice was frozen.

"For god's sake, look out!" screamed Holmes.

Just then the wind came roaring up off the bay, carrying away most of his words. But the urgency of Holmes's shout must have penetrated the gale, for at the last possible moment the group scattered and the ball landed harmlessly amongst them. Rattled by this near catastrophe, Taylor shanked his next shot into one of the odious little hazards called pot bunkers. He had to hit out backwards and recorded a 6 for the hole. He never regained his composure that round. His 86 placed him at equal fifth.

"I'll have to play much better than that if I'm to have any chance of defending," he said rather glumly when we were seated for lunch in the hotel. "It's not easy with this mystery hanging over me."

"You must place your trust in me," said Holmes. "Until the cup turns up, we can assume that whoever has it is keeping it with an eye to producing it at some appropriate time. Until we know his motive, we can't discern what that time might be. Now, since I've heard so much about haggis, I think I'll try a wee bit."

Boiled sheep innards do not appeal to me, and so I repaired to my room. When I knocked on Holmes's door on my way out to watch the second round, I was greeted by an awful groan. Entering I found my friend in bed, his face blanched and his head hanging over a wastepaper basket.

"What is it, Holmes?" I asked.

"Alimentary, my dear Watson, alimentary," he said with a sick smile. "The haggis seems not to have agreed with me. Go on with Taylor. I will catch up later, no doubt."

But I did not see Holmes again until that night. Where he spent the afternoon, I cannot imagine. Certainly I saw him nowhere on the course as I followed Taylor around. Taylor improved tremendously, shooting a 78, which left him five strokes behind Sandy Herd of Huddersfield. In the lounge bar afterward, Taylor was again in an expansive mood, speculating happily on his renewed chances of winning when Holmes walked in. He offered no explanations for his disappearance, no report on the progress of the case. He just sat down.

At that moment a waiter tapped Mr. Taylor on the shoulder and handed him a slip of paper. Holmes's eyes burned brightly as he watched Taylor unfold the paper.

*Who suffers deep longing?*
*He who knows Hell.*

I've got it," exclaimed Taylor, leaping to his feet. "If there is anything that makes this course special, it's the bunkers. Some are so famous they have been given proper names. Without a doubt, the most famous of all is Hell Bunker, on the 14th hole. It's a monster. You could hide a family of elephants in it."

"And is not the 14th known as Long?" said Holmes. "So the deepest part of Long is Hell, eh? This man is mocking us. Mr. Taylor, you no doubt need some sleep. Watson and I will visit Hell Bunker and see what's there."

I will never forget our walk that night out across the moonlit links toward what danger we knew not. Holmes had always been a vigorous walker, and it was now a challenge just to keep pace with him. The barren stretch of land, pocked by curious craters, resembled the lunar landscapes in one of Mr. Verne's fantasies.

There was no mistaking Hell Bunker: It would easily have held not just Mr. Taylor's elephants, but all of our Baker Street lodgings. As we peered over the brink, I could make out a small figure, a doll dressed in fawn tweed very much like the outfit in which Mr. Taylor had played that day.

Holmes climbed slowly down into the bunker, retrieved the doll and then scrambled back up its side. He showed me the doll and the pin someone had driven through its heart. "Not a word of this to Taylor," he said, "or he'll have no chance of playing well tomorrow."

That evening, as I was drifting off to sleep, I again thought I heard bagpipes and made a note to inquire about this curious phenomenon.

On the morning of the second day of play, Holmes was once more absent when I awoke. Miffed at finding myself excluded from his counsel, I decided to postpone breakfast until I had found him. Crossing the fairway of the notorious 17th, the Road Hole, I rounded the railway sheds and had begun to walk out on the wide meadows along the Eden River, where the golfers often practiced, when I beheld a sight that I had thought I would never see.

There was no mistaking the tall, gaunt figure standing on the practice tee. Holmes's swing was quite the opposite of Taylor's. Whereas our friend's traced a short, controlled arc, Holmes's had a loopy elegance to it. He used every inch of his height to generate power, and his follow-through lifted him clear off his feet.

I watched in amazement for 10 minutes until Holmes, apparently sensing my presence, turned and saw me. He seemed slightly irked at being discovered. "Just a bit of research," he said, lofting a shot high into the air, where the wind caught it and deposited it neatly on the green, some 10 feet from the flag.

"Shouldn't we find Mr. Taylor?" I asked.

"In a minute," he said, knocking out a high shot almost identical to the last. "You know, Watson, I suspect a skilled golfer might reduce this game to a set of scientific principles. Watch. I turn my hand in the other direction and. . . ." The ball jumped off the club, traveled 150 yards and then turned the other way.

"Holmes!"

"You're right, Watson. I suppose we should find Taylor." He hit one last towering shot, spun on his heel and started off in the direction of the hotel.

We were just making our way up the front steps when Mr. Taylor burst through the front door and thrust a slip of paper into Holmes's hands. Peering over his shoulder, I could see in an instant that it was written by the same hand as the other notes:

*Fancy a Beer?*
*Come to my Cottage.*

By now we knew how to interpret our adversary's clues. "The fourth hole is Ginger Beer," said Holmes, consulting his map of the course, "and yes, there's a bunker on it called Cottage."

Holmes saw me raise my eyebrows as I watched him check the revolver in the pocket of his coat. "Our friend has already demonstrated his fondness for word play," he explained grimly. "So far he has been content merely to mock us. But as this championship draws to a close, so does our adventure. I fear that the bier he is inviting us to is not social, but funereal."

With that grim thought, Holmes began to stride out across the course. As we approached the 4th hole, we could see a lone figure hunched over a ball on the green, putting, as it seemed to me. As we drew nearer I saw he was a tall, pale man, aristocratic in bearing. He dropped the putter and walked forward to meet us.

"Watson," said Holmes, "let me introduce you to Mr. Horace Hutchison, Taylor's greatest benefactor now turned his worst enemy."

"Really, Mr. Holmes," replied Hutchinson, "that seems a bit melodramatic, don't you think?"

From the first word I heard Hutchinson speak, the man's unctuous manner turned my stomach. "Why have you done this to poor Taylor?" I blurted out. "He's sick with worry. He describes you in far more generous terms than you deserve. Why have you done this?"

Hutchinson rolled his eyes across the sky, as if following the progress of one of Holmes's shots. "If Taylor wins here," he said, "he'll have a far loftier platform from which to publicize his awful populist views. When I encouraged him all those years ago, I had no idea the silly little bugger would get in his head to make golf a people's game like darts, football or cross-country running."

"Enough," said Holmes. "Where is the trophy?"

"And why should I tell you?"

"Because you have achieved your aim. Taylor stands little chance of winning now. He has lost whatever platform a win here might have given him. Shall we putt for it?"

"I didn't know you played, Mr. Holmes."

"I'm new to the game, but I'll take my chances."

To me, this seemed a foolhardy gamble, another example of my friend's confidence in himself, which at times seemed excessive. Not only did Hutchinson have years of experience, but he had been practicing on this very green as we approached. And this would be no easy putt: The hole was on the far side of a tricky ridge, perhaps 50 feet from where we were standing.

Hutchinson went first. He stood over the ball for a moment and then stroked it. It rolled up the ridge, then down its far side, gathering speed. It slipped past the hole on the right side by perhaps six inches and wound up another 18 inches beyond.

It was now Holmes's turn. Lighting his pipe, he walked all the way to the hole and back, examining the turf along the way. He then squatted, holding the putter vertically aloft and sighting along its shaft. Hutchinson seemed unnerved by Holmes's preparations, and he began to pace briskly back and forth just behind us.

"Hutchison, would you please stop moving?" said Holmes.

At last Holmes was ready. Standing over the ball with his pipe still in his mouth, he hit his putt with the same force Hutchinson had, but along a slightly different line. It traveled up the ridge, rolled along a swell neither I nor Hutchinson had noticed, caromed around the back of the hole and came to rest a foot away. Turning slowly, Holmes cocked an eyebrow at Hutchinson. "The cup?"

"Oh, blast!" said Hutchinson. "All right, all right. You're very nearly standing on it. This hole used to be known as the Hole of Cunnin Links–*cunnin* being old Scots for "rabbit." Under us is a vast rabbit warren. I stashed the cup down one of the holes to the right of the green. You'll find it there."

Sure enough, we found the cup in the third burrow we looked in. Holmes had to reach his arm all the way down into the hole to retrieve it. As we marched back to the hotel with our great prize in hand, we passed some of the early twosomes on their way out for the final round of the Open. We knocked on Taylor's door, and when he opened it, there, nestled in Holmes's arms, was the cup. Again I thought Holmes had overdone his penchant for surprise, as poor Taylor staggered backwards in shock.

"Great god!" he finally said. "Thank you, Holmes. Thank you, thank you, thank you. Wherever did you find it?"

"I will tell you later," said Holmes. "For now, you must concern yourself with other matters. To quote Robert the Bruce, 'I have brought you to the ring. Now you must dance.'"

With the cup now safely in his possession once again, Taylor was able to concentrate fully on his game in the round, and a magnificent demonstration he gave. Indeed, he could not have asked for a better day on which to demonstrate the effectiveness of flat-footed golf. The wind, risen up off the North Sea, came roaring across the course like a train. It played havoc with everyone's game but our friend's. Hole after hole, he planted himself firmly and then used his trusty mashie to punch his ball straight through the gale. Herd, who led by three shots as they started the round, suffered all the torments of the Scottish wind. He blew up to an 85, while Taylor finished magnificently, with a 78.

There on the 18th green–which in the first round had seemed destined to be the scene of his greatest humiliation–Taylor made an eloquent speech extolling the beauty of Scottish golf and of the Scots' generous desire to share it with all the world. He received a tremendous ovation and was toasted that night, I'm sure, in every pub in St. Andrews.

As we strolled home at midnight from a splendid celebratory dinner, I heard once again the music of my mysterious piper. Though Holmes did not seem especially interested in solving my mystery, I was determined to track down the midnight musician. I set off, with Taylor and Holmes jogging along behind me, using my ears to guide me through the dark, walled streets. Rounding a corner near the cathedral, I finally spotted him in the mist, a lone figure dressed in a kilt. "Good god," exclaimed Taylor. "It's Freddie Tait."

Tait, it turned out, was quite a golfer. In fact, in each of the next two years he would finish third in the Open. He also was quite a popular character among his townsmen, who found fault only with his fondness for midnight piping.

Holmes and I continued to follow Mr. Taylor's remarkable career. He did not achieve the dominance predicted for him after his triumph at St. Andrews. The following year another giant of the game appeared, Harry Vardon. The final round of the next year's Open was a corker, with Vardon making up three strokes on our friend, and then beating him in a 36-hole playoff.

The two of them, along with James Braid of Scotland, soon came to be know as the Great Triumvirate, which dominated British golf for 20 years. They would win 16 of the 21 Opens contested from 1894 through

1914. Our friend won his fifth and final championship in 1913 by the amazing margin of eight strokes!

Holmes and I, however, knew that he must have been equally satisfied by watching the game grow and spread through all the ranks of British society, thanks to the Artisan Golfers' Association and the National Association of Public Golf Courses, both of which he championed.

And Holmes? His mania–I know of no other word to describe it–for golf would last a lifetime. He tells people he has retired to the South Downs of Sussex to raise bees, but I know better. I visit him regularly and know the use he makes of the broad meadow behind his cottage, the true meaning of the tiny scallops cut from the turf. Holmes would never admit it, but I strongly suspect that the "James Sherlock" who finished sixth at the 1904 Open at Sandwich was none other than my estimable friend.

*Here is another boy meets girl story. Golf writers, perhaps inspired by the great Wodehouse, like their love and golf, golf and love. The lady's proposition is that a down-on-his-luck golf pro help a rich young lady develop her playing skills so she can enter a tournament . . . . Romance is lurking on the fairway. There was a popular golf movie in 1996 that is similar to this story—"Tin Cup," with Kevin Costner and Rene Russo in the lead roles.*

# THE LADY'S PROPOSITION (1955)

IT WAS TOO EARLY FOR players to show up, so I was tidying up the shop and eying the placard over the door that proclaimed me pro of this municipal golfer's mecca–nine emerald greens sprinkled over seventy acres of sunbaked cow pasture. Water's expensive in West Texas, and I had a yen to move my placard to greener fairways–someplace you could hit a decent wedge shot without displacing a shower of gravel; but most of all, someplace I could make enough money to hit the tournament trail.

Just at that disenchanted moment of my life the phone rang, and when I answered, Jack Simms' rusty baritone boomed over the wire.

"That you, Steve? How's the boy?"

"Barely solvent. What's with you?" Jack was one of my idols. As a kid I'd caddied for him some on the Texas pro circuit. Now, as pro at Dallas' plush Laurel Lane Country Club, he had it made.

"Thought I'd let you know Kelly's quitting in September to join the fly boys. Thought you might want to toss your hat in the ring." Kelly was Laurel Lane's assistant pro.

"Darn right, I would!" I said with some excitement. "Who's the big wheel?"

Jack chuckled. "Unc' Andrew Bond is president, but Renwick Farrow usually does the hiring. He's chairman of the golf committee. I'd write him."

"Swell, Jack. I'll get it off today. This place is drying up. Everybody buys their stuff wholesale, and nobody takes lessons. A guy could starve."

"It's different here, boy," Jack said gleefully. "There'll be lots of guys after Kelly's job."

"Yeah, I know. Laurel Lane, the land of mink and money."

Jack laughed. "Well, so long, kid. And good luck!"

I started digging around for something to write on; then suddenly out of the blue of this June morning a vision appeared.

"Are you Steve Carey?" the vision asked, looking me over with cool green eyes. "I hear you're a good player, and I'm stuck in this burg for the summer. Care to hear a proposition?"

I felt my hackles rising. Ansford is no metropolis but her tone implied we didn't even have inside plumbing. Curious, I motioned her over to the table in the corner of the shop.

She took off her little hat and patted her smooth blond hair. She was no golfer. I could tell that by her creamy skin and soft hands, and I couldn't help noticing the two-carat headlight she was wearing.

"Mr. Carey–" she began.

"Make it Steve," I amended.

"All right, Steve. I'm Patricia–Pat Kent. To get right down to brass tacks–by September I want to be playing par golf."

I gave her a wary look. "How good are you now?" I asked.

"I don't know. I've never tried."

I flipped. "What? I'm no miracle man; I could polish a ragged game, trim your score, maybe. But nobody–it takes years–constant practice," I sputtered.

"I told you I'm stuck here in Ansford for the summer."

"But what's the big–"

"I've got my reasons," she said. "Now. Will you give me a lesson every morning this summer for, say, five dollars a lesson?"

My confusion floated away like a mist. Money talk I understand. I guess every beginning golf pro thinks of himself as a poor man's Ben Hogan, just waiting for a big win to boost him into a four-figure bank account and a cushy job somewhere. But the waiting is sometimes long and it's usually pretty lean. My hand closed around the three quarters in my pocket. I couldn't even pick up my laundry until payday!

I bestowed on Patricia Kent a slightly mellowed look. "What have I got to lose?" I shrugged.

She was in the doorway when she turned around and said, "I might as well tell you that I hate golf. Simply loathe the game."

The back of my neck prickled with exasperation. "Please," I said without smiling, "you're speaking of the game I love."

She gave me a pitying smile. "See you in the morning!" she said crisply, and sailed out of sight.

Patricia Kent showed up the next morning wearing a pale-blue sweater and skirt, and a pair of marshmallow-white buck Oxfords. But I forgave her the shoes and even felt kindly toward her when she said, "You pick me out some clubs and whatever else I need–and I want the best you've got."

Delirious with this bonanza, I pulled a new cart, new bag and virginal, shiny clubs out to the practice tee, resolved to give this dedicated little chick the best I had to offer. But I gave her a week, two at the outside, to discover that golf isn't boarding-school hockey.

I spent thirty minutes showing her how to grip a five iron, and thirty more teaching her how to swing it. Then I dumped out a bucketful of practice balls and let her have at it.

For a raw recruit, she wasn't bad. Not bad at all. That afternoon she was back out on the practice tee, and after an hour she came in for a soft drink, holding up her hands for me to see two pearly blisters on her palms.

I handed her the drink and grinned. "You'll get used to it."

"You just bet I will," she said.

I wondered mildly, after she was gone, if she had a bet on or something, but I shrugged it off. Why should I care what her pitch was? I went back to daydreaming about my chances for the assistant's job at Laurel Lane.

Three days later I put my daydreams in cold storage for the summer when I got a letter from Renwick Farrow stating that applicants for Kelly's job would be interviewed at the club on September fifteenth. But with Jack in my corner, I still felt optimistic–could close my eyes and almost smell the fragrant turf that covered the laurel-lined fairways.

The first week Pat slugged away from the practice tee by the hour. At the end of the second week I had her wood shots grooved. Nothing exceptional, but she was hitting clean shots without a shadow of a slice, which is a good sign. Her irons were improving, too, but her putting was murder.

She couldn't have dropped a six-footer if the cup had been a washtub. I changed her stance, changed her putter, made her take off her sunglasses–and she kept right on, by-passing the bucket.

After a couple more weeks it began to get under my skin. "Holy mackerel!" I stormed out at her one morning right after she'd taken four putts to get down from twelve feet out. "You can bat those things out from the practice tee until hell freezes over and if you can't learn to putt you might as well take up hopscotch!"

Her chin went up, but she didn't say anything. We went on to the next tee, and with her chin still full mast, she stepped up and belted one to the corner of the dog-leg–two hundred and ten yards away. This surprised me, but I didn't toss her a bouquet.

After that we finished the round without a dozen words. Pat was getting twenty-five bonus yards on every drive, and she two-putted all the way in. It was the best round she'd had.

That afternoon she spent two hours on the putting green. And she didn't come in for a drink.

One morning, after we'd putted out on nine, we stretched out under the thin shade of a mesquite to rehash the round. Suddenly, Pat said, "Steve, I might as well level with you–fill you in on the whole thing. You've wondered, haven't you?" It was the first time she'd used a friendly tone since I'd made her mad.

I laughed. "Naturally. But it's none of my business; you're paying me."

"No more than you're worth. Steve, I'm going to make it. I know I am!"

I propped my head on my elbow. "You're doing fine, but don't get your hopes up."

Her eyes narrowed. "You want to know why I'm going to make it?"

"If you care to tell me."

"At Laurel Lane–"

I nearly choked on a blade of grass I was chewing. Laurel Lane, she'd said. She never told me she was from Dallas.

Pat, unaware of my bad moment, went on, "–at Laurel Lane, golf is to its members what horses are to Kentuckians. It's not only a game, it's a way of life!" Her short laugh had a bitter edge to it. She was leaning against the gnarled mesquite trunk, her lovely profile, framed by her windblown hair, outlined against the sky. I was acutely aware of how beautiful she was. *All right, Carey,* I told myself, *get back behind the counter.*

"Yeah, I know," I said. "The gentry type–three-day weekends and stuff."

She nodded. "The fellow I'm engaged to–he lives golf!" She sighed. "To him, everything is secondary to golf. Except money. He's gone to South America for the summer. Probably goes out and pars the Andes every day, or something." The glitter came back into her eyes. "I have no intention of playing second fiddle to a four iron the rest of my life!"

This had a familiar ring. A cute little redhead had handed me a pink slip a year ago on the same complaint. It's universal.

"How does it happen you're here in Ansford? 'Stuck,' you said."

"Oh, my aunt lives here. Her husband is on an engineering job in Monterrey and I'm staying with her. Nights, anyway," she laughed. "Since I'm out here most of the day, I had to confide in her too."

"Confide?"

"About Tracy. Tracy Herbert, I mean." So the guy's name is Herbert. Hideous name.

"Tracy's a newcomer at Laurel Lane–she–"

"She?" I cut in. "Tracy is a 'she'?"

"Quite a 'she,'" Pat said, sparks shooting from her emerald eyes, "and she's moving in on my territory."

"You mean the boy friend?"

She nodded grimly. "She's won every tournament the club's had that women could play in. Been on all the winning pro-am teams, mixed pairs–everything. And golf being the *pièce de résistance* at Laurel Lane–"

"I follow you," I grinned at her. "Hell hath no fury like–"

She banged her fist against the wheel of her cart. "Plat me no platitudes. I'm going to take the women's club tournament this fall and show her and my par-happy intended a thing or two!"

On that defiant note we called it a day, but she was back in the afternoon, banging out long iron shots with the perseverance of a robot.

July melted into August, and Pat, brown as an Indian princess, plugged doggedly away. She amazed me. In fact, there were a few times I began to think she'd hit a par round, but she never did. But she never doubted she was going to–maybe the very next day. At first, I was primarily interested in the long green she handed me every Saturday; then I got to pulling for her so hard the money no longer seemed important.

I kept reminding myself that this was purely business, but my heart and my head wouldn't concur. My head told me I was a cockeyed square to let myself get burned. Members of Laurel Lane weren't for the likes of me, even if they weren't already out of circulation, as Pat was. But my heart wouldn't listen. The summer was running out, and I knew when Pat left I was in for a sorry time of it.

We played our last round together the day before Pat went back to Dallas. Despite my grim determination all summer to follow along with Pat in keeping everything strictly business, I suddenly felt as though my entire life had been wasted. What would Pat look like in a fluffy formal? How would she feel, close in my arms, dancing–her head against my shoulder, lost in the enchantment of a moment that demanded nothing more than the moment itself?

All this was running through my mind when we teed up for our drives that sizzling last morning in August. Pat hit a clean, low drive that split the middle, and I grinned at her. "You've come a long way!"

She stood there smiling for a moment, watching the ball trickle to a stop, then nodded slowly. "You said I couldn't do it. And I haven't. Par, I mean."

"You will. Next summer, maybe, if you keep plugging."

Her smile faded. "The tournament is next week," she said simply.

"A gal with a one-track mind!" I gibed.

We were wilted down by the ninth tee, but Pat's eyes were shining. I knew why. She was even par through eight, but neither of us mentioned it–like keeping quiet when a pitcher has a no-hitter on the griddle. Number Nine is a long par five, with a lake about three hundred and fifty yards from the tee. It takes two Sunday shots to get over it and leave a short iron and two putts to get down in regulation.

The click of the club head against the ball told me Pat's drive was a honey. We both watched it roll down a swale and stop about two hundred and thirty yards down the middle. Pat's face took on a tense look, but she slipped her club back in the bag without saying anything.

I was wondering how she'd play the second shot. Up until today she'd laid up to the lake edge for a cinch crossing on three. This made a par most unlikely, unless the fourth shot carried the green into one-putt distance, and the back edge of the lake was a good hundred and seventy yards short of the green.

I stood by, watching, waiting. *Don't reach for an iron,* I breathed silently. She laid her hand for an instant on an iron, then resolutely drew out her two wood. *At-a-gal,* I applauded inaudibly, holding my breath as she carefully addressed the ball. Her swing was as fluid and graceful as the Hague's himself, and the ball skimmed true and straight for a hundred-and-fifty-yard carry, rolling to a stop twenty yards past the back lake edge.

"Good girl!" I yelled at her.

She laughed a breathless little laugh and we walked on. She was already playing her next one. That determined look on her face, I'd come to know too well–and to love, Lord help me.

Pat moved quickly to her ball and took a look at the promised land. She had to get on. She knew that, because she seldom one-putted: If she'd learned one thing well, it was how to plan a shot around her own limitations. I watched her take out her three iron. Never up, never on. She'd learned that.

The ball sailed in a low arc, hitting just short of the green and running on past the cup. Her face relaxed into a broad grin.

"Steve!" she said breathlessly.

"Remember your putting," I admonished her, but the grin stuck.

On the green her ball rested about eighteen feet from the pin. "If you three-putt this one," I told her, "I'm going to use your putter on you where it'll do the most good!"

She laughed and held up crossed fingers. She lined it up, stroked the ball and froze to watch it run three feet past the cup.

"Take your time," I cautioned her.

She took a deep breath and addressed the ball; stroked it. There was a resonant "clunk" as the ball dropped.

"Steve!" she squealed, dropping her putter and running right into my arms. "Oh, Steve, I did it!"

She kissed me hard on the cheek, and looking down at her, I saw the tears in her eyes. The summer flashed by again, like a meteor–the blisters, the practice rounds, the small talk. The damnable small talk that could've been sweet talk.

I put my arms around her and laughed. "Well, Pat, I never thought you'd do it."

"We, you mean! Oh, Steve, you're wonderful!"

"Yeah, I'm a great guy."

Back in the shop, we sat down to drink our ginger ale. Pat, relaxed and glowing, said, "Just think, Steve, the tournament starts the seventh–just a week off!"

"Keep me posted, will you?"

"I'll call you every night," she was saying, still bubbling over from her par round.

She was gone almost before I knew it, my cheek still tingling from the kiss she'd given me. More than anything in the world, then, I wanted that slot at Laurel Lane. That was where Pat would be.

Pat kept her promise to call every night, and I waited for those calls like a kid waiting for Christmas. The day of the qualifying round she carded an eighty-four, but it was good enough to make the championship flight. And luck smiled on her, because Tracy Herbert, medalist with a seventy-eight, was in the top bracket and Pat in the bottom one.

She won her first match, then her second, and when she called and told me she'd won the third round, I was as delirious as she was. Except she sounded a little strange. She told me she was playing Herbert in the finals and would let me know as soon as it was all over. As soon as it was all over–like somebody being wheeled into surgery with all the odds against her. I worried about it until I hit the sack, and it took me a while to go to sleep.

About midnight, the phone jangled me out of bed. It was Pat again. "Steve, I'm scared!"

"What gives?" I could tell she'd been crying.

"Everything's happened! Oh, Steve, can you come? I need you!"

The pulse beat in my ears sounded like a train thundering over a trestle. She needed me!

"Is Tracy trying to lace your highballs with cyanide?" I asked, trying to keep it light.

"The club's buzzing. They've got all sorts of bets going–and Renwick bet against me!"

"Renwick?" A cold feeling cleared the tumult in my head. I began to feel numb.

"Renwick Farrow, my fiancé. He's got his money on Tracy; we had a big fight."

I couldn't say a word. All I could think of was that interview coming up on September fifteenth with a man named Renwick Farrow. If I got involved in this hassle, my chances at the Laurel Lane job were cooked. For thirty seconds I floundered in the sea of irony that Fate had dunked me in. I groaned.

"Steve, are you there?" Pat's voice was sharp with anxiety.

"Yeah, sure. You hold tight, baby. What's your starting time?"

"One o'clock."

"O.K. Take it easy. I'll be at Laurel Lane by eleven. Go to bed and get some sleep."

She laughed a small, shaky laugh of relief. Her murmured thanks hung suspended in the darkness of the room after I'd hung up.

By seven the next morning I was highballing eastward toward Dallas, with four hours of turbulent solitude ahead of me in which to convince myself I was a congenital idiot with a talent for staying in the rough.

Jack Simms was at the fountain when I started toward the Laurel Lane shop. When I walked up, his broad grin told me he knew the whole story. "You sure fixed your clock, boy!"

"Yeah. It's a gift with me. Seen Pat?"

He jerked his thumb toward the putting green. "She's out there."

"You think she's got a chance?" I felt silly even asking.

Jack shrugged. "Maybe an outside one. I played a round with her a few days ago. She's game enough, but I figure the pressure'll get her. You can hear the current crackle when she and Tracy get within spittin' distance of each other." He chuckled.

"How's she hitting 'em?"

"Fine. Short irons, especially. She's layin' 'em up to the pin. Good thing. Steve, she can't putt!"

I was feeling sicker by the minute. "Her only chance is to stick 'em right under the flag, I guess."

Jack nodded. "Yeah. These greens are tricky, even when you're used to 'em."

I looked at him. I could tell he'd like to see the Herbert dame get hers. "Well, Jack," I sighed, "it would've been swell working with you."

He grinned, shaking his head, and I steamed off to find Pat.

Her face brightened like a new day when she saw me. She squeezed my hand and breathed a sigh. "Steve! Bless you! I don't think I could make it without you!"

She looked like a million in a tan skirt and blouse, with a scarf the color of her eyes knotted at her throat.

"What gives?" I asked.

"Not here, Steve." She glanced at the people milling about. "Let's drive out the highway and get some lunch. I didn't eat a bite of breakfast."

"That makes two of us," I said.

We got into my jalopy, which looked as out of place as a stevedore at a seminar, and roared off. Ten minutes later, over fried chicken and onion rings, Pat was bringing me up to date.

"It was at the dance last night. Boy! Is Tracy making a play for Renwick!"

"And Renwick?"

She sniffed. "He's used to it. All the girls go for him."

"And he put his money on Tracy's nose, huh?"

She nodded. "They've even got a pari-mutuel board set up. Right now the odds are six to one for Tracy. If anybody's playing Pat, the long shot, I don't know who!" She laughed, a little bitterly.

"Where're your folks?" Her family seemed conspicuously absent.

"There's just my Uncle Andy. I live with him. Unc's nearly seventy, but he'll be following me in one of the scooter cars."

"Pat"–impulsively I reached across the table and covered her hand with mine–"looks to me like a good way to parlay that three hundred you've paid me this summer into a small fortune!"

Her green eyes looked into mine, incredulous. "Steve! You wouldn't!"

I laughed. "Purely selfish on my part," I lied. "Always was a sucker for a fast buck." *And a lost cause,* I thought.

"You really think I can beat Tracy?"

"Sure!" I lied again. "And I'll be right here to see you do it."

Pat put her other hand over mine. "Steve, you're the best!"

"Yeah." *If you don't mind 'em dumb.* "C'mon, it's after twelve."

I hung around the fountain by the Number One tee while Pat went into the locker room. The gallery was gathering, and I was watching the tee for Tracy Herbert when Pat came out of the clubhouse flanked by a blond hunk of man with teeth like Liberace's. A quick appraisal told me he had a likewise bank roll.

From the tilt of Pat's chin I knew they'd just exchanged some verbal jabs, but she was covering beautifully when she introduced us. "Renwick–Mr. Farrow–this is Steve Carey, my angel." She slipped her arm through mine and beamed me a dazzling smile which I knew was calculated to give Farrow a twinge of jealousy.

Renwick laughed, flashing his pretty teeth. "Good job, Carey. Pat's giving me what-for for betting against her." His manner implied that while he didn't own the world, he was a major stockholder, and that he didn't get that way making sentimental bets.

"That so?" *Be pleasant, Carey. Keep quiet and you might bypass this booby trap yet.*

The starter was calling over the P.A. system, "Miss Tracy Herbert, Miss Patricia Kent, Number One tee, please!"

"You betting?" Farrow asked. Pat looked at me expectantly.

"Yeah, I'll take some of that six-to-one money."

Farrow's eyes narrowed ever so slightly. "How much, Carey?"

"Oh, say three hundred?" *It's only money, Carey. All you've got.*

"It's a bet, at pari-mutuel odds," he said, giving me a bone-crunching sample of his grip.

Pat glanced from my face to his, but her thoughts were masked, and we hurried on over to the tee. There, swinging her driver for a photographer was the Herbert, in a startling pair of white shorts and a halter bra. The size of the gallery no longer surprised me.

Farrow escorted Pat up to the tee with a hearty flourish and dropped back to say something to Tracy. Pat turned around and darted me a drowning look. I held up crossed fingers and grinned, but I knew her heart was in her throat.

The P.A. system blared, "Miss Herbert on the tee! Fore, please!" The Herbert babe hit a screamer–two hundred and forty yards, but hooking nearly to the rough. Pat, dead-pan, set up her ball. *Easy does it, baby.* I caught myself clenching and unclenching my fists. She cracked the ball solidly. Not long, but down the alley.

The gallery surged forward, and I moved with them. If Pat needed me, I'd be on deck. Otherwise, I was part of the scenery.

At the turn Pat was one down. They'd halved four holes, Pat had taken two and Tracy three. Everybody was surprised, including me. The six-to-one money still looked good, but not nearly so good as it did on the first tee.

Pat and Farrow were sitting on a bench drinking soda pop, but they weren't saying anything. She saw me and motioned me over.

"Any suggestions, coach?" Pat's light tone didn't hide the tension in her voice.

"You're on the ball. Stay there," I said simply.

Farrow jerked his head up. "She's scrambling, and you know it!" he needled smoothly.

My thermostat gave a sharp click. I shot him a look. He'd say that to his girl? Sure, he would–to save his frogskins. I felt a savage impulse to rearrange his gleaming molars, but a quick glance at Pat put out the fire.

Something else clicked. I remembered the day I'd jumped her about her putting–the way she'd steadied down and made me eat my words. She was wearing that same expression now, and I relaxed.

Forgetting my resolution to stay on the side lines, I laughed right in Farrow's face. "I say she's on her stick, Farrow, and I also say she's going to take the match!"

Pat grinned a tight little one-sided grin, then got up and walked to the Number Ten tee, where Tracy was already addressing her ball. As for me, I faded back into the crowd and tried to believe in my own propaganda.

Someday I may win the Open, Tam o' Shanter or some other big tourney, but there'll never be nine holes of match play that will gray my hair faster than the last nine of Pat's match. And all my agonizing was in vain. They came in all square on Eighteen, which meant only one thing: sudden death on Nineteen–Twenty–maybe Twenty-one, and the sticky heat and strain were telling on Pat.

The gallery had stopped its chattering, like the suspended movement and sounds around a roulette table when the wheel is slowing down. I wondered just how much lettuce was riding on this exclusive little battle, but I'd honestly forgotten I stood a chance to pick up eighteen hundred dollars.

Pat, back on the Number One tee, looked tired, but her drive was good. Tracy's was better, and again the crowd pushed on, the scooters trundling along the trails ahead of it. For an instant I grieved over my lost chance at the job, but when Pat hit her second shot I forgot all about it. She was in trouble. Number One, a par four, is heavily sand-trapped, and Pat's long iron was short and into a trap.

Tracy's second shot bit on the front edge of the putting surface and stopped eighteen feet from the cup. *That does it, Carey. Pat's slated for a bogey and Herbert's got a cinch par.*

The gallery got quiet again as it ringed itself around the green. Pat, holding her wedge, stepped into the trap. I could've almost reached out and touched her. She looked in my direction and I held up crossed fingers. She shook her head and addressed the ball.

The flying sand obscured the ball for an instant, but the applause from the spectators told me it was a recovery. Yes. There it was, fifteen feet from the pin. I felt sick. It wasn't good enough. She'd need to sink for a halve.

Tracy, away, stroked her ball carefully–too carefully. It stopped three feet short of the pin. They now lay alike, Pat fifteen feet out to Tracy's three.

Pat dropped to her knees on the shoulder of the green to study the roll, then moved slowly to the ball. She lined it up, then stroked it firmly. Never up, never in. I watched it break, curving toward the cup, held my breath as it hit the back lip and jumped–then, dropped. She'd cinched a halve. The match was still alive. Pat, grinning broadly, looked toward me, and how I grinned back!

The fringes of the gallery were already moving to the next tee. Tracy studied her putt, then walked up to tap it in. I held my breath again as she stroked it–and babied it! It hung on the rim of the cup. The match was over.

Everybody was pulling at Pat, even those she'd cost a lot of money. When I got near her, she reached for me, and I held her in my arms a short minute.

"Steve! If it hadn't been for you–" She was laughing and crying, and I was dying by inches, because I wanted to kiss her and tell her I loved her more than Renwick Farrow ever would or could.

Farrow pushed into the circle and the others began to drift back toward the clubhouse. "Great match, Pat! Congratulations!" His teeth were flashing from his perch on the new bandwagon.

"Thanks, Renwick," Pat said, her eyes shining. She put her hand on his arm. "And Renwick, here. I'm sure this will more than cover your bet with Steve."

While the moon and the stars and the planets swung crazily around my head, she slipped the big sparkler off her finger and handed it to Farrow. When I leveled off, a stocky, white-haired gentleman was giving Pat a big hug.

"Oh, Unc, this is Steve Carey. . . . Steve, my uncle, Andy Bond."

We'd already shaken hands before the name rang a bell. I gulped.

Bond's eyes were twinkling. "You guarantee the same results for all your pupils?"

Pat laughed. "He's the best instructor in the country, Unc."

"So Simms has been telling me," Bond said. "Maybe you could put a few patches on my game–maybe fix old Renwick's slice, huh?" He gave Farrow a hearty slap on the back that threatened to loose the storm that had gathered in his face. "How 'bout it, Carey? Still interested in Kelly's job?"

*You know it!* I almost shouted. I swallowed hard and managed to grin a "Yes" at him.

Farrow's face was now a study in pink granite. "You can pick up my check at the shop, Carey," he said, and wheeled toward the clubhouse.

"Pat–" I drew her to me. Unc Andy, being the perceptive old gentleman he is, ambled back to his scooter car, chuckling.

"Steve," Pat murmured, after I'd substituted action for words and kissed her a couple of times, "know something?"

"Plenty. What?"

"I love golf. Simply love the game!"

I looked deep into her green eyes. "You're talking like the gal I love."

*This courtroom spoof is a classic in golf literature. Don Marquis (1878–1937) was a well-known humorist in the twenties and thirties who wrote for the* New York Sun *and the* New York Tribune. *He is renowned for his plays, poems, novels, and short stories. One of his best is the satire* Archy and Mehitabel *(1927), about a love affair between a cockroach and a cat. Marquis liked to poke fun at politics and society by using his characters in parody. Other popular Marquis works are* Pandora Lifts the Lid *(1924),* The Almost Perfect State *(1927), and a collection of short stories called* Sun Dial Time *(1936).*

*Don Marquis*

# THE RIVERCLIFF GOLF KILLINGS, OR WHY PROFESSOR WADDEMS NEVER BROKE A HUNDRED (1921)

*I am telling this story to the public just as I told it in the grand jury room; the district attorney having given me a carbon copy of my sworn testimony.*

## The Case of Doc Green

QUESTION: Professor Waddems, when did you first notice that Dr. Green seemed to harbor animosity towards you?
ANSWER: It was when we got to the second hole.
QUESTION: Professor, you may go ahead and tell the jury about it in your own words.

ANSWER: Yes, sir. The situation was this: My third shot lay in the sand in the shallow bunker–an easy pitch with a niblick to within a foot or two of the pin, for anyone who understands the theory of niblick play as well as I do. I had the hole in five, practically.

"Professor," said Doc Green, with whom I was playing–

QUESTION: This was Dr. James T. Green, the eminent surgeon, was it not?

ANSWER: Yes, sir. Dr. Green, with whom I was playing, remarked, "You are all wrong about Freud. Psychoanalysis is the greatest discovery of the age."

"Nonsense! Nonsense! Nonsense!" I replied. "Don't be a fool, Doc! I'll show you where Freud is all wrong, in a minute."

And I lifted the ball with an explosion shot to a spot eighteen inches from the pin, and holed out with an easy putt.

"Five," I said and marked it on my card.

"You mean eight," said Doc Green.

"Three into the bunker, four onto the green, and one putt–five," I said.

"You took four strokes in the bunker, Professor," he said. "Every time you said 'Nonsense' you made a swipe at the ball with your niblick."

"Great Godfrey," I said, "you don't mean to say you are going to count those gestures I made to illustrate my argument as *golf strokes*? Just mere gestures! And you know very well I have never delivered a lecture in twenty-five years without gestures like that!"

"You moved your ball an inch or two with your club at every gesture," he said.

QUESTION: Had you really done so, Professor? Remember, you are on oath.

ANSWER: I do not remember. In any case, the point is immaterial. They were merely gestures.

QUESTION: Did you take an eight, or insist on a five?

ANSWER: I took an eight. I gave in. Gentlemen; I am a good-natured person. Too good-natured. Calm and philosophical; unruffled and patient. My philosophy never leaves me. I took an eight.

*(Sensation in the grand jury room.)*

QUESTION: Will you tell something of your past life, Professor Waddems—who you are and what your lifework has been, and how you acquired the calmness you speak of?

ANSWER: For nearly twenty-five years I lectured on philosophy and psychology in various universities. Since I retired and took up golf it has been my habit to look at all the events and tendencies in the world's news from the standpoint of the philosopher.

QUESTION: Has this helped you in your golf?

ANSWER: Yes, sir. My philosophical and logical training and my specialization in psychology, combined with my natural calmness and patience, have made me the great golfer that I really am.

QUESTION: Have you ever received a square deal, Professor, throughout any eighteen holes of golf?

ANSWER: No, sir. Not once! Not once during the five years since I took the game up at the Rivercliff Country Club.

QUESTION: Have you ever broken a hundred, Professor Waddems?

ANSWER: No, sir. I would have, again and again, except that my opponents, and other persons playing matches on the course, and the very forces of nature themselves are always against me at critical moments. Even the bullfrogs at the three water holes treat me impertinently.

QUESTION: Bullfrogs? You said the bullfrogs, Professor?

ANSWER: Yes, sir. They have been trained by the caddies to treat me impertinently.

QUESTION: What sort of treatment have your received in the locker room?

ANSWER: The worst possible. In the case under consideration, I may say that I took an eight on the second hole, instead of insisting on a five, because I knew the sort of thing Dr. Green would say in the locker room after the match—I knew the scene he would make, and what the comments of my so-called friends would be. Whenever I do get down to a hundred an attempt is made to discredit me in the locker room.

QUESTION: Well, you took an eight on the second hole. What happened at the third hole?

ANSWER: Well, sir, I teed up for my drive, and just as I did so, Doc

Green made a slighting remark about the League of Nations. "I think it is a good thing we kept out of it," he said.

QUESTION: What were your reactions?

ANSWER: A person of intelligence could only have one kind of reaction, sir. The remark was silly, narrow-minded, provincial, boneheaded, crass and ignorant. It was all the more criminal because Dr. Green knew quite well what I think of the League of Nations. The League of Nations was my idea. I thought about it even before the late President Wilson did, and talked about it and wrote about it and lectured about it in the university.

QUESTION: So that you consider Dr. Green's motives in mentioning it when you were about to drive–

ANSWER: The worst possible, sir. They could only come from a black heart at such a time.

QUESTION: Did you lose your temper, Professor?

ANSWER: No, sir! No, sir! No, sir! I *never* lose my temper! Not on any provocation. I said to myself, Be calm! Be philosophical! He's trying to get me excited! Remember what he'll say in the locker room afterwards! Be calm! Show him, show him, show him! Show him he can't get my goat.

QUESTION: Then you drove?

ANSWER: I addressed the ball the second time, sir. And I was about to drive when he said, with a sneer, "You must excuse me, Professor. I forgot that you invented the League of Nations."

QUESTION: Did you become violent, then, Professor?

ANSWER: No, sir! No, sir! I never become violent! I never–

QUESTION: Can you moderate your voice somewhat, Professor?

ANSWER: Yes, sir. I was explaining that I never become violent. I had every right to become violent. Any person less calm and philosophical would have become violent. Doc Green to criticize the League of Nations! The ass! Absurd! Preposterous! Silly! Abhorrent! Criminal! What the world wants is peace! Philosophic calm! The fool! Couldn't he understand that!

QUESTION: Aren't you departing, Professor, from the events of the 29th of last September at the Rivercliff golf course? What did you do next?

ANSWER: I drove.

QUESTION: Successfully?

ANSWER: It was a good drive, but the wind caught it, and it went out of bounds.

QUESTION: What did Dr. Green do then?

ANSWER: He grinned. A crass bonehead capable of sneering at the progress of the human race would sneer at a time like that.

QUESTION: But you kept your temper?

ANSWER: All my years of training as a philosopher came to my aid.

QUESTION: Go on, Professor.

ANSWER: I took my midiron from my bag and looked at it.

QUESTION: Well, go on, Professor. What did you think when you looked at it?

ANSWER: I do not remember, sir.

QUESTION: Come, come, Professor! You are under oath, you know. Did you think what a dent it would make in his skull?

ANSWER: Yes, sir. I remember now. I remember wondering if it would not do his brain good to be shaken up a little.

QUESTION: Did you strike him, then?

ANSWER: No, sir. I knew what they'd say in the locker room. They'd say that I lost temper over a mere game. They would not understand that I had been jarring up his brain for his own good, in the hope of making him understand about the League of Nations. They'd say I was irritated. I know the things people always say.

QUESTION: Was there no other motive for not hitting him?

ANSWER: I don't remember.

QUESTION: Professor Waddems, again I call your attention to the fact that you are under oath. What was your other motive?

ANSWER: Oh yes, now I recall it. I reflected that if I hit him they might make me add another stroke to my score. People are always getting up the flimsiest excuses to make me add another stroke. And then accusing me of impatience if I do not acquiesce in their unfairness. I am never impatient or irritable!

QUESTION: Did you ever break a club on the course, Professor?

ANSWER: I don't remember.

QUESTION: Did you not break a mashie on the Rivercliff course last week, Professor Waddems? Reflect before you answer.

ANSWER: I either gave it away or broke it, I don't remember which.

QUESTION: Come, come, don't you remember that you broke it against a tree?

ANSWER: Oh, I think I know what you mean. But it was not through temper or irritation.

QUESTION: Tell the jury about it.

ANSWER: Well, gentlemen, I had a mashie that had a loose head on it, and I don't know how it got into my bag. My ball lay behind a sapling, and I tried to play it out from behind the tree and missed it entirely. And then I noticed I had this old mashie, which should have been gotten rid of long ago. The club had never been any good. The blade was laid back at the wrong angle. I decided that the time had come to get rid of it once and for all. So I hit it a little tap against the tree, and the head fell off. I threw the pieces over into the bushes.

QUESTION: Did you swear, Professor?

ANSWER: I don't remember. But the injustice of this incident was that my opponent insisted on counting it as a stroke and adding it to my score–my judicial, deliberate destruction of this old mashie. I never get a square deal.

QUESTION: Return to Dr. James T. Green, Professor. You are now at the third hole, and the wind has just carried your ball out of bounds.

ANSWER: Well, I didn't hit him when he sneered. I carried the ball within bounds.

"Shooting three," I said calmly. I topped the ball. Gentlemen, I have seen Walter Hagen top the ball the same way.

"Too bad, Professor," said Doc Green. He said it hypocritically. I knew it was hypocrisy. He was secretly gratified that I had topped the ball. He knew I knew it.

QUESTION: What were your emotions at this further insult, Professor?

ANSWER: I pitied him. I thought how inferior he was to me intellectually, and I pitied him. I addressed the ball again. "I pity him," I murmured. "Pity, pity, pity, pity, pity!"

He overheard me. "Your pity has cost you five more strokes," he said.

"I was merely gesticulating," I said.

QUESTION: Did the ball move? Remember, you are under oath, and you have waived immunity.

ANSWER: If the ball moved, it was because a strong breeze had sprung up.

QUESTION: Go on.

ANSWER: I laid the ball upon the green and again holed out with one putt. "I'm taking a five," I said, marking it on my card.

"I'm giving you a ten," he said, marking it on his card. "Five gesticulations on account of your pity."

QUESTION: Describe your reactions to this terrible injustice, Professor. Was there a red mist before your eyes? Did you turn giddy and wake up to find him lying lifeless at your feet? Just what happened?

ANSWER: Nothing, sir.

(*Sensation in the grand jury room.*)

QUESTION: Think again, Professor. Nothing?

ANSWER: I merely reflected that, in spite of his standing scientifically, Dr. James T. Green was a moron and utterly devoid of morality and that I should take this into account. I did not lose my temper.

QUESTION: Did you snatch the card from his hands?

ANSWER: I took it, sir. I did not snatch it.

QUESTION: And then did you cram it down his throat?

ANSWER: I suggested that he eat it, sir, as it contained a falsehood in black and white, and Dr. Green complied with my request.

QUESTION: Did you lay hands upon him, Professor? Remember, now, we are still talking about the third hole.

ANSWER: I think I did steady him a little by holding him about the neck and throat while he masticated and swallowed the card.

QUESTION: And then what?

ANSWER: Well, gentlemen, after that there is very little more to tell until we reached the sixteenth hole. Dr. Green for some time made no further attempt to treat me unjustly and played in silence, acquiescing in the scores I had marked on my card. We were even as to holes, and it was a certainty that I was about to break a hundred. But I knew what was beneath this silence on Doc Green's part, and I did not trust it.
QUESTION: What do you mean? That you knew what he was thinking, although he did not speak?
ANSWER: Yes, sir. I knew just what kind of remarks he would have made if he had made any remarks.
QUESTION: Were these remarks which he suppressed derogatory remarks?
ANSWER: Yes, sir. Almost unbelievably so. They were deliberately intended to destroy my poise.
QUESTION: Did they do so, Professor?
ANSWER: I don't think so.
QUESTION: Go on, Professor.
ANSWER: At the sixteenth tee, as I drove off, this form of insult reached its climax. He accentuated his silence with a peculiar look, just as my club head was about to meet the ball. I knew what he meant. He knew that I knew it, and that I knew. I sliced into a bunker. He stood and watched me, as I stepped into the sand with my niblick–watched me with that look upon his face. I made three strokes at the ball and, as will sometimes happen even to the best of players, did not move it a foot. The fourth stroke drove it out of sight into the sand. The sixth stroke brought it to light again. Gentlemen, I did not lose my temper. I never do. But I admit that I did increase my tempo. I struck rapidly three more times at the ball. And all the time Doc Green was regarding me with that look, to which he now added a smile. Still I kept my temper, and he might be alive today if he had not spoken.
QUESTION (*by the foreman of the jury*): What did the man say at this trying time?
ANSWER: I know that you will not believe it is within the human heart to make the black remark that he made. And I hesitate to repeat it. But

I have sworn to tell everything. What he said was, "Well, Professor, the club puts these bunkers here, and I suppose they have got to be used."

QUESTION (*by the foreman of the jury*): Was there something especially trying in the way he said it?

ANSWER: There was. He said it with an affectation of joviality.

QUESTION: You mean as if he thought he were making a joke, Professor?

ANSWER: Yes, sir.

QUESTION: What were your emotions at this point?

ANSWER: Well, sir, it came to me suddenly that I owed a duty to society; and for the sake of civilization I struck him with the niblick. It was an effort to reform him, gentlemen.

QUESTION: Why did you cover him with sand afterwards?

ANSWER: Well, I knew that if the crowd around the locker room discovered that I had hit him, they would insist on counting it as another stroke. And that is exactly what happened when the body was discovered–once again I was prevented from breaking a hundred.

THE DISTRICT ATTORNEY: Gentlemen of the jury, you have heard Professor Waddems' frank and open testimony in the case of Dr. James T. Green. My own recommendation is that he be not only released, but complimented, as far as this count is returned. If ever a homicide was justifiable, this one was. And I suggest that you report no indictment against the Professor, without leaving your seats. Many of you will wish to get in at least nine holes before dinner.

*In the early days—before Palmer, corporate sponsors, and omnipresent television—golf was not a big-money game. Today, a top-notch tournament professional can make more money in a few months than the great Sam Snead made in his long career. Walt Smallens, the old-time protagonist of this story, is an aging tournament professional who realizes the game is up. It's a bittersweet story that originally appeared in the* Saturday Evening Post.

*William E. Pettit*

# DECISION ON THE FAIRWAY (1960)

RUTH BENT DOWN AND TOUCHED Walt's shoulder gently. He opened his eyes and rolled over on his back. "It 's four-thirty, dear," she said. "Do you want to practice?"

"Yes," he said, looking at her as she stood half bent over him and noticing the lines between her brown eyes. They were new, those lines, he thought; they hadn't been there at all a few years ago. "Yes," he said. "I have to. Especially today."

She smiled, straightening and turning to the tiny trailer stove, the breakfast on the drop-leaf table. "Go on," she said. "You could stay in bed all day and still qualify tomorrow."

"Maybe," he said, lighting a cigarette and smoking, his head on his arm, watching her. "But I don't feel right if I don't get out. Golf's a funny game, you know."

She laughed. "And you're a funny golfer. You don't vary two strokes a round on any course in the country from one year to the next, and you know it. But still you have to practice, practice, hours every day." She poured the coffee so it would cool a little–the way he liked it. Still smiling she said, "Old Deadeye Smallens. Old Consistency himself."

"Yeah," he said. "That's me, all right." He raised his knees, flexing slowly all the muscles in his legs, feeling, even after a good night's rest, that tiredness, that constant residue of fatigue that for several years had slowly been forcing itself upon his attention and that this year, at last, could no longer be ignored. He hadn't told Ruth about it yet–it was the only thing he could remember ever not telling her–and he thought this was a good time to plant a little hint. He said, "But it can't last forever, you know. Old pros wear out. Everybody has to go to seed someday."

"Go on!" she said. "Don't you talk that way. You'll play years and years yet, you'll see–unless you win fifty thousand dollars and want to quit."

He crushed out the butt in the ash tray resting on his chest and got out of bed. "Old dreamer, who are kidding? Me win fifty thousand dollars? I'd drop dead. Second-place Smallens, that's me. Never gets hot, never gets cold. Never get the breaks."

"Pooh," she said. "You don't play for breaks, remember? You play for accuracy and you're the best golfer of them all. Look at the records, they'll show it; nobody can match you for year after year after year. So what if you've never won first in a few big matches?"

It was like listening to himself talk, hearing a record of something he'd said over and over; and hearing it now, when he was painfully making his mind change, was uncomfortable. He washed his face in the tiny trailer sink, blew the drops of water explosively off his face and said, "Old Cheerleader, that's you. Twenty-four years on the circuits, and what's the most we've won? I ask you."

"Eighteen thousand," she said. "Twelve years ago."

"And since then?"

She shrugged. "The competition's getting tougher, that's all. More and more people are playing, so there's bound to be more good ones. But your game hasn't changed; the records show that."

"Records, schmecords," he said, hanging up the towel. He walked to her, grabbing her shoulders and squeezing them while he kissed her on the cheek. "Anyway, one thing I've decided. After this match you don't get up to get my breakfast. I'll get a bite myself and sneak out, and you sleep. You work twelve hours a day in those restaurants, on your feet all day, and then you get up two hours earlier than you have to, just to get me out." He sat down and began eating. "I don't see how you stand it anyway on your feet so much. I couldn't, especially these last few years. Every day, six days a week. Just to support me."

"Stop it," she said, sitting down suddenly. "I don't support you. You've always made more than I have, almost every year, and sometimes lots more." She relaxed her face and smiled at him. "Anyway, I don't mind. I'm made of iron, remember? You've said so often enough."

"Yeah," he said, shaking his head and thinking about his legs. "You sure are. I sure wish I was."

Twenty minutes later Walt, a small tight man whose face and hands and half-bald head were cured by the sun and the wind to a deep and permanent potato brown, was standing on the tee of the seventh hole, practicing. The fairway of this par-four hole went straight out between the trees and then bent back on itself to a small green, not visible from the tee. Walt was working–had been working every morning for a week–to shoot over the trees with his three iron and drop that ball on the green for a birdie–to save a stroke that could be the difference between fifty thousand dollars and the Crawford Cup, and second place. He was practicing to cut to zero the risk of what for anyone else would be a wild shot. And all the time he thought about his legs–his tired, tiring legs.

He set another ball on the tee, straightened and swung, each part of his body swinging around some imaginary axis, the clubhead going back along an imaginary curve he had plotted in his head. Then it came down, smoothly picking up speed, to the point where his wrists snapped the club around so quickly that even on the high-speed photographs Ruth once took of him, the motion of the head was an irreducible blur. He hit the ball and went on, turning until he ended with the shaft across his shoulder, his feet twisted, his body relaxed and almost falling down, limp like a straw man until he stepped back.

*This year,* he thought, *this year has to be it.* The tee was lying point up on the grass, broken in the middle as it should be. He turned his head up just in time to see the ball drop, from the peak of its rise above the trees, out of sight. Then he held his breath until he heard his caddie, standing under the trees near the green, shouting, "You're on!"

The caddie sounded chilly, Walt thought, and sleepy and bored now that Walt was hitting the green almost every time. But he knew all about sleepy, bored caddies–all the way back for years to one skinny young caddie named Walt Smallens, eagerly pocketing lost balls and hitting them, in his spare time, with a split and mended iron somebody in a temper had wrapped around a tree and tossed away. Walt had won the caddies' tournament when he was fourteen, won the county amateur at sixteen, turned pro at eighteen and married Ruth, whom he'd met at a tournament, the next year. And here he was, still at it, he thought. Old Second-place Smallens, the golfer's golfer, who'd won all the tournaments but the big ones, whose legs were wearing out.

He could stop playing of course, and take a year's vacation, hoping his legs would come back. But from all he knew of golfers, they wouldn't. Once the legs begin to go, that's it; and a layoff might even make them worse. Besides, there was this control of his, the edge of that peak he was sure he was now on. It was an extremely fine thing, like a violinist's technique or a brain surgeon's skill. Between the golf he was playing now and the golf he knew he could play was only a matter of two or three strokes. He'd been working toward that peak for twenty years or more and he'd figured that in three or four more years, playing his old way, he'd make it. But he'd figured wrong, figured without his legs giving out on him; so now everything was different.

For twenty-four years of playing he'd always prided himself on putting his shots where he wanted them, within a few feet. Now he'd discovered that by hitting harder, to make up for the lost snap in the muscles of his legs, he could get another fifteen or twenty yards, which meant he could play his second shot with a shorter iron, come in closer to the pin. But the extra push, the final surge of power threw his old swing out, blew his fine control away; so that he was never sure which way the ball would go. If there was a trap there or some trees–things which never would have bothered him before–he might wind up in them and lose the stroke he was taking such a chance to save. For Walt it was a new game, a crazy kind of golf he didn't like.

In spite of everything he'd ever believed in and lived for–playing golf accurately, with skill and science and taking out all the risk, like with this shot over the trees to the seventh green–this other idea, about winning one big one, got into his head. He'd made up his mind that in this last big tournament–and he knew this would be his last full year–this was the kind of golf he was going to play–risky, hitting hard, hoping for the breaks.

He hit a few more balls as the caddie yelled, "On," after each of them and then quit, sending his clubs back to the clubhouse and cautioning the caddie to be on time in the morning. He slept most of the day, sat talking with Ruth in the evening in the trailer, drank a cup of hot milk and two shots of rum and went to bed at ten o'clock. He fell asleep immediately, as he always did, and woke up at seven without needing an alarm clock. Ruth was already at work in the restaurant, and so he made his own breakfast, eating a little more than he usually did. He was calm all through his body. He had worked all this out so carefully years before, this routine before the start of a tournament so that he never felt, couldn't remember feeling, any nervousness at all.

The round was the qualifying round of the Crawford Open, the biggest cash prize of the year, and all the entrants but the top half dozen had to shoot under eighty to be eligible for the tournament. Some years ago Walt had been one of the few who hadn't had to qualify, he'd been so close to the top, but he didn't mind playing the extra round. Honors like that didn't mean anything to him; and now, with the new risks in his game, he was glad of an extra chance to practice. The others were avoiding tension and saving their best for the actual competition, and Walt was almost the only one of the more than one hundred players who was shooting as low as he possibly could–except for the over-the-trees shot on the seventh. He saved that for the last day.

He led the field all the way and went into the seventeenth a stroke ahead, but then the runner-up sank a thirty-foot putt and tied him. Somebody said, "Bad break, Walt."

Walt laughed and shook his head. "Those things roll in sometimes," he said. "For everybody."

The reporters were all for him, of course, and one of the papers said, "Walt Smallens looked good out there today, very good. Maybe this is the year we've all been waiting for," not believing it for a moment, but willing to go out on a limb a little in case a miracle was at long last about to happen. Ruth was so happy she jumped up and down. "Did you see what Powell wrote about you, Walt?" she said. "That this might be your year?"

Walt shrugged, carefully keeping his face calm. "He's a nice guy, Powell. I'll buy him a drink next time I see him. Anyway, honey, they're all my years, remember? You don't care if I don't win, do you, so long as I play my best?"

"Oh, go on," she said, making a face at him. "Of course I don't, and you know it. But after all, the law of averages; you've always been so close. And fifty thousand dollars. My, wouldn't that be nice?"

"Yeah," Walt said, looking down at his shoes. "It sure would."

The first day of the tournament was cold, and Walt's body was tight, his legs felt stiff. He kept putting more force into his downswing, using everything he had in his arms and shoulders, and his wood shots were flatter than they used to be, and the ball went out farther, ten or fifteen yards from his target spot. He was lucky–so lucky it made him sweat. He didn't land in any bad trouble spots and he finished the first round in third place, behind Snead and a big young fellow named Tucker.

Then the second day it rained a little, but not enough to call the tournament off, and Tucker blew some strokes. Walt went on hitting hard, to get the extra distance, and he finished second–two strokes away.

"Oh, Walt, honey, this *is* it," Ruth exulted. "I feel it, baby, I really do. This is the year we've been waiting for."

Walt shook his head. She didn't know what he was trying to do, the strain he was playing under; she thought he was playing his usual game. He said, "Let's not talk about it, will you? And let's go to a movie tonight. I don't want to get tensed up any."

Sunday was the last day–thirty-six holes in cold, fine rain. Ruth never worked the last day of a tournament because she couldn't stand not watching it; so she followed him around, carrying the things he needed. He felt all right going out on the first nine. He wore his gray sweater and a loose rainproof jacket and his rainproof hat. Every third hole he changed his socks and had a little swallow of rum and hot coffee from the vacuum bottle Ruth carried. His caddie, the same skinny boy, was shivering in the rain, but he kept Walt's clubs clean and dry.

Luck stayed with him all morning long, keeping her lovely eyes on his ball, stopping it just short of sand traps, dropping it safely under branches hanging out over the fairways as Walt wound his body back and strained his arms and shoulders and hit every long one just as hard as he knew how. It was as though the fickle lady, never having been wooed before by this man of iron will, was going to kiss him with her kindness when at last he needed her, when at last his own strength was proving not enough. Walt, after thinking about it for several moments, decided once more to play the seventh the regular way, saving his trick shot as the last possible ace in the hole. He parred the hole, parred or birdied every other hole and finished the morning eighteen even with Snead when the Slammer missed an eight-foot putt by less than a whisker. Ruth ran up to him as he came off the eighteenth green. "Walt, Walt! Oh, honey, it's–" She shook her head quickly, her eyes bright with excitement and hope and faith. She said, "How do you feel, honey; how do you feel?"

He laughed, squeezing her hand. "Tired," he said. "Dog tired." It was not only his legs that were aching, almost trembling, this time; it was his whole body. His arms, his shoulders, the big muscles up each side of his back, even the muscles in his belly–those that snapped the clubhead around that final, crucial few inches–were completely fatigued. He said, "I'm wrung out, hon; just sheer wrung out."

"It must be the weather," she said. "This rain. And the tension."

He shook his head. "I'm not tense, hon; you know that. And it's not the rain either. But"–he started walking toward the clubhouse, his arm through hers–"I'll tell you about it later."

"Why don't you lie down for a while?" she said, concerned. She was looking at him, noticing that his face, tanned though it was, showed how tired he was. "There're some cots down there, aren't there, in the locker rooms?"

"Just what I was going to do," he said. "I'll go right down the back stairs, so I won't have to gab with anybody. O.K.?"

"Sure," she said, slipping her arm away from his and smiling.

So while all the others–players, officials, spectators, reporters–were upstairs in the clubhouse laughing and talking excitedly, as tired people do near the climax of something big, something they've experienced together, Walt lay stretched out on a wooden bench in the locker room, which he'd found more relaxing than the soft cot, his head pillowed on his rolled-up jacket. He lay staring at the ceiling, not closing his eyes because he didn't want to fall asleep, and trying to pretend to himself that he wasn't thinking about anything–nothing at all.

He got up when he heard the applause outside and went up the outside stairs and around to the first tee. One twosome was already off, and Snead was on the tee; Walt glanced up at the big official scoreboard and felt, in spite of himself, a thrill in his stomach when he saw his name right under Snead's–four under par for all three rounds, fifty-four holes–and the nearest contenders bunched, three of them, five strokes behind. *They'll never catch up,* Walt thought. *None of them–not in the rain like this. So it's me or Snead, that's for sure.* Then Snead drove, and the crowd applauded; and Walt, who was in the next twosome to go, walked over to his caddie and took his driver, swinging it easily back and forth in his hands.

The hour's rest had helped a little, made him feel much less tired, but walking down the first fairway after a hard, low drive which had punched the ball away out through the rain, he knew it wasn't enough; he knew it wouldn't last. It would take more than an hour–it would take several days, just lying around, to wash all the fatigue out of him and all the aches out of his sore muscles. And going to the second tee, still even, he wondered if time would be enough, wondered if he'd ever feel rested and fresh again. He played on almost automatically, thinking only, *Sixteen more holes, fifteen more holes, a few more little hours, thirteen more holes. Twelve more. Man, how tired can you get? My back. And my poor old shoulders.*

He came up to the seventh tee and stood quietly looking down at the ground while his partner, who had no chance of finishing near the top at all, drove straight and short down the dog-legged fairway. Then Walt looked up at his caddie and nodded, smiling a little and winking. The boy, not bored at all now, grinned so widely Walt thought the top of his head would come off; and he handed Walt his three iron. Walt heard several excited people say, "Look, look, an iron. What's he going to do? Sh, sh-h." And then he could hear nothing but the soft sound of the rain and his own breathing; and he forgot everything, standing there leaning forward over the ball on its tee, gripping the leather-wrapped handle of his club. Then he prepared to swing. Nobody could understand all the tensions and adjustments and little readjustments he put into it. But he felt, as he twisted around into the backswing, his body all coiled around, something slip in his shoulder, like a knuckle slipping out of its joint; and a shot of pain went through his whole side that almost made him cry out. He didn't; he held his breath and swung. Then he heard the caddie cry, "You're on, you're on, you're on," and then heard the boy's straining shrill voice disappear under a roar of shouting and applause. Ruth ran over to him and she was crying, "Honey, honey, Walter! That was beautiful, oh, that was–I've never seen anything like it."

He looked up at her, smiling, feeling the pain subside in his arm, in his stomach; and he said very quietly, "Sure, baby, sure. Let's go on to the green, shall we?"

She walked beside him to the green, going around the point of trees. Then she stopped, waiting; and Walt went ahead to his ball. It was about twelve feet from the cup, on a level part of the green, just slightly downhill, with no breaks. Walt took his putter with his right hand and held it, sizing up the putt carefully from two directions; and then he putted, using his right arm mostly, as he always did, and was down in two putts, and a stroke ahead of Snead. The crowd raised a lot of fuss, of course, thinking that this stroke could mean something, everything; and Walt knew they were right, even with eleven holes to go. But all that seemed very distant now, even more distant than he usually tried to keep such things when he was playing out something tight. Instead he was listening, almost, to his shoulder, which had twinged out a sharp pain even when he putted; and he thought, *The bursae, maybe,* not really sure what the bursae were. He waggled the putter slightly, before he picked the ball out of the cup and felt the pain steady in his shoulder. And he knew that next time he took a strong swing it would hit again, harder and then harder. It wasn't feeling the pain that scared him–he knew he could stand that all right for the few holes that were left. It was the thought that his arm would pull or jerk and he'd ruin the shot completely.

Then the other thought came to him, the only really important one, and he couldn't believe he hadn't thought of it right away–if he went on playing, if he took just one more swing, he might ruin his shoulder, do some deep and permanent damage that would finish him forever as a playing pro, as a teaching pro, even as an old duffer in his sixties or seventies, swatting out a few on a bright spring Sunday morning. Was it worth that to go on, to take a wild fling at winning fifty thousand dollars? What was fifty thousand, anyway, for a man and his wife for the rest of their lives? It wasn't enough; it was only a small, small part of living, of what really made up living.

There was a man's work and the pleasure he got out of doing it well, and his sharing that with his wife and his friends. There was believing in something that was important to you and keeping your mind busy and alert and young. That was the way he'd lived, they'd lived, he and Ruth; and that was the way he wanted to go on living until they died–not as an old wreck washed up somewhere, with a cracked shoulder and an idle mind; a puny bundle of memories, half of which probably weren't true, and a small monthly check from the fifty thousand. Security–since when had he, Walt Smallens, had to be promised security before he'd walk out into the big world and take the next step?

He looked up. The gallery was going, rushing through the trees to get a good spot along the next fairway to watch him drive off. And Ruth, holding the vacuum bottle and all the other stuff she was carrying for him, was always carrying for him, was waiting, smiling. He took a deep breath and held it and then he handed the putter to the caddie; he began walking forward through the trees, toward the tee. The caddie, hurrying behind him, tried to hand him his driver because he knew Walt liked to have a club in his hands to swing gently as he approached his next shot; but Walt shook his head, saying, "Hang onto it, kid." He walked across the tee to the tournament official who was standing there, holding a clipboard with some papers on it, under a big black umbrella.

"Ben," Walt said, "I just hurt my shoulder on that tee shot back there–pulled something pretty bad and I'm going in to see the doctor. What's the rules say about that, if he should say I can go on all right? Am I finished if I leave the play?"

"That's too bad, Walt," said the official, a bald heavy man who'd been a pro himself years before, when Walt was growing up. "You don't want to take any chances with something like that, that's for sure. I was worried about something like that happening, the way you've been pushing it this week."

Walt, surprised, said, "You noticed that?"

Ben smiled. "Not much we don't notice, Walt, especially about guys we've been watching and worrying about twenty years or more." Walt felt a little guilty, a little ungrateful, realizing he'd been trying to carry this weight alone, when actually a lot of people had been carrying it with him all the time. He'd have to remember that, all right, when this was over.

Ben said, "You have some time of course, Walt; I'll have to check with Randy to see how much, because he's the boss on this one. And you'll have to finish out with somebody else, of course, because we can't hold up the whole–"

"Pardon me." It was a man in the crowds behind Ben, easing himself forward. He came up to them saying, "I overheard, Mr. Smallens; I hope you don't mind." He smiled a smile Walt liked immediately and said, "I'm Robert Halskins and I'm a doctor. I've had quite a bit of experience with things like this, and if you'd let me–"

He reached up toward Walt's jacket; and Walt, nodding quickly, unzipped it with his right hand. The doctor and Ben helped him slip it off his left shoulder, down his left arm; and as he turned to slip out of it, he saw Ruth standing there just behind him, her eyes fixed on his. *Damn,* he thought, as he smiled at her, *what a rotten thing to happen to her, just now of all times.* Then he jumped and grimaced as the doctor began feeling his shoulder, straining it back, prodding and poking. The pain was almost as bad as it had been when the shoulder slipped askew, and he tried to hold his breath until the man was through.

The doctor said, "I can't be absolutely sure, of course, without a more thorough examination and X rays and all that. I couldn't even be absolutely sure then; no medical man could. But I'd say that with complete rest" –he looked at Walt, pausing, and said again–"complete rest, and then starting off again very gently, you'll be able to play all right in a few months. Probably you'll always have to be very careful of it, because once these things happen–But as far as playing now"–he looked down at Walt's hands–"every stroke you play will mean that many more months you won't play and that much less chance your shoulder will come back completely. And by the time you've gone four more holes, you may not even be able to lift a club, much less control it."

Walt, looking at Ruth, nodded. "I see, Doc," he said. "Thanks. If you'll see my wife here and give her your address, she'll–"

"That's all right," the man said. "I'm just sorry that–if you'd like to check it with someone else right now–"

Walt shook his head, still looking at Ruth. "No, no," he said, "we don't have to do that. We know when we're licked, don't we, hon? And it's not just this shoulder, either, that did it."

"What do you mean, Walt?" Ruth said.

"I mean my legs have been giving out, hon, for a year or more now, and that's why I was pushing so hard today–to make up for it and to see if once, before I hung up my clubs, I could fix it so you wouldn't have to wait on those damned tables any more."

Ruth blushed and shook her head. She said, "That's not–never mind that; you know I don't mind. I just wanted once to win a big one so you could retire. I knew it was coming soon, when you couldn't go on playing the circuit like this; but I didn't know it was–"

He laughed. "Well, it's here. A man can't go on and on like a mule, stomping around and around the same track until he drops; and anybody who thinks he can ought to know better. Now I do. So let's–where's that kid?"

There was a flurry of turning and calling; and then the crowds opened again and Walt's caddie came hurrying up, holding tightly to Walt's clubs. He said, "Yes, sir, Mr. Smallens?"

"Take the bag into the clubhouse, kid," Walt said. "Be sure you dry them all off because I'm going to be using them again someday–showing somebody else how to play, probably," he added, grinning up at the official, Ben, standing just beside him.

"No problem there, Walt," Ben said. "Dozens of places just dying to get you. I heard somebody say just the other day they'd–"

The boy stepped forward, almost up against Walt, and said, "You're quittin', Mr. Smallens?"

Walt nodded, looking down at him. "Yeah, son. Right now."

"Gee, Mr. Smallens, I–" The boy's eyes filled with tears, and Walt smiled, knowing just how the boy felt, knowing down through many, many years just what was in the boy's mind and the great tragedy it seemed. But Walt knew now it wasn't so; he knew he was glad he could quit this way, right in the middle of almost winning the biggest match of his life.

And he knew he was glad he didn't have to think the first thought every morning about his legs, how much longer they'd last. He knew all that was over at last—and should have been over along time ago, if he'd only had sense enough to let go of what he'd once been. And he knew that for the next twenty or thirty or forty years there'd be another Walt Smallens, living a different kind of life—still golf, some end of it, of course, because that was what he knew and loved; and still the same Walt inside, but wearing an older pair of legs and a wiser head and not, he was sure, with Ruth working in restaurants.

He reached out and took Ruth's hand, pulling her close to him and turning to go, and he said, "Buck up, kid; it's not that bad. Nothing is."

"Yes, Mr. Smallens," the boy said, nodding and sniffling.

"Oh, hell, boy," Walt said, grinning and winking at Ben, "call me Walt." And he and Ruth walked away, and behind them the thick crowd of people, none of whom Walt knew personally, broke into a final, long, loud crackle of applause.

*The last and by far the longest golf story in this book is probably the most popular ever in Britain. Major Jacky Gore, who modestly attests to being "the finest sportsman living," decides to take up golf to prove a point or two. Gore's golfing and amorous adventures are told in a superb style that makes this story a benchmark of literary entertainment and quality. Author Robert Marshall (1863–1910) was a prominent British playwright.*

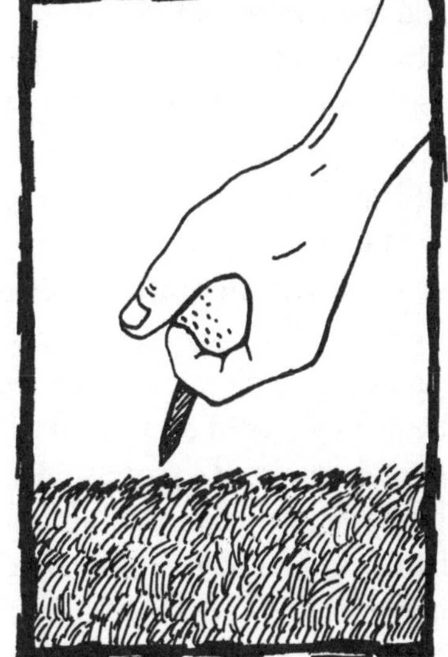

*Robert Marshall*

# THE HAUNTED MAJOR (1902)

## I: About Myself

I AM A POPULAR MAN and withal I am not vain.

To the people who know me I am an acquaintance of importance.

This is due to a combination of circumstances.

First of all, I am a youthful (aged thirty-five) major in that smart cavalry regiment, the 1st Royal Light Hussars, commonly called the "Chestnuts."

Secondly, I am an excellent polo player, standing practically at the top of the particular tree of sport; and again, I am a quite unusually brilliant cricketer. That I do not play in first-class cricket is due to long service abroad with my regiment; but now that we are at last quartered in

England, I daily expect to be approached by the committee of my county eleven.

I consider myself, not before taking the opinion of my warmest friends, the best racket player of my day in India; and I have rarely played football (Rugby) without knowing by a strange instinct (born, I feel sure, of truth) that I was the best man on the ground.

In the hunting field I am well known as one of the hardest riders across country living; and this statement, so far from being my own, emanates from my father's land agent, a poor relative of ours, and himself a fair performer in the saddle. As a shot, I will refer you to my own game book; and if, after examining the records contained therein, you can show me an equally proficient man in that special line, well–I'll take off my hat to him.

The trophies of head, horn, and skin at Castle Goresby, our family's country seat, are sufficient guarantees of my prowess with big game in all parts of the world; and when I mention that I have been one of an Arctic Expedition, have climbed to the highest mountain peaks explored by man, voyaged for days in a balloon, dived to a wreck in the complete modern outfit of a professional diver, am as useful on a yacht as any man of my acquaintance, think nothing of scoring a hundred break at billiards, and rarely meet my match at whist, piquet, or poker, it will be admitted that I have not confined my talents, such as they are, to any one particular branch of sport.

In fact, I am "Jacky Gore," and although the War Office addresses me officially as "Major the Honorable John William Wentworth Gore, 1st Royal Light Hussars," nothing is sweeter to my ear than to hear, as I often do, a passing remark such as "There goes good old Jacky Gore, the finest sportsman living!"

I take it for granted that the reader will accept this candor as to my performances in the spirit which inspires it, and not as a stupid form of self-conceit. I desire to be absolutely confidential and unreserved with those who peruse these pages, and a false modesty would be as misleading as it would be untrue to my nature.

For true modesty, as I conceive it, consists in an accurate valuation of one's own worth; an estimate of one's self that is conceived, not for purposes of advertisement, but rather to foster one's own self-respect. Thus, were these pages designed only for the eyes of sportsmen, there would appear no other description of myself than the laconic intimation, "I am Jacky Gore."

That, I know, would be sufficient to arrest electrically the ears of the sporting world. But as I desire my singular story to interest the whole range of human beings, from the Psychical Research Society down to the merest schoolboy who vaguely wonders if he will ever see a ghost, I must perforce be explicit, even to the extent of expounding my personal character as well as enumerating my achievements.

First, then, I am not a snob; I have no occasion to be one. I am the younger son of one of England's oldest earls, Lord Goresby, and my mother is the daughter of one of our newest marquises, Lord Dundrum. My friends are all of the very best, socially and otherwise. Indeed, I have established myself on a plane from which all acquaintances who have been financially unfortunate, or have otherwise become socially undesirable, must inevitably drop. For I hold that true friends are those whose position, affluence, and affection for one may be of material assistance in the race toward the goal of one's personal ambition.

If there is one thing that jars on me more than another, it is when a person of lower social status than my own presumes to associate with me in a style and with a manner that imply equality. I can readily, and I believe gracefully, meet people of higher rank than mine on their own platform, but the converse is, at least to me, odious.

Lest, from these candid statements, the reader might be inclined to consider me a trifle exclusive, I will frankly own that I often shoot, fish, or yacht with those *nouveaux riches* whose lacquer of gold so ineffectually conceals the real underlying metal. Still, a breadth of view of life, which has always been one of my characteristics, inspires me with the hope that the association of such people with one of my own type may in the process of time tend to the refining of the class from which they spring. Besides, one need not know people all one's life.

A keen eye for the artistic, a considerable talent for painting, a delicate and highly trained ear for music, and a quick perception as to what is of value in literature, have led me to frequent at times the houses where one meets the best class of so-called Bohemians. They are interesting people whom one may cultivate or drop according to social convenience, and useful as living dictionaries of the intellectual fashions of the moment. Sometimes I have thought that their interest in my experiences (as related in conversation by myself) has been strangely apathetic, not to say inattentive, due perhaps (as indeed I have been told) to their admiration of my physical points. In explanation I may point out that I have been modeled in marble as Hercules. It was a birthday gift I devised for my second cousin (by marriage) the Duke of Haredale, and I gave the commission to that admirable French sculptor, Moreau.

My means, viewed in proportion to those of my friends, are at least sufficient. For, although my allowance is nominally but £2,000 a year, my father has such a morbid sense of the family honor that he is always ready to pay up the casual debts that spring from daily intercourse with the best of everything. And as he enjoys an income of quite £150,000 a year, mainly derived from coal mines in Wales, there really seems no reason why I should not occasionally, indeed frequently, furnish him with an opportunity for indulging in his harmless hobby of keeping the family escutcheon clean.

I endeavor to keep in touch with society journalism and frequently entertain the editors of the more responsible sporting and smart papers. The Press being one of the glories of the age, I am ever ready to foster it; and though I care not one straw for the personal puffs of which I myself am so often the subject, still I know that they give pleasure to my friends, both at home and abroad.

As regards the literary style of these pages, I desire to point out that its agreeable flavor has been purveyed by a friend of mine, an eminent critic who writes for all the best daily and weekly papers both in London and the provinces. I have merely supplied the facts with such reflections and embroideries thereon as seemed to me both necessary and graceful. He has done the rest. Thus, if any adverse criticisms of my book should appear—an idea which I do not seriously entertain—the reader will understand that they are prompted either by professional jealousy or unfair rivalry, motives which, I am happy to think, have no place in the advanced and altruistic journalism of today.

And now, my reader, just before we plunge *in medias res,* I approach a subject which, if treated with candor, must also be handled with delicacy.

I desire to marry.

I desire to marry Katherine Clavering Gunter.

She is an American and a widow.

She is an enthusiastic golfer.

She is quite beautiful, especially in her photographs.

Since the day Carmody said, in the billiard room at White's, that she reminded him of a blush rose whose outer petals were becoming touched with the tint of biscuits, I have cut him dead. Her beauty is to me full of freshness, especially at night.

She has a fortune of £2,000,000 sterling, and I love her with a very true and real love. That is to say, I love her with a perfectly balanced affection; an affection based impartially on an estimate of her personal worth, an admiration for her physical charms, and an appreciation of her comfortable circumstances. I perceive that our union would further our respective interests in providing each of us with certain extensions of our present modes of living. I have long desired a place of my own in the country; and Katherine, I know, wishes to move freely in smart circles without having to employ the services of impoverished dowagers. In many other ways I could be of assistance to Katherine. I could tell her how to wear her diamonds, for instance, a difficult art she has not yet acquired. She is inclined on the slightest provocation to decorate herself in exuberant imitation of a cut-crystal chandelier.

There are, however, difficulties.

Prominent among these is the fact, already mentioned, that she is an ardent golfer. Except during the season in town, she spends her year in golfing, either at St. Magnus or Pau, for, like all good Americans, she has long since abjured her native soil.

Now golf is a game that presents no attractions to me. I have never tried it, nor even held a golf stick in my hand. A really good game, to my mind, must have an element, however slight, of physical danger to the player. This is the great whet to skilled performance. It is the condition that fosters pluck and self-reliance and develops our perception of the value of scientific play. It breeds a certain fearlessness that stimulates us not merely during the actual progress of the game, but unconsciously in the greater world where we play at Life with alert and daring opponents.

Now golf presents no such condition, and I despise it.

Once, by means of jocular query (a useful method of extracting such information as may not always be asked for bluntly), I gathered from Katherine that marriage with a keen golfer would probably be her future state; and this admission, I confess, was extremely galling to me, the more so as I had just been entertaining her with a long summary of my own achievements in other games.

I little thought at the time that before many weeks had passed I should be playing golf as heaven knows it was never played before. And this is how it happened.

## II: I Dine at Lowchester House

One warm, delicious evening late in July I was dining at Lowchester House. It was almost my last dinner engagement for the season, as all the world and his wife had suddenly got sick of the baking pavements and dusty trees of the great city and were making in shoals for green fields or briny sea.

The ladies had just left us, and we men were preparing to enjoy the heavenly hour that brings cigarettes, coffee, and liqueurs in its wake. Through the wide-open French windows of the dining room (which look out over St. James's Park) came softened sounds of busy traffic; a ravishing odor of sweet peas stole in from the garden, and the moon gave to the trees and shrubs without those strange, grave tints that are her wonderful gifts to the night.

As a rule such an environment impresses and invigorates me pleasurably. I enjoy the journeys of the eye as it travels lightly over polished mahogany, glittering silver, and gleaming glass, noting here the deep red of the wine and roses, there the sunsetlike effulgence of the hanging lamps, the vague outlines of the pictured oak walls, and the clearer groups of well-groomed men that sit in easy comfort under a blue canopy of lazily curling smoke. Or, as the glance passes to the scented garden without, noting the blue-green and silver wonderlands that the moon creates in the most commonplace and probably grimy of trees, and the quiver that the soft July wind gives to branch, leaf, and flower.

But tonight, somehow, such things had no charm for me.

And yet Lady Lowchester's dinner had been good. The cutlets, perhaps, a trifle uninteresting and the wine somewhat overiced; but, on the whole, distinctly good.

How, then, account for my mood?

Katherine was of the party, but at the other end of the table from mine. A tall, well-built, massive man, good-looking, and possessed of an attractive smile, had taken her in to dinner, and I have rarely seen two people so completely absorbed in each other.

Therein lay the sting of the evening.

I had eaten and drunk mechanically with eyes riveted, as far as good breeding would permit, on Katherine and her neighbor.

Who was he?

I know everybody that one meets in London, either personally or by sight, yet I had never before come across this good-looking Hercules. I must find out.

He was talking to Lowchester as, leaving my chair, I carelessly joined the group at the other end of the table.

"Yes, I first held the open championship five years ago," I heard him say.

I pricked my ears. Of what championship was he speaking?

"And again last year, I think?" asked Lowchester.

"Yes," replied Hercules.

I quickly inquired of my neighbor as to what championship was under discussion.

"Why golf, of course," was the response. "That's Jim Lindsay, the finest player living."

So that was it. No wonder Katherine was so deeply absorbed during dinner.

I hated the man at once. I lost not a moment. I darted my eyes across the table, caught his, and stabbed him with one of those withering knife-like glances that only the descendants of the great can inflict.

Then I discovered that he wasn't looking at me at all, but at one of my shirt studs which had escaped from its buttonhole. He drew my attention to it. I grunted out an ungrateful "Thanks!" and hated him the more.

Now, as a rule, after dinner–wherever I may be–I manage to hold the conversation. So much a habit has this become with me, that I can scarcely endure to hear another man similarly exploiting himself. Not, I am bound to say, that Lindsay was belauding his own prowess. But, what was worse, he appeared a center of enormous interest to the men around him. They drew him out. They hung on his words. They gaped at him with reverential admiration. Truly golf must have made many converts during the last three years I had been in India. Bah! And I knew it to be such a childish game.

"I've taken a house close to the links at St. Magnus for the summer, Lindsay," Lowchester presently observed. "And as you tell me you're going there next month, you must let me put you up. There's lots of room, and Mrs. Gunter will be with us during August and September."

"I shall be delighted; it will suit me exactly," replied Lindsay.

So Lowchester too had become a golfer! Lowchester–who used to live for hunting and cricket! Lowchester–the President of the Board of Education! Good heavens!

Presently we were all in the hideous gilded and damasked drawing room; for Lowchester House is a sort of museum of the tawdry vulgarities of the early fifties.

The rooms were hot. That no doubt was the reason why presently Mrs. Gunter and the champion were to be seen hanging over the railing of a flower-laden balcony; but the heat could in no way account for their gazing into each other's eyes so frequently, or so raptly.

I seized on a slip of a girl in pink, led her close to the window, and in tones that I knew must be overheard by the occupants of the balcony, began to relate how I won the Lahore Polo Cup for my team in '92.

I was well under way and just reaching a stirring description of the magnificent goal I scored by taking the ball the whole length of the ground, on a pony that had suddenly gone lame, when Katherine and the champion pointedly left the window and proceeded to another and more distant one.

So! My reminiscences bored them! Polo was nothing if golf were in the air!

It was enough. I could stand no more. I peevishly bade my hostess good night and passed through the rooms.

As I entered the great hall, which was but dimly lit, my eyes encountered a portrait of the famous (or infamous) Cardinal Smeaton, one of Lowchester's proudest pictorial possessions. The great Scotch prelate, I could have sworn, winked at me.

I was moving on, when suddenly, close to my shoulder, I heard the words, "I will meet ye at St. Magnus!"

I started and turned. There was no one near. I gazed fixedly at the portrait, but never was marble more immovable. I was about to investigate a recess and some pillars, near me, when I observed a footman at the hall door eying me with mild but interested scrutiny. He came forward with my coat and hat, and putting them on I passed listlessly into the courtyard and thence to St. James's Street, where I mechanically entered the doors of the Racing Club.

I rang the bell and ordered a brandy-and-soda.

## III: The Challenge

The Racing Club, as the reader knows, is the smartest sporting club in London, and the Inner Temple of the popular game of bridge. But tonight cards held no temptation for me; and I sat alone in the reading room, chewing the cud of a humiliation that was quite novel to my experience.

The incident of the Cardinal's wink and the unknown voice had already escaped my memory, and I was rapt in rankling memories of the unsatisfactory evening I had spent.

To me, it was inconceivable that even the finest exponent of a wretched game like golf could oust an all-round sportsman like myself from the circle of interest at a dinner table. It was not so much that I had not been afforded an opportunity to talk, as that when I did I was listened to with a wandering and simulated attention, suggesting that the listeners were only waiting for me to stop. The moment I paused between two anecdotes, someone precipitately led the conversation away to a channel that had no possible interest for me.

Then Katherine had indubitably avoided and ignored me.

It has always been understood between us that if I am in a room with her, mine is the first claim on her attention. Yet, tonight, there was, if not an open rebellion, at least a new departure.

It was extremely galling, and I ordered a second brandy-and-soda.

Must I, then, take to golf in self-defense?

Of course I could pick it up easily. There is no minor game that I have not mastered with ease, after about a week's hard application; and to acquire the art of striking a ball from a certain distance into a hole presents no alarming difficulties to the adroit cricketer and practiced polo player. Still, to go over, as it were, to the camp of the enemy, to apply myself to a game that I have openly and avowedly sneered at, was not altogether a pleasing prospect.

How it would tickle my pals at Hurlingham, Ranelagh, the Oval, and Lord's!

I took from the bookshelves the Badminton volume on golf and with a third brandy-and-soda applied myself to a rapid study of its contents. I admit that I was somewhat dismayed at the mass of printed matter and numerous diagrams that confronted me, but reflecting that I had often seen voluminous books on such trivial games as croquet or tennis, I concluded that the principle of sporting journalism is to make the maximum of bricks out of the minimum of straw.

I had not read more than three chapters when half a dozen men, including Lowchester and Lindsay, entered the room.

"My dear Jacky," said the former, "you left us very early tonight."

"Yes," I replied. "I found the atmosphere indoors a bit oppressive; and I'm not as yet a convert to golf, your sole topic of discussion during the evening."

"You ought to try the game," said Lindsay. "There's more in it than outsiders imagine."

"'Outsiders' in what sense?" I inquired, with an obvious courtship of a wordy wrangle.

"Oh! only as regards golf, of course. For aught I know you may be a celebrity in many other branches of sport."

"I am," was on the tip of my tongue, but I repressed it.

I felt strangely antagonistic toward this man. A sort of magnetic antipathy (if I may be allowed such a seeming contradiction in terms) warned me that we should influence each other's lives in the future, and that to the detriment of one, if not both of us. In fact, I felt myself being drawn irresistibly toward the vulgar vortex of a "row" with him.

"Golf," I suddenly found myself asserting after one of those deadly pauses that give an altogether exaggerated significance to any casual remark that may break the silence, "golf is a game for one's dotage."

"A period that sets in quite early in the lives of many of us," retorted Lindsay.

There was another pause. Lowchester was chuckling quietly. A club waiter with thin lips was grinning faintly.

"Which means?" I asked, with an affectation of bored inattention.

"Well, it means," was the reply, "that to stigmatize as only suitable for one's dotage a fine, healthy, outdoor sport, that employs skill and science, and exercises one's patience and temper as few other games do, suggests to my mind incipient dotage in common perception."

I did not understand this at first, so merely remarked, "Really," an ambiguous and useful word, which commits one to nothing.

But as I reflected on Lindsay's words, I perceived a deadly stab at my authority as a judge of sport. My blood tingled. I seized a fourth brandy-and-soda and drank it. It was Lowchester's, but I was only aware of this when the glass was empty. My lips compressed themselves. I recalled

Katherine and the champion hanging over the balcony. The thin-lipped club waiter was loitering with an evident desire to overhear what else was to be said. Lowchester looked at me with gently humorous inquiry in his eyes. The others regarded me with the sphinxlike calm that is the ordinary expression of the average Englishman when he is thinking hard but not lucidly. I had, in fact, an audience, always to me an overpowering temptation.

"I'll tell you what I'll do," I said, in the calm, deep tones born of a great determination. "After one week's practice on the St. Magnus links I'll play you a match on even terms, and I dare to hope lick your head off at your own game."

There was a pause of a moment. Then, as if to clear the oppressive air, a chorus of "Bravo, Old Jacky!" broke out from the bystanders. Only Lindsay was silent, barring, of course, the waiters.

"Well?" I asked him.

"I accept, of course," said he; "you leave me no alternative. But the whole scheme is absolutely childish, and, as I fear you will find, quite futile."

"I'll take my chance of that," I replied. "I can reach St. Magnus by August eighth, and on the fifteenth I'll play you."

"It's a match," cried Lowchester, and proceeded to enter it in a notebook. "Any stakes?"

"I will privately suggest to Mr. Lindsay the stakes to be played for," I answered. "May I ask you to come with me for a moment?"

Lindsay assented, and I led him to an adjoining room that was empty.

"The stake I suggest–and it must be known to none but ourselves is this. The winner of the match shall have the first right to propose matrimony to a certain lady. I mention no names. It is enough if we agree that neither of us shall propose to any lady whatsoever on or before August fifteenth, and that the loser shall further abstain from any such proposal till August twenty-second. This will give the winner a clear week's start, which really constitutes the stake. The subject is a delicate one," I hastily added, as I saw his surprise and evident desire to go further into the matter, "and I shall be obliged if you merely signify your assent or dissent, as the case may be."

With a certain bewildered yet half-amused air he replied, "I assent, of course, but–"

"There is nothing more that need be said," I hurriedly interrupted, "except that I shall be glad if you will join me at supper."

For at one of my own clubs, when a stranger is introduced, even by another member, I trust I can ever play the host with tact and grace. I asked Lowchester and Grimsby to join us, and during supper I was able to recount the chief exploits of my life to the attentive audience that a host can always rely on.

## IV: St. Magnus

I left London on August 6th, traveling by night to Edinburgh, and leaving the latter city at 9 A.M., on the 7th, reached St. Magnus a few minutes before noon. I had been recommended to try the Metropole Hotel, and accordingly took up my quarters there. It is quite near the St. Magnus Golf Club (for which I was put up at once as a temporary member) and is equally convenient to the links. Lord and Lady Lowchester were in their house, a stone's throw from the hotel, and amongst their guests were Mr. Lindsay and Mrs. Gunter.

St. Magnus, as the golfing world knows, is situated on the east coast of Scotland, and is second only in importance as a golfing center to St. Andrews, which, indeed, it closely resembles. It is a grim, gray old town, standing on bleak, precipitous cliffs that court every passing hurricane, and possessed in addition of a respectable perennial gale of its own. It is always blowing there. Indeed, I think a fair description of normal weather of St. Magnus would be "Wind with gales."

The ancient town boasts many ruins of once noble buildings. Cathedrals, castles, monasteries, colleges, and priories, that formed strongholds of Roman Catholicism before the Reformation, are now outlined only by picturesque and crumbling walls, held in a green embrace by the ever sympathetic ivy, and preserved mainly to please the antiquarian or artistic eye.

And many the tales that are told of the ghostly occupants of these dead strongholds.

The hotel was tolerably comfortable, although under any conditions hotel life is, to me, a hateful business. The constant traversing of passages that lead chiefly to other people's rooms; the garrulous noisiness of the guests, the forced yet blasé alacrity of the waiters, the commercial suavity and professional geniality of the proprietor, the absolute lack of originality in the cook, the fact that one becomes merely an easily forgotten number, these and a thousand other trivial humiliations combine to render residence in a hotel a source of irritation to the nerves.

The clubhouse, however, was airy and comfortably managed; and the older frequenters appeared to me to be good types of Scotch county gentlemen, or courteous members of the learned professions. Some of the younger men I met I did not quite understand. They had, to begin with, quite extraordinary accents. If you can imagine a native and strong Scotch accent asserting itself in defiance of a recently acquired cockney twang, you have some idea of the strange sounds these youths emitted. They were, however, quite harmless; and there really seemed no reason why, if it pleased them, they should not garnish their Caledonian and somewhat bucolic dialogue with misplaced "Don't-you-knows," or denude it, in accordance with a long defunct phonetic fashion, of the letter "g." They were quite charmed with my prefix "Honorable" and duly acquainted me of such people of title as they had either seen at a distance or once spoken to at a railway station.

The general society of the place was considered "mixed" by the younger bloods of the town; though, to my mind, these latter formed the most unpalatable part of the mixture. It numbered, to my surprise, half a dozen socially well-known people whom I frequently met in London. True, they pretty much kept to themselves and were not to be seen at the numerous tea parties, female putting tournaments, badly cooked but pretentious dinners, and other social barbarities that were—heaven help us!—considered *de rigueur* in this fresh seaside country town.

I, too, avoided all such festivities; though from the moment I set foot in the club, with name and condition advertised on the notice board, I was inundated with invitations; one of the many penalties, I suppose, of being more or less of a sporting celebrity. I felt, indeed, much as a great actor must when he goes "starring" in the provinces.

There is, however, one charming section of society in the gray old town, comprising mainly those learned and cultured people who own the city as their home. Mingling with these, some modern *littérateurs* in search of bracing health give a vivacity to the free exchange of ideas; whilst one or two staid but intelligent clergymen form a sort of moral anchor that holds cultured thought to the needs of the world rather than let it drift to the summer seas of imagination. In such society I should have been, of course, a welcome recruit; but I was in St. Magnus for one purpose only, and that was golf.

I have been writing calmly, but during the days that followed my challenge to Lindsay, my brain was in a fever. I had stipulated for but one week's practice, and, consequently, though dying to handle the sticks (or "clubs" as I find I ought to call them), I had been debarred from more than a study of the game, as set forth in the various published works on the subject.

I had taken a suite of four rooms in the hotel. One was my sitting room, another my bedroom, a third my servant's room, and the fourth I had fitted up as a golf studio. The latter is entirely my own invention, and I make no doubt that, after the publication of this volume, similar studios will become quite common institutions.

By arrangement with the proprietor, I had the room denuded of all furniture; and it was understood between us that during my residence no one, not even a housemaid, should be permitted to enter the chamber, with, of course, the exception of myself and my servant. I had no desire that St. Magnus should know the extent to which I was laying myself out to defeat my opponent.

A strip of coconut matting, lightly strewn with sand, represented a teeing ground, whilst a number of padded targets, designed to receive the balls as I drove them, almost entirely covered the walls. A fourth of the floor was boarded in with sand, eighteen inches deep, to represent a bunker. The remainder I turfed to represent a putting green. I constructed a small movable grassy hillock which could be placed in the center of the room for practice in "hanging" or "uphill" lies, and I imported whin bushes, sods of long grass, etc., to represent the assorted difficulties that beset the golfer. By day, and until I was finished with the studio for the night, the windows were removed in case of accidents; and altogether nothing was left undone that would conduce to complete and unobserved practice of the game.

In addition to this indoor preparation, I decided to do at least two rounds daily, starting at daybreak. Allowing two hours for each round, this could easily be accomplished before 9 A.M., and St. Magnus would be little the wiser. Then, if my progress should prove unsatisfactory, starting out about 5 P.M., I could edge in a third almost unnoticed round.

I had six volumes by different writers on the game, and from these I gathered that instruction from a first-class professional was practically indispensable to the beginner. By dint of offering extremely liberal terms, I secured the services of the well-known professional Kirkintulloch, it being understood that he was to coach me more or less *sub rosa,* and that in any case he was not to talk promiscuously of the extent to which I practiced. I exhorted him to spare no expense–an arrangement he accepted with evident and spontaneous alacrity, selling me a number of his own unrivaled clubs at what I have since learned were exorbitant prices. He also made a selection of other implements of the game from the best makers, that included fifteen beautifully balanced and polished clubs, four dozen balls, and several minor appliances, such as artificial tees, sponges, etc., to say nothing of a seven-and-sixpenny and pagoda-like umbrella. All these preparations were completed on the day of my arrival, and it was arranged that I should begin practice in deadly earnest at 4:30 on the following morning.

## V: I Begin To Golf

The morning of the 8th dawned with a warm flush of saffron, rose, and gold, behind which the faint purple of the night that was gone died into the mists of early morning. The pure, sweet air was delicious as the sparkling vapor that rises from a newly opened bottle of invigorating wine. The incoming tide plashed on the beach with lazy and musical kisses, and a soft, melodious wind was stirring the bending grasses that crowned the sand dunes on the outskirts of the links.

I inhaled the glorious air with the rapture of the warrior who sniffs the battle from afar.

[The literary grace of my esteemed journalistic colleague will be observed in the foregoing lines. "It was a ripping morning" was all I actually said to him.–J. W. W. G.]

Kirkintulloch was waiting for me at the first putting green.

I may say at once that during my entire stay in St. Magnus I never quite mastered this man's name. It became confused in my mind with other curious-sounding names of Scotch towns, and I addressed him promiscuously as Tullochgorum, Tillicoutry, Auchtermuchty, and the like. To his credit, be it said that after one or two attempts to put me right, he suppressed any claim to nominal individuality and adapted himself philosophically to my weakness; answering cheerfully to any name that greeted his surprised but resigned ears.

He was the brawny son of honest fisher folk. Of middle height, he was sturdily yet flexibly built. His hands were large and horny; his feet, I have no doubt, the same. At all events his boots were of ample proportions. He had blue eyes, with that alert, steady, and farseeing gaze that is the birthright of folk born to look out over the sea; sandy hair and mustache, and a ruddy color that suggested equally sunshine, salt winds, and whisky. His natural expression was inclined to be sour, but on occasion this was dissipated by a quite genial smile. His manner and address had the odd deferential familiarity that belongs exclusively to the old-fashioned Scotch peasantry. His face I soon found to be a sort of barometer of my progress, for every time I struck a ball I could see exactly the value of the stroke recorded in the grim lines of his weather-beaten features. In movement he was clumsy, except, indeed, when golfing, for then his body and limbs became possessed of that faultless grace which only proficiency in a given line can impart.

"It's a fine moarn fur goalf," was his greeting.

"So I suppose," said I. "Where do we go?"

"We'll gang ower here," he replied, as, tucking my clubs under his arm, he led me in the direction of a comparatively remote part of the links.

As we went I thought it advisable to let him know that, although not yet a golfer, I could more than hold my own in far higher branches of sport. I told him that I was one of the best-known polo players of the day.

There was a considerable pause, but we tramped steadily on.

"Whaat's polo?" said he, at length.

I gave him a brief description of the game.

"Aweel, ye'll no hae a hoarse to help ye at goalf."

"But, don't you see, Tullochgorum–"

"Kirkintulloch, sir."

"Kirkintulloch, that the fact of playing a game on ponies makes it much more difficult?"

"Then whaat fur d'ye hae them?"

"Well, it's the game, that's all."

"M'hm" was his sphinxlike response.

I felt that I had not convinced him.

I next hinted that I was a prominent cricketer, and, as a rule, went in first wicket down when playing for my regiment.

"Ay, it's a fine ploy fur laddies."

"It's a game that can only properly be played by men," I replied, with indignant warmth.

"Is't?"

"Yes, is't–I mean it is." He had certain phrases that I often unconsciously and involuntarily repeated, generally with ludicrous effect.

The reader, of course, understands that I was not in any sense guilty of such gross taste as to imitate the man to his own ears. I simply could not help pronouncing certain words as he did.

"Aweel, in goalf ye'll no hae a man to birstle the ba' to yer bat; ye'll just hae to play it as it lies."

"But, man alive," I cried, "don't you see that to hit a moving object must be infinitely more difficult than to strike a ball that is stationary?"

"Ye've no bunkers at cricket," he replied, with irrelevant but disconcerting conviction, adding, with an indescribable and prophetic relish, "No, nor yet whins."

I could make no impression on this man, and it worried me.

"I take it," I resumed presently, "that what is mainly of importance at golf is a good eye."

"That's ae thing."

"What's ae thing?"

"Yer e'e. The thing is, can ye keep it on the ba'?"

"Of course I can keep it on the ba'–ball."

"We'll see in a meenit," he answered, and stopped. We had reached a large field enclosed by a wall, and here Kirkintulloch dropped the clubs and proceeded to arrange a little heap of damp sand, on which he eventually poised a golf ball.

"Noo, tak' yer driver. Here," and he handed me a beautifully varnished implement decorated with sunk lead, inlaid bone, and resined cord. "Try a swing" (he said "swung") "like this," and, standing in position before the ball, he proceeded to wave a club of his own in semicircular sweeps as if defying the world in general and myself in particular, till suddenly and rapidly descending on the ball, he struck it with such force and accuracy that it shot out into the faint morning mist and disappeared. It was really a remarkably fine shot. I began to feel quite keen.

"Noo it's your turn," said he, as he teed a second ball, "but hae a wheen practice at the swung first."

So I began "addressing" an imaginary ball.

We wrestled with the peculiar flourishes that are technically known as "addressing the ball" for some minutes, at the end of which my movements resembled those of a man who, having been given a club, was undecided in his mind as to whether he should keep hold of it or throw it away. I wiggled first in one direction, then in another. I described eights and threes, double circles, triangles, and parallelograms in the air, only to be assailed with–

"Na, na!" from Kirkintulloch.

"See here, dea it like this," he cried; and again he flourished his driver with the easy grace of a lifetime's practice.

"I'll tell you what, Kirkcudbright–"

"Kirkintulloch, sir."

"Kirkintulloch, just you let me have a smack at the ball."

"Gang on then, sir. Hae a smack."

I took up position. I got my eye on the ball. I wiggled for all I was worth, I swung a mighty swing, I swooped with terrific force down on the ball, and behold, when all was over, there it was still poised on the tee, insolently unmoved, and Kirkintulloch sniffing in the direction of the sea.

"Ye've missed the globe," was his comment. "An' it's a black disgrace to a gowfer."

I settled to the ball again–and with a running accompaniment from Kirkintulloch of "Keep yer eye on the ba'; up wi' yer richt fut; tak' plenty time; dinna swee ower fast"–I let drive a second time, with the result that the ball took a series of trifling hops and skips like a startled hare, and deposited itself in rough ground some thirty yards off, at an angle of forty-five degrees from the line I had anxiously hoped to take.

"Ye topped it, sir," was Kirkintulloch's view of the performance.

"I moved it, anyhow," I muttered moodily.

"Ay, ye did that," was the response; "and ye'll never move that ba' again, fur it's doon a rabbit hole and oot o' sicht."

Nevertheless, I went steadily on, ball after ball. They took many and devious routes, and entirely different methods of reaching their destinations. Some leaped into the air with halfhearted and affrighted purpose; others shot along the ground with strange irregularity of direction and distance; a number went off at right or left angles with the pleasing uncertainty that only a beginner can command; whilst not a few merely trickled off the tee in sickly obedience to my misdirected energy. At length I struck one magnificent shot. The ball soared straight and sure from the club just as Kirkintulloch's had, and I felt for the first time the delicious thrill that tingles through the arms right to the very brain, as the clean-struck ball leaves the driver's head. I looked at Kirkintulloch with a proud and gleaming eye.

"No bad," said he, "but ye'll no do that again in a hurry. It was guy like an accident."

"Look here, Kirkincoutry," I said, nettled at last, "it's your business to encourage me, not to throw cold water; and you ought to know it."

"Ma name's Kirkintulloch," he answered phlegmatically; "but it doesna' maitter." (And this was the last time he corrected my errors as to his name.) "An' I can tell ye this, that cauld watter keeps the heed cool at goalf, and praise is a snare and a deloosion." Then with the ghost of a smile he added, "Gang on, ye're daein' fine."

The field was now dotted with some fifteen balls at such alarmingly varied distances and angles from the tee that they formed an irregular semicircle in front of us (one ball had even succeeded in traveling backward); and as I reflected that my original and sustained purpose had been to strike them all in one particular line, I began to perceive undreamed-of difficulties in this royal and ancient game.

But I struggled on, and Kirkintulloch himself admitted that I showed signs of distinct, if spasmodic, improvement. At seven o'clock the driver was temporarily laid aside, and I was introduced in turn to the brassie, the iron, the cleek, the putter, and the niblick, the latter a curious implement not unlike a dentist's reflector of magnified proportions. The brassie much resembled the driver, but the iron opened out quite a new field of practice; and my first attempts with it were rather in the nature of sod-cutting with a spade, varied at intervals by deadly strokes that left deep incisions on the ball.

As the clock of the parish church tolled the hour of 8:30, I returned to the hotel with an enormous appetite and a thoughtful mind.

## VI: I Continue to Practice

My practice in the studio was not attended with that measure of success I had anticipated. The turf got dry and lumpy, and when, by my instructions, my servant watered it liberally, an old lady occupying the room immediately below intimated to the proprietor that her ceiling had unaccountably begun to drip, and that strange noises from the floor above deprived her of that tranquil rest for which she had sought the salubrious breezes of St. Magnus. A gouty dean, whose room adjoined the studio, also complained that sudden bangs and rattles on the walls, intermittent and varied but on the whole continuous, had so completely got on his nerves that residence in that quarter of the hotel had become an impossibility; whilst a number of other guests pointed out that to walk beneath my window was an extremely dangerous proceeding, as golf balls and even broken clubs flew out on them with alarming frequency and exciting results. I admit that I had a thoughtless habit of throwing offending clubs from the window in moments of extreme exasperation, but I exonerate myself of any intentional bombarding of my fellow lodgers.

I myself suffered from this indoor zeal, for if a ball failed to strike one of the padded targets and came in contact with the wall (as often happened), it would fly back boomeranglike to where I stood, not infrequently striking me so hard as to raise grisly lumps on various parts of my body. Once I invited Wetherby, my servant, to witness my progress, and during the few minutes of his incarceration with me he was driven to execute a series of leaps and springs to avoid the rapidly traveling and seemingly malignant ball. It struck him, I believe, three times, which somewhat militated against his evident desire to pay me encouraging compliments, for these latter he condensed into a meager and breathless "Wonderful, sir!" as he dashed from the studio with an alacrity that was by no means constitutional with him.

The miniature bunker also gave rise to a certain amount of speculation on the part of inmates of the hotel, for as I generally practiced on it facing the window, casual loiterers below experienced brief but disconcerting sandstorms, and the porters and hall boys were kept busily occupied in sweeping the unaccountably sanded pavement.

I will not weary the reader with a description of my progress on the links from day to day. Suffice it to say that whilst I really made wonderful strides, it became borne in upon me, after five days' practice, that under no possible conditions could I hope to win the match I had set myself to play. For although I made many excellent, and even brilliant, strokes, I would constantly "foozle" others, with the result that I never got round the links under 100, whereas Lindsay, I knew, seldom if ever exceeded 90 and averaged, I suppose, something like 86.

What, then, was I to do? Give in?

No.

I would play the match and be beaten like a man. There was a remote chance that fortune might favor me. Lindsay might be seedy–I knew he suffered at times from the effects of malarial fever–or I might by some unlooked-for providence suddenly develop a slashing game.

At all events I felt I must confide in Kirkintulloch's ears the task I had set myself.

Accordingly, on the morning of Saturday the 13th, I intimated to him, as we started on our first round, that I had to play my first match on the Monday.

"Ay," said he quite imperturbably.

"Yes," I resumed, "and rather an important one."

"Weel, I'll cairry for ye. Whaat time?"

"Eleven o'clock," I replied; and then, plunging *in medias res,* I added, "I'm playing a single against Mr. Lindsay, Mr. James Lindsay."

Kirkintulloch stopped dead and gazed at me with blue-eyed and unceremonious incredulity.

"Jim Lindsay!" he cried.

"Yes," I growled doggedly.

We proceeded to walk on, but, despite his impenetrable expression, I knew that Kirkintulloch was charged with violent emotion of some sort.

"What's he giein' ye?" he asked presently.

"What?"

"What's yer hondicop?"

"None. I'm playing him level."

"Weel, of a' the pairfect noansense–"

"Eh?" I interrupted, with a certain dignity that was not lost on Kirkintulloch. But he again stopped dead, and for once in a way betrayed signs of some excitement.

"See here whaat I'm tellin' ye. He'll lay ye oot like a corp! D'ye ken thaat? Forbye ye'll be the laughin'-stock o' the links. Ay, and *me* cairryin' for ye! I've pit up wi' a' the names ye've ca'd me–Tullochgorum, Tillicoutry, ay, and Auchtermuchty tae–but I'd hae ye mind I'm Wully Kirkintulloch, the professional. I've been in the mileeshy, an' I've done ma fowerteen days in the clink, but I'm no for ony black disgrace like cairryin' in a maatch the tail end o' which'll be Jim Lindsay scorin' nineteen up an' seventeen tae play."

I am not vain, but I confess that this speech, the longest oratorical effort that I remember Kirkintulloch to have indulged in, wounded my *amour propre*.

"If you don't wish to cairry–I mean carry–for me on Monday," I said, "there is no occasion for you to do so. I can easily get another caddie, and whoever does undertake the job will be paid one guinea."

I watched his features keenly as I said this, and though he in no wise betrayed himself by look or gesture, there was an alteration in his tone when next he addressed me.

"It's like this, ye see," said he. "I ken ma business fine, and I ken a reel gentleman when I see yin, even when he's no whaat ye might ca' profeecient as a goalfer, an' I'm no sayin' I'll no cairry fur ye; a' I say is that ye're no tae blame me if Jim Lindsay wuns by three or fower holes."

With this change of professional attitude we proceeded on our way and were soon absorbed in the intricacies of the game.

That morning–how well I remember it!–I was pounding away in one of the deepest bunkers, filling my eyes, ears, hair, and clothes with sand, exhausting my vocabulary of language, and yet not appreciably moving the ball. I had played seven strokes with ever increasing frenzy. With the eighth, to my momentary relief, the ball soared from the sand to the grassy slope above, only–oh, maddening game!–to trickle slowly back and nest itself in one of my deepest heel marks. Under the impression that I was alone, I was engaging in a one-sided, but ornate, conversation with the ball–for it is quite extraordinary how illogically angry one gets with inanimate objects–when, suddenly, from behind me came the clear ring of a woman's laughter.

I turned and beheld Mrs. Gunter.

She was dressed in a tailor-made coat and skirt of butcher blue, and wore a tam o' shanter of the same color. A white collar and bright red sailor knot, adorable white spats, and a white waistcoat completed the costume. Over her shoulder she carried a cleek, and by her side was a caddie bearing her other clubs. Her eyes were sparkling with humor and enjoyment of life, her cheeks glowed with the bright fresh red that comes of sea air and healthy exercise. Her enemies used to say she was an adept at suitable complexions, but, personally, I give credit to the salubrious breezes of St. Magnus.

"Well?" she cried lustily (and she did *not* pronounce it "wal"). "How goes it?"

"Tolerably," I replied, as I mopped my perspiring brow. "You see me at present at my worst."

"Anna Lowchester is going to ask you to dinner on Monday to celebrate the great match. Mind you come. Say now, what are the stakes? You know it's all over the town you're playing for something colossal. You'll have quite a crowd at your heels. And tell me why you avoid us all?"

"I am here simply and solely to golf," I replied, with as much dignity as is possible to the occupant of a bunker that the merest novice could have avoided.

"Ye're keepin' the green waitin', sir," cried Kirkintulloch, as he appeared on the grassy slope in front of me.

"Then will you excuse me?" I asked Mrs. Gunter, and settling down again I proceeded patiently to maneuver under and round my ball. As I played the "eleven more," it rose in the air, and I left the bunker with a dignified bow to Katherine.

She passed on with a merry laugh and a wave of the hand, crying out as she watched the destination of my gutta-percha, "You poor soul! You're bang into another."

And so I was. For a passing moment I almost hated Katherine.

It was quite true that I had avoided the Lowchesters. I was in no mood for society, still less did I care to meet Mr. Lindsay. True, I stumbled across him frequently in the club, but we instinctively limited our intercourse to a distant "Good morning," or a perfunctory "Good night."

Moreover, I was becoming extremely depressed.

Katherine's flippant and unsympathetic bearing during my vicissitudes in the bunker; the certainty that for the first time in my life I was about to be made a fool of; the extraordinary difficulty I experienced in attaining to anything like an even sample of play; and the half-pitiful, half-fearful regard in which I was held by the guests at the hotel, combined to rob life of the exhilaration that I had hitherto never failed to enjoy.

## VII: I Meet the Cardinal

The morning of Sunday the 14th broke with a dark and stormy scowl. The sea was lashed to a foaming lather by frantic gusts of easterly wind, and great black masses of clouds sped landward and piled themselves in ominous canopy over the gray and bleak-looking city. A seething and swirling mist all but enveloped the links, and the bending grasses of the dunes swayed and swished with every scourge of the salt-laden gale. Hard-driven and drenching rain swept in furious torrents across land and sea. The ground was as a swamp; the wet rocks, cold and streaming, stood as black targets for the fury of the mighty and resounding breakers that, spent in impotent attack, rose in vast clouds of spray.

Not a soul was to be seen out of doors. The church bells, faintly and fitfully heard, clanged their invitation to an irresponsive town; indoors, fires were already crackling, pipes were lighted, magazines unearthed, and soon St. Magnus was courting the drowsy comfort that snug shelter from a raging storm ever induces.

I passed the time till luncheon in the golf studio, but, out of consideration for such Sabbatarian scruples as might possibly be entertained by the adjoining dean, I merely trifled with a putter, and indeed I had little heart even for that. The clamor of the gong for the midday meal was a welcome break to the black monotony of the morning, and, descending to the dining room, I partook freely of such northern delicacies as haggis (a really excellent if stodgy dish), crab pies, and oat cakes.

I then devoted a couple of hours to the perusal of my books on golf and copied out, on a scale sufficiently small to be easily carried in the pocket, a map of the St. Magnus links for use on the morrow. A glance at this before each stroke would show me all the concealed hazards with which this admirably-laid-out course abounds. The idea is, I believe, a new one, and I present it gratuitously to all golfers who peruse this veracious history.

Dinner at the Metropole on Sundays is a more pretentious meal than on weekdays. Game, cooked to a rag, figures on the menu, as also a profuse dessert of the cheaper and not quite ripe fruits of the season. Why this should be is not quite clear, as the golfer is robbed of his wonted exercise on a Sunday and therefore should be lightly fed. It may be that in view of the spiritual rations dealt out to the immortal part of man that day, the hotel proprietor, in the spirit of competition which becomes his second nature, feels it incumbent on him to provide for the mortal interior with a prodigality that will bear comparison. Be that as it may, I did full justice to my host's catering, seeing it out to the bitter end, and banishing my depression with a bottle of the "Boy" and a few glasses of a port which was officially dated '64. It may have been that this wine had reached the sober age claimed for it, but to my palate, at least, it seemed to retain all the juvenile vigor and rough precocity of a wine still in its infancy.

About 10 P.M. I proceeded to the smoking room and stretched myself luxuriously on a couch in front of a blazing fire, only to find that rest was not possible, and that I was the victim of what Scotch folk so aptly term the "fidgets." First, it appeared that I had been wrong to cross the right leg over the left, and I accordingly reversed the position. The momentary ease secured by this change was succeeded by a numbness in the right elbow which demanded that I should turn over on my left side. But this movement led to a stiffening of the neck, unaccountable yet unmistakable, and I turned for relief to the broad of my back, only to start a sudden and most irritating tickling in the sole of my right foot. I endured these tortures in silence for a time, attributing them, rightly, I imagine, to the fact that I had had no exercise during the day. The culminating point, however, was reached when the tickling sensation incontinently transferred itself to the back, suggesting to my now maddened imagination two prickly-footed scorpions golfing between my shoulder blades. I scraped myself, after the manner of cattle, against the wooden arms of the couch without obtaining appreciable relief, and finally sprang to my feet with a bound that startled a number of somnolent old gentlemen into wide-awake and indignant observation.

I must have exercise.

I drew aside one of the curtains and looked out on the night. The storm had somewhat abated, and the moon sailed brilliantly at intervals through the black and scudding clouds.

I decided on a walk, despite the weather and the lateness of the hour. I made for my room, arrayed myself, with Wetherby's assistance, in top boots, mackintosh, and sou'-wester, and thus armored against the elements I sallied forth into the wild and eerie night.

As I left the doors of the hotel eleven solemn clangs from the parish church warned me of the approaching "witching hour of night."

The town, despite the fact that most of the town councilors are interested in the local gas company, is extremely badly lighted; and by the time I had passed the hospitable and inviting rays that streamed from the doors and lamps of the clubhouse, I was practically in the dark.

I took the road that extends along the cliffs to the harbor, at times compelled to probe for and feel my way, at times guided by fitful splashes of moonlight. And the scene when the moon chose to break through her pall-like veil was superb. Before me, in cold and inky outline, stood the ruined towers and windows of cathedral and castle; to the left the sea, in a riot of black and white, still hurled itself with unabated fury against the adamant rocks and along the unresisting beach. The sky was an ever changing canopy of black and sullen gray, sparsely streaked with rifts of gleaming silver. Great trees bent and creaked on my right, flinging, as in a perspiration of midnight fear, great drops on the roadway below, sighing and screaming as if the horrid winds were whispering ghastly tales to their sobbing and tearstained leaves, tales not to be breathed in the light of day.

A profound sense of awe stole over me as, riveted by the scene each passing glimpse of the moon revealed, I stood my ground from time to time and held my breath in a frame of mind quite foreign to my experience.

[Here again will be observed the literary elegance of my gifted colleague. The preceding paragraphs have been evolved from my simple statement, "It was a beastly wet night."–J. W. W. G.]

So slow had been my progress that almost an hour must have passed before I reached the gates of the ruined castle. As I stood gazing up at the weather-beaten heights, faintly limned against the flying clouds, I became conscious of a sudden and strange atmospheric change. The gale inexplicably died; the trees hushed themselves into a startling silence; the moon crept behind an enormous overhanging mountain of clouds; and warm, humid, and oppressive air replaced the sea-blown easterly winds. A great and portentous stillness prevailed around me, broken only by a dull moaning–as of a soul in agony–from the sea.

The effect was awful.

I strained eyes and ears in an ecstasy of anxiety. I knew not what was awaiting me, and yet knew of a certainty that I was about to face some strange revelation of the night.

Above all a great and overpowering horror of the dead was in me.

I tried to retrace my steps and found myself immovable, a living and breathing statue clutching the iron bars of the castle gate, waiting–waiting for what?

Could it be that I, this quivering, powerless, quaking creature, was indeed John William Wentworth G–

Crash!–Crash!!

Within, as it seemed to me, a few feet of where I stood, a mighty blue and blinding flame shot out from the massive pile of clouds, firing sea and land with livid and fearsome light. Crash upon crash, roar upon roar of such thunder as I pray I may never hear again, struck up into the heights of the heavens and down again to the resounding rocks and ruins that fronted me. They broke in deafening awful blows upon my ear and stunned me. In a moment of utter collapse I fell through the gate and lay with closed eyes on the soaking turf within. But closed eyes had no power to keep out such burning fire, and each blue flash came piercing through the eyelids.

Gasping, and with a supreme and almost superhuman effort, I staggered to my feet and opened my eyes in bewildered and fearful expectation.

And what was the wild, weird thing I saw?

At the entrance to the castle, just beyond the drawbridge, holding aloft a wrought-iron lamp of ecclesiastical design that burned with a sputtering and spectral flame, stood the red-robed figure of a ghostly cardinal!

With a wildly beating heart I recognized at a glance the face of the long-dead Cardinal Smeaton, the cardinal whose portrait had arrested my eyes at Lowchester House!

## VIII: The Cardinal's Chamber

I shivered in every limb, and a cold beady dew sprang out on my temples as I stood with eyes riveted on the spectral figure before me. The light from the lamp fell on the left side of the Cardinal's head with a weird and Rembrandt-like effect, revealing a face with the tightly stretched gray-blue skin of the dead, and a fiercely flashing eye that seemed to divine the fear and horror that possessed me. Never to my dying day shall I forget that awful burning eye, glowing in what seemed to be the face of a corpse. I saw in its depths a grim triumph, a sardonic rapture, and a hideous relish of the blind horror betrayed in my blanched and streaming face.

The faded *vieux-rose* robes of the Cardinal (through which, as it seemed to me, I could faintly see the gray walls of the castle) only served to heighten the unearthly pallor of the face.

I swayed to and fro in the weakness of a sudden fever. My dry lips bit the air. I raised a hand to my eyes to shut out the appalling sight; but of strength I had none, and my arm dropped nervelessly to my side.

Presently–and I almost shrieked aloud as I saw it–his thin but redly gleaming lips moved, displaying a set of yellow and wolfish teeth.

"Come," he said, in hollow yet imperious tones; "it's a sair nicht, and there is shelter within."

"No! no!" I cried, in an agony of fearful apprehension. But even as I spoke I moved mechanically toward him, and no words can convey the horror with which I realized my unconscious advance.

The wind shrieked out anew, and a deluge of sudden rain beat down from the clouds above.

Nearer and nearer I drew, with staring eyes and parted lips, until, as I found myself within a few feet of the ghastly thing, I stretched out my hands toward it in mute and awe-stricken appeal.

In a moment the Cardinal's right hand shot out and fixed an icy grasp on my left wrist. I shivered violently to the very marrow, stricken powerless as a little child. The calm of despair came to me. I moved as in a dream. I was conscious that I was absolutely in the power of a spirit of the dead.

A flash of lightning and a crash of thunder heralded our entrance beneath the portcullis gate of the ruins.

I dared not look at the Cardinal's face. My eyes I kept on the ground, and I noted in a dreamily unconscious way the yellow pointed shoes of my ghostly guide as they slipped noiselessly from beneath the flowing draperies. At times, through his robes, I seemed to see glimpses of a white skeleton, and my teeth chattered loudly at the fearsome sight.

We had passed into the shelter of the archway that leads to the open courtyard of the castle, and on our right was a doorway that opened into a dark and damp recess.

Into this I was dragged, the bony fingers of His Eminence still eating into my throbbing wrist. At the distant end of the recess the Cardinal pressed with the open palm of his disengaged hand (for he had set down the lamp) a keystone that stood out an inch or so from the dripping and moss-grown wall. In immediate answer to the pressure a great block in the wall moved slowly inward, revealing a faintly lit staircase with a spiral descent, evidently cut through solid rock. This we descended, I half slipping, half dragged, until at length we reached a chamber lighted almost brilliantly with flickering tapers, and furnished in what had once no doubt been sumptuous fashion.

Here the Cardinal closed the old oak and iron-studded door with a clang that resounded eerily behind me and, releasing my almost frozen wrist, seated himself with grave dignity in a carved chair of ancient and pontifical design.

I looked around me.

The chamber, some sixteen feet square, was vaulted in the manner of a crypt, and the roofing stones were painted in frescoes, each panel representing the coat of arms of some old Catholic family. The walls were hung with faded and moth-eaten tapestry, depicting scenes of wild carousal, wherein nymphs, satyrs, and bacchantes disported themselves with cup and vine leaf to the piping of a figure that closely resembled his satanic majesty. In one corner of the room stood a *prie-dieu,* and above it a broken and almost shapeless crucifix, overgrown with a dry, lichenlike moss, and shrouded in cobwebs. In front of this, depending from the roof, swung an incense burner that emitted a faint green light and an overpowering and sickly aromatic vapor.

The floor was of plain, dull granite in smooth slabs, from which a cold sweat seemed to exude. The four chairs were of carved oak, with the high pointed backs of the cathedral stall, and on either side of each tall candles burned with sepulchral flames of yellow and purple.

In the center was a small square table of oak, the legs of which were carved to represent hideous and snakelike monsters, and on it stood a skull, a book, and an hour glass.

A sense of disconcerting creepiness was diffused throughout the chamber by the fact that it was overrun by numerous immense spiders, some red, some yellow, and others black. Indeed, so ubiquitous were these horrid creatures that once or twice I fancied I saw them running up and down the faint white lines of His Eminence's skeleton. But as the Cardinal himself evinced no signs of inconvenience from these intimate and presumably tickling recreations, I concluded that they were the fevered creations of my own heated imagination.

Another strange thing was that through the apparently material appointments of the chamber, I could dimly, yet undoubtedly, see the rough, dripping walls of the solid rock; and when, by the Cardinal's invitation, I seated myself on one of the chairs facing him, I was conscious that I passed, as it were, through it, and actually sat on a wet stone, to which the chair was seemingly but a ghostly and ineffective covering.

There was a certain sense of relief in this, for I argued that if my surroundings had no substance, no more probably had the Cardinal or the spiders. And yet a glance at my wrist showed me the livid imprints of His Eminence's bony fingers.

Presently I ventured to let my gaze fall on the Cardinal and was somewhat relieved to note in his otherwise inscrutable face a distinct twinkle of amusement. The corners of his lips suggested an appreciation of humor; and his eyes betrayed an ill-concealed merriment as, from time to time, I shifted uneasily on my seat in an endeavor to find the driest part of it.

I was reflecting on the strange calm that was gradually coming to me—for, oddly enough, I began to lose the overwhelming sense of terror that a few minutes before had possessed me—when my ghostly companion broke the silence, speaking in profound and dignified tones.

"When the moon is at the full, gude sir, and eke the tide is low, a body that spiers within the castle gates maun e'en be guest o' mine."

I did not quite understand this, but feeling it to be an announcement that demanded a response of some sort, I replied respectfully, if somewhat feebly, "Quite so."

That my answer did not altogether satisfy His Eminence seemed apparent, for after regarding me in contemplative silence for a moment he uttered the portentous words, "I'm tellin' ye!"

I quite felt that it was my turn to say something, but for the life of me I could not focus my ideas. At length, with much diffidence, and with a distinct tremor in my voice, I murmured, "I fear I'm inconveniencing Your Eminence by calling at so late an hour."

At this the Cardinal lay back in his chair and laughed consumedly for the space of at least a minute.

"Gude sake!" cried he at last. "The Sassenach is glib eneuch tae jest; wi' deeficulty nae doot, as indeed befits the occasion!"

It will be observed that my ghostly prelate spoke in broad Scotch, much as Kirkintulloch did, with, however, the difference that is lent to speech by cultured cadences and a comparatively exhaustive vocabulary. From the unexpected laughter with which my diffident remark had been received, I instinctively derived a cue. It seemed to me that the Cardinal appreciated the subdued effrontery that I now perceived in my words, though at the moment of their utterance, heaven knows, I only intended to convey extreme humility and deference. So I hazarded a question.

"May I ask," I ventured, with deferential gravity, "what keeps Your Eminence up so late?"

"Hech! sir," was the reply. "That's what liteegious folk would ca' a leadin' question. Forbye, I'm no just at leeberty tae tell ye. Ye see, folk maun work oot their ain salvation, and it's no permitted to the likes o' me, a wanderer in the speerit, to acquaint mortal man wi' information as to the existence of heaven, hell, purgatory, or–or otherwise."

"Then," I timidly pursued, with a good deal of hesitation, and beating about the bush to find appropriate terms, "I presume I have the–the–honor of addressing a–a spirit?"

"Jist that," responded the Cardinal, with a sort of jocose cordiality that was very reassuring and comforting.

His whole manner had incredibly changed and was now calculated to set one at ease, at least as far as might be between one representative of the quick and another of the dead. So conspicuously was this the case that I soon found the fear and horror that at first had so completely overwhelmed me replaced by an absorbing and inquisitive interest.

## IX: His Eminence And I

"From the exalted ecclesiastical position held in life by Your Eminence," I presently found myself saying, "I feel justified in assuming that you are now enjoying the well-merited reward of residence in heaven."

The Cardinal eyed me shrewdly for a moment and eventually replied in diplomatic but evasive terms–

"I'm obleeged for the coampliment, be it merited or otherwise; but I'm na' disposed tae enter into ony personal exposeetion of my speeritual career. This, however, I'm constrained to tell ye, that nine tenths o' the clergy and pious laity of a' creeds, at present in the enjoyment o' life, will be fair dumfounded when they shuffle off this moartal coil and tak' possession of the immortal lodgin' provided for them–lodgin's that hae scant resemblance to the tangible Canaans of their quasi-releegious but businesslike imaginations. Catholic and Protestant alike, they're a' under the impression that releegion is a profession for the lips and no' for the lives. As for Presbyterians, aweel! They'll find oot in guid time the value o' their dour pride in hard and heartless piety. They ken fine hoo tae mak' a bargain in siller wi' their neebors, but the same perspicacity 'll no' avail them when it comes tae–but Hoots! It's nae business o' mine." Then, as if to change the subject, he added, "I suppose ye've read a' aboot me in the Histories of Scotland?"

"Well," I replied, "I've read a good deal about Your Eminence. I've often pictured you sitting at a window of the castle, watching with grim enjoyment young Dishart burning at the stake."

It was an unwise remark to make, and I saw the Cardinal's eye flash balefully.

"Yer speech," he answered slowly and with dignity, "is no' in the best of taste, but it affords me an opportunity of explaining that misrepresented circumstance. Ye see, from a lad upward, I was aye fond of a bonfire, and what for was I no' to watch the bonny red flames loupin' up forenenst the curlin' smoke? Was that pleasure tae be denied me, a' because a dwaibly manbody ca'd Dishart was frizzlin' on the toap? Na, na, guid sir, I was glowering at the bonny flames, no' at Dishart. I saw Dishart, nae doot; still, and there had no' been a fire, I wouldna hae lookit."

During this speech my attention had been somewhat distracted by the creepy spectacle of two spiders, one red, one black, fighting viciously on one of His Eminence's white ribs. The sight affected me so disagreeably that I felt constrained to inform the Cardinal of the unpleasant incident.

"Your Eminence will excuse me," I said respectfully, "but I see two poisonous-looking spiders diverting themselves on one of your ribs, the lowest but one on the left side."

The Cardinal smiled, but made no movement. "I'm much obleeged," he responded, with grave amusement. "Nae doot ye're ruminatin' that sich internal gambols are no' compatible wi the residence in heaven ye were guid eneuch to credit me wi'." Then, with a certain air of resigned weariness, he added, "Dinna mind them, they're daein' nae herm; ye canna kittle a speerit, ye ken."

My seat was so extremely wet, and the damp was now penetrating my clothes in such an uncomfortable manner, that I resolved to assume an erect position at any cost. I may mention that we have rheumatism in our family. I cast about in my mind for a suitable reason for rising, and after some hesitation rose, remarking–

"Your Eminence will excuse me, but I feel it fitting that I should stand whilst a prelate of your exalted rank and undying celebrity" (this last, I thought, under the circumstances, a particularly happy inspiration) "is good enough to condescend to hold intercourse with me."

"Ay! Ye're guy wet," replied the undying celebrity, with a grasp of the situation that I had not looked for.

I stood shifting about on my feet, conscious of a rather painful stiffness in my joints, and wondering when and how this extraordinary séance would draw to a close, when the Cardinal, who had been lost for a time in the silence of a brown study, suddenly leaned forward in his chair and addressed me with an eager intensity that he had not displayed before.

"I'm gaun tae tell 'ee," said he, "what for I summoned ye here this nicht. Here!" he exclaimed, and rising he indicated the vaulted chamber with an imposing sweep of his gaunt arms and bony fingers. "Here! In this ma *sanctum sanctorum*."

He paused and eyed me steadily.

"I'm delighted, Your Eminence," I murmured feebly.

"Ye'll be mair than delighted, I'm thinkin'," he continued, "when ye ken ma purpose; the whilk is this. The moarn's moarn ye're playin', an I'm no mistaken, a match at goalf agin a callant ca'd Jim Lindsay?"

"That is so," I answered, in vague bewilderment at this sudden reference to a standing engagement in real life. For a moment a wild doubt swept over me. Was I living or dead? The dampness of my trousers gave a silent answer in favor of the former condition.

"Aweel!" resumed the Cardinal, "I'd have 'ee ken that he's a descendant in the straight line o' ane o' my maist determined foes–ye'll understand I'm referrin' tae sich time as I was Cardinal Airchbishop o' St. Magnus in the flesh–and ony blow that I can deal tae ane o' his kith is a solace to ma hameless and disjasket speerit. Noo, in ma day, I was unrivaled as a gowfer; there wasna ma equal in the land. Nane o' the coortiers frae Holyrood were fit tae tee a ba' tae me. It's a fac'. And here–here ma gentleman!" (and the Cardinal sank his voice to the low tremulous wail of a sepulchral but operatic specter, and his eyes gleamed with the sudden and baleful light that had first so riveted my gaze), "ahint the arras in this verra chamber is concealed ma ain bonny set of clubs!"

He paused and scrutinized my face to observe the effect of this announcement. I accordingly assumed an expression of intense interest.

"Noo," he continued, his eyes blazing with vindictive triumph, "I'm gaun tae lend ye this verra set o' clubs, an' I guarantee that an ye play wi' them ye'll win the day. D'ye hear that?"

"It is extremely good of you," I murmured hurriedly.

"Hoots! It's mair for ma ain gratification than for yours. In addeetion I'll be wi' ye on the links, but veesible to nane but yersel. Ye'll wun the day, and fair humeeliate the varmint spawn o' my ancient foe; and, eh! guid sir, but these auld bones will fair rattle wi' the pleasure o't! Will 'ee dae't?"

"I will," I solemnly replied. What else could I have said?

"Then hud yer wheest whiles I fetch the clubs."

With this His Eminence turned to the tapestry behind him, and, drawing it aside, disclosed a deep and narrow cavity in the rock. From this he extracted, one by one, a set of seven such extraordinarily unwieldy-looking golf clubs that I felt it in me to laugh aloud. Needless to say I indulged in no such folly. I examined them one by one with apparent interest and simulated appreciation, as, fondling them lovingly, my companion expatiated on their obviously obsolete beauties. A strange and almost pathetic enthusiasm shone in his eyes.

"Nane o' yer newfangled clubs for me," cried the Cardinal; "they auld things canna be bate. Tak' them wi' ye back tae whaur ye bide; bring them to the links the moarn's moarn, and as sure as we stand here this nicht–or moarn, fur the brak o' day is close at haun'–I'll be wi' ye at the first tee, tae witness sic a game o' gowf as never mortal played before. But eh! guid sir, as ye'd conserve yer body and soul frae destruction and damnation, breathe nae word o' this queer compact tae man, wumman, or bairn. Sweer it, man, sweer it on this skull!"

His bloodless hands extended the grinning skull toward me, and I, repressing an involuntary shudder, stooped and kissed it.

A gleam of malignant triumph again lit up his face as I took the oath. Then he seized the weird-looking clubs and, caressing them with loving care, muttered to himself reminiscences of bygone years.

"Ay, fine I mind it," he cried, "when young Ruthven came gallivantin' tae St. Magnus and thocht his match was naewhere tae be foond. We had but five holes in thae days, ye ken, and ilka yin a mile in length. Hech, sir! what a match was that! I dinged him doon wi 'three up and twa tae play. Ye'll no be disposed to gie me credence, but it's a fact that I did yin hole in seventeen!"

"That was unfortunate," I replied, mistaking his meaning.

"Ay, for Ruthven," was his quick and peevish rejoinder. "For he took thirty-seven and lost the hole."

I had not grasped that he considered his own score extremely good.

"Of course I meant for Ruthven," I stammered, with the vague and silly smile of clumsy apology.

"Ye didna," replied His Eminence; "but I'm no mindin'. Ruthven, wi' a' his roughness, was an affectit callant in thae days, and rode his horse atween ilka shot. He moonted and dismoonted seeventy-fower times in three holes that day." And the Cardinal chuckled loud and long.

He related many other tales of his prowess with great gusto and enjoyment. We were now on such unaccountably familiar terms that I ventured to tell him of the marvelous goal I had won, playing for the Lahore Polo Cup in '62, when, of a sudden, he interrupted me, crying out–

"The oor is late! Ye maun hae a sleep. Awa! man, awa! For ony sake, tak' the set and awa!"

And indeed I needed no second invitation; so, seizing the seven weird clubs, I made a low obeisance to His Eminence, and turning, found the door behind me open. I fled up the stone-cut staircase, passed like a flash through the recess to the archway, and, with a cry of such delight as surely never greeted mortal ears, I hailed the faintly dawning day. With the joy of a captive set free, or the rapture of one who has returned from a living tomb to bustling life, I inhaled the precious air in deep lung-filling draughts.

The storm had passed, the sea was calm, birds twittered in the gently whispering trees, the world was waking, and I was on its broad earth again.

But my thoughts were chaos. My brain refused to work. I had but one desire, and that was to sleep. In wretched plight I reached the doors of the hotel, where the astounded night porter eyed me, and more particularly the hockey-stick-like clubs, with a questioning surprise and bated breath.

I made him bring me a stiff glass of hot whisky and water. This revived me somewhat, and telling him to warn my servant not to call me before 10 A.M., I staggered to my room, flung the clubs with a sudden, if scarcely surprising, abhorrence into a wardrobe, got out of my dripping clothes into welcome pajamas, and, pulling the bedclothes up to my chin, was soon at rest in a dreamless sleep.

## X: The Fateful Morning

I woke to find sunshine streaming in at the windows, a cloudless sky without, and my servant Wetherby busily occupied over his customary matutinal duties.

With a sudden flash of memory I recalled the weird scene of the night that was gone, only, however, to dismiss it as an unusually vivid dream. For a time I felt quite sure it was nothing more. But presently, as my eye fell on the empty glass that had held the hot whisky and water, I began to experience an uneasy doubt.

Ah! Now I remembered!

If it were a dream, there would be no clubs in the wardrobe.

I lit a cigarette, and asked Wetherby the time.

"Ten o'clock, sir," was the reply; "and you've no time to lose, sir. The match is at eleven."

I sprang from bed and casually opened the wardrobe.

Good heavens! It was no dream! There they were! Seven of the queerest clubs that antiquarian imagination could conceive.

So it had actually happened! I had been the guest of Cardinal Smeaton's ghost, and had entered into a compact with him to use his ridiculous clubs in order that he might revel in a trumpery revenge on the house of Lindsay.

Be hanged if I would! I remembered vaguely that in law an oath extracted from a party by threat or terror was not held to be binding, and I determined to ignore my unholy bond with the shadowy prelate. I would play with my own clubs and be defeated like a man.

I jumped into my bath. The pure morning air swept through the open window, the sunlight streamed in on the carpet and danced in circles of glancing gold in the clear cold water of the bath, and a glow of health and vigor (despite the late hours I had kept) sent the blood tingling through my veins. Indeed, what with the ordinary routine of dressing, my servant's presence, the hum of life that came from the links, the footsteps of housemaid and boots hurrying past my door, and generally my accustomed surroundings, I found it all but impossible to believe that I had really gone through the strange experiences of a few hours ago.

Yet, undoubtedly, there stood the clubs. Curious and perplexing ideas flashed through my mind as I dressed, ideas that clashed against or displaced each other with kaleidoscopic rapidity.

Was such an oath binding? Was the whole incident a dream, and the presence of the clubs an unexplainable mystery? Was there mental eccentricity on either side of my family? Had my father, the son of a hundred earls (or, more correctly, of as many as can be conveniently crowded into a period of a hundred years), transmitted to me some disconcerting strain in the blue blood that filled my veins; or, had my mother, with her less important but more richly gilt lineage, dowered me with a plebeian taint of which absurd superstition was the outcome? Or had the combination of both produced in myself a decadent creature abashed at his first introduction to the supernatural? How could I tell? Was there really a spectral world, and I its victim? Was I reaping the harvest of years of cynical unbelief? Was I myself? And, if not, who was I?

I gave it up.

I determined to ignore and if possible to forget entirely my creepy adventure in the vaults of the ruined castle. In this endeavor I was assisted by the pangs of healthy hunger. There is something so homely, so accustomed, so matter-of-fact in a good appetite, that I felt less awed by the unwilling oath I had taken, when Wetherby announced that an omelette and a broiled sole were awaiting me in the next room.

I was endeavoring to force into my tie and collar one of those aggravating pins that bend but never break, and alternately wounding my neck and my forefnger in the process, when, through the open window, my eye fell on a dense and apparently increasing crowd that surged on the links behind the first teeing ground. A dozen men held a rope that must have measured close on a hundred yards, and behind it the entire population of the town seemed to be gathering.

What could it be? Possibly a popular excursion, a public holiday, or a big professional match.

I asked Wetherby.

"I understand, sir," replied that phlegmatic youth, "the crowd is gatherin' in anticipation of your match with Mr. Lindsay, sir."

"Oh! Is it?" I murmured vaguely.

"It's been talked about considerable, sir."

"Has it?" was all the comment I could muster.

I was appalled at the sight. There was a horribly expectant air in the crowd. Their faces had that deadly going-to-be-amused expression that I have seen in the spectators at a bullfight in Spain. Many eager faces were turned in the direction of my windows, and I shrank instinctively into the seclusion that a muslin curtain affords.

That dim recollection of the bullfight I had seen in Cadiz haunted me.

Was I to be a golfing bull?

Or was Lindsay?

Was I to be the golfing equivalent of the wretched horse that eventually is gored to death, to the huge delight of thousands of butcher-souled brutes?

Well, if so, they would see a bold front. I'd show no craven spirit.

I began to wonder if the seven queer clubs had the properties that the Cardinal claimed for them. And then an idea seized me. I would have them near me on the links, and if the game went desperately against me I'd put them to the test.

"Wetherby," I said, as I put the finishing twist to my mustache, "I should like you to carry these odd-looking clubs round the links in case I want them. I don't propose to use them, but it is just possible that I might."

"Yes, sir."

I handed him a capacious canvas bag. I had purchased three similar bags from Kirkintulloch by his advice, one for fine weather, a second for wet, and the third (which I now gave Wetherby) an immense one for traveling. Kirkintulloch had informed me that without these my equipment as a golfer was incomplete.

"I don't wish them to be seen, unless it happens that I decide to use them, so you needn't follow me too closely," I added.

"I understand, sir."

"But you'll be at hand should occasion arise."

"Certainly, sir."

And shouldering the seven unwieldy weapons, Wetherby left the room with a twinkle in his eye that I had never remarked before.

I took another furtive glance at the crowd, and my heart gave a leap as I saw way being made for a party that included Mrs. Gunter and Lord and Lady Lowchester.

I passed mechanically to my sitting room and sat down to breakfast.

I began to eat.

Thanks to the discipline of daily habit, my hands and jaws performed their accustomed tasks, but my mind was in a condition alternately comatose and chaotic, so much so that it was a matter of surprise to me when I found my eyes resting on the bones of my sole and the sloppery trail of a departed omelette.

I drained my coffee to the dregs and lit a cigarette.

I began to feel a sense of importance. The knowledge that one's personality is of interest to a crowd is always stimulating, but I was haunted with the uncomfortable reflection that sometimes a crowd is bent on jeering, not to say jostling. Ah! if only I could manage that those who came to laugh remained to–well to laugh at the other man.

Presently the door opened and Wetherby presented himself, with the smug deference for which I paid wages at the rate of sixty pounds a year.

"Mr. Lindsay's compliments, sir, and if you are ready, sir, he is."

"I am coming," I replied, as, passing a napkin across my lips, I pulled myself together for the impending ordeal.

As I walked through the hall of the hotel I saw that the entire domestic staff had gathered together to witness my exit. There was an uncomfortable sort of suppressed merriment in their faces that was not encouraging. The waiter who attended me at meals had the refined impertinence to blush as I passed. The boots seized his lips with two blacking-black hands, as if to deny his face the satisfaction of an insubordinate smile. A beast of a boy in buttons winked, and the general manager bowed to me with a deference so absurdly overdone as to be extremely unconvincing.

I passed through the folding doors and stood on the steps of the hotel facing the crowd.

A tremendous cheer greeted me. When I say "cheer," possibly I don't quite convey what I mean. It was more of a roar. It was a blend of delight, expectation, amusement, derision, and exhilaration. Every face was smiling, every mouth open, every eye glistening. As the first hoarse echoes died a sound of gratified mumbling succeeded, as when the lions of the zoo, having bellowed at the first glimpse of their food, merely pant and lick their lips till the raw meat is flung to them.

Kirkintulloch was waiting for me at the foot of the steps. He looked a trifle shamefaced, I thought, and I fancied I heard him say to a bystander as I went toward him, "Aweel, it's nae business o' mine!"

Presently it pleased the mob to adopt a facetious tone, and as Kirkintulloch elbowed a passage for me through the crowd, I heard on all sides cries of "Here comes the champion!" "He's guy jaunty-like!" "Eh! but he looks awfy fierce!" "Gude luck ti ye, ma man!" "He's a born gowfer!" "Gude sakes! He's a braw opeenion o' himsel'!" "The puir lamb's awa tae the slaughter!" "It's an ill day this for Jim Lindsay!" (this with a blatant laugh intended to convey irony). "Ay! His pride'll hae a fa', nae doot!" and the like.

## XI: An Expectant Crowd

Of a sudden my heart stood still, and for a moment I stopped dead. There in front of me and approaching by a series of jinks and dives amid the crowd, was the ghostly figure of the Cardinal. Faint and ill-defined as the apparition seemed in the brilliant sunshine, there was no mistaking the cadaverous features or the flowing robes. In less time than it takes to tell he had reached my side and was whispering into my ear.

"Dinna mind thae folk," he said, "they'll sing anither tune afore the day's dune. And dinna mind me. I'm no veesible to livin' soul but yerself, and nane but yer ain ears can hear what I'm sayin'. But if ye've a mind tae speak tae me, a' ye've got tae dae is to *thenk;* tae speak in tae yersel, as it were; for I can thole the jist o' yer thochts, wi' no sae muckle as a soond frae yer lips."

I was flabbergasted.

"Sic a clanjamfray o' vermin!" he added, as he swept a contemptuous glance over the noisy mob.

But his presence exasperated me beyond endurance. My nerves were strung to all but the breaking strain, and I found a relief in venting my spleen on this self-appointed colleague of mine.

"Look here," I said, and I was at no pains to conceal my ill-humor, "I'm fed up with you! You understand, I'm sick of you and your devilish wiles. I'm no longer in your power, and I snap my fingers at you. Get out!"

I had neglected His Eminence's instructions only to *think* when I addressed him, and the crowd naturally regarded my words as a sally in reply to its own ponderous wit.

The result was a babel of words, furious, jocular, jeering.

"Did ye ever hear the like?" "Ay! Did ye hear him say 'deevilish wiles'? An' this a Presbyterian toon forbye!" "Mercy on us! An' ma man an elder in Doctor MacBide's kirk!" "Awa wi' the bairns; a'll no hae their ears contaminated," and so on.

"Hoots toots!" was the Cardinal's response, "and you a gentleman! I'm fair ashamed o' ye. But ye canna win awa' frae yer oath, ye ken. It wad mean perdeetion to yer soul an ye did, though I'm far frae assertin' that ye'll no receive that guerdon as it is."

I stopped again, with the intention of arguing out the point once and for all, when I realized that if I went on addressing this invisible specter, I might possibly be mistaken for a madman. I therefore contented myself with a withering glance of abhorrence at the prelate, and a few unspoken words to the effect that nothing in heaven or earth would induce me to have further truck with him. I then walked calmly on, but I was conscious of the ghostly presence dogging my steps with grim persistence, and several times I heard the never-to-be-forgotten voice mutter, "Ay! We'll jist see," or "M'hm! Is he daft, I wonder?"

At last I reached the inner circle of the crowd, and at the teeing ground Lindsay came forward, looking, I am bound to admit, the picture of manly health and vigor.

He held out his hand.

I accepted it with dignity, then looked about me, bowing here and there as I recognized acquaintances. This section of the crowd showed signs of better breeding. There was neither vulgar laughter nor insolent jeering. On the contrary, its demeanor was so extremely grave as to suggest to my sensitive imagination a suspicion of covert irony. I recognized many celebrities of the golfing world. There was Grayson, who wept if he missed a putt and spent his evenings in chewing the cud of his daily strokes to the ears of his depressed but resigned family. There too was Twinkle, the founder of the Oxbridge Golf Club, whose "style" was as remarkable as his mastery of the technical "language" of the game. Near him was General Simpkins, who, having had a vast experience of fighting on the sandy plains of the Sahara, now employed his old age in exploring the sandy tracts of the St. Magnus bunkers so assiduously that he seldom, if ever, played a stroke on the grass. He was one of the many golfers who find a difficulty in getting up a "foursome." Not far off was Sir William Wilkins, another notable enthusiast, whose scores when playing alone are remarkably low, though he seldom does a hole in less than eight strokes if playing in a game or under the scrutiny of a casual onlooker. I nodded to Mr. Henry Grove, the celebrated actor-manager, and a keen golfer. I didn't know that he was celebrated when first I met him, but I gathered it from the few minutes' conversation that passed between us.

Standing near the Lowchesters was Mrs. Gunter, in a heavenly confection of shell pink and daffodil yellow, a sort of holiday frock, delicate in tint, and diaphanous as a sufficiently modest spider's web. She greeted me with the brightest of smiles and laughingly kissed her finger tips to me. Certainly she was the most charming woman present. Her bright color and gleaming hair seemed to defy the wind and sunshine, though I fancy that rain might have proved a trifle inconvenient. There was no manner of doubt that I loved her. She represented to me a sort of allegorical figurehead symbolizing affluence, luxury, and independence. That is, assuming that she would consent to occupy the central niche in my own ambitious temple of matrimony.

Even the University of St. Magnus was represented in the gathering by a group of its professors, rusty-looking gentlemen who betrayed no indication of anything so trivial as a bygone youth; but, on the contrary, closely resembled a number of chief mourners at the funeral of their own intellects. A notable figure was the genial and cultured Doctor MacBide, one of the ablest and most popular divines that Scotland has given to the world, one in whom is to be found the rare combination of an aesthetic soul allied to a fearless character, a man who, keeping one eye on heaven and the other on earth, has used both to the benefit of the world in general and St. Magnus in particular.

Mr. Monktown, the more or less distinguished politician, was also in the crowd. His eyes had the faraway look of a minor celebrity on whom has been forced the conviction that due recognition of his talents will never be found this side of the grave. On the other hand, his charming and brilliant wife conveys the impression that she will continue to lustily insist on the aforesaid recognition until a peerage or some such badge of notoriety is administered as a narcotic by a peace-at-any-price premier.

But to enumerate all the interesting people in the dense crowd is an impossible task. Suffice it to say that such a constellation of golfing stars could be seen only on the links of St. Magnus, with perhaps the single exception of those of St. Andrews.

How little did the crowd guess that, unruffled and confident as I seemed, I yet knew that I was destined to a humiliating defeat; and how much less did I know what a bitter thing is defeat to a man of my sanguine temperament and former achievements!

## XII: The Match Begins

I was startled from a brief brown study by the sound of Lindsay's voice.

"Shall we toss for the honor?"

"As you please," I replied.

He spun a coin.

"Head or tail?"

I chose the head.

"It's a tail," he said, as, pocketing the coin, he took the driver that his caddie handed.

Then he drove. It was a magnificent shot, straight and sure, and the ball landed halfway between the public road and the stream that bounds the first putting green. A murmur of approval rose from the crowd.

Then I took up position.

Again a murmur arose from the crowd, but not a reassuring one.

Kirkintulloch endeavored to inspire me with confidence as he handed me my driver by whispering in a hoarse, spirituous undertone that must have been audible to everyone near, "Dinna mind the crowd, sir. Just pretend that ye *caan* goalf."

I was about to address the ball when my eye caught sight of the Cardinal. His face was livid with rage, and I could barely repress a chuckle as he shrieked in a voice that apparently only reached my ears (for the crowd never budged), "Tak' the auld clubs, I tell 'ee!"

Afraid of betraying myself by vacant look or startled mien, I ignored His Eminence's fury and precipitately drove the ball.

I topped it.

It shot along the ground, hurling itself against casual stones, as if under the impression that I was a billiard player desirous of making a break in cannons.

Then we moved on.

As we walked over the hundred yards that my ball had traveled, the Cardinal sidled up to me, and thrusting his face (through which I could clearly see a view of beach and sea) close to mine, exclaimed, "Ye're a fule!"

I took no notice. I was beginning to enjoy the discomfiture of one who had caused me such acute sufferings a few hours before.

"D'ye hear?" he persisted "Wi' yer ain clubs ye're no match for a callant like Lindsay! For ony sake, tak' mine. Are ye feared the folk'll laugh at sic antediluvian implements? Ye needna mind the mob, I assure ye. If ye win hole after hole, ye'll turn the laugh on Lindsay, nae maitter what the clubs be like. Forbye, there's yer oath."

I still ignored him, and I saw the yellow teeth grind in silent fury.

Meantime, behind us plodded the crowd, the dull thud of their steps on the spongy grass almost drowned by their voluble and exasperating chatter.

There are no words in my vocabulary to express the humiliation that I felt as I played. I was at my worst. My second shot landed me about a hundred yards further; Lindsay dropped his onto the putting green. With my third the ball traveled to the burn and stopped there, embedding itself in the soft black mud. This incident afforded unbounded delight to the mob, and I fancied that I heard Mrs. Gunter's silvery laugh. The only satisfaction that I experienced was in the uncontrollable rage of the Cardinal. He danced and leaped about me, gesticulating wildly, alternately pouring sixteenth-century vituperation into my ears and imploring me to use his accursed clubs. He even indulged in weeping on the off-chance of softening my heart, but I saw no pathos in the tears that flowed down his spectral cheek from eyes that never lost their vindictive glare.

Lindsay behaved extremely well. He showed no sign of triumph as he won hole after hole, and several times he turned upon the crowd and upbraided them roundly for the howls of laughter with which they received my miserable efforts. Kirkintulloch became gradually more and more depressed and eventually took the line of a Job's comforter.

"It's jist as I tell't ye. He's layin' ye oot like a corp," said he.

"Well, let him," I growled.

"It's mesel' I'm thinkin' o'. Ye see I've a poseetion tae keep up. They a' ken I've been learnin' ye the game, forbye I'm the professional champion. I'll be fair howled at when I gang in tae the public hoose the nicht."

"Then the simple remedy is not to go there," I argued.

"Whaat? No gang tae the public hoose?"

I had apparently propounded a quite unheard-of course of action, but I stuck to it, and said, "No."

"Aweeel," he resumed, "a' I can say is ye dinna ken oor faimily" (which was true). "Ma faither never missed a nicht but what he was half-seas over in the 'Gowfer's Arms,' an' it's no in my blood to forget the words, 'Honor yer faither and mither,' an' a' the rest o' it. So I just dae the same, and it's a grand tribute to the memory o' my kith and kin. Forbye–I like it. I canna sleep if I'm ower sober."

I leave the reader to imagine my feelings as Kirkintulloch thus unfolded the hereditary tendencies of his family to one ear, and the Cardinal poured violent anathemas into the other. The crowd was convulsed in spasms of derisive delight at each of my futile strokes, and certainly Mrs. Gunter seemed furtively amused when I ventured to glance in her direction. Only Wetherby was unmoved. Bearing the Cardinal's clubs, he followed me at a discreet distance, with an inscrutable expression that would have done credit to a priest of the Delphic Oracle.

I got into every possible bunker, to the noisy gratification of the mob which, despite the frequent remonstrances of the better class of people present, had now abandoned itself to the wildest hilarity. The match was, in fact, a harlequinade, with Lindsay as the clever clown and myself as the idiotic pantaloon.

I seemed to tread on air, with only a vague idea of what was going on.

By a lucky fluke I won the short hole, albeit in a rather undignified manner. Mr. Lindsay's caddie, though some distance off, was nevertheless slightly in front of me as I drove, and my ball (which I topped so that it shot away at right angles) struck his boot, on which Kirkintulloch loudly claimed the hole.

At the "turn" (*i.e.*, the end of the first nine holes) I was seven down; and at the end of the eighteen–let me confess it at once–Lindsay was sixteen up.

The first round over, the garrulous crowd dispersed in various directions, gabbling, cackling, laughing, and howling with an absence of breeding truly astounding.

Even the "society" section no longer concealed its amusement. I have never understood the limitations of that word "society." It seems to me such an elastic term nowadays, that if a person says he is in it, then *ipso facto* he is. Formerly it applied exclusively to my own class, *i.e.*, the aristocracy; but since we latter have taken to emulating the peculiarities and tendencies of the criminal classes we are possibly excluded.

An interval of an hour and a half was allowed for luncheon, and it was arranged that we should meet for the final round at 2:30.

I refused all invitations to lunch at the club or at private houses, and retired to a solitary meal in my own room.

But it was only solitary in a sense.

I had just begun to tackle a mutton cutlet and tomato sauce when, raising my eyes for a moment to look for the salt, I beheld my ubiquitous Cardinal seated opposite me.

This was a little too much, and seizing a decanter of claret I hurled it in his face. His shadowy features offered so little resistance that the wine eventually distributed itself over Wetherby, who seemed for once mildly surprised.

I muttered an apology to that irreproachable domestic, explaining that the liquor was corked, and then I desired him to leave the room.

I was alone with my tormentor, and I determined to have it out with him. But His Eminence anticipated me, for whilst I was framing in my mind a declamatory and indignant exordium, he leaned across the table, and with a singularly suave voice and subdued manner addressed me as follows:–

"I apologize, young sir, if I have caused you ony inconvenience on this momentous occasion. I was ower keen, an' I tak a' the blame o' yer ill fortune on ma ain shoulders. Just eat your denner like a man, and dinna fash yersel' wi' me; but when ye've feenished, an ye'll be sae gude as to hear me for the space of five meenits, I'll be obleeged. Mair than that, I'll undertake that ye'll no' be worrit by me again."

This was an important offer, and a certain unexpected charm in my unbidden guest's suavity turned the balance in his favor.

"Do you mean," I asked, "that if I grant you a short interview when I have finished luncheon, you will undertake to cease annoying me by your enervating companionship and intemperate language?"

"That's it," replied the prelate.

"Very good," said I; "I agree."

I continued the meal. Wetherby returned with a fresh bottle of wine and a custard pudding, brought me cigarettes, coffee, and cognac in due course, and though in the discharge of his duties he frequently walked through the dim anatomy of my ecclesiastical patron, his doing so seemed to afford no inconvenience whatever to that perplexing prelate.

As I ate and drank in silence my red-robed friend paced the room with bent head and thoughtful mien, in the manner adopted by every Richelieu that I have seen on the stage. I fancied that I detected a wistful glance in his eyes as from time to time I raised a glass of wine to my lips, but I may have been mistaken.

It must seem odd to the matter-of-fact reader that I could golf, talk, eat, drink, and generally comport myself as an ordinary mortal whilst haunted by this remarkable specter; but the fact is, I had no choice in the matter. Suppose I had drawn the attention of my neighbors to the fact that I was pursued by a shadowy Cardinal! It was abundantly clear that none but I could see him, and I should only have been laughed at. And, after all, a man of my varied experiences and quick intelligence adapts himself, through sheer force of habit, to any situation, though at the time he may utterly fail to comprehend its *raison d'être* or significance.

At one period of the meal I was on the point of asking Wetherby if he saw no faintly defined figure, robed in red and standing near him. But just as I was about to speak to him he advanced with the coffee, and in setting down the tray actually stood within the same cubic space that the Cardinal occupied. That is to say, I distinctly saw them mixed up with each other, Wetherby passing in and out of the prelate's robes quite unconsciously. Nor did His Eminence seem to mind, for not only did the coffee and cognac pass through the region of his stomach, but also the tray, cups, saucers, and cigarettes.

## XIII: I Test The Clubs

My luncheon over, I pushed back the plates, drank a glass of cognac, poured out a cup of coffee, and lit a cigarette.

The combined effects of the fresh air of the links and the moderately good wine I had drunk during lunch had braced me up, and as the first puff of pale blue smoke left my lips, I leaned back in my chair and contemplated my guest. "Well, old man," said I, with perhaps undue familiarity, "out with it!"

He turned and swept me such a graceful bow that I felt a sheepish shame at the flippant and vulgar tone I had adopted.

"I will noo mak' ye a final proposal, young sir," he said. "Ahint the hotel is a secluded field, and if ye'll tak' ma clubs there and try a shot or two, I ask nae mair. If so be ye find a speecial virtue in them, gude and weel; if no', then a' thing is ower atween us, and the even tenor o' yer way'll no be interfered wi' by me."

I saw what he meant. I was to try the clubs and test the marvelous qualities that he insisted on.

Well, there was no harm in that.

I rang the bell and told Wetherby to carry the clubs to the field indicated by my ghostly counselor.

It was a good grass meadow of some ten acres, and not a soul was near, with, of course, the exception of the Cardinal.

I teed a ball, and selecting a club that most resembled a driver (though it was more like a gigantic putter than anything else), I began to address the ball.

As I did so I experienced a curious sensation.

I suddenly felt as if I had been a golfer all my life. There was no longer any hesitation as to where my hands or feet should be. Instinctively I fell into the right attitude.

I was no longer self-conscious. I found myself addressing the ball with the same easy grace I had observed in Kirkintulloch. A sense of extraordinary power came over me. My legs and arms tingled as if some strong stimulant were flowing in my veins. The club had taken a mastery over me. I swung it almost involuntarily, and the first shot was by far the finest drive I had ever made. I tried again and yet again, six shots in all, and each was as straight and sure as the very best of Lindsay's.

I was amazed and dumfounded.

"Weel! Did I no' tell ye?" cried the Cardinal, as he hopped about in a grotesque and undignified ecstasy. "Try the putter noo!"

I took the putter. It was something like a flat-headed croquet mallet, and very heavy. Then I threw a silver matchbox on the ground to represent a hole and began to putt.

I simply couldn't miss it. A sense of awe came over me.

No matter from what distance I played, nor how rough the ground was, the ball went straight to the box, as a needle to a magnet. I even tried to miss it and failed in the attempt.

I looked at His Eminence, and words fail me to describe the childish yet passionate exultation that shone in his face.

"I can dae nae mair!" he cried. "Ye see what they're like. Play wi' them, and ye'll win as sure as my name's Alexander Smeaton! It's a fact. Ay! And ye've time to wander into the clubhoose and lay yer wagers, if ye're minded to mak' a wheen siller. For the love o' ma auld bones, dae as I tell ye, man!"

I didn't at all love his old bones, but my mind was made up.

"I'll play with the clubs," I said, and the old man staggered in an intensity of delight.

"Hech! sir," he cried, "this'll be a grand day for Sandy Smeaton! When the match is ower I'll be there to compliment ye, and then–aweel, then I'll no fash ye till ye 'shuffle off yer mortal coil,' as auld Bacon has it. When ye're like myself–a speerit, ye ken–ye may be glad tae hae a freend at court, an' I'll dae what I can for ye. I can introduce ye to a' the canonized saints. They're a wheen ponderous in conversation and awfy orthodox in doctrine, but on the whole verra respectable. Hooever, that'll no' be for a while. Meantime, young sir, win yer match and humeeliate this varmint spawn o' the hoose o' Lindsay. So–*'Buon giorno'*–as we used to say in the auld Vatican days–*'A rivederci!'*"

With these valedictory remarks the Cardinal left me, and returning the clubs to Wetherby, who had been standing some hundred yards off, I returned to the hotel.

It was two o'clock.

How shall I describe what I felt? I could win this match–of that I felt absolutely sure. I cannot explain this curious sense of certainty as to the issue of the game, but I knew by a sort of prophetic inspiration that I could not lose.

The Cardinal had hinted at wagers. Well, why not?

I could turn the tables on some of the crowd who had smiled in pity at my efforts of the morning, and there is no revenge so sweet as that of scoring off men who have laughed at one. I decided to get a little money on the event, if possible.

I strolled leisurely over to the club and entered the smoking room, an immense room with bay windows that open onto the links. It was crowded. The members had finished luncheon and were discussing coffee, liqueurs, cigars, and cigarettes, amid a noisy jingle of laughter, talk, clinking of glasses, tinkling of cups, hurrying footsteps of waiters, and general hubbub.

My entrance had something of the effect that oil has on troubled waters. Everybody near me ceased laughing. No doubt I had been the bull's-eye for their hilarious shafts of wit. They hemmed and hawed as if I had detected them in some nefarious plot. A few bowed to me, and one or two invited me to have a drink. But I was bent on business, so, joining a group in which I saw a few acquaintances, I asked casually if any bets had been made on the match.

"Not one, don't you know!" replied O'Hagan, a Scotch youth of Irish name, who cultivated a highly ornate English accent with intermittent success.

"Anybody want a bet?" I asked, adding, "Of course I should want very heavy odds."

There was a general movement on this. Members gathered round me, some laughing, some chaffing, some whispering. Lowchester came up to me and growled in an undertone, "Don't make a fool of yourself, my dear chap; you can't possibly win."

"Still, I don't mind making a bet or two," I persisted. "Will anyone lay me fifty to one?"

"I'll lay you forty to one in fivers," said Mr. Grove, the actor, no doubt considering the publicity of the offer as a good advertisement.

"Done!" I replied, and took a note of it.

"So will I!" "And I!" "Put me down for the same." "In sovereigns?" "Yes." "Tenners if you like!" "Done!"

These and other cries now sounded all round the room till the babel reminded me of the Stock Exchange, and I think quite two thirds of the men present laid me the odds at forty to one in sovereigns, fivers, or tenners.

I suppose they considered me a madman, or at least an intolerably vain and eccentric person who deserved a "dressing down." A hurried adding up of my bets showed me that I stood to lose about £250, or win £10,000.

It was now past two o'clock, and we moved off to the links. The crowd was not quite so dense. Evidently many people considered the match as good as over, and the interest of those who remained was almost apathetic. The heavy midday meal that is eaten in St. Magnus may account to some extent for this lethargy.

I found the faithful Wetherby waiting for me, at a discreetly remote distance, and telling him that I meant to play with the clubs he was carrying, I walked up to Kirkintulloch. The latter had all the air of a martyr. His head was thrown back, as if in the act of challenging the world in general to laugh at him. He glared suspiciously at everyone near him and with difficulty brought himself to touch his hat at my approach.

I chuckled inwardly.

"Whaat's this I hear, sir?" he said. "Ye've been wagerin', they tell me."

"I've made a few bets, if that's what you mean," I answered.

"Weel, sir, as man tae man, if ye'll excuse the leeberty, ye're fair demented. It's no' possible to win. A'body kens that. As for mesel', I'm the laughin'stock o' the toon. I huvna had sae muckle as time for ma denner– "

"Why not?" I asked.

"I've been busy blackin' the een and spleetin' the nebs o' yer traducers. I've been fechtin' seeven men. It's a caddie's beesiness to stand up for his maister, nae maitter what kind o' a gowfer he is."

"Ah, well!" I answered, "you'll make them sing to another tune tonight. I am going to play with these."

And uncovering the canvas flap that concealed them, I exposed the weird-looking clubs to his gaze.

I think he thought I was joking. He looked first at the clubs, and then at me, with a half-questioning, half-stupid twinkle in his hard, blue eyes. Then he spat.

I apologize to the reader for mentioning anything so unpleasant, but it is an uncomfortable habit that certain classes indulge in when they desire to punctuate or emphasize their views. Amongst themselves, I believe, it is considered highly expressive, if employed at the true psychological moment.

"What kin' o' things are they?" he asked, after a portentous pause.

"The clubs I mean to play with," I replied.

"Aweel!" he answered, "that concludes a' relations atween us. I may be daft, but I'm no' a fule, an' I'm seek of the hale stramach. Ye mun get another caddie, I'll no cairry the likes o' thae things."

"My servant is going to carry them," I answered quickly; and I fancied Kirkintulloch looked a trifle crestfallen at such an unexpected exhibition of independence.

"I'll be glad, however," I added, "if you'll accompany me round the links, and I promise you the pleasing sensation of astonishment if you do."

With this I left him, but I could hear fragments of a voluble explanation that he apparently deemed it necessary to make to the bystanders.

"There are leemits, ye ken–it's no' for the likes o' me to say–I've been a caddie twenty-fower year–the man's no' richt in the heed–no' but what he's free with his siller an' a born gentleman–I wouldna say he wasna–but ma name's Kirkintulloch, an' I've a poseetion tae keep up."

The clock of the parish church boomed out the half-hour, and I advanced to the teeing ground, with Wetherby at my heels. The flap had been replaced over the heads of the clubs, and the bag looked ordinary enough, though my new "caddie" was so faultlessly attired in his well-cut gray suit as to be a target for the derision of a number of Kirkintulloch's professional friends.

## XIV: The Second Round

The "honor" being Lindsay's, the first drive was his. It was a clean-hit ball, but a wind had arisen that carried it a trifle out of the course.

Then I took my stand and received from Wetherby the Cardinal's driver.

Of all hearty laughter that my ears have ever listened to, none could equal that of the bystanders who were near enough to see the club. If I had made the most witty joke that mind can conceive, it could not have elicited more spontaneous, prolonged, or uproarious appreciation. Mrs.

Gunter's mezzo-soprano rang out in a paroxysm of musical hysterics. Even Lindsay edged behind me that I might not see the smile he found it impossible to repress. Members of the club and their friends, who had behaved with decorous gravity during the morning, now abandoned themselves frankly to unrestrained laughter. The infection spread to the masses of the crowd who were not near enough to see my curious club, and they gradually pressed closer and closer, anxious to share and enjoy any new source of merriment, so that it took the men with the rope all their time to maintain the semicircle that divided the spectators from the players.

Under ordinary circumstances I should have resented such behavior, but somehow it didn't seem to affect me. I even felt inclined to join in the general hilarity. I certainly felt the humor of the situation. As it was, I approached the ball with perfect composure and the ghost of a sardonic smile.

And then I drove it.

Away it winged, hard-hit and fast, traveling straight in the line of the hole. I had never, of course, played such a magnificent shot, and the effect on the crowd was electrical. Laughter died of a sudden, as if choked in a thousand throats. Broad grins seemed frozen on the upraised faces round me. Mouths opened unconsciously, eyes stared vacantly at the flying ball. For the moment I was surrounded by so many living statues, transfixed in mute amazement.

I think it was Lowchester who first spoke. "A fine shot," I fancied I heard him say mechanically.

We moved on, and the act of walking loosened the tongues around me. A confused murmuring ensued, gradually increasing in volume till everybody seemed to be talking and arguing, agreeing with or contradicting each other at the pitch of the voice.

I caught stray phrases from time to time.

"I never seed the likes o' that." "Man, it was a braw drive!" "He'll no' dae it again, I'm thinkin'." "By Jove! that was a flyer–but what an extraordinary club!" and so on.

I had outdriven Lindsay by about sixty yards–no small feat when one bears in mind that he has the reputation of being the longest driver living.

His second shot was a good one, landing him some thirty yards short of the burn. As we reached my ball, I selected the Cardinal's ponderous and much-corroded cleek. There were faint indications of amusement at the sight of it, but a nervous curiosity as to my next shot was the predominating note.

I played the shot quite easily. As before, the ball flew straight as a bird in the line of the hole, crossed the burn and dropped dead within a few feet of the flag. An unwilling murmur of admiration rose from the crowd, and Lindsay, no longer smiling, said very frankly that he had never seen two finer strokes in his life.

I think it only right to admit that he is a sensible, manly, and modest fellow.

He took his lofting iron and with a very neat wrist shot dropped the ball dead, within a foot of the hole.

A hearty cheer greeted the stroke. It was quite evident that he was the popular favorite. Well, I could wait, and I meant to.

Arrived on the putting green, I advanced with the odd-looking putter. One or two of the spectators indulged in a cynical, though somewhat half-hearted, snigger at its curious lines, but for the most part the crowd was quite silent, and one could almost feel in the air the nervous tension of the onlookers. My ball was about seven feet from the hole. With complete self-possession I went up to it and glanced almost carelessly at the ground.

There was a dead silence.

I played, and the ball dropped lightly into the hole. I was one up on the second round. I had holed out in three.

I half expected a murmur of applause for the putt, but a bewildered stupor was the actual effect produced. In all that concourse of people only two appeared to be quite calm and collected, namely, Wetherby and myself. I caught a glimpse of Kirkintulloch's face. The features were there, but all expression had departed.

For myself, I walked on air. The outward calm of my demeanor gave no index to the wild exultation that I felt. Truly there is no more satisfying or stimulating anticipation than that of a coming revenge. The sentiment, I am aware, is not a Christian one, but at least it is eminently human. I felt no desire to be revenged on Lindsay. Any hostile feeling that I had entertained toward him had passed away. But I did desire to score off the crowd. More, I desired to humiliate Mrs. Gunter. Her callous treatment of me, her silvery but malicious laughter, her avowed admiration of Lindsay, had galled me to an extent the expression of which I have carefully kept from these pages. *Noblesse oblige!* One cannot be rude. But I wanted to annoy her–a very common phase of love.

As the match proceeded I won hole after hole, often in the most astonishing manner. Twice I landed in bunkers close to the greens (the result of exceptionally long shots), and in each case the Cardinal's iron lifted the ball from the sand and deposited it in the hole. I cannot take credit to myself for such prodigious feats; they were undoubtedly the work of the clubs.

At the eighth hole, however, I experienced an important reverse. It is, as everybody who knows the St. Magnus links is aware, the short hole. I took the iron and dropped the ball within a yard of the hole. Lindsay followed and landed some twenty yards off; and then, by a splendid putt, he holed out in two. I, of course, had no difficulty in doing likewise, and we halved the hole; but the awkward fact remained that I must now gain every hole to win the match, for my opponent's score was nine up, and there only remained ten holes to play.

If the match was intensely exciting–and to me it was more than that–the demeanor of the crowd was no less psychologically interesting. The tag-rag and bobtail, with the fickleness that has ever characterized the emotions of the unwashed, and even of the occasionally clean, now began to acclaim me as their chosen champion, and each brilliant shot I made was hailed with a vociferous delight that might have turned a less steadily balanced head than my own. The reason of this is, of course, more or less obvious. There is more pleasurable excitement to be derived from making a god of the man whose star is in the ascendant than in continuing allegiance with falling crest to one whom we have placed on a pinnacle by an error of judgment, to which we are loath to attract attention.

But if the crowd was a source of ever increasing interest, what shall I say of the demeanor of the men who had made heavy bets with me?

It is not strictly true that Scotchmen are mean in money matters, any more than it is to say that they can't see a joke. As regards the latter point, it is my experience that a Scot won't laugh at the average jest that amuses an Englishman, simply because it isn't good enough. And since he doesn't laugh he is supposed to have missed the point. In support of my theory is the fact that there is an established vein of Scotch wit and humor, but I have yet to learn that England has evolved anything of the sort. True, England has many comic papers, and Scotland has none. But it must be borne in mind that the statements announcing such periodicals to be "comic" emanate solely from the proprietors.

There is, however, a substratum–or rather a perversion–of truth in the aphorism that deals with the Scotch and their money. And I take it the real truth is that a Scot cannot bear to part with money for which he gets no return of any sort–a very natural and proper feeling. Again, he dislikes any extra or unusual call on his purse. For the rest he is generous, hospitable, and public-spirited to a degree. It may be argued that if this be the case the Scot ought never to make a bet; the answer to which is that as a rule he doesn't, unless something almost in the nature of a certainty presents itself. Then he forgets his nationality and becomes merely human. And that is precisely what happened to my Caledonian friends in the smoking room of the club. An apparently unprecedented opportunity of making a little money had presented itself, and they had accepted its conditions with a noisy humor intended to lacquer their inbred acquisitive propensities.

And now, as I casually watched their faces, I saw an interesting awakening. Their faces were as those of infants who, having been roused from a long and profound sleep, gaze about with inquiring but stupefied wonder. They were quite silent for the most part, as with every shot I played they seemed to feel the sovereigns melting in their pockets. Ah! this unhappy craze for gold! I have seen the same set faces at Monte Carlo, when, as the croupier cries out, "Rouge, Pair et Passe!" the bulk of the money is staked on "Noir, Impair et Manque." How deplorable it all is! And I stood to win £10,000–a most exhilarating prospect.

## XV: In the Throes

As the match progressed I continued playing an absolutely faultless game, and there was no manner of doubt that Lindsay had become more or less demoralized. At the end of the fifteenth hole his score was reduced to two up, with three more holes to play. That is to say, so far I had won every hole of the second round, with the exception of the short one which we had halved. I had only to win the last three holes to gain the match, nay more, to break the record score of the links!

A curious change in the crowd's bearing was now apparent. They preserved a complete silence. Each shot, whether my own or Lindsay's, was played in a profound stillness. An intense suppressed excitement seemed to consume every soul present. Even during the marches from shot to shot scarcely a word was spoken; only the dull thud of thousands of feet gave audible token of their presence.

The news of the sudden and extraordinary change in the fortunes of the game had evidently traveled backward to St. Magnus, for as we worked homeward the mob was increased at every hole by such vast numbers that it seemed impossible for the men with the rope to control so great a concourse.

Once or twice I glanced in Mrs. Gunter's direction, and I should have thought her face was pale but for two vivid splashes of a most exquisite carmine that glowed, or at all events dwelt, on her cheeks. Her jet-black eyebrows formed two thoughtful lines below the golden cloud of her beautiful hair. How resplendent she was! I have never seen a complexion at all like hers except on the stage. What wonder that Lindsay should be demoralized, with the prospect of being forestalled hanging over him like the sword of Damocles?

Only once did I catch sight of the shadowy Cardinal, and that was at the end of the sixteenth hole, which I had won easily. As we walked toward the teeing ground of the seventeenth I chanced to let my eyes fall on the railway shed built against the wall bounding the links, and there–executing the most extraordinary and grotesque fandango of delight–was His Eminence. He was evidently in a rapture of delirious intoxication, for, in the passing glimpse I had, I saw him standing on his head, so that the ghostly robes fell downward to the roof of the shed, leaving his white skeleton immodestly bare and feet upward in the air. It was not a pleasing exhibition, and very nearly unnerved me; but the mere handling of my marvelous driver seemed to steady me in a moment. And fortunately none but I could see the antics of my ecclesiastical patron.

Reader, do you know what it is to be outwardly as calm as a blasé policeman, and all the time quivering with inward excitement? If I could have yelled once or twice it would have been an immense relief, but I had a part to play, and I meant to play it. As it was, I puffed carelessly at a cigarette, professed to admire the view, glanced carelessly at my watch, and generally indulged in such little bits of byplay as were calculated to indicate extreme *sang-froid.* [I ought to mention that I am a very capable amateur actor, and at our annual Thespian Club theatricals always take the leading part. I founded the club and manage it.]

That I played my new role of champion golfer with credit was evident. The seething crowd had originally assembled to jeer, but it remained to accept me at my own valuation–always a pleasing change to find registered in the barometer of public opinion.

My drive at the seventeenth hole (the last but one to be played) was a perfect shot, whilst Lindsay's was comparatively feeble. He was now but one up, and at the end of the hole we ought to be "all square and one to play." But the strain on my nerves was beginning to tell. I felt like Hood's Eugene Aram–

*"Merrily rose the lark, and shook*
*The dewdrop from its wing;*
*But I never marked its morning flight,*
*I never heard it sing;*
*For I was stooping once again*
*beneath the horrid thing!"*

I was conscious in a vague somnambulistic fashion of the green links, the blue sky, the purple crowd, splashed here and there with the bright colors of frock and parasol. My eyes took in mechanically the onward movement of the people, the rosy light that caught the spires of the old gray town, the shrieking railway train, the red blaze of the sun in the windows of St. Magnus, and a hundred other ocular impressions. Yet all these things seemed unreal; the dream background in a land whereof the Cardinal, Lindsay, and I formed the sole population.

Moreover, pressing as it seemed on my very brain, came the humiliating conviction that I was nothing short of a fraud, a charlatan, a ghostly conjurer's accomplice.

Was it an honorable game that I was playing? Would I be justified in taking the money I stood to win? Was it fair to usurp the throne of champion by the aid of a supernatural agency, whose purpose I could not even pretend to fathom? Could I look Mrs. Gunter in the face if, crowned with a stolen golfing halo, I asked her to be my wife? And if I couldn't, what more deplorable type of lover was possible? Ought I to burden myself with a secret that I should have to carry with me in silence to the grave? Was the nominal prefix "Honorable," with which my parents had dowered me without either warrant on my part or inquiry on their own, to be a prefix only? These and many other thoughts flashed through my mind as we played the seventeenth hole.

I got on the green in three, Lindsay in four. He then played the "two more," and by a remarkably good putt holed out in five.

I took the putter, and in a profound and most impressive silence holed out in four. A stifled gasp rose from the crowd.

The score was now "All square, and one to play."

I stood on the teeing ground of the eighteenth hole. The landscape in front of me was blurred and blotted; the dense crowds on either side of me were as mere inky blotches. The ground at my feet seemed miles away. Only the teed ball was in focus. That I saw clearly.

It was a test moment in my life. I could lose the match if I chose, and keep a clean conscience.

I could play the last hole with my own clubs!

And if I did–well, I'd lose; but, by heaven! I'd still be an honorable gentleman.

I caught sight of Lindsay's face. It was white and set, but he looked a manly fellow for all that. It was a cowardly trick to tear the laurels from his brow as I was doing. He had won them after a lifetime's devotion to the game.

And I–?

Faugh! I would not touch the accursed clubs again. For aught I knew, to win was to sell my soul, and become a servile creature doomed to the tender mercies of a phantom's patronage.

"Ye fushiomless eediot!" I suddenly heard the words ring in my ears, and at the same moment I saw the Cardinal's deadly face peering into my eyes as if to read my very soul. "What's come ower ye? Are ye daft? Nane o' yer pauky humor at this time o' day. Tak' ma driver an' catch the ba' the bonniest skite of a'! Whaat?"–and his voice rose in indescribable fury–"Ye'll no do sic a thing? Ye lily-livered loon, if ye dinna dae as I tell ye I'll hae ye back in the castle vaults and wring the neck o' yer soul wi' ma ain bony fingers! Ay, an' haunt ye till the day ye're deid!" (What good purpose could be served by haunting me till the day of death, after wringing the neck of my soul, was not quite clear.) "Mind that!" he continued. "I'm no' to be trifled wi'!"

I turned on him and answered deliberately, "You fiend!"

"Beg pardon, sir?" said Wetherby. I had forgotten for the moment and spoken aloud.

"Give me the driver from Kirkintulloch's bag," I replied.

Kirkintulloch heard me and elbowed his way to my side. He was shaking with excitement. I feel certain he had never been so sober for years.

"Will 'ee no jist gang on wi' the one ye've been playin' wi'?" he urged. "Ye're daein' fine!"

"Give me the driver with which I played the first round this morning," I persisted.

During all this the Cardinal was moving and shrieking round me in a whirlwind of red draperies and white corroded bones.

Reluctantly Kirkintulloch drew the driver from his bag and handed it to me.

"I think ye're wrong, sir," he whispered very earnestly in my ear, mixing himself up with the demented prelate in doing so.

"For heaven's sake let no one speak to me!" I cried. "Get out of my way!" I added fiercely–really to the Cardinal, though Kirkintulloch, Wetherby, and everyone near seemed to take it to themselves, and drew back hastily. Then I gave a vicious kick at His Eminence's shins. Lowchester has since told me the action appeared most inexplicable and uncalled for, inasmuch as I apparently kicked at space.

I addressed the ball.

His Eminence promptly sat on it. Then, stretching his arms in front of me, he cursed me wildly and volubly in Latin. What the exact words were I cannot tell, and could not have translated had I known, but the general effect was awful.

Crash through his bones–not that such a trifle could inconvenience my intangible enemy–went the club.

The ball, feebly struck on the top, shot along the grass and dropped into the burn!

The match was as good as lost.

A shriek, whether of delight, dismay, relief, or anxiety, I know not, rose from the mob. I believe everyone in that crowd was suffering from the same nervous strain that affected me.

Then Lindsay stepped to the front.

He drove a magnificent ball, and, strange as it may seem, the mere sight wrought a complete upheaval of the altruistic pedestal on which I had perched myself. I was suddenly conscious of a wild exasperation at having thrown my chances to the winds. For, after all, my objections to winning had been purely sentimental, not to say childish. It is marvelous how the realization of our best intentions very frequently betrays the insincerity of the moral mood that inspired them. It is easy to be magnanimous if we don't foresee the unhappy but common result of poignant regret.

The vision of a heavenly and luxurious life with Mrs. Gunter seemed to fade. I turned and looked at her. She was as white as a sheet, save for the faithful discs of carmine. Ah, what a fool I had been!

But the game was not yet over; and even as the thought flashed across me, Lindsay made his first serious mistake. It was a mistake of judgment.

"Thank heaven," he exclaimed, with an ill-bred grunt of relief, "I've cooked your goose for you at last!"

I have no doubt this thoughtless and ill-timed speech was the result of the strain he had been put to. Perhaps I ought to have made allowance for it. In point of fact, it reawakened in me the most consuming desire to win, and I cursed my extravagant magnanimity.

Meantime a rapt and beautiful change had come over the faces of the men with whom I had made bets. Frowns were dissipated as by a ray of beatific sunshine, and lively smiles and chuckles were the order of the moment. There was even a touch of insolence in their sidelong glances. They began to chatter volubly. I could hear the drift of their sudden recall to speech.

"I knew he was bound to break down in the long run," said somebody.

"Undoubtedly; still he's played a remarkable game." "I win ten pounds"–"And I a fiver," and so forth. My miserable drive had acted on their tongues as the first round of champagne does at dinner.

We were walking toward the burn as Lindsay spoke, and I was about to answer when–springing apparently from nowhere–the Cardinal again appeared, or rather shot up before me, in a state of incontinent frenzy. None the less, he seemed to divine the thoughts that were chasing each other through my mind, for, bending toward me, he whispered in hoarse, trembling tones, and with the utmost intensity–

"Tak' ma club! Tak' ma club!! Tak' ma club–ye eediot!!! He's dealt ye a black affront; but, by a' the buried bones o' the Smeatons he hasna yet won the day!"

"You think I still may win?" I silently asked him, albeit in a state of incredulous stupefaction.

"Try, man–try!" he shrieked in reply; "I'll see what I can dae!"

And with that he caught up his skirts and flew off in a series of amazing leaps and bounds in the direction of the last hole. What this change in his tactics meant I was at a loss to conjecture.

I wish I could adequately describe the extraordinary flight of the prelate across the green turf of the links. He seemed to be borne on the wings of the wind, and each leap he took must have covered at least twenty yards. He gave me the impression of a grotesque competitor in an unearthly game of "Hop, skip, and leap." At length, after an elapse of perhaps fifteen seconds, I saw him halt in the distance about twenty yards from the red flag of the hole. Then he turned and faced us, as if patiently awaiting the next shot. I little guessed what his purpose was. His figure was clearly outlined against a distant crowd of some two or three hundred assembled behind the final hole to witness the end of this unprecedented struggle.

## XVI: An Exciting Finish

My ball was duly fished out of the burn and dropped behind my shoulder. I returned my own faithless driver to Kirkintulloch and once again took hold of the Cardinal's. As I did so a telepathic throb of excitement passed through the bystanders.

I played the shot.

It eclipsed all my former efforts. I never have seen, nor shall I ever see again, such a hard-hit ball. With a trajectory scarcely higher than that of a rifle bullet at a medium range, it winged its way straight to the hole, dropping eventually within a yard or so of His Eminence. And then, straining my eyes, I saw a sight that startled me into a sudden realization of the latter's purpose. He had, so to speak, fielded the ball–that is to say, he had dashed toward it as it fell; and now, by a series of nervous but skillful kicks, he was directing its course straight to the hole! The red skirts were held high in his hands, and the white bony legs hashed to and fro as he sped in the wake of the running globe. I could not, of course, actually see the ball, but, by an intuition that admitted of no doubt whatever, I knew what he was up to. I held my breath in an agony of suspense as nearer and nearer to the red flag flew the gaunt figure of the Cardinal. I swear my heart stopped beating, and the paralyzed crowd seemed similarly affected, though the sight that I saw was mercifully denied to its eyes. There was no doubt about it. The Cardinal had so manipulated the ball that I had holed out in three.

But the match was not yet over.

What Lindsay's feelings at the moment were I know not, but he managed to play a clever second stroke that landed him on the green, some seven feet from the hole.

And now came the supreme moment.

If Lindsay holed his putt we halved the match, if he failed I won the day.

Such was the pressure of the excited crowd that only the most strenuous efforts enabled the rope holders to maintain a clear circular space round the hole. It measured about fifteen yards in diameter, and within this charmed circle stood Lindsay and his caddie, Wetherby and Kirkintulloch, old Jock Johnson (the keeper of the green), Hanbury-Smith (the captain of the golf club), and myself. All other spectators were without the pale, with the important exception of the Cardinal.

I looked about me. My part in the game was over. I had but to watch and wait. I was thankful the final shot was Lindsay's and not mine.

The faces of my betting friends had changed again in expression and become drawn and strained. The unfortunate gentlemen no longer chattered and chuckled. The magnet of luck was again slowly but surely attracting golden coins from the depths of their purses, and such pangs could only be borne with dumb fortitude.

The crowd was so terribly congested that two women fainted. I looked anxiously at Mrs. Gunter, but–thank Heaven!–the rich carmine still glowed on her cheeks.

At length, putter in hand, Lindsay approached his ball, and even the breathing of the crowd seemed to be suspended.

I moved to a spot some six feet from the hole, on the opposite side to Lindsay. As I did so my eyes fell on the ground, and I saw a startling and curious sight.

My terrible ally, the Cardinal, had stretched himself at full length, face downward, on the turf, so that his ghastly head was directly over the hole and his shadowy feet close to mine.

A sense of faintness crept over me.

As in a red mist I saw Lindsay strike the ball. I saw it traveling straight and sure to the hole!

And then—heavens above us!—I saw the Cardinal take a quick and gulping breath, and blow with might and main against the skillfully directed ball! It reached the edge of the hole, trembled a moment on the brink, and then ran off at an angle and lay still on the turf a couple of inches from the hole!

I had won the match.

A tumult sounded in my ears, the sky turned a blazing scarlet, the crowd swam before my eyes, and of a sudden I fell prone on the turf with my nose plunged in the fateful hole!

When I came to myself I found kind friends grouped about me, and my head resting luxuriously in Mrs. Gunter's lap. I think I should have been perfectly happy and content with this state of things, had I not unfortunately just at that moment caught a glimpse of the ubiquitous Cardinal standing ridiculously on his head and kicking his heels in mid-air in an ecstasy of frenzied glee.

The sight so upset me that I went off a second time into a dead faint.

## XVII: And Last

Again I was myself, and this time I felt revived and strong. I rose to my feet. Immediately the crowd closed round me and acclaimed me with cheers and yells. Presently I found myself being carried shoulder-high by a dozen lusty caddies, Kirkintulloch heading their progress with proud bearing and gleaming eye.

A thousand voices were howling "See, the conquering hero comes!" A thousand hats and handkerchiefs were waving in the air. A thousand smiling faces beamed up into mine.

Mrs. Gunter cried out to me, as I passed her in triumphal procession, "You'll dine with the Lowchesters tonight, won't you?"

And turning a smiling and radiant face to her, I answered, "I will."

I was the idol of the hour, not—I may add—an altogether new experience.

At length, after what seemed an eternity of acclamation and adulation, I was set down in the great bay window of the club and immediately surrounded by all members who had *not* made bets with me. Fulsome flattery, genuine congratulation, and general admiration were showered on me. At writing tables in distant corners of the room I saw my betting friends busily writing out checks. They did not seem inclined to participate in the enthusiastic ovation. But what did I care?

Surfeited with the overwhelming tributes to my achievement (and, I fancy, to my personality), I broke away from my friends, only to be seized again by my escort of caddies and carried shoulder-high in the direction of the Metropole. The sturdy fellows finally deposited me on the top step of the main entrance to the hotel, and I stood facing the seething crowd.

Here a fresh outburst of applause greeted me from my fellow guests and the domestic staff.

I bowed incessantly right and left.

"Speech! Speech!" now rang out on every side from a thousand throats, and I felt that if only to get rid of them, I must say something. So holding aloft my right hand as a token that I accepted the invitation, and in the profound silence instantly produced by my action, I said–

"My friends, I thank you. I have excelled in all other games, and why not in golf? Again I thank you."

The simple words completely captivated them, and I retired indoors to a volley of tumultuous and long-continued cheers.

As an example of how trivial things often imprint themselves on our dazed memories during crises in our lives, I remember noting, as I passed through the hall to my suite of rooms, an immense pile of luggage, evidently just arrived, and labeled "The Prince Vladimir Demidoff." I had not heard of his intention to visit St. Magnus. In fact, I don't think I'd ever heard of the man at all.

Reaching my room, I stretched myself on a couch, lit a cigarette, and got Wetherby to bring me a stiff brandy-and-soda. At last, thought I, I had breathing space. Imagine, then, my consternation and irritation when, on opening my eyes–I had closed them for a moment as I reveled in the first deep draught of my "peg"–I beheld, seated opposite me, His Eminence!

"Upon my soul!" I cried, "this is too bad. You swore–"

"Hud yer wheesht!" interrupted the Cardinal. "I'm here to thank ye and bid ye gude-bye."

"I'm glad to hear it," I muttered, sulkily.

"Ye've focht a grand fecht," he proceeded, "an' I'm much obleeged tae ye. But, man, there's ae thing that worrits me extraordinar'. Ye ken, I had tae cheat! I aye played fair in the auld days, and it gaed agin' the grain tae blaw on Lindsay's ba' at the last putt, but what could I dae? Hooever, it canna be helpit. The queer thing is that noo that my revenge is complete, it doesna seem to gratify me muckle. Hech, sir!–life moartal or speeritual's guy disappintin'. For a' that I'm much obleeged, an' ye'll never see me mair. Gude-bye!"

And with that he faded into space, and, truth to tell, he has honorably abstained from haunting me since.

Sheer physical fatigue precluded the possibility of anything in the nature of psychical research, or even of attempting to think out the weird supernatural experiences I had gone through.

I was dozing off into a gentle sleep when Wetherby opened the door and informed me that Kirkintulloch was waiting below and would be proud if I could grant him a short interview.

I consented, and presently Kirkintulloch appeared.

"It's no' for the guinea I've come, sir," he began (I've no doubt, by way of a gentle reminder); "I thocht ye'd be glad o' a card wi' yer score, an' I've had it made oot."

He handed me a card, and on it I read the score:

| | | | | | | | | | | | |
|---|---|---|---|---|---|---|---|---|---|---|---|
| Out, | 3 | 3 | 4 | 3 | 4 | 5 | 3 | 2 | 3 | • | 30 |
| In, | 3 | 2 | 3 | 4 | 5 | 3 | 3 | 4 | 3 | • | 30 |
| Total | | | | | | | | • | • | • | 60 |

"Ye're a credit to my teachin', sir," he continued, "an' I'm real prood o' ye. The record for thae links is seventy-twa, and ye're jist a clean dozen below that. The likes o' it was never seen. It's a fact. Ay! an' long after a'body here's dead ye'll still hud the record. I little thocht I had pit ma ain style sae coampletely into ye! Ye're a pairfect marvel!"

"Thank you," I muttered wearily.

"I see ye're tired, sir, an' I'll no keep ye, but jist afore I gang, wad ye mind showin' me thae queer-like clubs ye played wi'?"

"By all means," said I. "Wetherby, where are the clubs?"

"Ain't you got 'em, sir?" asked the latter, with some surprise.

"Not I!" I answered. "You had them."

"Well, sir, I can't quite tell 'ow it is, but in the crowd I suddenly felt 'em slip out from under my arm, and look as I would I couldn't lay eyes on 'em after that. I supposed some friend of yours had taken them out of curiosity and meant to bring 'em to you, sir."

"Dinna fash yersel'," broke in Kirkintulloch; "if they're in St. Magnus I'll lay hands on them, never fear. Gude nicht, sir!"

And so that admirable caddie passed out of my life. I tipped him well (and I've since been told he paid me the high–if deplorable–compliment of a week's continuous intoxication), but from that day to this no mortal eye has seen the bewitched clubs of the ghostly Cardinal Archbishop of St. Magnus.

Much revived by two hours' sound and dreamless sleep, I dressed at half past seven, and a few minutes before eight I started for the Lowchesters' house.

It had somehow got abroad that I was dining there, and a large crowd had assembled in front of the hotel. I was again received with an outburst of cheers and subsequently escorted to my destination to a lustily sung chorus of "For he's a jolly good fellow!"

Arrived at the Lowchesters' gates, I bade the kindly crowd good night and retired from their sight to a final volley of echoing cheers.

I need not describe the welcome I received from my host and hostess, Mrs. Gunter, and the other guests. Even Lindsay spoke to me tactfully on the subject of our match, expressing genuine admiration of my performance, though I was slightly startled when he said, "In fact, I consider your play today nothing short of supernatural."

So did I, but I didn't venture to say so.

The dinner was delightful. Excellent food, perfect wine, charming people, and myself the center of interest. I ask no more at such a function.

I took my hostess in to dinner of course but on my other side was Mrs. Gunter, exquisitely dressed in a Parisian triumph of eau-de-Nil velvet with groups of mauve and purple pansies. Her wonderful complexion was more ravishing than ever in the soft lamplight. Indeed it seemed to have specially adapted itself to the requirements of her delicately tinted gown. Her hands and arms had the bloom of peaches, and her luxuriant hair, dark underneath, was a mist of ever changing gold on the top.

Several times during dinner I saw the jet-black lashes raised and felt her glorious eyes regarding me with the rapt gaze of hero worship.

Well, tonight I should know, for weal or woe, what fortune the Fates held in store for me.

When the ladies had left us I drew Lindsay aside on the pretense of examining some engravings in the hall, and as soon as we were alone I touched on the subject uppermost in my mind.

"I think it only right to tell you, my dear Lindsay," I began, "that tonight I shall propose to Mrs. Gunter, and if by any chance she should dismiss me, then I leave the field clear for you. I have to thank you for all the courtesy you have shown during my visit to St. Magnus, and I sincerely trust that whatever may happen we shall always remain friends."

"As far as I'm concerned you may be sure of that," replied Lindsay. "But it does seem to me that you've been laboring under a delusion. I've never desired to propose to Mrs. Gunter. And even if I wanted to, I couldn't. I'm a married man, with three of a family. More than that, I'm very deeply in love with my wife, and not at all with Mrs. Gunter."

"But–good heavens!" I exclaimed, "surely we agreed–"

"If you remember," he interrupted, "that night in the Racing Club, I wanted to explain these things, and you simply wouldn't hear me."

"Then," I continued blankly, as in a sudden flash of memory I recalled the fact he alluded to, "we've been fighting for nothing?"

"Exactly," he replied.

In silence we shook hands, and the matter dropped.

Presently we joined the ladies in the drawing room, and after a decent interval I drew Mrs. Gunter aside. We sat by each other on a couch concealed from view by a group of palms. A pretty girl in white was playing the "Moonlight Sonata."

I admit it at once–my heart was beating. I wished I had rehearsed the role I was about to play. Then I reflected that I had often witnessed proposals on the stage, so taking a leaf from that reliable book I cleared my throat.

"Mrs. Gunter," I began, "may I say Katherine?"

"Ah! So it has come to this!" she murmured, lowering her eyes with the most captivating grace.

"Yes, this," I whispered passionately. "This, that I love you and only you! This, that I am here to ask you to be my wife!"

"It can never be!" she murmured conventionally, and a low cry, half sob, half sigh, escaped her.

"Katherine!" I cried. "Why not?"

"Because," she answered slowly, and as if the words were dragged from her, "I have lost every penny of my fortune. And a penniless woman I cannot, will not come to you. Unless–" and her voice trembled into silence.

She was wearing several thousand pounds' worth of diamonds at the time, but somehow I didn't grasp the sparkling contradiction.

Now I am a man of quick resolution. I can grasp a situation in a moment. In a flash I realized that I alone could never afford to keep this beautiful creature in surroundings worthy of her, at least not without such personal sacrifice as at my time of life would be extremely inconvenient. I am but a younger son. To force her then to marry me under such circumstances would be a cruelty to her and an injustice to myself.

Afraid, therefore, that the murmured word "Unless–" was about to open up possibilities not altogether desirable, I broke the silence with–

"And so you dismiss me?"

She looked at me for a moment in blank surprise.

Then the ghost of a faint smile flickered over her face, as she answered–

"Yes, *so I dismiss you!*"

I gave a suitable sigh.

The "Moonlight Sonata" was over, and poor Katherine rose.

I followed her to a group of guests in the center of the room, and as I did so she turned and said–

"I was going to say, '*Unless* you can induce my future husband to give me up,' when you interrupted me."

"Your future husband!" I exclaimed aghast.

"Yes," she answered serenely; "let me introduce you to him."

And touching the sleeve of the good-looking foreigner who had taken her in to dinner she said–

"Vladimir, let me present Major Gore," adding to me, "Prince Vladimir Demidoff. Didn't you know that we are to be married next week?"

I murmured confused words of congratulation and escaped to Lady Lowchester's side.

"Are they really going to be married?" I asked her.

"Of course they are!" replied my hostess. "Why shouldn't they?"

"But–but," I stammered, "she's lost every penny of her fortune!"

"Not she!" replied Lady Lowchester, with a merry ringing laugh. "That's what she tells every man who proposes to her. She says she finds it an excellent gauge of devotion."

"I see," I answered.

I stood still for a moment. Then I walked over to Lowchester and asked him which was the best morning train from St. Magnus to London.

I did not feel justified in keeping for my own use the £10,000 I had won, but it may interest the reader to know that with it I founded the now flourishing and largely patronized Home for Inebriate Caddies.

# PERMISSIONS ACKNOWLEDGMENTS

Grateful acknowledgment is extended to the following authors and publications.

P. G. Wodehouse, "The Clicking of Cuthbert," from *Wodehouse On Golf,* originally published in *Collier's,* March 1910.

John Kendrick Bangs, "The Phantom Card," originally published in *Harper's,* 1900.

"The Pro," from *Museums and Women and Other Stories* by John Updike. © 1972 by John Updike. Reprinted by permission of Alfred A. Knopf, Inc.

Ring Lardner, "Mr. Frisbie," reprinted with the permission of Scribner, a division of Simon & Schuster, from *Round-Up,* by Ring Lardner. © 1928 by Ellis A. Lardner, renewed 1956 by Ellis A. Lardner.

Charles E. Van Loan, "The Ooley-Cow," originally published in 1918.

Everett Rhodes Castle, "Pay As You Play," originally published in American Magazine, January 1932. © 1931 by The Cornell Publishing Company.

Kevin Cook, "Lee and Me At the Open," originally published in Playboy Magazine, June 1982.

Glynn Harvey, "Who Wants to Marry Money?" © 1955 by Crowell-Collier.

E. C. Bentley, "The Sweet Shot," from *Trent Intervenes* by E. C. Bentley, originally published by Curtis Brown, Ltd.

Stephen Leacock, "The Golfomaniac," from *The Iron Man and the Tin Woman,* published in 1929 by Dodd, Mead, and Company.

Bernard Darwin, "The Wooden Putter," originally published in *The Strand,* 1924.

P. G. Wodehouse, "Archibald's Benefit," originally published in *Collier's,* March 1910.

Charles Dickinson, "My Livelihood," © 1982 by Charles Dickinson. This story was originally published in *Esquire Magazine* and appears in the author's collection, *With or Without,* published by Avon Books. Reprinted by permission of the author and his agent, Robin Straus Agency, Inc., New York.

W. G. Van T. Sutphen, "The Hong-Kong Medal," originally published in 1898.

"The Year of Getting to Know Us," from *Emperor of the Air.* © 1988 by Ethan Canin. Reprinted by permission of Houghton Mifflin Company. All rights reserved.

"Farrell's Caddie," from *The Afterlife and Other Stories* by John Updike. © 1994 by John Updike. Reprinted by permission of Alfred A. Knopf, Inc.

Stephen Leacock, "A Mediaeval Hole in One," from *The Leacock Roundabout, A Treasury of the Best Works of Stephen Leacock,* published in 1952 by Dodd, Mead, and Company.

Paul Gallico, "Golf Is a Nice Friendly Game," reprinted by permission of Harold Ober Associates. © 1942 by The Curtis Publishing Company. © 1942 by Paul Gallico, renewed 1969 by Paul Gallico.

P. G. Wodehouse, "Sundered Hearts," originally published in *McClure's,* December, 1920.

Merrell Noden, "The Adventure of the Treacherous Traps," reprinted courtesy of *Sports Illustrated,* July 24, 1995. © 1995 by Time Inc. All rights reserved.

Earlyne S. Browne, "The Lady's Proposition," used with permission from *The Saturday Evening Post.* © 1955.

"The Rivercliff Golf Killings," © 1921, 1928, 1929, 1930, 1934, 1935, 1936 by Don Marquis. From *The Best of Don Marquis* by Don Marquis. Used by permission of Doubleday, a division of Bantam Doubleday Dell Publishing Group, Inc.

William E. Pettit, "Decision on the Fairway," used with permission from *The Saturday Evening Post.* © 1960.

Robert Marshall, "The Haunted Major," originally published in 1902.